MIDNIGHT SKY

(SKY BROOKS SERIES BOOK 7)

MCKENZIE HUNTER

This is a work of fiction. Names, characters, businesses, places, events, and incidents are either the products of the author's imagination or used in a fictitious manner. Any resemblance to actual persons, living or dead, or actual events is purely coincidental.

McKenzie Hunter

Midnight Sky

© 2018, McKenzie Hunter

McKenzieHunter@McKenzieHunter.com

ISBN: 978-1-946457-71-4

ACKNOWLEDGMENTS

To my family and friends, I want to thank you for your help and unconditional support. I want to offer a special thanks to my sister and mother for being my sounding boards and helping me through the writing process. It was a tremendous help and I just can't thank you enough.

Elizabeth Bracker, Sherrie Simpson Clark, Robyn Mather, and Stacey Mann, you are wonderful beta readers, and I appreciate the constructive feedback you provided. Emerson Knight, working with you is a delight and I appreciate the hard work and dedication you put into Ethan's POV.

Thanks to Oriana for the beautiful cover and Luann Reed and Doreen Martens, my editors. I appreciate the time and effort you put in helping me tell Sky's story and making it the best that it can be.

To everyone who followed Sky's journey, you will always have my gratitude. It can never be truly expressed in words how fortunate I feel to have readers like you. I enjoyed writing Sky Brooks Series and truly enjoyed discussing the characters and story with you all through messaging, email, and in my readers group. Thank you for allowing me to entertain you with my stories.

CHAPTER 1

*E*than paced the room, running his fingers through his hair, mussing it. Despite his injuries he moved with his typical predaceous grace—purposeful, long strides as if he was a caged animal, restricted, edged into acceptance of his situation. In a way he was. It had been four hours since Sebastian had informed him that the Alphas and Betas of the South and East and the Master of the vampires' Northern Seethe were missing, and he was waiting to hear back about the West. It was an attack that didn't make sense.

"Why Demetrius?" Ethan said aloud, trying to figure out the anomaly in the pattern. The same question that went through my mind was displayed on his face: why hadn't they come after the Midwest Pack?

"You said this is worse than the Red Blood," I probed.

He nodded and took one look at me before taking a long breath, a failed effort to calm me. My heart was pounding, and slowing my breathing took a great deal of effort. Our mating had connected us in a manner I wasn't prepared for. I felt his emotions as if they were my own. I'd felt them before, but on what I now knew was a superficial level. It came from him being a strong wolf; pack members felt the emotions of their stronger fellows. Since Ethan would have been an Alpha in any other pack, he was a strong broadcaster. The anomaly of the situation was me, and how my emotions affected the pack. When Steven had been arrested and I'd thought we were going to be outed, I hadn't been able to tamp down my anxiety. The pack had felt it—apparently, it not only had a feel to it but a distinctive smell as well.

A cloud of frustration lay heavily on Ethan's shoulders. A dark cast marred his features as he took a seat next to me. He started slowly, and I knew he was trying to remove the carefully placed filters from the story. Such constructs barred me and anyone else from gaining information he felt we shouldn't be privy to. We struggled with that habit. No, *he* struggled. It was a delicate and complicated dance to go from being part of his pack and a person he kept information from to his mate, whom he felt compelled to share with.

I didn't push. I waited for him to speak.

He slumped back into the sofa and frowned. "It happened seven years ago. We were accused of abducting and killing off smaller packs in the area in an effort to assert our dominance and let our presence be known." His hand scrubbed over the light beard that covered his jaw, and he remained silent for a few beats. "The accusation wasn't taken lightly. We didn't have a problem with smaller packs in the past." He smiled grimly. They hadn't had a problem with small packs until I'd been attacked by one. Then things changed. Fringe packs were no longer allowed.

"We had to look into it, but the trail went cold. Someone was picking off the Alphas of the smaller packs, along with their Betas and a few of the thirds. We couldn't find the culprit."

My heart pounded harder and I knew he could feel my panic. I didn't have it in me to calm it. My thoughts immediately went to Winter. Maybe the abductors were going to forgo the

Alpha and Beta of the Midwest and go for her. Ethan grabbed his phone from the coffee table and called Winter before I could suggest it.

"I'm fine," she said immediately once she was on the line. "Sebastian called already. Don't worry about me. If someone comes through my door, they will be exiting without body parts that I assure you they will likely miss. That is, if they manage to leave." I heard the click of metal in the background. Winter's home was set up as if she was expecting a siege at all times. It was a peculiar way to live, but at the moment I was appreciative of her paranoia and over-the-top protection efforts.

"Winter's fine," he offered, tossing his phone back on the table. He continued as if his story had never been interrupted. "They were missing and the trail was cold. We had no idea who was taking them, until they made a fatal mistake. They took a witch."

"A witch? Were they just collecting supernaturals?"

He shook his head. "No, they were hunting were-animals. For sport, and people paid a lot of money for the privilege. The witches were just for entertainment." He grimaced. "Asking a level one witch to perform magic equivalent to the tricks that a children's magician or cruise ship entertainer does is insulting to them. It's about as insulting as someone wanting to keep one of us as a pet. Or hunt us like natural animals." Steel gray overtook his eyes and he closed them, taking a moment to calm himself.

My thoughts immediately went to David and Trent and their fascination with Josh and his magic. They weren't above asking him to perform trite tricks. I groaned softly. "David and Trent ask Josh to perform magic all the time," I admitted.

Calmed, Ethan gave me a half-smile. "Josh isn't that easily offended. Besides, he likes Trent and David."

"Who took the witches and the were-animals?" I prompted.

"Ronan Everest. We still don't know how he found out about

us and why he went the route he did. I guess he'd planned to find success in the underground entertainment industry. He gave hunters the opportunity to hunt animals that were smarter than the ones you find in nature. We had no idea what he was going to use the witches for, other than entertainment. He knew enough about were-animals and our dynamics to know to go after the smaller packs. They didn't have the same resources as the larger ones. I'm not sure that he wouldn't have become more confident and tried the larger packs. The smaller packs could have been practice."

"You were able to find his location by tracking the witch's blood?"

He nodded. "The witches were more than happy to help us do it."

Apprehension made me hesitate before continuing with my questioning, partly because I knew the answer. "Is he still alive?"

Ethan shook his head. "Nor are any of the people who thought it was okay to hunt us." His voice held no remorse and I didn't expect any.

"You think it's a copycat? A friend, maybe even someone who worked with him in the past?"

"It seemed as if he was working alone. He'd had a few Hunters help capture were-animals, but they were just work-for-hire, not part of his plan."

"What happened to them?"

"Chris is what happened to them. She's dedicated to her job and even more so to the reputation of Hunters. Others working for humans and ultimately hurting people in the otherworld wasn't good for business. She can be ruthless when crossed."

I didn't know we were back to stating the obvious. *Welcome back, Captain. I've missed you.*

. . .

An hour had passed and Sebastian hadn't called back, nor was he answering any of Ethan's calls. I cringed each time Ethan passed me as he traveled the length of the room. His frustration, anger, and anxiety had started off as a nagging feeling that had quickly escalated to a raging firestorm of emotions. Ethan's hands were clenched into balls. I figured it was just a matter of time before he needed to do something to expend some of the energy pinned inside of him.

"Sebastian should have called by now. Something's wrong." He stopped pacing. "I have to go see." He grabbed his phone and headed for the door.

He stopped abruptly when I grabbed my things and started to follow. "Sky, you can't go."

"Ethan, we don't have time to debate this. It's not a bad idea to have someone to back you up. If Sebastian is in danger, I can help."

"I can't do anything while worrying about you."

"We can spend time arguing about this, or we can go. I can take care of myself."

Ethan's jaws clenched hard enough to make diamonds. After several moments of deliberation, he reluctantly conceded. In the car, however, I was met with a litany of instructions. The growing theme of each one was that if things got out of control or became too dangerous, I was to leave. I listened. There was no harm in listening, but there was absolutely no way I was leaving without doing what I could to help. Looking straight ahead, Ethan exhaled several ragged breaths, seemingly aware that nothing he could say would change my mind. "Sky, I need you to be careful."

I nodded. I'd be careful, but I wasn't leaving him behind under any circumstances.

It was dusk but seemed later as we drove down the long driveway, bordered by a crowd of trees so thick I could barely see the homes beyond them. Sebastian's home reminded me of the pack's. Neighbors were separated by miles of land; each house might as well have been its own subdivision. If the extended boundaries of Sebastian's property weren't enough to discourage visitors, then the long crawl up his driveway to the large, sand-colored brick home might. The house itself made a statement. And the statement was: "I don't want to be bothered."

Although off-putting, Sebastian's home had a cosmopolitan, urbanely elegant air. Tall, overstated pillars reminiscent of Greek architecture surrounded the brick neoclassic home. Huge windows provided an unobstructed view of the lush trees that encircled his property and the meticulously manicured shrubbery that skirted it. The place *was* Sebastian. The Alpha who embodied many complexities and contradictions: ruthless and cold when necessary, but capable of kindness, gentility, and warmth as well. A man who headed the strongest pack in the country, while possessing a deep appreciation for fine food, unconventional art, and literature. His home was a conflation of those things.

The front door had been rammed open; splinters of wood littered the foyer floor. We entered warily. Windows had been broken, and shards of glass covered the hardwood floors. Remnants of something toxic lingered in the air.

"Gas?" Ethan said, his hand covering his nose. His sense of smell was more acute than mine. The odor was tolerable because of the breeze coming through the broken windows. Chunks of plaster were scattered about and there were body-shaped holes in the walls. There was blood everywhere. I was cautious as I navigated around it, leaning in to take a whiff.

None of it was Sebastian's. Ethan knew it, too. Relief softened his grimace as he continued to assess the house. Ariel, startled by our approach as we entered the kitchen, flicked a menacing bolt of magic in our direction. It slammed into the protective field that I'd quickly erected.

6

A gasped apology was smothered by the hand she placed over her mouth.

"What are you doing here?" Ethan asked.

Ariel's white, airy shift dress exposed parts of her toned shoulders through cutouts. It fell only mid-thigh, revealing toned legs enhanced by pastel-print stilettos. The relaxed V-neck of the dress offered a slight peek of a pale pink, satin and lace bra that pushed up her breasts.

"I had a meeting with Sebastian. He told me to just let myself in when I arrived," she said when my gaze went to her coat, lying across the arm of the sofa.

Meeting? Is that what the kids are calling it these days? If Sebastian is comfortable telling you to let yourself in, this isn't the first time.

"Meeting?" I asked, with an inquiring brow. *No meeting is complete without a beautiful dress, stilettos, and a push-up bra.*

I took in the scene and inhaled to pick up the other subtle scents in the home. It looked as if Sebastian had been preparing dinner for their "meeting." A bottle of red wine and two glasses were set out. The scents of cinnamon, sage, roasted meat, onions, and vanilla permeated the air in the room. I wasn't sure why she didn't want to admit it was a date—she couldn't possibly believe we thought this was a "meeting."

"I haven't been here long. Once I realized he wasn't here, I erected a ward to protect me while I investigated." She shook her head, and I could feel the heaviness of her emotions. "I should have known something would happen to him when London informed me of the other missing were-animals." She made a face and looked around the room.

The scent of blood mixed with the acrid smells of medicine and metal. Had they used tranquilizers? The drugs worked on us but had to be given in very heavy doses and wouldn't last long. That wouldn't matter if they had braced him with silver. Not only did it weaken were-animals; it also prevented us from healing. Silver aversion was something I didn't have, as a result of my unusual background.

Sebastian's home was decorated similarly to his office. Avant-garde art and nature scenes decorated neutral-colored walls. The expensive, dark wood furniture that lined the walls was splattered with blood. A large coffee table had been flipped over and one of its legs was missing. After a quick scan of the room I located the battered leg, which seemed to have been used as a weapon. The wall-mounted television was cracked. Sebastian was gone, but he'd put up a hell of a fight.

Ethan's phone rang. "What's wrong?" he asked, instead of giving a greeting.

"Sebastian's gone," came a panic-strained Quinn's voice.

"I know—"

"No ... you don't understand. When everyone started going missing, he said he had a tracker with him. I had him for a while and then it just shut off."

"You think they found it?"

"Maybe, but it's in his mouth. It's a cap that goes over the tooth. Sebastian said it was uncomfortable, but he'd wear it just in case."

"It was moving from the house, right?" Ethan asked.

"Yes. But then it stopped. If he'd lost it, then its position would be stagnant. It just went blank on my screen."

Ethan's brow furrowed and then his eyes narrowed. I heard the sound, too. "I'll call you back."

He ended the call and headed toward the back of the house. Ariel and I trailed behind him. He stopped to turn in my direction, and I knew he planned to tell me either to stay behind or leave. I fixed him with a look that made my point. I wasn't going anywhere, and I damn sure wasn't staying behind.

Ethan backtracked and used the side door of the house to leave. There were sounds coming from the front and the back. Ariel slipped off her heels and signaled that she was going to the front. Sparks of magic laced around her fingers, and with slow, silent movements she eased to the front of the house.

Ethan turned his head, listening intently to the sounds around us. I walked quietly, surveying the area by allowing my senses to fully take over. The various smells that lingered provided the most information. I inhaled: the smell of gunfire, iron, evergreen mixed with chemicals, probably cologne. Wind whistling through the branches, bristling sounds from the tufts of grass and swaying leaves, and noises of small animals living in the wooded area that surrounded Sebastian's home all competed as a distraction.

Slight, indecipherable noises came from the distance, followed by the sounds of booted feet tramping hard against the ground, coming toward us. Ethan went east, I moved west. Suddenly, a sharp cry shot through the air. It came from the direction I'd seen Ethan go. Soon after that, a wail of pain and the distinct sound of bone breaking.

Ariel shrieked. I followed the direction of the sound, and darted toward the front of the house. Magic seeped into the air. Sounds of violence and aggression came from Ethan's direction. I heard the familiar thud of a body being slammed to the ground.

I had a fraction of a moment to decide whether to continue following the magic in Ariel's direction or the sounds coming from Ethan's direction. A gunshot made the decision for me. I followed it toward Ethan and found three men on the ground. One's head was twisted at an odd angle that no one could survive. Another's leg was wrenched into a painful bend. Face grimaced and eyes screwed shut, he bit down on his lips to suppress wails of pain. The third was in the best condition, suffering from what looked like a broken ankle and a punch to the throat; his hand was pressed to his neck as he struggled for each breath. Ethan was crouched over him, prepared to finish the job.

Four men dressed in military-style clothing and holding assault weapons charged Ethan.

"Put your hands up. Now, dammit!" one of them demanded.

Ethan was slow to move. After another command and the cock of a gun, he stood. His eyes lifted to my direction as he pondered their request to put his hands up. I jumped when someone shot. Not one of the men surrounding him, but someone a few feet away. A dart was embedded in Ethan's arm. He blinked several times, struggling to keep his footing, but eventually collapsed to the ground. I used magic to send the men holding the assault weapons back. Two hit the tree. The other two hurtled back, causing weapons to go off in the air, bullets raining down.

"Contain her!" the man with the dart gun yelled, making an effort to come to his feet. Another sweep of magic and his legs collapsed under him. It took an exceptional amount of magic to hold them all down, and I was starting to feel the effort. Footsteps resounded against the ground and I whipped around, striking the first man in the nose with the heel of my hand. He crashed into another man, whom I grabbed and threw to the ground with a hip toss. I spun and kicked the gun out of the hand of another. He stumbled back. I swiped his leg out from under him before he could regain his footing. When he crashed to the ground, I lunged for his discarded gun but came to a quick stop when I felt metal pressed against the back of my head.

"That's enough of that." The voice was as hard and cold as the gun barrel pressed against my skull.

"She has dark hair," someone from the group pointed out.

"Turn around," another commanding voice said. The gun bumped against my head to urge me to move. I turned to face a taller man. With salt-and-pepper hair, cropped short, and golden, weather-marked skin, he looked as cold, calculating, and cruel as his voice.

The salt-and-pepper man, who had to be the lead on this, moved closer. "She has dark hair and green eyes. This is the one we can't take," he informed the men. Focused, glacial eyes that seemed bronze instead of brown studied me. "*Cómo te llamas?*" What is your name?

He asked my name in poorly pronounced Spanish with an American accent. I wasn't sure if he didn't know I was Portuguese or thought the languages were similar enough that I would understand. Perhaps he didn't know or care to know there was a difference.

"Your name?" His tone had a serrated edge to it when he asked again in English.

I pulled my lips tight, defiant.

Darkly amused, he chuckled. "If you're the person we were instructed to leave alone, you might want to give me a name. Otherwise"—his eyes flickered with cruelty—"you'll be going with us."

My eyes trailed in Ethan's direction. He had three darts embedded in him, and a man was now leaning over him, injecting him with something. I had to suppress my anger in order to make a decision based on logic and not emotions. If they took me, I would have to rely on others to find us. But the advantage of going would be that they'd take me to where they had Sebastian and the others, or at least I hoped. Then we could escape together. I had to consider that if it were that easy to escape, they would have. If I stayed behind, I had the resources to find them and figure out who the gun-toting militia was.

"Sky ... Skylar Brooks."

Smiling, he nodded. "Well, Ms. Sky ... Skylar Brooks, you are a very lucky woman. A lot of very important people want you alive." He leaned in, assessing me, as if trying to determine why I was being spared. What about me warranted amnesty from this? Based on the unsated curious scowl, he hadn't figured it out.

"Leave her, but you will have to cuff her," he ordered

someone behind me. "Use the same type you used on the witch. Bind her legs, too. I'm sure someone will be here soon to retrieve her." I assumed the witch they were talking about was Ariel, which would explain why she hadn't retaliated. The leader turned away and headed toward Ethan.

I wasn't confident that the man with the gun pressed against me, who kept bumping it against my head, was okay with the command. It was doubtful he'd follow the order unless he was under the commander's scrutinizing gaze. My hands were positioned behind me, and someone slipped manacles on my wrists. They weren't heavy enough to be iridium, and I was thankful for that. I would have access to magic.

"Wrong ones. They need to be exactly like the ones you use for witches. Those are iron; iridium is heavier and paler in color," someone from my left informed him. I heard the clank of metal as they shuffled through what I suspected was a bag of metal restraints. The gun stayed pressed firmly against my head until the other cuffs were replaced. Playing it safe, they made sure the second pair was on before removing the first.

My attention was on Ethan as they jerked him up and carried him away, when a red-headed woman obstructed my view. She studied me with the same curiosity as the man who'd asked my name.

"I thought she's one of those things that turn into an animal." Her disgust was apparent even without the frown that crinkled her wide features. Her accent was peculiar, as if she'd forgotten to mask it in the middle of the sentence, so it was an odd Australian/American English mixture. My face scrunched at the change in her dialect. Noticing it, she shot me a sharp glare.

"Yeah, she's supposed to be one, too, but also a witch of some kind. Don't care. We were just instructed to leave her behind," the man who had been holding the gun to my head informed her as he holstered his weapon.

The woman continued to look at me with morbid curiosity,

removing her attention only to catch the zip tie tossed in her direction. I could see her intent before she did it, so I swiped her leg at that moment. Whoever wanted me alive probably didn't specify in what condition. I stomped on her leg and heard it crack. She howled on the ground, rolling and grabbing her fractured leg. I whipped around and kneed the man with the gun in the groin. When he doubled over, I smashed my knee into his head. He'd feel that later. He dropped to his knees, grimacing but refusing to fall to the ground. I helped him by kicking him squarely in his chin.

He went down at the same time something hard hit my shoulder, with enough force to send me crashing to the ground. Without my hands to brace myself or help with my balance, I fell on my side. Another hard impact went into my leg. The rubber bullets striking me hurt like hell.

"Ms. Brooks," said another man, slowly approaching me, carrying the shotgun that I suspected had delivered the shots. He had a similarly rough, hybrid Australian/American voice, as commanding and forceful as that of the commander who'd asked my name. "We were instructed not to bring you with us or kill you. There are a lot of ways we can leave you here without killing you but definitely making you regret your actions. Do you want us to do that?"

I remained silent as he moved over me and pointed the barrel of the shotgun at my face. I didn't want to feel that anywhere near my face. I shook my head.

He instructed someone to secure my legs. I lay on the ground, trying to commit all the smells and sounds to memory, hoping they would help me in the future. Each face that came into view, I studied. I looked at their guns, their weapons, the brand of the bags they carried. I knew who had an accent, who faked a Midwest one, the color of their hair. I knew the brand and type of hats they wore, and every identifying thing about them I could perceive. I committed it all to memory. They moved away from me, taking the same route they had taken Ethan, a small path in the woods. I assumed it had been made by Sebastian's constant use. When they were gone, I wiggled myself into a seated position. Among all the things I'd memorized, the one that stuck out the most was that someone wanted me alive and all the Alphas and Betas out of the picture.

CHAPTER 2

he people behind the attack might have spared my life, but they wanted me helpless, I thought as I jerked at the cuffs, trying to break them. It was highly unlikely I'd get out of iridium, and with my legs zip-tied I didn't have the option to run for help. Despite the surge of hopelessness, I worked on the handcuffs, twisting and jerking them. The salt-and-pepper man's words replayed in my head in a continuous loop: "A lot of very powerful people want you alive."

But who?

Ethos was the first person to come to mind—but he was dead. I'd cut off his head, and Ethan had finished the job with a spell. My second suspect was Dexter, who had the financial resources to execute such an elaborate abduction of Demetrius and the strongest were-animals in the world. He was financially secure enough to discard a pair of iridium cuffs as if they were cheap handcuffs from the costume store. He'd be at the top of the list if I hadn't seen him shot to death. Dexter would have hired Hunters, not people who didn't know the difference between iridium and iron cuffs. There were too many people involved. This would have taken more than the seven Hunters that I was aware of near us. These people seemed military—maybe mercenaries. A lump formed in my throat. Whoever the hell they were, they knew we existed. Would they become a bigger problem?

It came down to either the Red Blood or Ronan Everest, who'd been responsible for the abductions years ago. Ronan was said to be dead, and I was positive that wasn't something Ethan would have left unconfirmed.

"Ariel!" I yelled.

"Yes." Anger reverberated in her voice, and I knew it came from being divested of her ability to use magic. Josh had been cuffed once and been so agitated by it that we'd had to pull over the car we'd been riding in to take them off. Magic was the very essence of powerful witches, and taking away their ability to use it was as devastating to them as inhibiting a vital organ.

"Are you okay?"

"I'm fine, but I have to get these handcuffs off me," she responded with a painful grunt, no doubt trying to either yank them apart or squeeze her hand through the brace. Inch by inch, I made my way toward her. It was going to take forever to get to the front of the house where she was. I'd made it a foot when I heard voices: Gavin and Winter.

"You want some help?" Gavin asked, walking toward me.

"No, I just want to stay bound in the back of Sebastian's home," I mouthed back.

"Okay, well, let me go help Winter with Ariel until—"

"Gavin, help me," I grumbled, annoyed.

"Make up your mind," he snapped back—but there was an undercurrent of humor to his tone. He was working hard at making the dire situation lighter. I realized it was not for him, but for me. When my emotions rode high, they affected the pack.

Slowly he moved around me, getting into position behind me, observing his surroundings and inhaling the air.

16

"They had guns?" he asked, but with his keen sense of smell, he knew. "And sedatives?"

I confirmed, staying still as he wiggled tools behind me, making disgruntled noises as he worked on the lock.

"Did you see their faces?"

"Yes, they weren't trying to hide them."

He made another unpleasant sound. "They're arrogant and feel they are untouchable. Confident that a visual ID isn't possible. They probably aren't from around here," he growled through clenched teeth. His anger and frustration were showing in his handling of the cuffs. I had a feeling he wasn't very good at picking locks.

"Do you need help?" Steven asked, coming into sight as well. He wore the same grim look he'd had since he'd learned of the disappearance of his mother, the Southern Pack leader. "Winter just got Ariel loose, and she said the locks were difficult."

I heard the lie in his voice, so I knew Gavin did, too. Steven was always the amiable one and would do what was necessary to spare someone's feelings.

A little over five minutes later I was free and rubbing my raw wrists while Gavin, Steven, and Winter surveyed the area and questioned Ariel and me.

Magic hummed off Ariel. Her cheeks were ruddy and her lips pulled so tight, I knew she was itching to use magic, probably violently. So much of it had been pent up while she was restricted by the braces. Her movements were rigid and stiff while she gave a visual demonstration of everything that had occurred. The visual wasn't needed, but it seemed to help get rid of that energy.

While she went over the events, I worked on staying calm, slowing my mind to make sense of things. I had to find Ethan and the others.

Josh and London popped in just as I was looking over the area again. Josh released London and surveyed the area. His

17

hard-pounding heart was too distracting to ignore. Slowly he walked over the area, surveying the scene as his breath became labored and sharper.

"Josh," London whispered, approaching him as he scanned the area, checking his phone periodically.

"I'm fine," he lied in a tight voice. He was far from fine, as the sparks of magic coming off the hand without the phone and his increasingly labored breathing indicated.

"What happened?" he asked, still searching the grounds slowly and with purpose. I followed him, giving him a rundown of what I'd witnessed and what Ariel had revealed. He listened but was obviously distracted by whatever he was looking for. Eventually he knelt down and showed me Ethan's damaged phone.

The destroyed phone snapped the tenuous control he had over his emotions, and he bowed his head. "I have to find my brother." My eyes shifted from him; I was unable to bear the look of pain etched on his face.

"We will," I promised.

CHAPTER 3

I pushed back the wet hair that was obscuring my view of the information Quinn had pulled up on his computer. Removing the dirt and grime from my body had helped calm me, and I preferred the smell of vanilla bath wash over that of blood, metal, and grass that had clung to me. Driving back to the pack house had helped relieve some of my anxiety. I'd sped along through the streets, windows open, allowing the cool air to inundate my senses and distract me. Or distract me as much as was possible. Which only meant I wasn't anxiety-riddled or ready to rip anyone apart with my bare hands. The ride had added discernment to my anger, and I wanted to be very specific about whom I ripped apart.

"This is everything you have on Ronan?" I asked.

Quinn nodded, frowning. "His body was found. Attacked by an animal. It's not him doing this."

He clicked a few keys on the computer, bringing up police reports, a death certificate, autopsy, and will. His eyes slid to the side to look at my face, expecting a show of disapproval. There wasn't any. I needed Quinn and all his ethically questionable tactics. I was operating in the gray and knew I would have to, in order to find everyone.

I paced, my attention drifting about the office occupied by the Worgen, new additions to the pack after Sebastian decided he would no longer allow fringe packs after I was brutally attacked by one. They weren't much of a pack to begin with, rather geek squad, and they stood out among the members of our pack. Peculiar posters covered the walls. Life-sized superheroes were in every corner. Gaming laptops were stacked on a chair and a side table. On another desk, on the other side of the massive room—the result of a wall being removed to give them space to work—were stacks of board games I'd never heard of. I'd overheard them tell Gavin they had purchased them at a board game convention, something I hadn't been aware existed. It seemed Gavin had been in the dark as well, but he hadn't had any compunctions about telling them how little he cared about the new information.

Quinn clicked a few more keys, and all the information switched to the screen on the wall so we all could look at it. Winter stood to my right, Gavin to my left, and Steven was closer to the screen, studying it intently.

"What do we do next?" Winter asked me.

Shocked, my head snapped in her direction. Why was she asking me? I expected her to take the lead.

"Do you want me to look into the Red Blood?" Quinn asked me.

I nodded.

"Is it okay if I start questioning people? I'd like to talk to Mason and Gideon. They might have heard something," Gavin asked.

Um ... okay? I wasn't sure why he was asking me but I was more than happy that he was willing to do it. The last thing I wanted to deal with was Gideon, formally known as the Prince of Mischief and now the new leader of the elves. I definitely didn't have the patience to handle the embittered former leader, Mason. *Have at it.*

"Sky, I think that's a good idea, don't you?" Chris's voice came from behind us. I turned around to find Kelly escorting her in. Kelly gave me an inquiring look, as if she wanted to know whether it was okay or if she needed to escort her out. I nodded assent.

"Chris." Winter said her name with a practiced hospitality.

It seemed to amuse Chris that Winter was making an effort to be polite and congenial. Gnawing at my gut was the feeling that the Hunter-turned-vampire could have used the abductions as a way to get rid of Demetrius. We'd settled into a comfortable place of being reluctant associates, and I guessed since I'd played a part in her plot to take over the Southern and Northern Seethes, I was her accomplice as well.

"Chris," I said, walking toward her. Jerking my chin toward the door, I invited her to join me in the hallway. We walked down the hall toward the infirmary and then into one of the recovery rooms, where I closed the door behind us.

The words didn't come immediately because I struggled for a way to ask without sounding rude; depending on the answer, it might get violent.

"Ask me, Bambi," Chris urged in a cool, even voice.

I frowned. "Did you have anything to do with the abductions?" Her eyes widened, but it wasn't the question that provoked that response; it was my voice. Laden with fire and steel, it sounded raw with malicious intent and rage. So much so, that Chris took a step back.

"No. I didn't have anything to do with this, and I want to help because I think the same people who took your people are the ones who took Demetrius. I need him back."

"Why? This is perfect. He's gone. You now are free to take over the North—" I stopped myself abruptly. I was about to tell her to take over the South by force if needed. That feeling of drowning in a swamp overtook me, and I sucked in a sharp breath. Was it my hate for Demetrius that was the root of it, or had I devolved into a person who cared only for my pack? It seemed I wasn't just toeing the gray line—I'd stepped over to black.

"You're right, we need to find Demetrius, too," I conceded, but it didn't make me feel better. He wasn't a priority, but if the same person who'd abducted him had taken our Alphas and Betas, he would be rescued as well.

Chris gave me a sympathetic smile, as if she knew the dark place where my thoughts had ventured.

She shrugged. "His abduction is at an inopportune time. He hasn't presented me to the Seethe as the Mistress. I need him to do that. Until he does, I care very much about his safety."

Oh, so you really do *need to find him.*

"Does Chase get the position if Demetrius doesn't return?"

She nodded. "And taking the North from him would be harder—much harder. I need to find Demetrius. And he needs to be in a condition capable of 'presenting' me to the others." I didn't ask what "presenting" meant. As we made our way back to Quinn's office, I snickered at the image of Demetrius presenting her to the other vampires the way the Lion King presented the cub Simba. The image was so vivid in my mind that I laughed out loud, earning me a sideways glance from Chris.

"I'll follow your lead as the Alpha of the pack," she informed me, bringing my laughter to an abrupt halt. I still had my hand on the knob of the door I'd just opened.

"What?"

"The Alpha is missing but not presumed dead, which means his responsibilities go to the Beta. You're the Beta of the pack, since Ethan is only missing, not declared dead."

That explained the reverence people were giving me and the way they were running tactical suggestions by me. The image of the Lion King was gone and, for a brief moment, my mind was blank. Completely blank. I'm not sure if someone had asked my name at that moment I'd have been able to give it to them. *I* was to take on the Alpha role.

Chris smiled and nudged me through the doorway, where I'd stopped to let the situation sink in. I'd be whatever I needed to be to get everyone back, but I didn't want to be the Alpha. I'd never felt more out of my depth, but I refused to show it. Putting on false bravado to mask my rampant insecurities, I walked down the hall and back into the Worgen room with purpose.

"Gavin, I think you should talk to the elves and anyone else you think might know anything. If you find that anyone else is missing, no matter how minor their role is, please let me know as soon as possible. Right now, the pattern's thrown off because of Demetrius. Why would they take Demetrius and not—" I stopped and directed my question to Chris. "Alexander isn't missing, correct?"

"Not to my knowledge."

I continued my first thought. "And not Alexander. That just doesn't make sense."

"Could Alexander be involved? Maybe he wanted to get rid of Demetrius so he could be the Master of both the North and the South."

Chris shook her head. "Something like this is too strategic for him. You're giving him far too much credit. He's an irresponsible man-child with fangs, nothing more."

It wasn't Alexander or Mason. Gavin assured me that it wasn't Gideon, but I knew that before he'd given me his findings. Gideon had proved to be a good ally and ever grateful that we'd saved his life. He showed his appreciation at every chance.

Gavin's anger and frustration had been barely controlled when he'd returned from seeing Gideon and informed me that Abigail was no longer in the country. She'd taken a vacation to Amsterdam to visit family.

I wasn't ready to check Abigail off my list; that she was visiting family right now seemed too coincidental. She was manipulative and capable of very calculated, elaborate plans. I recalled the appalled innocent-bystander look she'd put on when an assassination attempt was made against her brother—an attempt she was responsible for. We'd also discovered her role in organizing an army to get rid of the were-animals, in the event that we weren't able to "fix" things after a violent altercation involving Steven was caught on tape.

I didn't trust Abigail.

Gideon's shocked face was expected when I barged my way into his home, past the assistants who'd answered the door. He greeted me with a reverence that shocked me, bowing his head in acknowledgment before shifting his attention to Winter and Steven, who stood on each side of me.

"Skylar, how are you?"

"How do you think I am? My Alpha and my mate are missing. And I just found out your sister is missing as well. How convenient for her."

"She's not missing; she's on vacation," he corrected. "She was overdue for one. My dear sister has been far too involved with my transition, and it was taking a toll on her." I could sense the secrets behind his peculiar violet eyes and the strain on his slight features. His lips were pulled into a tight line, as if he believed the truth would be spilled if he dared relax them. I wasn't sure if it had anything to do with us or something else. His sister had her hands in so many things, he might have sent her away to protect her from her actions involving someone else. Or she'd left on her own—gone into hiding.

Gideon's stature, tall and thin as a waif, made him seem deceptively harmless. He was able to control the elements and had a mischievous nature. Once hailed as the Prince of Mischief, he'd never wanted the position of leader of the elves. He'd taken it but didn't adhere to the same rules as his predecessor—his father. I wasn't sure if that made him a good leader or a dangerous one. He'd been on our side—an ally—but I imagined as an enemy he could be formidable and probably as cunning and duplicitous as his sister.

No matter how angry I was, diplomacy was needed.

"I need to speak with your sister," I informed him in a low, even, stern voice. His eyes flashed and lightning crackled outside. Apparently, the diplomacy I wanted to demonstrate hadn't translated in the delivery.

Taking several moments to find his composure, he gave me a faint, apologetic smile. "I know my sister had met with Cole several times. I'm not sure if she was the last person to see him before he went missing." Gideon sighed. "I can assure you she didn't have anything to do with it."

"Then why is she gone?" Steven interjected in a poorly controlled growl. Gold coursed over his eyes and his hands were balled at his side. His mother was missing and if Gideon was withholding information, it wasn't going to end well for him. Taking a few steps, I put myself between the two.

"You can imagine this doesn't look good for Abigail. Our Alphas and Betas are missing and she decides to take a vacation," Winter offered, displaying remarkable control. A contrast to what she'd shown in the car, which was several detailed plans of her murderous intentions toward Abigail if she was in any way involved.

"She didn't decide to go; I sent her when I heard that Cole was missing," Gideon admitted. His tone and presence commanded the room now, and he stood taller, his eyes as frosty and indomitable as he'd become. "I am not blind to my sister's ambition and some of her less-than-admirable behavior as of late. But she would not be involved in something like that."

"I would like the chance to ask her," I said.

"You won't get that chance. Do you know how I know your Alphas and Betas are missing? The otherworld is aflutter." He took a breath but I could tell he was using that moment to gather his thoughts to present them judiciously. "People are just concerned because when you all feel attacked, you aren't discerning about who is injured by the machine you use to protect yourself." Again, he took a moment, and when he spoke, his voice was even and held a hint of sympathy. "I've admired Sebastian for a long time and respect the measures he takes to protect his pack." His gaze traveled to Winter and Steven and then back to me. "The lengths you all go to—but they are not without consequences. The reluctant or uneasy acceptance of your past behaviors by others and the secrets that surround your pack have left you with more enemies than you may suspect."

"Do you know who's behind this?" I asked.

He shook his head. "I don't." His voice lowered. "I'd tell you if I knew, not because I trust you any longer but because I am bound to you for saving my life."

Shocked by his response, I felt my mouth drop open. He held up his hand to prevent me from speaking. "Only a fool would ignore your history or the myriad of dubious things that have happened over the years that suggest your pack's involvement. Long-standing curses removed from the vampires and the Tre'ases. The death of Tre'ases who'd been here for hundreds of years. Were-animals who are oddly connected to the dark forest and can subjugate the vilest of creatures in it with their presence. You are able to perform magic—strong magic. And so can your mate." He gripped his lips between his teeth and then released them, leaving them rose colored. A dark shadow moved over his features and made its way into his words. He frowned. "We can't ignore that the Faeries returned and your pack are who they came for. I can't help but wonder if we were fighting against the very people who might have returned to protect us. Perhaps they know something we don't. Maybe they can see what the future may hold, or remember what it's like when a small group obtains great power."

"You're taking a bunch of unrelated events and attributing them to us—and making more of them than there is," I asserted in defense.

"Am I?" he scoffed, adding a humorless laugh. He seemed to have aged in the few minutes I'd been there. Hardened and weighted, carrying a burden that had pushed away the carefree person I'd known when we'd first met. What had put that look on his face? His position, or the perceived danger he suspected my pack to be?

"We aren't a threat."

"Ms. Brooks, you are not a fool. You know what your pack is capable of, the power it wields, the lines that are crossed to protect it, the alliances you form to further your self-interest. And eventually we will have to deal with whatever is produced by your union with Ethan. Understand, people are watching."

Eyes closed, I absorbed the information. People were watching me, Ethan—us. Our union wasn't just a surprise to me, but undesired by others. We were the villains in so many people's stories, and no matter how I attempted to brush the insult aside, it lingered heavily, creating a burden I couldn't just shrug off.

My mind raced, and sorting out the many thoughts that traveled through it became increasingly difficult under Gideon's disapproving gaze.

I turned and headed out of the door. "I need to speak with

27

your sister. This isn't a request you should ignore," I demanded, putting enough steel in my voice that it left no room for debate.

If it meant finding Ethan and the others, I'd be the villain in this scene. No matter what I'd decided to do to find the Alphas, it was difficult shrugging off Gideon's words. Defensively, my mind worked overtime to justify my pack's actions, though my conscience knew it was utter BS.

CHAPTER 4

The next day I paced in Quinn's office under the watchful gaze of those present. My mind raced, trying to process everything. There were probably more players in this than I'd initially suspected. My eyes flicked toward Chris, who'd come bearing more bad news: Alexander, the Master of the South, had been taken just a few hours earlier.

Quinn was slouched at his seat at the computer, his brows furrowed in concentration and his hands moving, deftly rotating the Rubik's Cube in his hand. He had a lot of nervous quirks, but this was by far the oddest. He'd finished three and stacked them on the table next to him.

"They didn't kill them on sight," I mused, breaking the tense silence. All eyes were on me. "If they just wanted to get rid of them, they would have killed them on the spot. They want them for something." Abruptly, I stopped pacing.

Quinn became motionless. "But Ronan didn't have any partners that I could find, and his estate went to his sisters. I've checked them out and there isn't anything suspicious about them or their accounts, except for the large sum of money they received from their inheritance."

"And the Red Blood?" Winter asked, pushing up from the wall she had been leaning against.

Quinn set the Rubik's Cube on the table, then picked up his laser pointer and aimed it at the screen on the wall. "They're still active, but sticking with their same schtick of exposing us to the world, planning more kidnappings and videos of us shifting. But because of what happened with your abduction, no one's willing to bite the bullet and do it again unless they are absolutely sure. They were so sure about you, Sky." He smiled with admiration. "You didn't change, which has shaken their confidence. They thought they could pick us out. Apparently, we don't look human and demon magic makes us *so* alluring and enchanting." Quinn rolled his eyes and made a mocking face.

They weren't wrong; I'd felt it the first time I'd encountered a were. I suspected that they were so used to feeling like that around one another that they didn't sense the predator's allure that emanated from them. It was nebulous and subtle. People found themselves drawn to a person who piqued their interest even while their body's alarms were going off, signaling them to run like hell. The were's magnetism silenced the warnings. I understood what they were talking about—even Quinn and his pack of super geeks possessed it.

"So, do we mark them off the list?" Steven asked.

When the line was crossed through their names, a heaviness returned, as it had with each person we marked off. What if I was wrong?

We'd marked off Gideon, but not his sister, Abigail. Mason was marked off the list but the reasons were flimsy at best and I went back and forth on whether to keep him on it. He hated were-animals and wouldn't have bothered abducting them. He'd have killed them on the spot, especially Ethan and Sebastian. He seemed to be waiting for a reason to get rid of the were-animals because he thought we were going to out ourselves to the humans. Mason had hired mercenaries and Hunters to "contain us." But the pieces didn't align because Demetrius and Alexander were missing, too.

The witches were excluded because, at that moment, they were in the other room trying to perform a locating spell, using Josh's blood, to find Ethan. I just couldn't believe that anyone could be so deceitful as to offer assistance while being the culprit. I thought of Abigail, who'd played the grief-stricken sister with an award-winning performance, all the while being responsible for the assassination attempt on her brother. But it was easy for one person to pretend. Could every one of the witches be that great an actor? Chris had pointed out that they didn't have the financial resources to conduct such a massive abduction.

Chris had eased herself into a corner, attempting to be unobtrusive, something quite difficult. Her vampire prowess was showcased in an outfit of all black: sleek fitted leather pants and a button-down shirt that had several buttons open to reveal a cross necklace. The latter contradicted the belief that her kind couldn't be exposed to symbols of religion. That might have been a new development, the result of our removing the spell that ultimately lifted their aversion to sunlight as well.

"It's safe to say it's not the Red Blood," Chris said, pushing herself up from the wall. She picked up a dossier of the group's members that one of the Worgen pack had made. "They don't have the cash. If the assault team was as elaborate as Sky reports —iridium handcuffs, weapons, access to drugs strong enough to disable you all—then you are looking at someone with money. If they're spending this type of money and it's not to kill you, it's for something that's very important or can bring them more money than what was spent." Face rigid with contemplation, she continued, "I suspect there is someone else doing what Ronan tried. If my information about what happened before is correct, then this could easily be a payoff close to seven figures. Before, they had were-animals from small packs, which wouldn't pull the same type of money as Alphas, Betas, and the Masters of the Seethes."

"You think they're going to hunt them like animals?" I asked incredulously.

Chris nodded, her attention on the wall of information in front of her. "Exactly. Now we have to figure out who."

I wasn't ready to let Abigail off the hook so fast, although I suspected that Chris was right. My curiosity was still piqued in regards to Abigail. Why had she met with Cole? Had that precipitated the chain of events? I didn't have a chance to pose my question before my phone rang. It was an unknown number.

"My brother said you wanted to speak with me," Abigail said in a soft, melodic voice, shot through with notes of irritation.

"I'd prefer it to be in person."

"I'd prefer not to have my vacation ruined by your inane accusations. Do you really believe I'm responsible for Cole's disappearance?"

"I'm not sure, which is why I wanted to talk to you, but I guess on the phone is just as good. You're so skilled at acting innocent, I doubt seeing you would help me determine the truth."

"If she's opening her mouth, she's probably lying," Winter grumbled from across the room. Abigail might have missed Winter's comment since elves weren't known to have preternatural hearing, but she had to be aware of Winter's feelings. After their relationship ended Winter had never attempted to mince words when dealing with Abigail.

"Why were you meeting with Cole?"

"No reason in particular. We have a lot in common," she offered aloofly.

"That is?"

"We both find your pack's secrets and the lengths you go to

in order to keep them dangerous. Obviously someone else feels the same way, which is why your people are missing. Do you all ever think about the consequences of your actions, or do you really feel immune to them? Your pack's the reason the Faeries resurfaced. Did you think that would go unnoticed?"

"Are you really in a position to chastise us over ethics and behavior?"

Several beats of silence passed and I wondered if she was having a moment of self-reflection.

"I made the situation for our people better. My brother is a better leader than anyone they would have put in place. He has mended the relationship between the elves and Makellos—"

"There isn't a mend; it's conditional and the Makellos are only playing nice because of your brother's relationship with us. While you choose to point out our many faults, you might remember that if there were to be a civil war among the elves your brother can call on us if needed. Liam's certainly aware of it. However, I will make sure that we don't answer any future call if I find out you had anything to do with the disappearances. I will find the people responsible and make them pay, especially if it's you."

"I had nothing to do with it." The cold, hard realization of the situation took the arrogance out of her voice.

"Do you know anything that can help us find them?"

There was another long pause before she responded, "No."

We hung up, and I looked over my shoulder for confirmation that Abigail was telling the truth. Weres had exceptional hearing, but Abigail was such a prolific liar and performer that none of us, not even Winter, could be sure.

I refocused on the information before me. "People know about us." I wasn't sure why that suddenly surprised me. My neighbors knew supernaturals existed, the vampires' garden knew, and so did the Red Blood. We weren't as concealed as we once liked to believe.

33

"That's nothing new, Sky," Chris offered. "Small pockets of people knowing about us or suspecting our existence isn't a problem. However, there are some that know who use our desire to stay secret to their advantage. This is one of those cases. We are limited on what we can do. In most cases like this —mass abductions—federal agents or local police could be called. We don't have the advantage of using those resources."

She was right; we were at a disadvantage.

"I need a moment," I said, excusing myself.

I needed more than just a moment, I needed fresh air. My mind was too crowded to sort out and I had to find something to clear it.

Standing at the back of the house, I looked over the expansive forest. Lush trees, vibrant green grass that managed to look lively and healthy despite being trampled constantly by us. I inhaled, taking in the earthy scents of oak and dirt. It wasn't as calming as it usually was: now the trees weren't a refuge but perches for hunters to wait for Ethan and the others. The thick flourish of leaves obscured the full view of the sky, nothing more than camouflage for a hunter. Scents that I'd formerly enjoyed could mask another—the hunter's.

"What's going through your mind?" Josh asked from behind me. My arms hugged around me. I kept my eyes on the woods. He moved toward me, cracking fallen branches and snapping me out of my fugue state. I was grateful for it. The visions of people being hunted for sport seemed too real.

"I guess the locating spell didn't work?" I asked.

"No," he croaked out in a disappointed whisper. Using Josh's blood to find Ethan had been a long shot, but it had been worth trying. Josh's fear, anguish, and frustration were palpable, and I didn't know how to ease them. His brother was missing and he was doing an exceptional job of holding it together. But the mask crumbled, and I saw the pain.

"There's no sensing him, either. I thought I'd be able to do it," I said grimly. While they'd been taking him, part of me thought that would be the way I could find him. But in place of feeling him, there was a void.

"If he's still heavily sedated"—Josh seemed despondent and his eyes were heavy with sorrow, making me curious how I looked to him—"you won't be able to." He scrubbed his hand over a shading of beard. "Do you think Chris is on to something? Is it similar to what Ronan did?"

"I don't know. It's possible, but that doesn't seem to add up and I'm not sure why."

"Because there isn't a why?" he offered.

"Exactly. Why now, of all times? What was the inciting incident?"

"Does it matter?"

"I suppose it doesn't, but knowing will prevent it from happening again."

"Killing the person responsible the first time didn't. I doubt it will this time," he pointed out.

"I guess you're right." But I couldn't let it go; something had to be the provoking incident. Had this been planned all along? The ambush and abduction were well orchestrated. But their knowledge or lack thereof about the difference between iridium and iron was troubling. Wouldn't that be something they should know? They'd taken Cole while he was here and not at home in Maryland, timing it perfectly—both he and his Beta were in the Midwest. They knew that Ethan had to be braced with iridium. And they left me behind. Who would take all of the others and order me to be left behind?

Then I looked back at the forest. The pack's land was huge, lots of space for us to roam and hunt on. We were never bothered by a neighbor or anyone accidentally traversing the land. It was off a single-lane, obscure road, hidden away from the rest of the world. From the streets you saw a long stretch of driveway and groves of trees. We went unnoticed because all anyone saw was woods. But the group that had taken our members could follow the same strategy of isolation and concealment.

"I need you to give me the locations of all forest property in the area, aerial views if you can," I called out as I rushed out into the Worgen office again, with purpose.

I was treated to multiple looks of confusion.

"If in fact the abductors plan on using their captives for a hunt, they'll need a forest similar to what we have. They can't do it in a field, they wouldn't have an advantage. We can narrow down the search areas."

Directing my attention to Quinn: "If you can get me any information about the person who owns the various properties, that would help a lot."

Chris started to back out of the room. I moved in her direction. "Where are you going?"

"I'm going to interview several Hunters. They could have been approached first."

"They wouldn't have. Ethan said that you handled the others that helped with Ronan's attack. I'm pretty sure they wouldn't want to be included in the cleanup once this mess is over." *If it is ever over.*

"Some retire and new ones crop up to take their place." Her lips lifted into a cynical half-smile. "I'm not as infamous as you seem to believe. Cautionary tales don't really work on us—the payoff if you succeed is worth the risk. And everyone has a price."

I had no doubt that was true in her case. A cautionary tale only increased the asking price.

"How long will it take you to get that information?" I asked Quinn.

He shrugged. "I can have a full report in an hour." I knew what the glint in his eyes meant. He'd have the information but he'd be using some questionable methods. I didn't care. The lines between black and white were blurring and I didn't have it in me to sort them and walk that delicate line. My toe eased over the line, where it would probably stay.

~

A dirty white gate at the entrance was unlocked, so we eased it open. It hadn't been much of a deterrent, but the steep dirt road leading to an old, dull-blue farmhouse was. Navigating around various chunks of metal, nonworking vehicles, lawnmowers, and other equipment was slow going. The junk minefield was a less-than-subtle way of saying the occupants didn't want to be bothered.

We were at the home of the third Hunter on Chris's list. The other two visits had made it obvious that she'd been modest when she said she wasn't infamous. The first two Hunters showed admiration that bordered on fandom when she showed up at their doors. Our first stop had been the residence of Sean, Chris's self-proclaimed replacement after she'd been changed to a vampire. She'd once described him as an entitled twit. I agreed. He'd been Ethan's and my first stop when we were trying to find out more information about Tre'ases. We'd gone to him first, a waste of time. And once again, seeing him was a waste of time. He was full of useless information, an obvious attempt to impress Chris. Ingratiating himself in hopes of her taking him on as a mentor—or so I suspected.

He knew her history and a great deal about her mentor. He was unable to stop displaying his knowledge of it as he prattled off clips of information about her past. He also blatantly expressed his desire to learn more about her process and potential retirement. He was so focused on his agenda that he missed the flare of Chris's irritation at the mention of retirement. I figured death would be the only thing that would retire her.

The second Hunter hadn't been approached by anyone meeting our description but said that it was doubtful she would have been. While Chris had a more favorable opinion of her, Ann had been humble about it. We left with the name of someone Ann felt might have been approached for a job involving were-animals.

"She could replace me," Chris acknowledged as we left Ann's. She attempted to sound nonchalant but I heard the yearning in her voice—deep, mournful, and born of fondness and regret. "She *has* replaced me," she whispered, with a tinge of pain.

"I'm fine, Bambi," she snapped before I was able to comment. She wouldn't meet my eyes, as if she was ashamed that I'd seen the emotions. As if I'd stripped away something and left her bare and exposed to the world, and she didn't appreciate it.

We parked several feet away from the front door. Chris, Steven, and I were quiet as we got out of the car and approached the house. We ascended the stairs, hoping we could be at the door before the residents knew they had visitors. The third Hunter was actually a father-daughter team.

Steven and I stayed a couple of steps behind Chris as she moved to the door and knocked.

Chris knocked harder when no one answered. "I can hear you breathing," she said through the door. She stepped in closer, her brows pinching together, and I could hear the murmur of whispers and furniture moving. When the door finally opened, I was surprised to see a burly, older man. His sun-weathered skin was ruddy along his cheeks, a peculiar contrast to his deep olive tone. His nutmeg-colored hair was gray at the temples and he had a short, salt-and-pepper beard.

"Chris"—then his gaze immediately went to me—"Sky"—and then skated over to my right—"Steven." It wasn't a greeting but a display of his knowledge.

In silence, he stepped aside to let us in. I cringed the moment we were standing in the middle of the room and his hand settled in his pocket. A high-pitched noise made my head pound, the pressure so excruciating it felt as if my head was moments from exploding. Judging from the distressed look on Steven's face, he was experiencing the same.

Chris's cool brown eyes met the Hunter's cedar-colored ones. "Turn it off," she commanded through clenched teeth.

"I have no idea what you are talking about."

"Fine. I'll find what you have 'no idea' what I'm talking about. Since you are unaware of it, the thousands it will cost to replace it will be a non-issue." She smiled, baring her fangs. "Are you going to play nice, or are you going to continue being an ass?" Her gaze bounced around the room and landed on a spot several feet away.

The older man scowled at her, slipping his hand in his pocket once again. The piercing noise tapered off. It didn't completely stop—a low nagging noise remained—but it was tolerable. It was his act of defiance, but I wouldn't give him the satisfaction of knowing it bothered me. His home was more bothersome than the noise. The walls were wood-paneled, and the hardwood floor was bare with the exception of one rug, a long stretch of animal skin. Hanging over the stone fireplace and along the walls were the heads of several game animals, and in the corner stood a stuffed bear. There was a collection of guns on another wall, and a hatchet blade hung over a small writing desk. The two computers on the desk were the only modern things in the room. Everything else had a minimalist, frontier feel. It was deceptive. He used technology and was having fun with it: the noise increased. I shuttered and the noise quickly lessened. When I returned my attention to him, I found him looking at me with dark amusement.

"Frank, where's your daughter?" I asked.

"Obviously, she's not here," he retorted with a razor-sharp tone.

I didn't have the patience to deal with him, and I was positive he'd have changed his tone if he knew how perilously close he was to awakening the wolf.

"You know who I am. I'm going to assume you know why I am here."

"I've never had great luck. My game never comes to me. I have to work for every kill. So, I'm guessing you're not here to buy your contract."

"Buy her contract?" Chris and Steven asked at the same time.

"Sanders, what the hell are you talking about?" Chris asked.

"Oh, come on, as if you've never had a contract purchased," the aging Hunter snapped back.

"I'm getting bored with you. Don't let the many techniques I've learned to break a bone become one of the ways I entertain myself," Chris snapped back.

He moved his hand from his pocket to the gun holstered at his side. "I know they don't kill vampires but bullets hurt like hell, don't they?"

As Chris seemingly calculated her speed and her ability to disable Sanders, I intervened. "There's a contract on me?"

"You have to know that. Nearly seven figures. Higher than your boyfriend's." He shrugged. "But since rumor has it he's been caught and presumed dead, I figured you'd be around to buy your contract from me." He shrugged.

I made an attempt to wipe off the look of disgust at him speaking so casually about a contract to murder me, as if he was telling me he forgot to get napkins for my takeout order.

Counting slowly didn't help and warmth crept up my neck, my skin prickled, and my body was threatening to change. Not to escape from the situation, but to use claws and fangs rather than hands on this man who was so blasé about my and Ethan's deaths.

"I'm not sure what kind of mind games you're playing, but I'd start talking, or you won't have to worry about Chris entertaining herself." A honed wolf's glare was fixed on him.

That only made him more defiant, the kink in his lip lifting higher. He didn't go for his gun; his hand slipped into his pocket, and the noise blasted higher. Steven and I screamed. Cringing, we fought the urge to double over in pain. Steven sprung into a lunge from his folded position to catch the arrow soaring in my direction. Chris was a flash of movement as she charged at Sanders, knocking him to the ground. I dashed out toward the woman, who had tossed a bow aside and run toward the door. Stout like her father, she was faster than she looked and was out the door before I could grab her.

Chasing someone who'd been paid nearly seven figures to assassinate me brought out the predator. I unleashed her, aware that she was too ravenous to control. I was more wolf than woman. The only thing human about me at the moment was my form. Snarling, I pushed faster and grabbed the back of her shirt. With one quick jerk, I tossed her back over my shoulder. She hit the ground with a powerful thud, gasped out a breath, and groaned. She'd just caught her breath when I leapt on her, my hands around her neck.

She struggled for every breath I allowed to slip through my stranglehold. I loosened my grip and asked, "What's your name?" She didn't answer until I reapplied some of the pressure.

"Samantha," she choked out.

"Samantha." Repeating her name with more roughness and menace than I intended, I softened my voice some when I spoke again. "I'm going to loosen my grip, so you can talk. If you choose not to answer my questions, know that these might be your final breaths. Do you understand?"

She didn't acknowledge, so I let her struggle for breath longer. I needed her to understand how serious I was and how merciless I planned to be if she was difficult.

"Let's try this again. Do you understand?"

Face ruddy and eyes wide and teary, she nodded.

"Where is Ethan?"

I loosened my hold enough so that she could speak.

"I don't know," she sputtered out. I tightened my hold on her neck. She used one hand to claw at mine, while the other patted at her side. I snatched the knife she was searching for and tossed it out of reach.

I loosened my hold again and repeated the question.

"I don't know. We wouldn't have taken a job like this, but the money was too good to pass up. Someone is going to do it. As far as we know, someone has already gotten the other one and you are the last. They came specifically to us this morning."

"Who came to you?"

As if she was anticipating me choking her again, she took several more rapid breaths. "South African woman. Thin, older. Dusky brown hair."

My breath caught and I could feel the blood rush from my face. She was lying. It had to be a lie. There was no way Claudia would put a bounty on mine or Ethan's head. Never Ethan's. My mind raced. I patted the Hunter down and found cuffs I knew she would have if she was good enough to approach Ethan or me. Undoubtedly, like Chris, she had an assortment of weapons on her. I divested her of all of them and snapped the handcuffs on her.

Refusing to stand, Samantha was dead weight as I dragged her back to the house. She had to regret her choice as I jerked her up the three steps into the house. I placed her next to her father, whom Steven had secured facedown on the floor.

A light raspberry-colored bruise was starting to show on Sanders's face. The room was in disarray, wooden chairs broken, the peculiar fur rug flipped over to reveal the underside, which proved it had been taken from an animal and wasn't a fake.

Arms crossed, Chris glared at the father-daughter team. "Let's try this again. Who hired you all to kill Sky and Ethan?"

Neither one spoke. The dark cast that overtook Chris's face matched her ominous voice. "I broke my finger once," she started out slowly, as she stretched out her long thin fingers, examining them with casual interest before directing her attention back to Sanders. "I was fortunate. Vampire blood helps it heal much faster. I had a donor. But when humans break their bones, it hurts like hell. They take a long time to heal."

She slithered to the floor, more snakelike than Winter in animal form. On the right side of Sanders, she took his trigger finger in her hand. "Hunters need their fingers. A blade is hard to hold when you don't have use of them. I'm sure, since you were the one they came to, you're good at your job. It will be a shame to force you into retirement."

Rigid and defiant, he seemed to welcome any reprisal we handed out as a sign of his resilience. If I saw it, so did Chris.

A cruel smile curled Chris's lips, and her movements once again made me hate vampire speed. The flash of movement that made their actions nearly indecipherable until it was too late. The horror and wash of helplessness, when I realized there was nothing I could do to stop the action that was about to happen. I heard the crack of bone breaking and saw a finger angled anatomically incorrectly. Sanders suppressed his cries of pain for longer than I'd expected before he let out a bloodcurdling scream.

Then Chris had Samantha standing and braced against her. She sank her teeth into the Hunter's neck, drawing blood. Sanders's eyes widened, and so did mine. I was about to say something when Chris fixed me with a quelling look. As much as I'd wanted to believe I was ready for the gray areas and prepared to cross over to black and leave my morals at the door along with any remnant of humanity, I wasn't sure I was able to. Chris lived on those lines, walked them like a gymnast on a balance beam. Navigated through the swamp of gray and black and dabbled in white when it suited her interest.

I swallowed, but my throat was too tight to say anything. These people had been paid to kill me. Would they have given me the same consideration? I was nothing more than a big paycheck for them. My gaze flicked in Chris's direction but settled behind her, giving the impression that I was looking at her. I couldn't look, but I wouldn't show that I was weak and unprepared to go the distance.

"Let's try this again, Sanders," Chris said, as she showed him his daughter's neck. "This is small. I don't need to tell you that these"—she exposed fangs—"can be used like a knife. I could sever the artery right now."

He whimpered, but I believed it was for his daughter's suffering and not for the pain in his finger.

"Who sent you?"

He repeated the same thing his daughter had, verbatim. It hadn't been Claudia, but I had no idea why whoever had hired them wanted to blame her. "That's not the truth. We need the truth."

They both remained silent. I sighed. "Bye, Samantha," I whispered.

Chris moved her head roughly; Samantha fought as much as she could but wasn't a match for Chris, and the vampire's mouth covered her neck again.

I headed for the door, hoping my act of indifference would give him a nudge.

"I don't know who it is. They gave us half and told us if we were ever asked who hired them to describe the South African woman," he blurted.

"Witch, elf, vampire, mage, fae? Do you have a name?" I probed.

"I think she was a witch. She kept touching a little emblem dangling from a charm. I've seen other witches with something similar. No one else. She didn't have fangs." Sanders's eyes moved to his daughter, the dark arrogance and defiance gone. He tried to turn to face me but was restricted by Steven. I nodded and Steven gave him room to move. "I don't think she was acting alone. The way she spoke wasn't the same as the way the person who contacted me did."

"How did they contact you?"

"E-mail, and said they'd send someone with the money. Half upfront and the remainder when the job was completed."

"They must have been confident in your success," Chris mused.

"Yes, I'm good at what I do," he asserted confidently.

Steven's eyes kept roaming around the room, taking in Sanders's displays of his love of hunting.

"Have you been invited on a hunting excursion recently?"

He shook his head, but I heard the jump in his heartbeat and the change in his already rapid breathing. "You're lying," Steven said, closing the distance between him and the man.

"No, I'm not. But I know of one. It's"—he looked at his daughter, who was still in Chris's hold—"I can't afford it, but … I know someone who was invited."

"Name?" I asked.

His lips pulled in a tighter line and I couldn't figure out if it was defiance or fear. "If you are afraid of the people who are responsible, don't be."

"Bethany James. She enjoys less-traditional sports."

Yeah, hunting people for sport isn't traditional at all.

I removed the cuffs from Samantha and Chris slid her to the ground. She looked pale, but she'd be okay in a few hours. Sanders's finger looked painful, really painful. Chris was headed out the door when I stopped her.

"We can't leave him like that," I whispered. She ignored me and continued out the door.

"Chris!" I snapped before she got in the car.

"Look, Bambi, fixing him isn't going to change his feelings about you. You were a job, get over it. If things had been handled differently, you would be dead, they would have a paycheck, and they wouldn't have thought twice about their actions. That's what we do."

Her brusque tone softened and her lips curled into a sympathetic smile. "There will be casualties in situations like this. There are *always* casualties. You will have to accept that. He has a broken finger—that will heal. Samantha will be fine in a couple of hours. I'm pretty sure he has the necessary connections to take care of himself."

I looked back in the door. Steven was heading toward the car, looking as unbothered by the situation as Chris was.

When I didn't move, Steven backtracked to me, placed his hand on the small of my back, and nudged me toward the car. I pushed the thoughts of Sanders and Samantha out of my head and thought about us being ambushed earlier and the people who had carried it out. We had a suspect.

Once I was in the car, I called Quinn and gave him the name Bethany James.

CHAPTER 5

$\mathcal{W}$e returned to the pack's house to find visitors. Three were-animals that I suspected were from the East Coast Pack—I didn't recognize them—and four from the Southern that I did recognize. Among them was Taylor, the were-cheetah who had become Joan's shadow after Joan had nearly sacrificed her own life to save her. She'd cut off several inches of her once-long blonde hair, now in a short ponytail pulled to the nape of her neck. Her eyes looked as severe as her appearance, but they softened when she saw Steven come in behind me.

They had a peculiar relationship. When he visited his mother in the south, whatever went on between them resumed. The first time I'd encountered them, Steven had her secured against the wall, her legs wrapped around his hips, leaving no doubt what they'd been doing. He later told me it had been a sparring session that had gotten out of hand. He responded with a blush and a smile when I pointed out the many times I'd sparred with Winter and never ended up playing naked Twister with her.

Taylor was just inches from him, her hand resting gently on the side of his face.

"Are you okay?" she asked softly.

I waited for the obligatory "yes," but it never came. "No," he admitted, shedding the poised mask he'd donned.

"We'll find her," she assured him softly. It was comforting to have her around even if for no other reason than to be there for Steven. I was going to have to start entering rooms with my eyes covered, in hopes of not catching them *comforting* each other or *sparring* as a distraction.

My gaze trailed over the new faces in the room. "We don't have anything yet," I informed them, aware of the reverence and attention each gave me. I didn't understand how Sebastian and Ethan dealt with people looking at them with the expectation that they were going to fix it or have the answers. Perhaps they weren't looking at me like that at all and it was just a self-imposed burden that I carried. "I'll let you know as soon as we do. Please make yourself at home."

As I made my way to Quinn's lair, I stopped at the library, hoping to find Josh. He was there, along with London and Nia. I wondered if the latter's participation was offered willingly or was a task given to her by Ariel. The look she gave me quickly answered that. Nia wasn't fond of us, especially after discovering the history of the Faeries and blaming us for their resurfacing. She'd accused us of being reckless and irresponsible with magic, and she wasn't wrong. But this didn't have anything to do with us being reckless. Sanders had said a witch was the intermediary for whoever had hired him, and it had to be someone who knew about Ethan's relationship with Claudia.

I poked my head in. "Josh, may I have a moment?"

His expression changed when he looked up from his book. He looked concerned and quickly stood and followed me down the hall. I would have used Sebastian's office, since it was soundproof, but so were most of the rooms.

"Do you trust them?" I asked, once we were secure behind the door of a room several feet from the library.

"I've become a cynic—I can't completely trust anyone," he admitted. His voice was mild, but the optimism he always displayed had been snuffed. The events of the past months had made him wary.

After I told him about our meeting with Samantha and Sanders, he sighed heavily. "I don't doubt that a witch is involved, but I don't think that it's Ariel. There are still those who were dedicated to Marcia and her initial vision. You and Ethan are wrong in their eyes, and that's not going to change."

I speculated whether it was more. Did people blame us for Marcia's death at Josh's hands after they'd kidnapped several people and were-animals in hopes of finding a way to nullify our immunity? That's what facilitated the change between the two sects. The new witches versus the old ones. Were the older witches holding a grudge and using Ethan to hurt Josh?

I frowned. "Do they have the resources to do this?"

"Maybe not those who no longer align themselves with us."

Us. It seemed so peculiar coming from Josh in relation to the witches. He'd been an outsider to them for so long, not to mention a valued member of our pack. Once again, he was splitting his loyalties and commitment.

Rubbing my temples didn't stave off the headache I was getting from trying to process it all. No matter what was happening, finding the Alphas and Betas was my first priority.

"We can't find a locating spell that will work without Ethan's blood, and using mine didn't work—" He cut himself off.

Ethan and I were anomalies: born of witch mothers, yet we didn't have the same benefits of being a witch. It wasn't guaranteed that we could be found by tracing our blood.

To find the others, I had loosened the reins on Quinn and the others, which were minimal and had been put in place by Sebastian only to placate me. I didn't even have plausible deniability now. Quinn clicked away at his computer, occasionally giving me a coy smile. He'd made a show of being abashed by my request to hack into Bethany's records, a factitious effort to appear morally challenged about what he was doing, but his customary prideful deviance won out. The way his pack had survived before joining ours was by skimming a few dollars off of others' bank accounts; this was just another day at the office for him and his crew. The former Worgen Pack was now a well-assembled tech team led by Casper, the moniker given to Quinn because of his ability to hack into anything without leaving a digital footprint. I had to look beyond the dark brown khakis and, for him, irony-free bright yellow Darth Vader t-shirt for anything that gave him away as a were-animal. He was all lean muscle, probably from minimal physical effort; I'd never seen him or any of the other Worgen near the gym. He kept looking over his shoulder at me for a hint of disapproval as he moved around the other screens instructing his minions. I watched in awe, lost as to how they got there, but seeing financials, legal documents, social media accounts, and membership records of clubs and associations. They really should have been a little more ashamed of admitting to their criminal proclivities.

I couldn't have been prouder of or more thankful for the little band's skills when Quinn showed me everything he'd compiled within a matter of hours.

"What am I looking at?" I asked, leaning into the computer and seeing several identical wire transfers into one account.

"You're looking at the people who have our Alphas."

And the Betas, more importantly.

"This is Kitsboro Corp.'s business account. Owned by Bethany James. And it's a sister company." He stopped and made a face, and my heart skipped a beat.

Please don't let this be who I think it is.

"Bolten Corporation," he said.

"Dexter's dead. He can't be behind it," I said, exasperated. I'd watched the mage get shot and killed. There wasn't any way he'd come back from that. For a brief moment, my thoughts became erratic as I considered all the possibilities. Had he been resurrected with a spirit shade? That wasn't possible; he'd been dead too long. Did one of the witches do a *rever tempore* and reverse time? No, Josh would have known about that.

"Ronan and Dexter went to the same college and were in the same fraternity, along with this guy." He brought up a name but moved on so quickly I knew it was inconsequential. "And this woman is his sister"—another click of the mouse and more pages popped up—"and her business partner. Bethany and Sonja. Sonja hunts for sport. I suspect this was her idea." A deep growl reverberated from Quinn's chest. It was understandably upsetting. They had reduced us to animals that people could hunt for sport, and they'd get paid an exorbitant amount of money to allow others that privilege. It was barbaric and cruel.

I waited for the big reveal. Quinn and the others' faces were bright with pride in their investigative skills. Another of the Worgen intervened, a woman just a few inches shorter than Quinn. She wore a hat that paid homage to whatever game she'd decided to promote, and crinkled, poorly controlled ash-colored hair peeked from under it.

"These are all the properties linked to them." It wasn't a long list, just five. Three were in other states and two were in Illinois.

Chris and Winter moved closer to one of the screens.

"Two more transfers have been made for the same amount as the last five," Winter pointed out.

I scanned the pictures I had of the properties and the relevant land surveys. I glanced at the payment. Eight people had been taken. Seven payments, which meant they were waiting on one more—unless Sonja decided to participate as a hunter. My chest tightened, and bile crept up my throat. I had to make a decision.

"Chris, can you have Chase and Gabriella look at this property?" I handed her the information. "We'll go to the others."

"A moment?" Chris asked, shifting her head toward the door before heading that way. She moved with slow, measured steps, likely an effort not to look so obviously vampire. Were-animals had a turbulent history with vampires, our pack especially with her, and she'd know not to draw attention to herself.

"You don't trust Chase and Gabriella?" I asked.

"I trust them, but they are aware that Demetrius will be doing a Presentation ceremony soon. If anything happens to Demetrius after that, the Seethe will be under my rule. Before that, it will more than likely go to Chase. The animosity they have toward you for killing Michaela will also be a disadvantage in this situation."

"Then I'll split them. Half of the vampires and weres in one location and the rest in the other. I don't want to give the kidnappers an opportunity to know that we've found them, nor do I want to risk someone getting caught."

She smiled. "You're not bad at this, Bam—Sky."

CHAPTER 6

The next day, it didn't take long to determine that the first property wasn't the location we wanted, and the vampires quickly joined us at another. *Please let this one be it,* I thought as we moved along poorly formed trails, through thick tufts of grass and large trees. Last night we'd debated extensively whether to try to retrieve the captives at night or during the day. The debate quickly became contentious and would have persisted well into the morning if I hadn't intervened.

I was getting used to my commands being listened to without question but couldn't wait to relinquish my role as protector of the pack. I stood by my previous belief that it wasn't a position worth fighting for. To Sebastian it was everything, but I'd never understand that.

The smell of metal, foliage, and a strong stench that I couldn't quite make out tickled my nose. This had to be the place. It was perfect. Long stretches of fallow land separated it from the nearest neighbor by miles. One narrow trail of trampled, dull-looking grass led to an opening obscured by more trees; wide leaves from low-hanging branches masked the entrance and made it easy to miss. It was definitely intentional.

If you weren't supposed to be there, they were going to make it difficult to find them.

The trail wrapped around, but we'd parked close to the entrance, allowing an easier and quicker exit.

"We have to split up," I directed everyone. I separated them into four groups, making sure each consisted of vampires, were-animals, and magic wielders. We barely had enough of the latter, since we only had Josh, Ariel, London, and me.

I led a group consisting of Steven, Gavin, Chase, and a were-fox who was functioning on a razor's edge, ready to pounce on anyone or thing that got in her way. Her coiled frustration and aggression made me nervous, but I knew it was because of me. Dousing my emotions was getting harder and harder.

The cluster of trees thinned, revealing a large cabin. I ran and tried to open the door. Locked. I used magic to blast it open, sending splinters of wood everywhere. In my peripheral vision I could see the were-fox turning a ruddy color and inhaling the air. I had to get my emotions under control or this was going to turn catastrophic. Did anxiety, frustration, and anger smell as bad as the expression she made?

Whatever my expectations were, they hadn't adequately prepared me for what I saw. All ten of the cabin's rooms had dead-bolt locks. The doors to eight of the rooms were open, and I could see unlocked braces mounted to the walls. The potent odor of medicine and strong metallic smell of silver were thick in the air, along with hints of smoke. I also caught hints of Ethan's and the others' scents among noxious ones that I couldn't decipher.

"They're not here." I rushed out of the cabin, past Gavin, who'd started to back away. He scanned the area.

"Look to your right, in the tree; there's someone in there." Perched on a large branch was a man, crossbow in hand, dressed in camouflage that made me wonder why he'd even bothered. He didn't blend in with the environment. The green and brown in his clothing were distinctively different than the flourishing leaves on the branches. Focused on his target, a Beta, he smiled, his fingers pressed on the crossbow's release. I pelted him with a sharp blow of magic. Shock was woven into his features as he toppled from the tree. Gavin was upon him when he crashed to the ground, covering his mouth and silencing his scream. I knew we'd decided our plan was going to be absolute and what that entailed, but it didn't make hearing the crack of a broken neck any easier to deal with.

That's one. But I wasn't sure how many there were. Seven payments, but I had a strong feeling Sonja wouldn't want to sit this one out. I was operating on the belief that there were eight hunters we needed to find. Shots rang out and I followed them to my right; Gavin wasn't far behind. Winter came from the opposite direction. The sound still carried in the air. I smelled blood and heard a painful groan but didn't see the shooter. Moments later, I heard the bristle of leaves being crunched underfoot. Just as I started toward the sound, I felt that undeniable tug.

Ethan.

Comfort washed over me. At least he wasn't sedated. Whatever they'd given the captives had worn off, but it was doubtful they were at their full potential. I was torn between going after Ethan and the wounded were-animal.

"Ethan?" Winter asked, gauging my dilemma.

I nodded.

"You go find him; I'll find the wounded," Winter said.

It took me a few moments to move.

"Go," she urged. She unsheathed her sword and headed deeper into the woodland.

I followed the nebulous tug, which pulled me in the opposite direction. It was weak, a nagging feeling in the pit of my stomach. What if it wasn't him and just my nerves? Doubt had edged its way firmly into my psyche. No, this wasn't nerves, it was him.

The feeling began to ease. I was satisfied that I was closing the distance. The smell of blood and metal cloaked the air. Were they using silver in their arrows and bullets? It wouldn't surprise me. I whipped around at a sound behind, to find myself staring down the barrel of a gun.

"Skylar Brooks," mused the woman behind the gun before she lowered the weapon. Her hunter-green safari hat was pulled down, but wisps of red flyaways fell from it. Based on the dossier of information I'd received from the Worgen, the cruel-looking woman was Sonja. Her lips pulled into a cold smile. "Well, we were warned that there would be a rescue attempt. I figured it would be a good thing, more game for the next one. Did you bring the strongest of the pack?"

I remained silent, and her smiled widened. "Good, I'll be able to charge just as much." Then she frowned. "I'm not sure what we'll do with the witches." Her lips twisted in consideration. "Vampires don't bring much. No one really cares to pursue them."

Why the hell was she talking to me like we were friends? "Ah, you mean your participants can't convince themselves they are just hunting another animal? Tell me when I should start feeling sorry for your dilemma," I snapped.

My cold, narrowed gaze didn't waver under her assessing one.

Giving me another long once-over, she said, "If you stop this, the agreement made to protect your life is forfeited. I'd advise you to take your ragtag group of rescuers and hide, in hopes that you won't be in the next game."

Darkly amused by her arrogance, I knew my voice held the same threat of unbridled violence as my eyes. She took a step back, her finger wagging, *tsking* me. "Honestly, I'm not sure why —" A massive light-gray wolf crashed into her from the side.

Cole. Her finger was still on the trigger, and a shot was released as she hit the ground.

She started to raise her weapon, and I moved quickly on her, snatching it away and aiming at her. I didn't like guns, had only shot one a couple of times, but I was close enough that there wasn't any way I could miss. Well-warranted fear washed over her face, as if she could see everything I was thinking. Even if she could only catch half of it, she didn't know the things I wanted to do to her were worse than anything she could imagine.

"Who wanted me alive and why?" I demanded.

She pursed her lips together, splitting her attention between me and Cole.

"Sonja, I guarantee you don't want me to make you talk. Who. Wanted. Me. Alive."

Her eyes were fixed on mine, which had gone full-on primal. I allowed her to come to her feet and get a better view of me. Now her eyes widened with fear. I asked my question again. She remained silent. Magic hit her in the chest and she soared back, airborne for several moments before she crashed to the ground. Standing over her, I gave Maya free rein: darkness overwhelmed me, and magic crackled in me like a live wire. I welcomed Maya's draconian ways and unrestricted thirst for mayhem. Usually two people far removed, we now acted as one, with the same motive and desires. My hand touched Sonya's chest, her mouth parting as she felt the oxygen slowly being pulled from her, her heart slowing to a pace that could no longer sustain life. She'd die slowly. I'd done this once before, but this time it was different. I felt the energy, invigorated by it as if I was an electronic device in need of a charge. Sonja's eyes rolled back as she choked out a breath.

Defiance seeped from her quickly. When I removed my hand and gave her space, she scuttled back, using the heels of her feet.

I let her stand. Her hand remained over her heart, probably to appreciate that it beat normally and didn't drag.

"You're not a were-animal," she gasped out.

"I am."

"Iridium," she whispered, as if she was just figuring out why it had to be used on me. Revulsion marred her face as she took a few more steps back.

"Answer my question," I demanded.

For a brief moment, the fear was gone, and she went for a knife at her side. I hit her with another jolt of magic, far more controlled than the first.

I quickly positioned the gun and shot at the ground near her foot. It was far more impressive to her because she didn't know I'd been aiming for her foot. Shocked, she opened her mouth to speak, but silver fur blurred past me as the massive wolf careened into her.

"Cole, leave her alive!" It was too late. Her blood covered his mouth and nose, and some splattered on me. Using the back of my hand, I wiped it off. Feral eyes softened as they continued to look at me. I crouched down as he approached me. I examined him; he didn't have any noticeable injuries.

"Are you okay?" I asked.

He nodded but stumbled a little. He rested his muzzle against my shoulder to steady himself. It must have been the residual effect of the sedatives. When I attempted to move back, he whimpered. It was hard to stay heartless with someone who'd gone through what he had, even though there was a part of me that felt he deserved it.

"Okay." I buried my fingers in his fur before stroking, soothing. "I need to find Ethan. The others are here. Do you think you can make it out?"

He moved back, and I figured he was about to change. Alpha or not, being drugged and kept captive and possibly given a limited amount of food was going to affect his ability to change. "Don't change. You'll be stronger in this form."

"Her name was Sonja," I offered, tipping my head toward the body.

He nodded.

"She has a partner." I gave him a description of the photo Quinn had found of her. "Have you seen anyone fitting that description?"

He confirmed with another nod and pulled back his lips to display his teeth.

His head jerked back; he sniffed and took off running. I ran after him until he came to a full stop. Turning to face me, he nudged me away.

"You want me to find the others?"

He shook his head, then moved closer. The massive animal pressed his head toward the inner part of my thigh in a suggestive manner. I shuffled back and hoped I was getting the message. "Ethan. You want me to go find Ethan?"

He made a sound that I assumed was agreement and nudged me away again.

"Be careful," I said. It was out of my mouth before I could bite it back. I needed to hate Cole. I wanted my disdain for him to resurface even in the moment. He was safe, but I still didn't like him. Finding Ethan and the others took precedence over anything else. I called Cole's name. "If you find Bethany before I do, make sure I'm able to talk to her first. It's important."

Cole's wolf regarded me for a moment, intense predaceous eyes boring into me. He made a low growl of assent, or what I thought was agreement, before he trotted away.

I ran in the opposite direction, covering several miles of the dense woods. I stopped when an arrow soared just to my side, aimed at something behind me. I caught it and returned it in the direction from which it had come, hard and fast enough to shock the hunter, who saw it spiraling in his direction. Taking one hand off his bow, he raised it to protect his face. The jaguar he was targeting embedded claws in his arm. Joan didn't stop clawing and biting until he had stopped moving. She collapsed next to him.

With all the commotion, I knew that I wouldn't be able to keep my earpiece in to communicate, but I had to now. "Steven, Joan's here. I'll wait here until you get here." Fifteen minutes out of my time looking for Ethan, but it was worth it to see the relief that washed over Steven's face.

"We have Sebastian—he was shot in the leg and arm, but he seems to be okay. Ariel left with him already. We found my mother's Beta and Cole's Beta," he informed me.

"I saw Cole, but he left. He's in animal form, so I couldn't get much out of him. Take your mom back to the house. I'll get Cole and Ethan," I said.

Staring down at the massive animal, he seemed to be trying to figure out the best way to carry her while in animal form.

He knelt down and eased his hands under her to lift her, and she stirred. Raising her head, she moved it toward him and brushed her face against his shoulder. His body folded into relief before he wrapped his arms around her in an embrace. Within moments, she had shifted and was wearing Steven's shirt, which he'd given her as soon as she'd changed. She declined his shoes, but accepted the support when he placed his hand at her waist. I scanned her: she didn't look injured, but she walked slowly, and I didn't know if that was from fatigue, malnutrition, or the drugs. Whichever it was, it was something she would recover from.

They were a few feet away when Steven called me. "I'm not sure if you care, but we found Demetrius, too. Well, Chris found him. He was going through reversion and one of the witches gave him enough blood to hold him over."

It was a good thing the witches had accompanied us, because if I was the only source of nourishment, I would have been fine with watching the full process until Demetrius was nothing but dust.

I nodded and continued my search for Ethan, ignoring the off-putting smells of blood, iron, and again an unfamiliar, over-powering odor that was strong enough to mask anything lighter, like a body scent. The only thing I had was the meta-physical pull.

"Ethan," I whispered, hoping it would carry enough for him to follow it. Did he feel it, too? Before our mating, he'd always been able to find me, but I'd attributed it to his skill as a hunter. As I advanced on a large tree, the only thing stronger than Ethan's presence was the smell of blood in the air.

"Please be okay," I whispered to myself as I moved closer to it. His head rested back against the trunk of the tree. His hands were battered and bloody, and he had an arrow protruding from his right shoulder and another in his thigh, where he'd been shot from behind.

"Is the person who did this to you still out there?"

He gave me a faint smile. "Yes, but they are in desperate need of medical attention."

"Did they shoot you while you were like this?" Bile crept up my throat as I waited for him to answer. They could have pretended that they were going after an animal if he'd been in wolf form. But this was just murder. They were hunting people. "I changed after I was hit in the leg. It's easier to pull out." He inhaled a sharp breath. "The second one I got after I'd changed. Both men are down. One severely injured and the other dead. Or that was my assumption."

One of the arrows hadn't gone all the way through, so Ethan had iron in him. I leaned in and kissed him lightly on the lips. "Close your eyes," I whispered.

He shook his head and flashed me a weak grin. "Not a chance. I want to see your face when you do it."

I scoffed. "I just saw a couple of people mauled by animals. I can handle a little blood from an arrow."

But it wasn't a little blood. It was Ethan's grimace that got to me when I had to push the one in his thigh through the muscle to get a hold of the head to break it off.

He looked at the blood that covered his clothing. "I should try to change," he said.

I considered it. If Joan could tolerate changing from her animal form, then he could change into his. I would be with him in case we ran into trouble.

"If you can do it."

With great effort his body started to tremble as he transitioned. He grimaced and bit back the pain as his body contorted into his animal form. It looked awkward and painful. I was used to his change being smooth, elegant, and beautiful, a graceful shedding of his human shell, and it was hard to watch. In his wolf form, his movements were lumbering and ungainly, the polar opposite of his usual fluid, lithe movements.

Every so often, as we ambled back to the car, he needed to take a break. A few feet from the entrance of the forest, Josh approached us. He knelt down and gently touched his brother's head before his hands glided over Ethan's sweat-drenched coat and traced the openings of the arrow wounds on his shoulder and leg. He frowned, grim.

Maintaining a gentle touch on his brother, his voice was just as easy when he spoke—calming, sensing that was what his brother needed. "We have everyone except Cole." He looked at London and smiled. Their interaction always hinted at a shared history. "London did most of the cleanup." Again he looked at her, sharing a smile. "Once you return, we'll go over it again."

There were very few people left behind. I assumed Steven had gone with Joan. Ariel had taken Sebastian, and I suspected Winter had taken the others. Left behind with me were Gavin, London, and Josh. Gavin watched me, intrigued, as if he could see my inner battle. I so desperately wanted to leave Cole behind—but I couldn't. We were here to rescue the pack and that included him.

As I started to back away, Ethan made a grumble and began to walk with me. I unsheathed my sword.

"I'll be fine, Ethan." I gave him a reassuring smile, which didn't stop him from following behind me, limping.

I halted. "Ethan, if I run into any trouble it will be harder for me because I'll be worrying about you. I came to get you," I reminded him. "I can handle this." I backed away before turning around and easing into a full run until I was in the middle of the woods. Scent wasn't going to help me. There was too much of that pungent odor and the smell of blood wafting through the air. Briefly, I closed my eyes and listened to the sounds. The light rustle of wind through the leaves, the crunch of small creatures' feet over the tufts of grass, light but melodious sounds of birds at a distance. I focused as hues of magenta and blue shone through my closed lids. I heard the approach of light steps toward me. Sword in hand, I turned around, ready to slice into anything within my reach. The blade was just a few inches from Cole's neck before I identified who he was. His bare chest was crimson with smeared blood. Sanguine fluid ran from cuts down his right arm and his abdominals. He also had a stab wound to his thigh.

I sheathed my sword as he stumbled in my direction. He rested his head on my shoulder, and I raised my hand, looking for a place to put it on his blood-soaked skin. He buried his face in the curve of my neck, nuzzled it, and inhaled. It was too intimate for me, something Ethan would do. I stepped away and placed my hand at his shoulder to steady him.

"Is there anyone left?" I asked.

He shook his head.

I sidled in next to him, allowing him to wrap his arm around me for support as he tottered toward the exit. "Bethany, too?"

"She didn't make it. I know you wanted her alive, but it wasn't possible."

Dammit. I'd really wanted to question her. There were so many missing pieces, and I'd hoped that she would be able to fill in the gaps in the puzzle. If she hadn't been willing to do it freely, I had been prepared to do whatever I could, including enlisting the fae that Ariel had once used to coerce a noncompliant witch to help us.

As Cole used me as a human crutch, I kept eyeing his wounds. They were bad, but so were Ethan's. If Ethan could change, so could Cole.

"You probably should change, to walk easier," I suggested.

He shook his head. "I've changed twice already. Hurts too much," he breathed out.

"I can help."

"If you don't want me to touch you, fine," he snapped as he unhooked his arm from around my shoulder and struggled to walk next to me.

I didn't want him to touch me, but an Alpha admitting he needed help had to be humbling.

"No, I'll help." I eased closer to him and he put his arm around my shoulder.

He eyed me for a moment, his gaze roving slowly over my face, taking in my features as if he was trying to commit them to memory. "Thank you," he whispered. "I do think even I am undeserving of you."

No need to take this conversation to Creepytown.

Ethan was relaxed back in the SUV, but at my approach he sat up, watching me intently as we moved toward the car. His gaze periodically slipped in Cole's direction before he redirected it to me. He conjured up a faint smile, forced. It was still there when I eased Cole into the car.

"Thank you," Cole said again, his hand still on my arm before it fell from me, his head lolling to the left. He looked noticeably worse than Ethan. His skin was now ashen, lips taking on an anemic bluish color, and perspiration glistened along his hairline and forehead. His skin was warm, fevered.

~

Cole was dead weight as we moved him to the house. All the color had drained from his face, and his hair was sweat-drenched. When we laid him on the bed, his hand batted at the open space until it found mine. He held it, and desperation spilled over his face when I attempted to tug it away. I didn't want to be the one to offer him comfort and looked frantically around the room for someone to take my place. They all looked a little pallid and the warmth that radiated off them from the silver poisoning made the room warmer by several degrees. Ethan sat on a bed across the room, his eyes locked on Cole's hand. He frowned at it, and I shrugged. Denying Cole something as simple as a touch seemed cruel.

Lying back on the bed, clinging to life, he didn't look like a calculating viper but rather a wounded person. A wounded Alpha and an extension of our pack. I remained by his side as Dr. Jeremy looked over his injuries, assessing him, a perplexed frown etched into his face as he saw the distinct difference in the way he looked compared to the others. He had the same wounds I'd seen earlier, and they weren't any worse than those the others had sustained, but his response was different. In a few days, there wouldn't be any reminders that they'd ever been injured; the way Cole looked, I wasn't sure he'd be alive in a couple of days.

Dr. Jeremy looked concerned, prompting everyone else to be as well. Kelly and Dr. Jeremy examined everyone, bandaged their wounds, removed the silver, and hooked them up to IV drips to help flush out the remaining silver. I curled up next to Ethan on the bed, and only then did he relax. The smell of blood clung to his clothes, and his injuries hurt more than he wanted to let on. He cringed when he moved to pull me closer and wrap his arms around me.

"You're going to make it worse," I warned him.

He made a noise of satisfaction when I was close enough that he could rest his chin on top of my head. "I won't hurt anything," he said confidently.

"Mmmm, I see you still think that a JD is very similar to an MD degree. I'm sure Dr. Jeremy will be very excited to know that. Maybe he should look over the contract for the next business venture?"

"Sky," he breathed into my hair. Saying my name was equivalent to saying "whatever," but without the debate that would follow.

I nudged him with a finger. "I know what that means," I shot back.

His chuckle made his chest rumble. Minutes later, he fell asleep, and I watched him. Finally, the weight of the situation lifted. All the fear, doubt, insecurities, anger, and frustration that had made me feel as though I was carrying a boulder vanished. We had found them and, I hoped, discouraged anyone from ever trying a hunt again.

CHAPTER 7

*T*wo days after the rescue, I heard Dr. Jeremy and Kelly conferring with Sebastian as they headed toward his office.

"He's not healing," Dr. Jeremy said, exasperated. His voice sounded as fatigued as he looked. His silver hair was mussed and his salt-and-pepper beard was the longest I'd ever seen it. Dr. Jeremy rarely wore a white lab coat, but when he did, it was usually crisp and professional, as if he was about to pose for a stock photo: the stereotypical sophisticated, courtly looking older doctor. That wasn't the image he presented now. He looked disheveled. Kelly was the much-needed shot of pep, in bright purple scrubs. The color softened grave news, or maybe the fact that his nurse looked like a life-sized Jolly Rancher was intended as a distraction.

Before they could close the door, I slipped in behind them. Sebastian's arms crossed over his chest, he gave me a castigating look, and his eyes narrowed on me.

Yeah, yeah, Mr. Alpha, I'll just put that in the bag with the other disapproving looks I've collected over the year. Let's get on with the information.

"Ethan's not here, so I'll be his stand-in," I said.

Sebastian nodded once.

Did that actually work? That's my response for everything from now on.

Based on the look Sebastian gave me, it hadn't.

Sebastian's wounds were bad, from bullets and an arrow, and they had been injected with silver. Enough to slow healing, but not critical amounts.

"Do you need me to assist with healing him?" he asked.

Dr. Jeremy declined, emphatically. "You aren't in a position to do so. Let me continue to work on him. In two or three days, when I feel you are a hundred percent, then we can explore that as an option. His symptoms and response to treatment are quite peculiar. He's behaving as if he has silver poisoning, but the fluids I gave him should have flushed it, and I've searched and there isn't any. I have no idea what it could be."

"The others?" Sebastian inquired.

"They are recovering. Once the silver was removed, they healed as expected." Dr. Jeremy shot a disapproving look in my direction. "As you know, Ethan went home yesterday, against medical advice." Then he returned his stern gaze to Sebastian. "As with you."

Sebastian actually seemed apologetic for his actions. Not remorseful, but he held Dr. Jeremy in high esteem and valued him. He was one of the few people Sebastian never pulled his Alpha status on. I assumed it was like that in all the packs. Some auxiliary positions carried a special autonomy and prestige.

"Fallon, Cole's Beta, is doing well and can be released if it's okay with you."

"It's your call."

Dr. Jeremy nodded. "I'd like to keep Joan longer, but ..." He gave Sebastian a rueful half-smile.

"But she's as contrary and stubborn as you are and has made

arrangements to leave today," Kelly blurted out. She was still having trouble adjusting to pack order and propriety. Well, that was the excuse everyone was giving. I suspected that, as with medicine and anything else she had an interest in, she knew the rules like the back of her hand and chose not to follow them.

Sebastian's brows rose as he shot her a sharp look that didn't put a dent in her armor of defiance.

"I'm not sure why you all can't take two or three days to care for yourselves. Nope, I'm Mr. or Ms. Alpha and I do whatever the hell I want. Protocols and recommendations be damned," she huffed out. "I mean, seriously, it's a day or two, the world isn't going to crumble while you take those days." She was on a rant and walked to the door to let herself out, denying Sebastian the privilege of asking her to leave. "We've been doing this for years, but your WebMD-search medical degree is better than what we have." She wasn't even talking to anyone, just going off on one of her speeches that I was sure she'd learned from Dr. Jeremy. He was known for going on a tangent about his skills and mastery being underappreciated.

Instead of censure and anger at Kelly's outburst, Dr. Jeremy had the glow of paternal pride. We could hear the continued hum of her mini-tirade as she walked down the hall.

"What do you think?" Sebastian asked Jeremy.

"I think she's going to leave no matter what you say. Steven will go with her and promised to stay a couple of days."

Days? I hoped it was just days, but with everything that had occurred in the last few months between them, it could very well be permanent. I shut my eyes and attempted to push the thoughts away, but they wouldn't budge. They were persistent. I was going to lose Steven. The pain felt surreal.

I was grateful for Sebastian's deep baritone breaking the silence. It pulled me out of my head. "Perhaps you are right, but let me talk to her."

They started out the door, and I was right behind them. Sebastian sighed. "Sky, will you get the door?"

"No one's at—" Before I could finish the sentence, the door-bell rang.

No one needs the smug smile. It's not very becoming, you know.

Dr. Jeremy and Sebastian went to the recovery room where Joan was, and I answered the door to find Ariel there. She had returned to her uniform of all white. Her smile was cordial but professional. She looked past me, waiting for an invitation, I assumed. She nodded appreciatively and entered once I'd moved aside.

"It is my understanding that a drug was used to trigger their change."

I nodded. It was something we hadn't addressed yet, too busy trying to deal with six injured Alphas and Betas.

Brows furrowed, she frowned. "I didn't think that was possible." She fidgeted with her bracelet as she became distracted by her thoughts. "How is everyone doing?"

You mean, how is Sebastian doing? Let's not be coy.

"*Everyone* is doing fine," I said, with a knowing smile.

"I'd like to speak with Sebastian. It will probably be a good idea if we discuss this situation. If they can trigger a change in you all, what's to say that someone won't do it to cause someone to out themselves? Change in public, in front of an audience."

That thought had gone through my mind repeatedly since Ethan had told me about it. Especially when he'd admitted he hadn't been able to stop it. Triggering a change without us being able to override it would prove to be disastrous. It would be a problem for us, but I wasn't sure why Ariel was worried about it. I wasn't naïve enough to think that her worry extended beyond the well-being of the witches. No matter what her interest in Sebastian might have been, her first priority was to protect her own. Sebastian's was to protect the pack, which might be why they were drawn to each other. Mutual respect for the protection of their mutual sects.

"Where is Sebastian?" she asked, looking around.

Joan's voice was heard first, and pronounced interest shone in Ariel's gaze. I knew Sebastian was with Joan. Ariel's jaws clenched. Sebastian and Joan's peculiar interactions made it difficult to determine if they were colleagues with an inappropriate closeness, ex-lovers who still had feelings for each other, or friends whose intimacy blurred the lines. Ariel was taking in the ambiguity at that moment.

Joan wore a pair of jeans and a shirt that were definitely not her style, so I assumed they were something Steven had gotten for her. The jeans weren't as flattering to her tall, sleek form as the clothing she usually wore. She'd never wear a pink shirt that clashed with her red hair, which was pulled up in a loose ponytail. She and Sebastian were just outside the infirmary doors, several feet away. Far enough that their conversation couldn't be heard, especially by someone with normal hearing. They'd perfected their whispers so that I couldn't hear, either. Along with Ariel, I was treated to their unexplained closeness. All personal space was eliminated, and they stood just inches from each other as Sebastian spoke to her and she responded with a series of nods and headshakes. Ariel sucked in a ragged breath when Sebastian cradled Joan's face in his hand and leaned in to whisper something to her. She smiled, and he kissed her gently on the forehead. Steven had kissed me several times on the forehead, and this wasn't anything like it. An unintentional intimacy —or maybe it wasn't unintentional, but it definitely wasn't platonic, like the kisses Steven had given me. The curiosity that I had about Joan and Sebastian resurfaced. He moved his hand from her face to her waist, casually placing it there as if it was second nature.

Ariel's second sharp inhalation drew his attention.

"Ariel, I wasn't expecting you."

"Um ... I ..." She was flustered, her gaze bouncing from his hand on Joan to his impassive face. "I wanted ... I wanted to discuss what happened with your animal being triggered." She took a deep breath, which seemed to allow her professional confidence to reassert itself. Her voice became cool and detached. "It seems like something you need to get ahead of before it becomes a big problem for us all."

"I agree."

"If you need to discuss it, I can have another witch available to see what can be done about it. I suspect magic was involved." With that, she turned and let herself out.

Was he really as shocked as he looked by Ariel's abrupt departure? He couldn't possibly have missed that huge social cue. *Okay, Mr. Alpha, you're getting a social interaction book, too.*

Sebastian might have missed it, but Joan hadn't. She moved away from his hold, greeted me with a quick nod of recognition, and padded up the stairs.

"That was strange," Sebastian acknowledged, his brow furrowed before he headed toward his office.

"Are you kidding me?" I chortled incredulously as I followed him into his sanctum, closing the door behind me. He could hear footsteps from a great distance, smell someone's fear from ten feet away, and detect physiological changes a body made when a person lied, and he couldn't sense that Ariel was bothered by his touchy-feely display with Joan.

He continued to stand, his thick brows furrowed as he regarded me for several moments. When I didn't immediately continue, he crossed his arms over his chest. Bulging muscles stretched the seams of his shirt and made him seem uninviting, unapproachable. I figured that was the point, but I'd dealt with him and the were-animal personality so much that I'd built up an immunity to it. Unfazed by his cool exterior and the dark, foreboding amber eyes that stared at me, I sat and relaxed back in a chair.

"What's strange is that you saw Ariel and didn't have the wherewithal to remove your hand from Joan."

"Why would I do that?" he asked, his voice tepid, even bland. Bewilderment stretched over his features.

"Because you were feeling up one of your girlfriends in front of the other."

He rolled his eyes. "I didn't move my hand because I wasn't doing anything wrong. I was comforting an Alpha. Joan is just settling into her role as an Alpha, and this situation was hard for her."

I'd seen him comfort others: it was more of a nod, a quick pat on the back, and a dismissal. With Joan, things were always different, and any time I asked about their past relationship, people directed me to the source—Joan or Sebastian.

"Were you two ever lovers?" I asked.

A glint of shock and irritation sparked in his eyes, followed by a look of disbelief. The only thing he could do was avoid answering the question—or kick me out of his office. I had a feeling both were about to occur.

"Is there a reason you are in my office?"

I nodded. "Yes, I want to figure out why you were so touchy-feely with an ex in front of your current girlfriend. Why didn't you go after Ariel?"

"Why would I do that?" he asked earnestly. "We are allies, nothing more. It's strictly professional."

"And I'm a princess and nothing more," I piped back in a cloying, hyperbolic tone. "You should see me in my tiara."

Eyes narrowed on me briefly before looking at the door, his less-than-subtle way of asking me to leave.

"There isn't anything 'strictly professional' about you and Ariel, and even if I didn't know that, seeing how she dressed for your 'meeting' at your house only confirmed it," I said.

"I really don't think my personal life is any of your concern," he offered coolly.

Stop looking at the door, I'm not going anywhere.

"It's not. I don't care who you are having 'meetings' with or about your past with Joan." That was just partially true. My curiosity was piqued concerning the latter, but it would have to go unsated because of more pressing matters. "When Josh was hurt, it was the witches who saved him. Now, if there is something out there that can force us into a change, one that even an Alpha can't override, we're going to need them—"

"I screwed up," he interrupted.

I blinked several times. Had I heard him right? Then I blinked again because that wasn't enough to lift the feeling that I'd been swept into an alternate world. Had he admitted to being wrong? Was he going to take my advice? I sucked in a ragged breath, waiting for the apocalyptic fire and brimstone that I was convinced was about to rain down. This couldn't possibly be Sebastian.

"What?"

"I screwed up," he repeated in a low voice. "When it comes to Joan and her well-being, I tend to have tunnel vision." He moved over to the door. "I appreciate you coming by."

There he is. Welcome back, Sebastian, I missed you for the three seconds you were gone.

Scrutinizing him and then the door, I wondered if he was just placating me because he knew I was rooted to the seat, defiant, and would refuse to leave until I'd been heard. That was always the problem when dealing with someone like Sebastian; you weren't sure where you stood. He smirked at my dilemma, and I felt sure he was aware of everything I was thinking and that I was dissecting every moment of our conversation. With a vulpine grin, he opened the door wider, inviting me to leave.

I stayed seated.

"Get out of my office, Sky."

"Geez, you can't put a *please* somewhere in that request?"

His grin widened. "You'll be quite pleased with the direction of this conversation if you leave now. Is that better?"

This guy. Leaving, I gave him another look over my shoulder and took in the smug look on his face. I'd won. Why was he looking so pleased?

CHAPTER 8

houghts of the Sebastian and Ariel drama quickly slipped from my mind. They didn't necessarily slip but were replaced by something more pressing—the price on my head. For the past few days, I'd remained cautious and kept that information to myself, not because it wasn't important but because how it was handled would mean the difference between amity and war. I didn't want a war between the were-animals and the elves. The violence, death, and cruelty I'd experienced up to this point were enough to last me a lifetime.

Optimism burrowed its way into my thoughts, and I allowed it to have its way with my plans as I drove up the circular driveway to a white colonial-style home. The tan, brick-lined entryway gave it a stuffy feel, and the sharp lines of the rectangular pillars that boxed in the front door made the house look stately and a little pretentious. Mason's abode was the essence of who he was. It could have been a coincidence when a gentle rain started as I approached the house—I wasn't sure if Mason was an elemental elf like Abigail and Gideon.

After three hard knocks, Mason answered the door. Cool

eyes regarded me with disdain as I pushed my way past him into the foyer.

"We need to talk," I said.

"It wears the shell of a woman, but underneath it is still a beast," he mumbled to himself as he closed the door behind me. His deep, gruff Australian accent didn't take the bite out of his insult.

He wasn't going to make this easy. I'd rather have greeted him with a face-pounding than a smile, but I tempered that emotion. I was there to be amicable. To prevent a war, not hasten it.

"Call them off," I asserted the moment he turned his attention to me.

Regarding me for an exceptionally long time, he finally spoke. His response was gentler than I had expected, which unnerved me. Was this the calm before a tempestuous storm or simply relief at being found out? "The Faeries were a small group of people who terrorized many. For those of us who concern ourselves with the past, understand it's just a slip, one ignored anomaly, a wrong that is left unchecked that leads to devastation."

"What the hell are you blathering on about?"

"You and Ethan are wrong. We are being foolish by allowing it to continue. The witches accepted the frowns and ridicule but have pride because they knew they were doing what we all should have been courageous enough to do."

"You may consider infanticide courageous, along with the many other psychopaths who populate the world, but it is never going to be considered an admirable act. Never. Why—because those babies had the potential to become something powerful, uncontrolled, and dangerous? I'm sure you started off quite harmless, and look what you have become," I rebutted, venom lacing each word.

"The insults from the cursed will never mean much to me. The witches see the dangers that we chose to ignore."

"You all call us cursed and in no uncertain terms continue to say we don't have a place in this world. For a person who claims to know his history, you would know that it was the 'cursed' who saved your asses. It is because of us that you are able to stand here and be an insufferable, smug bastard. Since you don't want to be polite, there's no reason for me to, either."

His lips pulled into a tight line before coiling down into a resentful frown. "Yes, you all did save us, but for us to pretend that your existence is beneficial is still foolish. Wearing the shell of man and woman doesn't change what is underneath. Give animals power, they exploit it. Give them magic, and they abuse it. Everything you have done is for one reason—to protect your own. Our survival was wrapped up in your desire to thrive unrestrained. The Faeries were our only weapon against you all."

I wasn't in the mood for a debate. Not with a person who was so comfortable in his pretentions and able to overlook the horrors of his kind. The elves created creatures so vile that they had to be contained by magic, and yet he flung his derision at us.

"You're not going to get a world without were-animals, so get over it and mark it off your list for Santa. But if you manage to find some semblance of common sense, you may keep your life," I said. "I don't want to see you hurt or in a war because you let an ideology cloud your judgment."

Mason scoffed. "Not an ideology. I'm not the one who's blind—you and Ethan are. Your mothers were witches, and by all accounts you shouldn't be able to use magic. Spirit shades should not be able to use magic through you all, yet they can. The safety nets that we relied on and thought would protect us are slipping." He shook his head and laughed bitterly. "He had the magic of a dark elf, and only because of another were-

animal with the ability to use magic was he able to be rid of it."
He shuddered at the idea.

Being able to kill people with a touch wasn't a gift, and changing to animals didn't mean we were cursed. Even if I pointed out the flaws in his thinking, they would have gone ignored. The very people he hated because of perceived wrongs and abominations against what he considered normal in the otherworld were the ones who were righting these things. He sneered at me with disgust for several minutes; I held my tongue as long as I could. "And yet it seems we are the ones who clean up each wrong that has occurred. But, please, stay on your high horse and tell me how we shouldn't exist and that we are wrong, and abominations."

"I've accepted the existence of pure were-animals. It's yours and Ethan's existence that I loathe. You two should be killed, especially now that you are together." He looked as if he'd taken a whiff of something so putrid that he was about to vomit. "What will the two of you create? Will we survive that abomination?"

No longer able to be civil, I closed the distance between us. Magic sparked from my fingers. Loud crackles filled the room and the sky opened as hard rain battered the home. Okay, that was different, but I pretended it was intentional. I had my answer: Mason was an elemental elf and I knew I no longer needed a person's blood to mirror their magic. Fear and concern would have doubled me over if I wasn't so vehement about holding things together. I couldn't give Mason the satisfaction of being right. My magic wasn't evolving over generations; it was doing it in real time, in me. There weren't enough fucks for me to spew to make me feel better.

I shored up my determination and eased into the power, the new magic, the evolving abilities. I let the thunder crackle in chaotic, violent cacophony, the wind thrash and whip through the sky, and the rain pour violently, knowing it was only Mason's home being affected.

He didn't seem fearful of my display but pensive, as if he was seeing the world he knew being destroyed in a voracious fire or succumbing to a natural disaster and he couldn't do anything but watch helplessly. "I would have preferred you all to remain as you were. The way the history books depict you. At least we knew what we were getting. These new shells are deceptive." He looked away, distraught, as if he couldn't handle the deception.

I cursed myself for allowing this to affect me, but it did. I hated that we were viewed as nothing more than animals in human shells. My anomaly and Ethan's were threats warranting swift and brutal reprisal.

Sighing, I relaxed, easing the wind and rain, and the magic that twined around my hand.

"Mason, is this really the hill you want to die on? If you kill me or Ethan, there will be consequences. Consequences you won't live through. For what, the *possibility* that Ethan and I will spawn some kind of magical wunderkind? What if it goes the other way and everything cancels out and it's just a child? A plain, simple, nonmagical, vulnerable human child?"

I hadn't completely moved in with Ethan and people had already planned our future, complete with an unconquerable hybrid child that would end the world as they knew it.

"But at least one of you will be dead, or better yet, both. Then we have a few more years of hope."

The breath I sucked in was ragged and thick. I nearly choked on it. It wasn't the breath, it was the realization that I was going to have to end it. Stop Mason permanently. All the bloodshed and violence that I'd experienced over the past few years flooded my mind. Was this my life now? A little voice responded, *Yes.*

The inner turmoil and sudden influx of conflicting emotions

obscured the scope with which I looked at this situation. It made me needlessly introspective, and I hated him for it.

Finally, fatigue became the most prevalent emotion. I was tired of being the villain in everyone's historical recollection of events, when in fact we were just flawed champions. It was insulting how many people disregarded us as just were-animals. That led to more conflict—they considered us murderers, and at that moment I was complicating things by being just that. It pushed me to refuse to use violence and to try diplomacy with him.

I stepped away. "I've lost count of the number of people who've tried to kill me, yet here I stand." My gaze roved slowly over him in consideration. "I can assure you that my death won't be at your hands. I'm giving you a chance to walk—"

A bolt of lightning shot through me. My body vibrated with pain and, before I could recover, I was hit by another. It wracked through me and brought me to my knees. I'd bitten my tongue and the taste of blood filled my mouth. Sparks flickered from Mason's hand; I erected a protective field, and the next assault hit it. The field wavered, colorful sparks jumping off of it as he assaulted it with elemental magic. I held it, feeling the layers stripped away with each attack. Lightning battered it. Brutal gusts of wind raged against it. And not just the wind, but various items struck my shelter. Statues and art crashed into it. A coffee table slammed into it and then rebounded, making a large hole when it hit the wall. I focused on keeping my bulwark up, but it took great effort.

I'd expected him to tire, considering the amount of magic he was using—but he didn't. He seemed invigorated as he examined the damage his attack had caused on his house.

He chortled, and when he spoke his Australian accent was so thick, it took effort to understand him. "I witness the debauchery of your existence."

Hypocrisy runs rampant in zealots.

"Gideon aligns himself with you because of self-preservation." I wasn't sure why that wasn't a good thing, but he spouted it with such contempt, he made it seem like the vilest thing imaginable. "His father would have never done such a thing. And he will be his father's legacy. The elves and their army of beasts. I aligned myself with witches, and he with animals. Yet, no one could see the stark differences in our leadership, in our choices—choices that would affect the well-being of our people. I chose pure magic and he—"

"Are you kidding me!" I snapped. "You're throwing a big-boy tantrum because you don't get to be king of the elves anymore? And Gideon's allies are the yucky were-animals, while you were cuddled up with the witches. Is that what this is about?" I laughed at the absurdity of it. This was a political ploy. He'd ramble on about the wrongness of me and Ethan and how he was the only one, despite being stripped of his leadership, to do what was right for his people. All the while, our death by an elf would lead to a war. A war that would leave them weakened, us culpable, and a long-abandoned hatred rekindled. I suspected he planned on restoring his position as leader of the elves once everyone turned against Gideon. I was so tired of the political BS and maneuvering, of being a cog in the political wheel that people manipulated to get what they wanted.

The introspection gave me clarity that made me truly see Mason. Seeing the changes in my demeanor, he altered his stance. Squaring his shoulders, he focused on me. My attention went to the small cyclone forming in his hand. A calculated and portentous smile lifted the corners of his lips.

The circular motion of the cyclone continued, but his attention remained on me. I watched him as closely as he did me, forming a strategy. Mason stepped back, distancing himself from the weapon of destruction he was about to release. It would destroy my protective field. I crouched into position and, before he could release it, I dropped the field and within seconds was in wolf form, soaring in his direction over the spiraling wind. I'd nearly missed the cyclone as I soared over it, taking flight like a bird. The top edge of it clipped one leg, nudging me hard to the left. Thrown off balance, I sprawled onto the floor. The cyclone was erratic—pulling the drapes from windows, furniture and home décor hurtling in my direction—but under the direction of its cruel master. I moved, darting and jumping around the refuse, keeping enough distance from the small force not to be swept into it. Giving it all that I had, I thrust myself at Mason, crashing into him and sending us both to the ground.

He howled when I bit into his leg. I sank my teeth in so deep that if I was pulled away from it, so would part of his flesh. The blustering wind stopped. Mason pounded indiscriminately, trying to get me to release him. When he made a move toward my eye, I let go and jumped away from the attack. He rolled away and grabbed a piece of broken furniture, held it out, assumed a defensive position. Limping as I rounded him, I moved to get a better striking angle. Before I could gain the advantage, the front door blasted open, and a gust of wind followed. It was strong but not as strong as the one that sent Mason flying into the wall. His head hit it hard. Gideon and two uniformed men, dressed in military-style uniforms similar to ones worn in Elysian, stormed in. Then Mason was pelted with sharp shards of ice, leaving marks and cuts on his body. The assault didn't yield until Mason was slumped against the wall.

Gideon waited patiently until Mason lifted his gaze to meet his. "You are no longer the leader of the elves. It is time that you behave as though you realize that," he asserted in an even, tight voice.

"Sky, I'm glad you weren't injured too badly. Please accept my apology for Mason's actions. Although I share in his concerns, I don't condone the actions used to deal with it."

Gideon's arresting violet eyes moved from Mason's to mine.

He no longer had the androgynous beauty of the man who was once hailed as the Prince of Mischief. His narrow features were now more handsome than pretty as he diligently performed the duties of the position he'd grudgingly accepted. He kept looking at me. My cue to leave.

I wasn't surprised to find Sebastian there, his arms crossed over his chest, when I trotted outside. He turned around once I was close enough to the car to retrieve the clothes I had stashed in the trunk. I shifted and dressed.

"How did you know?" I asked.

"Winter told me that someone had placed a bounty on you and Ethan, and I figured it had to be Mason. Once I knew that, I knew you'd try to handle it yourself." He sported the universal "you're so predictable" look. He could deduce it was Mason from the limited information I'd given Winter but couldn't figure out that Ariel was upset with him? I'd never understand Sebastian.

"I was handling it," I shot back, irritated.

"I'm sure you were, and more than likely diplomatically, but situations like this require more than that. Letting Gideon handle his own is"—he searched for the right words—"less messy." I was quite surprised that he'd come up with something so simplistic. And with that, he nodded his head in my direction, got in his car, took another look at Mason's home and the rain that was concentrated just over it, and drove away.

ess messy. Was there such a thing? Things always seemed to be messy and to have consequences, even Ethan and me mating. My body ached and I wanted to eat, shower, and sleep, I wasn't sure in which order. I was surprised that I seemed to have drifted and found myself in my neighborhood instead of Ethan's, pulling into David and Trent's driveway. Relief flooded me when I saw their windows were open. They were home. They didn't have a specific work time and sometimes weren't available. They hadn't been home the last few times I'd called. It only reaffirmed how much I needed them, not just the human aspect of who they were, but the fact things were always "less messy" with them. It was simple, normal, pedantic, and the most fun. They had a life I had once thought I'd have, or at least some semblance of it. They got to walk away.

The door swung open before I could make my way up the stairs. "Kitten," David cooed.

I narrowed my eyes, glared, and growled at him.

"Oooh, so scary. Not a kitten at all, but rather a bloodthirsty wolf. I should have slammed the door and run for my life," he teased, before pressing his lips to my forehead. He crooked his finger under my chin, inspected me, then took a step back and gave the rest of me the same once-over. Most of my bruises were hidden by my clothes, except for the one on my left cheek.

David's brows lifted in inquiry.

"It looks worse than what it was," I lied.

He nodded, quickly accepting it, and we found ourselves entrenched in our mutual denial. It was a comfortable place; after he and Trent had nearly died in a Faerie attack, I'd vowed to expose them as little as possible to my world. David seemed content with me doing so.

He examined his wineglass, one of the small ones he used when he wanted to pretend he was just a wine sipper; the ones he and Trent used most of the time could hold nearly half a bottle each. He grinned, pulled out the Big Gulp wineglasses, uncorked two bottles of red, and filled glasses. Slowly I made my way to the living room, balancing my glass and Trent's.

Trent took his absently and focused on my ring finger. He looked distraught. I quickly realized why. "No, the band broke."

"How did you break the band, cupcake?" David asked, handing me a literal cupcake. Now if only he could call me a frosted cinnamon bun and make that happen.

I contented myself with my cupcake, the cheese and fruit platter, and the vegetables and dip he set on the table. Instead of indulging in the cake, I had a few carrots, celery, and broccoli first, because I was a responsible adult.

"I forgot to take it off when I changed." I didn't elaborate, and they were content with that explanation. Trent had delved into our cave of denial. We were all content, happy with the simplistic world we pretended was the only one that existed.

"Wonderful, so we can eat, drink, and be merry." Trent pressed a few buttons on the remote and the TV came to life. The first thing I saw was a woman saying, "Yes to that dress."

"How long have you had that one in the chamber?" I asked,

realizing that he'd saved enough episodes of various shows to make a night of it.

"Ever since you showed us that big-ass ring," he shot back indignantly. I'd forgotten that Trent couldn't be shamed like a normal person. He was too comfortable with everything he did.

"No one gets a ring like that and doesn't have a wedding."

Three hours, four bottles of wine, and two trays of cheese and grapes later, I wasn't drunk but slightly buzzed and being wooed by David and Trent into having a wedding.

"We're not having a wedding," I confirmed, despite the surely practiced wide-eyed puppy-dog looks they gave me. "We're mated; the ring was just a romantic gesture."

"A necklace is a romantic gesture, sentimental gifts are romantic gestures, and *actual* romantic gestures are romantic gestures. A diamond like that is a proposal deserving of a wedding," David asserted, taking another draw from his glass.

"We're mated; that's better than being married. It's for life. ... It's different."

David shrugged, stood, and drained his glass. Then he strode over to where I sat in the chair, nudged my t-shirt off my shoulder to expose skin, and bit me. I was shocked into silence. My mouth fell open and remained that way even after Trent, taking David's lead, did the same to my other shoulder.

"There," Trent huffed with indignation. "Now we're mated, too. I guess you'll have to have a wedding." David grinned. I wished I hadn't gone into detail about it. I recalled the frown of confusion that came over their faces when I'd tried to explain the nuances and the bonding process of being someone's mate, along with the pack politics that came along with it. Apparently, they didn't really understand it; if they had, I wouldn't have had two red marks on my shoulder from them biting me.

"Hmmm. Are you two embroiled in some contest where you're trying to see who can make things the weirdest?"

They laughed. "We try," Trent said and grinned. I knew the

debate was far from over, but we settled into a comfortable silence as we watched the shows. The wine was wearing off, but so was my resolve—I kept reminding myself that they could make preparing a wedding fun.

David and Trent noticed the decline as well, and after a while, it was just them watching me watch the shows.

"We'd help," David offered.

Before I could answer, my phone buzzed. A text from Ethan: "When are you coming home?"

"Is that Ethan?" David asked.

I nodded.

"Should you tell him we're mated, or should I do it?"

"I'll tell him. He might not be too happy that he's in a polygamous relationship with two other men," I teased.

"All this can be avoided if he's your husband," David pointed out with a dramatic wave of his hand.

I returned his text to let him know soon.

Ethan was sitting up in bed, a book in hand, when I returned home. It was a few minutes after two in the morning. I would have been home sooner but I'd had to shift several times to get rid of the alcohol haze. I showered, then crawled into bed naked. I didn't bother putting on pajamas most of the time because, once in bed with Ethan, it was only a matter of minutes before they were in a pile on the floor.

He pulled me closer. I rested my face in the curve of his neck, taking in his strong masculine scent, with a slight hint of oak and evergreen. He'd been for a run in animal form; I could subtly feel his wolf being unleashed and given free rein, and the hum of aggravation and frustration with being restrained behind his human form. I nestled in closer, pressing my lips to his chest. I kissed it. My tongue slipped out to taste his warm skin. His groan urged me on. He rolled to his back, bringing me with him. I continued to kiss, tracing the indentations of his abs, nipping at his skin. Tasting him. Inhaling him. Taking in not just his intoxicating scent but the metallic hint of his blood. It was a siren, calling to me, and I craved it as much as I desired Ethan. He kissed me hungrily, entwining the fingers of one hand in my hair, while the others slowly roved along the curves of my body. I sheathed him in me, finding our rhythm, my fingers curled into the thick cord of muscles along his back. My nails bit in and broke the skin. He groaned at the pain; desire and unsated hunger swelled in me. Again, I inhaled, this time ignoring one scent and craving the more enticing one. Ethan saw the hunger, felt it in my frenetic movements. The gyration of my hips, me searching to feel more of him, to be connected even further, to have more of him. Sex couldn't squelch it. The harder I moved, the more frenzied I became. The kisses were intense, but the movement wasn't intimate enough. I needed more—a lust born out of more than just eroticism.

The feeding had become part of our joining, such that Ethan no longer recoiled or discouraged it. He turned his head and I bit, spilling blood. I tasted him again, and my body shuddered, sated. Ethan pulled me to him, kissing me, exploring my mouth. He rolled me to my back, his hips jutting into me, his face buried in my neck, finding the pulse, where he licked. I imagined him doing the same as I had done to him. I waited in anticipation. He simply nipped, and it was enough. I shuddered again under him, and soon Ethan found his pleasure before resting on top of me. The warmth of his body enveloped me.

He rolled off and pulled me into his arms, where I stayed. There wasn't the uncomfortable silence there'd been the other times when I'd needed more than just sexual satisfaction. It wasn't often, but it had been happening more since we'd mated. Neither one of us seemed open to exploring what that meant. Maybe it was nothing, but I was probably being naïve.

CHAPTER 10

*A*t eight the next morning Ethan was drinking a cup of coffee, e-reader in hand, perusing what I assumed was the paper. Ethan was the type to have a morning ritual. Up at six, morning run, shower, dress, coffee, breakfast, and the news delivered electronically. The night routine was similar, except instead of the news it was stock reports and business figures.

He had already dressed meticulously in dark blue slacks and a blue-gray shirt, ready to take on the morning, while I'd managed to amble out of bed, make the bed, shower, and lumber into the kitchen in a fog. Ethan loved to cook, so I just warmed up whatever he left for me, or made my way to the table if it wasn't too late.

He grinned as I sauntered to the table, taking in my purple fitted shirt and black yoga pants and fluffy socks. His grin became a look of derision at the unicorn on my shirt. "So sexy," he purred.

Even when he didn't have to go to the office, which he did infrequently, he was always dressed as if he was ready to go to it, or to court.

I looked down at the shirt, made a face, and grabbed sausage from a plate. "Be happy I have on clothes."

His brow rose. "Is there a no-clothes option? If so, I want that one." He stood and came over to my side of the table and kissed me. The fluidity of his movements had improved significantly since yesterday. They were still stiffer, lacking some of his usual grace, and I could tell he was still injured.

He placed my ring next to my plate. He'd gotten it repaired.

"You're not going to put it on me?" I complained, extending my hand and waiting for him to put it on my finger.

"I put it on you when I proposed. That's tradition. How hard is it to put it on your finger now?" he asked.

I wasn't sure why this was the battle I chose to fight—there wasn't any rhyme or reason to some arguments I took on—but I really wanted him to do it. Ethan was defiant at times for no apparent reason and took a stand on things based on some obtuse principle that I didn't understand. I guessed that it was rooted in his belief that Steven and Josh never denied me anything, so he'd made it his personal mission to deny me, just to maintain some weird cosmic balance or keep me humble. I didn't know the reason, but it bothered me.

Time ticked by, my arm tiring, as he stood a few feet from me, arms crossed and steadfast. I put my arm down and then slid my ring to the middle of the table and kept a defiant glare on him as I ate breakfast. Then I cleared the table, leaving the ring where it was. He moved to the table, lifted the ring off of it to clear away a few crumbs, then returned it to its location.

"Are you going to work today?" he asked.

It seemed so wrong to call what I did at the pack's bar with Josh "work." But after I'd spent several days there, it turned out Josh did more than drink with the beautiful people, chomp down edibles, and be the center of attention when the club was open. Surprisingly there was more to what he did behind the scenes, but since most of his time was consumed sipping on a drink, playing music while chair dancing, and texting on his phone, I had a hard time deciphering when he was working.

"I thought I'd go by the house first—"

"To check on Cole?" Ethan inquired; his tone was even but there was a sharp edge to it.

"He might die. It seems cruel to ignore him and let him be alone."

"Dr. Jeremy has been there around the clock, and so has Kelly. Just because his preferred guest is you doesn't mean being there is the right thing to do."

He sighed heavily, and I could see his frustration. I replayed every vile thing Cole had done that was worthy of my hatred, but it all withered away when I thought of him pale, fighting the hopelessness he had to be feeling as he suffered from an ailment not even Dr. Jeremy could cure. I didn't possess the level of coldness needed to abandon him, and I searched Ethan's face trying to figure out if he did. I'd caught him in the room once, watching Cole, and the air of abhorrence wasn't there.

"Where are we with finding out what they used to change you all?" I asked, changing the subject.

Ethan rubbed a hand over his face. "We were all sedated. We awoke in animal form, unable to change back. I was in the woods when I regained the ability. We didn't have clothes and there wasn't an adequate sample of any substance in our system," he admitted.

"Where does that leave us?"

"Screwed. If someone has the ability to force us to change and we're unable to stop it, what if it's done while we are in public?"

He'd voiced the very concern I had. We'd barely avoided being outed before; now it might happen, and there wasn't anything we could do about it.

"Maybe the formula died with Sonja and Bethany," I

suggested, hopeful. Being foolishly optimistic wasn't the best course of action, but it was all I had at the moment.

"Let's hope so, but I'm looking into it." Ethan finished his coffee, stood, and put the cup in the sink. The wayward grin that overtook his face as he walked toward me was one of the more obvious similarities between him and his brother. He picked up the ring and gently took my hand in his. He kissed the back of my hand and turned it over and did the same to my palm as his intense gunmetal gaze bore into me. With great care he stretched out each of my fingers. He kissed the tip of my thumb, his warm breath sending a chill through me. He gave each finger the same delicate attention, and I shivered each time his tongue slipped out to taste my skin. When he got to my ring finger, he nipped at the tip of it. He dropped the ring in my hand and folded my fingers around it.

He was heading out the door before I could give an adequate rebuttal, reducing my response to a searing sound of irritation. His deep, rumbling laughter lingered a few minutes after he was gone.

"Betahole," I breathed out, slipping the ring onto my finger. *Ethan—one, Sky—zero.*

Josh had been running his fingers through his hair for the last five minutes, looking at the paper in front of him in the office of the club. I knew he wasn't going to get any work done and all his energy was going to be directed to pack business.

He shook his head. "I don't know how they changed them without a spell," he finally admitted. It was the puzzle he'd being mulling over for the past two hours.

"An Alpha or a stronger were-animal can trigger or stop a change. A powerful witch can only stop one, they can't trigger one."

"Not just a witch, a powerful one. I couldn't stop a change on my own, but several level three witches, maybe five or six, would have the strength to do it." He stood and began pacing the floor. "A formula that can trigger a change without magic will be disastrous."

All the possible scenarios were filing through my brain, and not one of them was good.

Josh plopped down in the chair, back again to studying books in his office while I took over the bar's responsibilities: stocking liquor, scheduling bands, contacting employees about monthly meetings. Josh would handle the social media part, finding a way to be the charismatic witch even through social media.

His face brightened when London poked her head into the office. "Grilis herb," she said, placing a bag and a large spell book on the desk. "It's rumored to have been used in archaic shapeshifting spells."

"You all can make people shapeshift?" I inquired, shocked.

They both made faces. "I do believe this is one of the more creative tales out there to make us seem more powerful than we are. If we are, then I haven't met anyone with that particular skill. It might be one of those abilities that very few witches possess. I know of two witches who can compel people to truth," London said.

She opened the bag and pulled out a green and purple, grainy-looking plant. She took out a small stone bowl, three vials with herbs, and a grinder. Josh moved from his desk, giving her space to work. After a few minutes of mixing the herbs together, she looked at the bowl's contents and then at the book several times. Frowning, she lifted her eyes to mine. "Will you try it?"

I wasn't too keen on them trying archaic potions on me, but we had to find out.

There were several moments of strained silence before I

nodded. She scooped some of the mix in her hand and blew. A coating of bluish dust filled the air, fluttering over my face and on my nose. I sneezed. They waited. Nothing happened. Determination moved over London's face, peculiarly similar to Josh's when he was given a magical puzzle. A spark and joy lit; they were always ready to stretch the boundaries of their skills and knowledge.

She blew the powder at me again; nothing. She tried four more configurations of magical dust before finally conceding, "It's not the grilis."

"What else could it be?" I asked.

They didn't know, and we still needed to find out. I left London and Josh working on the project and, based on our conversation, my next stop was the library in the pack's home. That made me think of Cole. Two mysteries that needed to be solved.

"Dammit," I grumbled as Demetrius's black car came up behind mine before I could pull out of the parking lot at work. My commitment to ignoring him crumbled when he moved his car even closer. I would have to acknowledge his presence even if it was just to tell him to move out of the way.

Demetrius was a vision of midnight as he got out of his vehicle. His dark hair was shorter than it was when we'd found him after the aborted hunt. Standing, he tugged at the sleeves of his black shirt and brushed out nonexistent wrinkles from black slacks.

I kept my window up, even after he lowered himself so that he was at my eye level.

He tapped on the window. I raised a brow in acknowledgment but kept the window where it was. He could hear me tell him to screw off just fine through it.

"What?" I asked sharply.

"Can we talk?"

What in the world did we have to talk about? Curiosity overrode my anger. "Talk," I urged.

He looked around the parking lot, where a delivery van was already parked, along with Josh's Jeep and a large blue truck belonging to the head bartender, who'd arrived early to set up training for two new hires.

"Not here. Can we go somewhere private?"

It took a long time for me to answer because my thoughts were dominated by visions of me reversing my car, running over his foot, and, once he was on the ground, edging forward just enough to get momentum to back over him. The hate I had for him ran deep, and for a brief moment I wanted to succumb to it and be as reckless and cruel with his life as he'd been with Quell's. I felt sordid pangs of guilt and self-loathing. Not about how much I detested Demetrius—he deserved it—but how much it had darkened who I was. Would talking to him only intensify those feelings or assuage them? I exhaled a long breath as if it would clean my thoughts and lighten my mood. It didn't.

"There's a cafe around the corner. We can meet there," I instructed after several moments of consideration.

He nodded and quickly made his way to his car. Moments later, the black Porsche streaked away, mirroring its owner's swift and powerful movement.

At the bakery, Demetrius made a face of contempt as the cashier rang up my order: a small coffee, three muffins, six cookies, three biscotti, a cinnamon roll, three adorable cake pops, a black and white cookie, and a brownie. He gritted his teeth when the cashier gave the total and I jerked my head in his direction, implying he was paying. I planned on being on a sugar high the entire time I was with him.

I took a seat while the Master of the Northern Seethe brought over my assortment of baked goods.

"You can't possibly eat all of that in one sitting."

"Nope, I can't, but you said you wanted to talk. You talk, and I'll listen and eat. As you pointed out, I can't eat all this, so I'll need a carryout box. Will you be a lamb and get me one?"

He struggled to keep his composure, obviously not used to receiving orders and definitely not ones that reduced him to a woolly, errand-running, docile farm animal. For several beats he struggled with it before forcing a smile and exposing his fangs.

"You should put those away since there is no way you are going to use them here—especially on me." I grinned, remembering the conversation where he'd said doing anything to me would be more trouble than it would be worth since he'd have to deal with my pack and, most of all, Ethan. I was being obnoxious, but if anyone deserved to be the recipient of such objectionable behavior it was Demetrius.

He returned with two containers and a coffee for himself. I would have had him box it up for me, but I didn't want him to touch my food. After I'd put away everything but a few items, I took a sip of my coffee and a bite of my cinnamon roll. "What do you want to talk about?"

"How did Chris take my absence?" he asked softly. He wouldn't keep eye contact and let his gaze drift to the empty space next to me. I never thought I'd live to see the day when Demetrius would drop his shield of entitlement and arrogance to show something as human and fragile as humility and awkwardness. But there they were. He seemed embarrassed by his inquiry. At that moment it took a great deal of effort not to drop my armor and feel compassion for the person sitting across from me, who was obviously in pain.

"She helped find you." It was all I could offer. I was in a quandary. I wanted to tell him that the only reason she wanted him alive was to present her as the new Mistress. If it had been a title given to her prior to his abduction, I doubted she would have been as involved in finding him. But I wasn't sure of it.

"Why did you convince her to come back?" he inquired, his voice faltering with emotions and uncertainty.

Damn. Lies always came back to bite me in the butt. I had nothing, and my skills as a storyteller weren't sufficient to come up with anything plausible. My jaws clenched as they bit back the truth.

She wanted to come back with the sole purpose of taking the South. I want her to take the North. Take it from you.

"You should ask her," I suggested evasively.

"I did, and she said I should be more concerned with the fact that she's back."

"Sounds like a good answer to me." I shrugged, shoving another piece of cinnamon roll into my mouth with the intention of keeping it full for the rest of the visit so I'd be limited to nods, headshakes, and shrugs.

"I created her," he whispered.

I guessed I wasn't going to be able to eat and shrug my way through this. "And you feel that gives you permission to treat her the way you do? You locked her in a box! What type of person does that?"

"Am I to believe you have never been placed in one of those cages you all seem to be so fond of? It's my understanding there aren't many of your kind who haven't seen the inside of one— given your tempers and propensity to give in to your primal side. I hear that it is done to protect, no matter how cruel it seems to others. And make no mistake, I find the practice abhorrent."

Remaining civil was becoming increasingly difficult, and I found myself under his judgmental gaze. "It's no more abhorrent than locking a person who clearly has a problem with being in small places in a box." Chris's panicked and hurt face when she'd blurted out what he'd done flashed in my head. She'd looked broken. All the while, he'd seemed entitled, expecting no consequences for his actions.

His lips tightened. "I have very few rules and the ones I do have I expect people to respect, even Chris. She is no fool and recognizes my feelings for her and is quite willing to exploit them to her advantage." A small smile full of admiration and respect flitted across his lips. It quickly disappeared when he saw the look of disgust on mine as I tried to figure out if he was a sadist or a masochist or a peculiar combination of both. *If I throat-punched him, would he hate or love me?* Quickly I abandoned the idea of jumping down that rabbit hole and getting lost in the vampire's world of dysfunction.

"You care about her. There should have been some leniency," I asserted, looking at the exit and longing to use it. I was starting to think that the more time I spent with him, the more soot I'd have on me. Or worse, I'd start to understand the dysfunction and possibly accept it.

He looked down at the coffee he'd been stirring periodically. He relaxed the disapproving line of his lips enough to continue. "She tried to kill Alexander, and the reason wasn't acceptable. As Sebastian will tell you, there will be those who test your authority, push the boundaries to test how pliable they are. I don't hide my desire for Chris. If I was willing to punish her so cruelly, they now know how merciless I would be with them. It had dual benefits."

Several minutes passed as he watched me stare at him with loathing. Not about what he was saying but the mere fact that I saw some similarities in what the pack did, my pack. We weren't without our questionable tactics or so different from the Seethe.

Demetrius's gaze wandered away from mine. "She hates small spaces: cages, coffins, closets, and rooms. Chris gets claustrophobic and loses herself in her panic. It's her weakness. Now she knows that, even under the cruelest conditions, she can survive them." He shifted his eyes toward me as if asking for some form of understanding. Maybe guidance? I had no clue.

This moment couldn't have gotten any weirder if everyone had broken out in song and dance.

"I've created her in more ways than she will ever know. The length of her human life was because of me as well. Not just the blood I shared with her—I am the reason she survived her first job after Ryan died. It was my intervention that kept her alive. Though she was tenacious and resourceful, she still had her hang-ups and fears. But there was always potential." His voice was nostalgic, and I assumed his thoughts were drifting back to that day. I only knew bits and pieces of it, things I'd heard in passing or as part of another story.

He shook off the memories, and his hand closed around his cup, seemingly appreciative of the warmth it provided. It was odd watching him enjoy something as trivial as a warm mug. It was the most human I'd ever seen him look. Deceptively gentle, with a somnolent longing. Uncomfortable, I shifted in my seat and pulled to the front of my thoughts every bad image of him that I could think of to chase away the image before me.

No sympathy. He will not get an iota of sympathy from me.

"During one of her jobs, the room she was in was set on fire, and as smoke filled the room, she gave in to fear rather than respond logically. She almost had it." He looked up. "She had gotten close enough to the water pipes to douse the fire, and if she hadn't lost those minutes panicking about being in a small space, she would have done it without my help before the smoke overwhelmed her."

I tore my eyes from the dark pool of emotions on display. So very human—a frailty that I'd thought he was devoid of. It masked him with a beauty that wasn't physical.

My attention went to the creamy brown liquid in my cup as I battled the fascination I had with a very vulnerable, emotionally beautiful, gentle Demetrius. Where was that damn meteor when you needed it?

"Why are you telling me this? It won't change how I feel. So what? You saved her life only to feel as though it's yours to do with as you please. In fact, you've said that several times. When you care about someone, you do things for them because you care for them. Their life doesn't become yours and you don't get to treat them however the hell you please because of it." It came out as hard as I had intended. I hoped it would deter him from telling any more stories that would whittle away at my wall of hate. It was inches thick and I planned to keep it that way.

"You have every reason to hate me," he said solemnly, his dark eyes meeting mine as his head tilted to appraise me.

I swallowed quickly. "Thank you for your permission, but I was doing a good job without it."

His voice was now cool and detached, and that was familiar and welcomed. "If I knew what I know now, my first encounter with you would have been different. It should have been different."

"Oh great, in hindsight you wouldn't have killed my mother. Should I now nominate you for a humanitarian award?" I lowered my voice when I realized I'd raised it and the few people in the café had looked in our direction.

"My instruction was to get you, and the loss of your mother's life was regrettable … is regretted." He closed his eyes. "For that, Michaela's life was indeed payment."

The anger roiled in me as he ripped open old wounds that I'd worked so hard to heal. I couldn't stay there. Continuing the conversation would only end with a scene and, given the way I felt, a violent one. I grabbed my bag and my purse and stood. "We're done here." I rushed out of the cafe with Demetrius close behind. The cool air washing over my face felt good. The sugar-laced high was another comforting sensation.

"Why the hell are you following me!" I snapped, turning to face Demetrius, who had passed his car and was heading toward where I'd parked.

"You are still in pain, human pain, and that is understandable. But will you not give me credit that my actions are responsible for who you are today? And what I see before me is quite impressive. Far better than what you were before. I guess, in a way I am as much your creator as Chris's." He paused, taking in the new revelation. "You're welcome."

You're welcome!

I thanked him. I thanked him as hard as I could. I slapped him. Flashes of red consumed me and anger piloted my actions. It wasn't until I did it the third time and still he stood without moving or retaliating that I stopped. "It is the height of arrogance for you to attribute who I am today to what you've done."

"Arrogant, perhaps. But it doesn't make it less true. Maybe I don't deserve gratitude, but I don't deserve your hatred. I've atoned for my misdeeds, and I assumed you bringing Chris back was to atone for yours and what you did to Quell. Do you feel absolved of your guilt, now that you have hit me?" Condescension laced his question.

I'd feel absolved once I kicked him in his man giblets.

"What *I* did to Quell!"

My palm tingled with the urge to either slap him again or to pummel him with magic. The rage, violence, and unfettered, cold, destructive ire that I was feeling I attributed to Maya or my wolf. I liked to think that my humanity kept me tethered and incapable of something like this, but it didn't. It wasn't my wolf or Maya who wanted to yank open my car door, grab a stake, plunge it in him, and watch him struggle for life while I stood over him eating a cake lollipop. Sucking in a deep breath, I closed my eyes briefly, hoping that I could find the resolve not to act on any of the thoughts that were rampaging through my mind. There was a plan. Chris needed to be presented as the new Mistress. He needed to feel and deal with something far worse than just a stake through the chest. He would not rob me of my vengeance. I wanted him to mourn, feel sorrow, and go through stages of grief—or whatever the other things were. I mastered my anger.

"You think because I didn't show my affections for Michaela the way you show it for others that I didn't care?" he asked.

"Did you feel those affections before or after you rolled out of the bed of whatever poor soul you were using for the night?"

His lips slipped into a small, thin line and he glowered. "You think a relationship where you can't share your body with others for fear of losing the affections of your mate or the dissolving of the relationship is stronger and better than one that can survive that?" he inquired, with hints of dark, patronizing amusement.

I wasn't going to discuss the sanctity of marriage, mating, and relationships or what was the right way to love with that degenerate.

"This conversation is over." I turned to get in my car.

"You killed Quell before I even took that sword to him." Those were his parting words, or rather what he *wanted* to be his parting words. Demetrius seemed determined to end our meeting with another slap—or a stake.

"What?" I challenged through clenched teeth.

He looked bored.

When he spoke, his tone was smooth, unbothered. "You've been elevated to a status in the Midwest Pack that I haven't seen in my lifetime. Unlike others, *I* do not believe you are naïve or harmless. In fact, I'm sure you are quite formidable; therefore, I don't believe you weren't aware of Quell's feelings for you. They exceeded those he had for Michaela, his creator, and me. You played your game well with him. Giving him just enough to feel cared for … loved, luring him into the Sky trap. Just a taste of Sky and what he desired. But in the end, you ended up with Ethan, the person who could give you status that you'd never have with Quell. He desired nothing more than to just live, be part of the Seethe, and have you. I suspect you wanted more."

"I did *not* choose Ethan because of his status or what he could do for me. I love him." I hated that I was letting Demetrius's words get to me. Was that the narrative that people saw, or was Demetrius just saying whatever was needed to get the information he wanted? What he was accusing me of was similar to what Chris was doing. I wondered if his assertion meant that he knew and was doing this to get me to admit it. I was unable to get a read on it as I stared into his emotionless face and tepid eyes. He was over a century old, and I doubted he'd held on to his position and become as dreaded as he now was by being naïve.

"I loved Quell, but it was different than what I feel for Ethan. No matter how much you twist the story, I loved him, and you killed him."

He opened his mouth to speak and I lifted my hand to stop him. "We have nothing more to say."

With that, I quickly got into my car. My eyes watered as they fought a losing battle to keep my tears at bay. I didn't know what to think.

Demetrius's words dominated my thoughts as I drove to Ethan's home—I meant my home. Had I done something wrong? Was Demetrius right? The moment I stopped in the driveway, I jumped out of the car and started removing my clothes. I felt bound and in dire need of shedding not only my clothing but also my vulnerable human shell that thought too much and felt too many emotions. I wanted to run, to be nothing more than fur, claws, fangs—a feral and uncomplicated being who only wanted to run, eat, and meet my basic primal needs. A servant to my id.

In animal form, I sprinted into the massive forest behind Ethan's—our—house, giving myself a reprieve from everything that had transpired over the last few days and getting lost in the dense forest. Fallen branches broke under the pressure of my heavy paws. I ran away from the thoughts, the emotions, the conflicting feelings, and the betrayal that I felt I'd inflicted on myself by having any empathy for Demetrius. I felt submerged and drowning, choking on feelings that weren't mine to own. I didn't kill Quell. Demetrius did. I didn't force Quell to love me. He chose to. It wasn't my fault that the love I felt for him was platonic. No matter how I sped through the dense forest, took in the thick, oaky scent of the trees, the strong odor of the dirt I kicked up, and the crisp smell of the grass, it wasn't enough of a sensory overload to erase my conversation with Demetrius. I needed it to disappear from my mind.

Instead, the conversation looped through my head, along with a replay of Demetrius killing Quell. My mind decided to be egregiously cruel, intermittently replaying the images with me in Demetrius's position, giving me visions of me as Quell's murderer.

It was dusk by the time I'd finished. I estimated that my run had lasted at least three hours. No longer running, I was able to feel the full effect of the hours of activity. My body was so tired, I knew my estimate was correct. I was ready for food and sleep. Ethan was waiting for me at the entrance of the forest, sitting by a large tree, my clothes draped over his lap.

I padded up to him and plopped half of my body on him and rested.

"Change," he said softly.

I whimpered a response.

"Sky, change." There was more of a command to his voice. "Now. You've been out here for hours. Your clothes smell like Demetrius, and right now I'm itching to go over to his house and kick his ass. I should know why I'm doing it." He looked grim and frustrated. "What happened between you and Demetrius?"

I moved onto all fours, then shifted to human form and reached for my shirt. Determined to keep me in my naked state, Ethan held on to it as I tugged at it. Slowly his gaze moved over the curves of my body, spending an exceptionally long time looking at my breasts.

Really? I snatched the shirt from him, slipped it on, and took a seat next to him. My eyes closed and I rested my head on his shoulder, inhaling his strong, musky scent. Potent, it reminded me of the woods, a soothing redolence. I took in another whiff.

I rested my face in the crook of his neck. The steadiness of his breathing and heart rate became a welcome distraction. A gentle, melodic beat that nearly lulled me to sleep. Ethan's fingers gently stroked my hands, and then he kissed my hair.

"What happened?" he finally asked. It was the first time I was the one willing the silence to continue.

"Nothing."

"Sky, there is no way we are not having this conversation, and 'nothing' isn't going to cut it. You come home and go straight to the woods for hours. Something happened. What?"

I had no idea how to broach the subject. My relationship with Quell was a sore spot, and I knew his death only bothered Ethan because it hurt me. Any sympathy that Ethan had for Quell was connected with the feelings Ethan had for me. Nothing more, and I'd go as far as to say he was happy to have Quell out of the picture.

"He said that I had killed Quell long before he did."

"Hmmm."

Hmmm? I was expecting more than just a "hmmm." I wanted him to tell me that Demetrius had just had a big helping of crazy flakes, on his way to there-is-no-way-in-hell-ville, driving his ridiculous-thinking-mobile, while singing "I'm a dumb ass." And he hit me with a "Hmm."

Ethan gave my hand a squeeze.

"I was expecting a little more than a 'hmmm,'" I whispered. I was tired, emotionally and physically.

Shifting, he lifted me and repositioned me until I was straddling his legs and facing him. "He was in love with you, Skylar."

Skylar? This is going to be an interesting conversation.

"It might have been platonic for you, but it wasn't for him. If he'd lived, he'd have spent his life looking for someone to fill his Sky-sized void. His donor looked so much like you it was creepy. It was like looking at a picture of you. When he went on his feeding binge, did the women not resemble you?"

I remained silent, aware that he already knew the answer.

"It's not my fault."

"I never said it was, but *you* think it is. No matter what I say to you, any comfort I attempt to give you won't be enough. I'll just pose the question: What could you have done to save him from those feelings? To make things better for him? Be with him?"

Ethan's brows rose, and I dropped my head, avoiding his gaze because I didn't have the answer. I had an answer but it would have been hurtful—I wouldn't have told him about Ethan.

As if he had read my thoughts, he lifted my chin until our eyes met. "He would have found out about me. Are you happy with me?" he whispered.

"Of course I am."

Studying me, he frowned. "This is your least favorable quality."

"Hey!" I shrieked, hitting him in his chest. It was intended to be a playful jab but was harder than anticipated. "The whole 'kicking a person while they are down' thing applies."

"It's not my intention to do it, but you've always had a Pollyanna way of looking at things. Willing to sacrifice your own safety and happiness for others. While most people find it endearing, I am not one of them."

"Hey!"

His lips quirked into a sinful grin. "You're the one who wanted total honesty, and that's it. No filters. I love you, but every day when I walk through the door, I wonder what stray cat, dog, person, vampire, elf, fae, witch, or whoever you've picked up for the day with the intention of 'saving' will be there. The loyalty you have for the people you love is admirable, your best trait. The other thing, not so much."

"I got it. Let's move on," I sniped back.

He kissed me. I might have smelled like Demetrius, but it didn't deter him from responding to me being barely clothed and straddling him.

"Why did you agree to meet with Demetrius?" he asked. The miscreant smirk told me he knew the real answer. "Everyone doesn't deserve your time or sympathy. I tell people to go to hell all the time."

"Like you don't enjoy doing it."

He laughed. "I do. But there's a freedom to it. You should be more like me."

"If I were like you, I doubt we'd have ended up together."

He considered my comment for a moment and gave me a wicked smile. "I don't know, I like me—it can't be too hard to be with me."

I let out a long, exaggerated sigh. "It's exhausting." In just my shirt, I headed to the house and went into the shower, knowing that it would only be a matter of time before Ethan joined me. Showering was something he'd prefer we didn't do alone. It always led to us making love, and this wasn't an exception. Ethan's phone was chiming when we got out. Ethan answered it. I moved closer, to hear nothing but Sebastian's practiced low voice, which made it impossible to make out any words. After several exchanges, me hearing one side, Ethan's voice had dropped to being barely audible. Then he hung up.

"They found out what's wrong with Cole. He's healing."

CHAPTER 11

*C*ole was healed. It was as if I was looking at a different person. Moving closer to Ethan at the doorway of the infirmary, I studied Cole with intense curiosity while he sat on the edge of the bed, leaning over a three-dimensional chess game he was engaged in with Sebastian. Both of them analyzed the board with such concentration, it seemed to be about more than a game. Unwritten stakes, a quiet battle between the two Alphas.

Cole moved a piece and then shifted his attention to me. The warm color had returned to his cheeks; the wolf that had been subdued by illness was revived and livelier. His mesmeric gray eyes glinted with the shrewdness of a predator. His voice softened to a sultry whisper as he said my name. I hated how intimate and wrong it felt for my name to come from him in a slow, seductive drawl. He raised his hand, his fingers slightly bent in a wave. Then he mouthed, "Thank you." A diminutive, easy smile lifted the corners of his lips. It was disconcerting how he made such an inconsequential action seem amorous, as if we were sharing a moment. There were too many deceptive facets of his personality. I didn't want to share anything with him—not even a moment.

Cole had something undeniable about him. It was more than the allure of the predator; it was a magnetism that dominated his personality. It was the reason Winter had considered him a confidante, a kind person, the guy that had her back, only to be proven wrong when he'd challenged Ethan not once, but twice. The last time after Ethan had been injured.

Cole's gaze remained pinned on me while Sebastian studied the board. Ethan wasn't hiding his disdain. Pleased by Ethan's reaction, Cole widened his smile. I wouldn't provide more fuel for the flames. I made my way over to Dr. Jeremy, who was at the other side of the room, in the corner where he kept his microscope. Hearing my footsteps, he looked up. His face folded into a series of frowns and scowls as he split his attention between what was under the microscope and the chart next to him. Lines creased his forehead, and his glower deepened each time he looked at the chart. Whatever feelings of apprehension he may have had toward Cole were shelved momentarily, and understanding Cole's recovery and his ailment was of the utmost importance. I knew it was more than medical curiosity; it was to uphold his reputation as the guy who cured people who would have died under anyone else's watch. He looked down into the eyepiece of the microscope.

"I have no idea what this thing is that I found in Cole."

"May I see it?"

He nodded, moving aside. I didn't understand why he'd put it under the microscope. It was tiny, just a little over an inch, but could have easily been seen by the naked eye. Sensing my curiosity, he took out a metal examining tool and pressed the small, cylinder-shaped creature. A massive amount of silver leaked out of it.

It was like the Tod Schlaf, and I was sure it could only be found in the dark forest. Was it a coincidence that Abigail was the last person to see Cole? Speculation and theories were like a wildfire rapidly raging through my mind. Cole and Sebastian were still engaged in their game of chess, a test of each other's stratagems. While I saw it as banal and trivial, they approached it with vehemence, as a display of their mastery. Their Alphaness. I moved past Ethan, who'd been swept up in the game, scrutinizing the board and the players—especially Cole.

Cole looked aggrieved after Sebastian made a move. His lips strained into a taut line, and frustration and defeat coursed over his features. He went from casual arrogance to ennui in a matter of seconds.

Cole's hand pressed against his stomach. "Perhaps we should save the rest of the game for later. I'm not feeling well," he said.

"Of course." Sebastian moved the table out of the way. "I'll leave the board so you can study it. We can always learn something from the moves we made that didn't have favorable results, right?"

"I agree," Cole replied. Clearly he didn't, and he hadn't put a lot of effort into making it sound convincing. I started to leave when he called my name. I couldn't pretend that I hadn't heard it, because I'd stopped the moment he'd said it. His voice was always too soft, raspy, and intimate. It was another weapon in his quiver to annoy Ethan. How could I explain Ethan attacking Cole because he didn't like the way he said his mate's name? He always had a look of self-satisfaction when Ethan glared at him, and this time was no different.

"What?" I demanded.

"Is there a way I can get a laptop?"

Before I could answer, Dr. Jeremy strode across the room and dropped a small laptop on the bed. In silence. He lowered the head of the bed until Cole was lying flat.

"I need to check your bandages," he said.

"I looked at the wounds earlier," Cole offered. "They're almost healed. Whatever you put on them worked its magic."

"I still need to see them."

Moving toward the exit, I ignored the conversation. It had been the same one for the past three days.

"Bye, Sky," I heard Cole purr as I exited. I stiffened and over-came the urge to turn around and snap at him. Whatever interest Cole had in me seemed insincere and calculated. Was it to have me because of his clear disdain for Ethan? More than anything, he seemed to long for something in the Midwest Pack and I suspected it was Sebastian's position—his entire position. It was not out of the realm of possibility that Cole wanted to be the Elite and the Alpha of the strongest pack in the country. Our pack had access to magic and essentially two Alphas.

Finding out more about the silver-spurting creature was my priority. I didn't believe in coincidences. I allowed all the possi-bilities into my mind, sorting them out, trying to make sense of them, extrapolating the necessary information from the chaotic mess in my head.

Distracted by my thoughts, I nearly ran into Gavin and stopped short just shy of crashing into him. He shuffled back several feet and tucked his hands to his sides as if he feared that I would touch him. Dark eyes narrowed on me as he brushed his hair out of his face. His straight, black hair grew so fast that he'd given up on taming it, allowing it to freefall over his face, something Kelly complained about often. In the last few conver-sations of theirs that I'd overheard, she'd been brushing his hair out of his face and urging him to cut it short or secure it with a band. He'd conceded to a lot of Kelly's requests, most of them centered on showing a modicum of cordiality: "Don't tell people they are boring." "It's rude to walk away from people while they're speaking just because you find them tedious or long-winded"—something that I'd been treated to on multiple occa-sions. It wasn't that Gavin didn't *know* not to do this, it was that he didn't *care* not to do it. There was a difference.

"I need to talk to someone," I said.

"Where's Ethan? Steven? I can get Kelly or Winter for you," he offered. I couldn't tell Ethan yet, because if I was right, it needed to be handled. If I was wrong and Ethan acted on it, that could be problematic. Then there were Steven's and Ethan's personal feelings about Cole, and my thoughts would not bode well. They would react with emotion, and that was the last thing we needed when dealing with Cole.

"I'd rather talk to you."

He made a face, a combination of surprise, concern, abhorrence, intrigue, and wariness.

"Why?"

"Because you're objective and I need a sounding board. This is happening. Deal with it," I chided before he could respond.

He stiffened when I took hold of his wrist and guided him away from the infirmary and upstairs to one of the bedrooms on the second floor.

"What's wrong?" His voice was heavy with unease.

I paced, trying to work things out in my head. Perhaps he was right; maybe I should be speaking with Winter, but one attribute they had in common was cynicism about a person's motives. "I think Cole is responsible for the abductions, and he made himself sick." The words rushed out.

His eyes widened and then his brows pinched together; he was obviously curious about how I'd come to that conclusion. "If Sebastian wasn't the Elite Alpha, who would you peg for being the next one?"

"Ethan."

"Then who?"

"Joan, then her Beta."

"The West Coast wasn't ever involved. Demetrius and Alexander were taken, too," I said.

Before I could explain Demetrius's role in this, Gavin spoke up. "Demetrius killed Quell, and Cole knows it. He knows that you were distraught about it. Demetrius's death would have made you happy."

Gavin rested back against the wall, one long leg outstretched and crossed over the other. He looked past me, his features wrinkled in concentration. "But if Demetrius was dead, Chase would more than likely take over as Master and he would be just as big of a pain in the ass. It would have been easier to leave Demetrius in place."

He was doing exactly what I'd hoped, challenging my thoughts. All the pieces were there; I just needed to put them in the right places. Gavin was right. Why not leave Demetrius for me to handle personally?

Gavin's eyes were heavy on me as I started to pace. I probably looked the way Josh often did when he was trying to come up with a spell. Instead of biting into my nail beds, which was something I'd only seen him do, I gnawed at my nails. Chewed them to nonexistence.

I stopped pacing abruptly. "Chris," I blurted out.

"What about her?" The heightened curiosity in his voice made me look up.

"We all knew that she would be made Mistress, but none of us knew it wouldn't be official until the Presentation. If we didn't know, I'm sure Cole didn't, either. He knows that Chris and I are—" I stopped abruptly. I almost said *friends*. We weren't that. But we weren't enemies. Allies? Indentured allies? Used-to-hate-each-others? Frenemies? Barely-hate-buddies? "We help each other out when necessary. And..."

I was reluctant to continue with the rest of my hypothesis because it delved slightly into implausibility, more fantastical than my other revelations.

The quiet stretched too long and Gavin became noticeably agitated. "And?"

"His injuries seem self-inflicted. Think about the others' wounds. Scratches from running in the woods. Ethan had injuries on his back, and so did the others. Every injury inflicted was from an awkward position, obviously a result of an external source. Cole's were puncture wounds in his arm and stomach." I reenacted the scenario I suspected had occurred.

Gavin's face twisted into a scowl as I waited for him to tell me I was being ridiculous. But he didn't. Instead he rested his head back in consideration. "They knew to put iridium cuffs on you and to pump Ethan with it and brace him. How would they know that? Someone had to inform them of it."

"And they left me behind," I added.

I was grateful for the understanding in his eyes. It meant he didn't need details. Cole's obsession with me wasn't something easily understood, and telling others of it made me feel like I was being arrogant. Sorting out how it made me feel was difficult. I didn't want to say that Cole was obsessed with me and that was the reason I was spared.

"You have to tell Sebastian and Ethan."

I was heading for the exit before he suggested it, and he was hot on my tail.

Sebastian, Steven, Winter, and Ethan were heading up the stairs as we were heading down. A cloud of frustration, concern, and anger hung over them.

"Gavin, we just received a call from the Council. We have to meet with them. Now. They've given us a two-hour time window to make an appearance." Sebastian's voice remained level but his stern look showed the effort he put into doing so.

"For what?" Gavin asked.

"We don't know, but they want to see all ranked members."

The torrent of restrained emotions they'd fought to keep at bay overtook them. Gavin took a sharp breath once he felt it. Ethan brushed a quick kiss on my cheek. "We should be back in a couple of hours." They all headed for the front door.

Ethan stopped, but my gaze went past him to Gavin. I needed assurance that he would let me be the one to tell Ethan and Sebastian about my suspicions. He nodded slightly, and I knew he understood. He confirmed it when he quickly pressed his finger to his lips. Silence.

I mouthed a thank-you. They filed out of the door toward Dr. Jeremy, who was getting into a large SUV. The presence of all five ranked were-animals wasn't unusual, but the request for the presence of the pack's physician was unheard of.

I watched as they drove away, the SUV slowly moving out of the driveway, seemingly as reluctant to leave as the passengers were.

"Do you know what that's about?" Cole asked from behind me. When I turned around, I found him just a few inches from me. He was freshly showered. The fragrant scent of redwood drifted off of him, and a white V-neck t-shirt clung to his chest where he'd failed to completely dry himself. One hand ran through his damp hair, ruffling it, while the thumb of his other hooked in the pocket of his jeans.

"No."

He choked out a rough, incredulous scoff. "Are they keeping secrets from you again? Do you ever wonder how many secrets others keep from their mates? I'm sure it's significantly less than what Ethan keeps from you." He sauntered closer. "What more can you do to prove your value to this pack? You saved us. Nothing should be kept from you. Sky, you are just as integral to the strength and survival of this pack as Sebastian ... as *Ethan*."

Cole's vulpine smile unfurled into a wide grin when I backed up to increase the distance between us.

"How are you feeling?" I asked, changing the subject.

"Better." He lifted his shirt, exposing his chest and unmarred skin. "Not a scar in sight. Dr. Jeremy cleared me to go home tomorrow."

"Good," I responded coolly.

A brow hitched and the devious, arrogant smile returned. He spoke, his voice low and sultry and inviting. "Is it good that I'm better or that I'm leaving?"

"Both. If you weren't better you wouldn't be released to leave. And I want you gone."

"Why is that, Sky?"

"I don't trust you."

"Because I challenged Ethan?"

"I don't like you because you challenged Ethan. I don't trust you because you're the reason he was injured."

"I've said before, I did what I thought was best in that situation. I saved Steven because I didn't want to see you hurt if he were killed. Ethan seemed like he had the situation under control, so I made a split decision. It was the wrong one and I can't apologize enough for it. I don't want to see you hurt, and Steven dying would have hurt you," he said quietly, moving forward and narrowing the distance between us another few inches. So close I could feel the warmth that radiated off his body.

"And killing Ethan during a challenge would have hurt me more."

"Ethan made that choice, not me. If you have issues with the way it was handled, hold Ethan, *your mate*, accountable, not me." He moved past me toward the kitchen. "I'm hungry; if you want to continue this conversation, then you can join me in the kitchen. If not, take care."

Curiosity killed the cat. I kept thinking about that as I followed him into the kitchen. *But not every cat,* my curiosity retorted. Looking at how comfortable Cole was in our house, our kitchen, our business, it was hard to forget he was an interloper. He didn't belong. He had his own business, house, and pack to tend to. But the comfort he displayed in ours was as if he'd already claimed it as his own.

In silence, I stood at the entrance of the kitchen and watched him take leftovers from the fridge, along with three steaks that he quickly seasoned and cooked just long enough to lightly brown. He added a heap of leftover pasta salad to his plate, took a seat at the kitchen table, and started eating.

"Why me?" I finally asked. "Is it the challenge because I don't want you? Or is it that you hate Ethan?"

Cole studied me in silence for several moments, taking thoughtful bites from the food on his plate. He nudged his foot against the chair in front of him, kicking it out. An invitation to sit down.

"I'm fine here," I said crisply. This wasn't a social visit.

"I'm not going to yell at you from across the room. It's rude."

"We're not even fifteen feet apart. We can hear each other just fine."

He returned to eating, ignoring me. Something I was sure he'd continue to do until I was seated in front of him. Reluctantly, I slipped into the chair, arms crossed over my chest.

"We have a quarterly meeting. It's usually short; we discuss any issues with the packs and new members. We give a brief background of what we know of the new members. I remember Ethan's face when your name came up. The fleeting look of betrayal and concern when Sebastian brought you up. It was as if Sebastian had disclosed a secret between them and had deprived him of something essential. Like a slice of happiness was snatched from him. I'd never seen Ethan respond that way to any woman. It definitely piqued my interest. After all, I was very aware of his reputation, not just as a rumor but in practice." He marked his words with a frown of derision.

When I didn't dignify his comment with a response, he continued, "I was curious about the woman who had seemingly brought Ethan to his knees. One that his wolf wanted to protect and the man desired. I'd seen that look very few times. It wasn't lustful—which surprised me. It was longing, and infatuation."

Cole looked darkly amused and intrigued. His voice dropped, a deep drawl. "From Ethan, nonetheless. He quickly hid it and pushed it from his face. *But* for that fraction of a second, it was all about you. We'd heard about the Midwest's new mysterious member, and the rumors were plentiful. Sebastian and Ethan spent the remainder of the meeting evading questions about you. Knowing Ethan, I knew his infatuation would lack true depth, so I knew you'd be beautiful. Perhaps by some considered unobtainable. I had to meet this Skylar who had captured Ethan's interest."

He sat back in his chair, fingers clasped behind his head, watching me with renewed interest. I fidgeted in my chair under his relentless attention and allowed my eyes to wander throughout the kitchen. I found other things to focus on rather than Cole. I didn't return my attention to him until he started to speak again.

"So I made a visit." His eyes were distant, wistful. "I watched you throughout the day."

"The first time we met was the first time I'd ever seen you," I pointed out.

"I saw you. You never saw me."

"That sounds like the beginning of so many crime shows. I'm pretty sure half of *Criminal Minds* episodes start off just as you described."

He shrugged off my comment. "I was curious. Then I met you. You are beautiful, but I've seen and had better."

"Good for you. Your award is in the mail," I snarked back. "Do you want a cookie, gift basket, a gold star or something— because you seem to be looking for accolades." I did an exaggerated slow clap. "Good job. You've dated and probably screwed a lot of pretty women. Do you now feel justly celebrated?"

"You're getting me and Ethan confused," he hissed. "I don't

need trophies. It's Ethan who has the shelf that's always in need of something or *someone* to put on it. Oddly, he was indeed infatuated with you. Intrigued. Enamored. Enthralled by the enigmatic wolf that was now part of his pack. The one he had to have." His face grew solemn and held a hint of bitterness. "And he did."

His voice dropped. "I was told that when you meet your mate, even if you haven't claimed her, you know. I always thought it was a foolish, irrational belief. I was wrong. I knew it was true when I met you."

"I'm Ethan's mate."

"You weren't when we met. I knew it when I finally met you. He sensed it, too. He mated with you so that I couldn't have you. Why did he choose to do it after I made my intention to challenge him known? His interest in mating with you heightened when I arrived. Before, he toyed with you—because that's what you were to him. A toy."

"You want me to believe Ethan mated with me so you couldn't have your true mate? He decided to be with a person that he was only 'infatuated with' and saw as nothing more than a 'trophy' for his shelf until his death, just to keep *you* from having the person you believe is your true mate? Is that what you want me to believe?" I asked, incredulous. "Come on, Cole, you're getting sloppy with your little kernels of deception and sabotage. This theory is beneath you."

"'Until his death,'" he scoffed. "Forever—do you think there's a forever for Ethan? You can't possibly believe he takes the mating seriously. He'll be faithful to you this year; after all, it's the honeymoon phase and you still interest him. It's only a matter of time before his shiny new acquisition isn't enough. He'll cheat. And you'll make concessions and stay with him. Because *everyone* makes concessions for Ethan." The latter part was pushed through clenched teeth. Rigid coils of tense muscle bunched along his neck and chest, and he took a moment to calm himself. Cole's cool, calm, collected mask dropped. He was an unrestrained ball of resentment. He really hated Ethan.

It took more time than I'd expected before he donned his self-assured, calm façade again. He eased out several breaths, and an easy calm eventually overtook him, but I'd seen before that he was able to mask his pure hatred for Ethan, raw and unfiltered.

Mate. It irked me that anyone considered me in that capacity other than Ethan. Frowning, I debated whether I'd heard enough. I wanted a confession and needed to figure out a way to redirect the conversation.

He kicked his legs out and relaxed back in the chair. "Did you know that until five years ago the Alpha could reject a challenge from another pack? It was changed because Sebastian abused it to protect Ethan. Twice he rejected my request. *Twice* he protected Ethan and his position. It was one that should have been rightfully mine. That's Ethan's world. Everyone makes his life easy. Sebastian sacrifices the safety of his pack to protect Ethan, swaddles them in lies and secrecy to protect Ethan. Creates allies of people they should shun and enemies of those who should be befriended because he does whatever is necessary to shield Ethan. This behavior has made Sebastian unworthy of his position." Cole's voice sizzled with ire and frustration. His fingers ran through his hair, rustling it.

"Or Sebastian could have been protecting you. Ethan won the first challenge and it should have been to death. Are you sure you would have won the others? Never underestimate Sebastian and his motives. I suspect it was *your* life that was being protected, not Ethan's."

He scoffed at the idea, but clearly, the thought wounded his ego. For a brief moment his lips parted in disbelieving awe. He'd spent years believing Ethan was the one being protected, when in fact it was him. He'd reveled in the perception that Ethan was weak, shielded by privilege and his Alpha. Now the narrative had changed. The cool, confident Alpha arrogance withered away. The self-assured lift in his lips dropped. Inflated confidence deflated for a moment as his eyes and face went blank. He was thinking about it. Dealing with the realization that the story he'd carried around was a false chronicle of how things really were. He swallowed, part of his pride going down with it. For several minutes I watched him reconcile the new story, but it didn't take long before arrogance reasserted itself. I wasn't sure if he'd found his peace by simply disregarding my story as false and believing that Ethan couldn't best him and his previous victory was simply an accident. An Alpha's ego was a dichotomy: inflated and fragile.

"What happened with Bethany? Why couldn't you bring her in alive? It should have been easy. She was human," I asked, redirecting the conversation to get the information I wanted. As long as Ethan was the subject, Cole would be distracted by resentment, and I wouldn't get any more information.

"I tried. But I was injured and was just trying to keep her from hurting others."

"How did you get your injuries?" I tried to sound nonchalant as I sat back in the chair, waiting for him to answer.

"I was poisoned, hungry, and injured. I'd rather not relive the moments that I was at my most vulnerable," he sighed.

Resigned to the idea that I wouldn't get anything more from him, I stood to leave.

"I know you'd like the humans to be alive, because you owe them a great deal. Ethan has kept his position because of them."

I whipped around to face him. "What?"

"If I hadn't gone missing, you would have had to fulfill the challenge. You would have lost Ethan's position. I didn't want to hurt you, but if I'd had to in order to claim a position that is rightfully mine, I would have."

"You wouldn't have won," I assured him. I headed for the door.

"There's one way to find out. We spar. If you win, I never challenge Ethan again. I'm injured and you have the advantage. Will you take it?"

I *so* wanted to take it. But not to protect Ethan's position—I just wanted to kick Cole's ass.

CHAPTER 12

*I*n the basement of the pack's home, I was smothered by Cole's scent as he stood just inches from me. It was too close. "I thought we were sparring. No one spars this close together." Placing my hand in the middle of his chest, I pushed him, harder than he expected, and he stumbled back but quickly regained his footing.

Slipping his shirt off, he tossed it to the side. He turned his back to me, examining the swords hanging on the wall, the various weapons in the corner, and the bruised walls that had seen more than their share of crashes and battery.

"If I win," he started out slowly, "I have one request: a kiss. Just one."

"That wasn't part of the deal and I won't agree to it."

He smiled. "Don't tell me you're not the least bit curious. I've seen the way you look at me, Sky. You are curious even if you won't admit it to yourself."

"You're confusing disdain for attraction. I'm not sure why. They are very different. Not remotely the same. Why can't you understand that I'm not interested?"

"He was your first, wasn't he?"

"That's none of your business," I snapped.

"You will wonder. I promise, you will. You'll be curious about the pleasures a man can bring you when he sees you as his equal. When he gives himself completely to you. I see it, Sky. That fear that maybe I'm right. You don't want to admit that deep down you know I'm the person you should be with, and I understand that." He closed the space between us, standing so close his warm breath brushed against my lips. "Just one kiss. He'll never know. Between us." His voice slithered around me like the snake that it came from. It rang sincere, a reminder of what Cole was capable of.

"It's not about whether *he'll* know. *I'll* know that I did one of the most reprehensible things I can think of—and that's kissing you."

I slammed my foot down on his. He moved back, and I swiped his leg. He hit the ground with a thud and rolled out of the way and got to his feet as my leg whipped around in a spin kick. Distancing himself from me, he wagged his finger in ridicule and *tsked*. He walked over to one of the cabinets and pulled out an iridium manacle. One that was used on Ethan during their challenge. He tossed it at me. "We have to keep you honest. If this were a real challenge, you'd wear it."

I glared at him as I knelt and clasped it around my ankle.

"Don't expect leniency from me, Sky," he warned, fixing me with a hard look.

Aw. I think I hurt his feelings.

I had a moment of fear as Cole seemed to switch from the man who just moments ago wanted a kiss as a reward for a win to something altogether different. I was seeing what Ethan and anyone else who'd challenged him or had been challenged by him had. An Alpha. Unmistakably Alpha. Predatory grace, powerful agility, undeniable stealth, and poorly controlled wolf.

The nebulous line between man and wolf nearly indistinguishable. It was demonstrated in the power of his movements, the grace in his steps, the mastery of his body as he advanced toward me. It was something I'd seen over and over again. The wolf and man becoming one predaceous, vicious being.

Fear tightened my muscles and I stretched them a little, still keeping my distance from him as I tried to coax them into relaxing. I'd challenged him before. This wasn't any different. It wasn't to death.

I hesitated before engaging, seeing more behind the menace and predatory alertness in Cole's eyes: desire. Unsated desire, and I hated the way it remained directed at me. I pushed aside the uncomfortable way his eyes ran over the planes of my face, the curves of my body, and held mine in an entreating way. It angered me more than anything else. Shallow affections that were based on something in his head. How he'd pursued me despite my objections. Claimed me as his mate and continued to work so hard to put a wedge between Ethan and me, placing doubt and making me insecure.

Cole closed the distance between us, his hands placed at his sides as if he'd forgotten why we were there. Pangs of doubt gnawed at me so much that the words escaped. "Did you have anything to do with the abductions?"

I listened for changes in the steady beat of his heart, an increase or decrease in his breathing. Something that would give me the truth when his words wouldn't. There weren't any tells.

His voice was soft and steady. "You think I had something to do with this? I was taken as well. Injured more than the others. I killed the guilty parties so they could never do it again."

Cole was right. That list of things didn't seem like it belonged to a man who was guilty, but I couldn't shake the feeling. My instincts were heightened, knowing that I had a cunning and opportunistic predator close by. His features were so deceptively innocent, if I hadn't seen his ploys firsthand— and felt the lust for power draped around him like a shawl—I wouldn't think he was capable of guile.

In my mind, he was guilty until proven innocent.

Since it seemed like Cole was content with us just standing in front of each other, rounding, gazing into each other's eyes, I struck first. Moving quicker than I'd anticipated, he dodged, jamming his hand into my striking arm and then swiping my stance leg. I crumpled to the ground on my side. Spinning from my position on the ground, I swiped his leg. He landed a few inches from me. We rolled to our feet around the same time. I jumped back, just missing his front kick, but the spin kick came too fast for me to avoid. It hit me hard in my chest. I expelled a sharp breath and doubled over from the pain. Several harsh breaths later he was in front of me, my face cradled between his hands as he lifted my head until my eyes met his.

"Are you okay?" His warm breath wisped against my mouth as he spoke. His lips were inching toward mine; I jerked away, removing myself from his hold.

"Yeah." It just startled me. No, it surprised me. Cole was stronger and faster than I was. His skill as an Alpha was apparent.

"Do you want to continue?"

I nodded, returning to my offensive stance.

In an attempt to throw Cole off, I asked, "Who was she?"

His brow rose.

"Who was the woman who chose Ethan over you and left you feeling jilted and bitter toward him?"

A rough, baleful sound rumbled in his chest and filled the room. "I've lost one woman to Ethan and, unfortunately, she's currently putting herself in a position to be hurt by me. I'm not enjoying this situation."

My plan backfired. I was the one thrown off. Each time he spoke of me as if I were his or he was looking for a chance to make it so, it rattled me. I swallowed and distanced myself, moving to the left to get out of his line of sight.

"I don't think I'm the one who's going to get hurt," I told him confidently.

"I'm not going to go easy on you."

"I don't expect you to."

After several moments of consideration, he advanced toward me. Strikes, parries, and kicks were exchanged. I can't say that I gave as well as I got, but as Cole wiped blood from his nose from an elbow strike and left jab to his lips, I guessed he'd probably learned that I wasn't as easy to subdue as he'd thought.

"Beautiful and dangerous. Ethan is a very lucky man."

He advanced: a front kick that I dodged. I blocked a spinning kick and landed a well-deserved strike on his leg. He winced and stepped back, hissing at the pain.

Sliding his tongue over his lips, he removed the remnants of blood from earlier. "Very lucky," he whispered. When he charged this time, I attempted to block a strike, which was unfortunately a false move that he used to sweep my legs from under me, sending me crashing to the ground. In a flash of movement that was just short of vampire speed, he was crouched over me. One of his hands bound my arms over my head; the other rested on the bottom of my face. He lifted my chin at an angle and gave it a light jerk. "*If* this were a challenge, this is the part where I'd break your neck," he whispered against my ear.

He released my face but didn't move. He hovered over me, his free hand inching under my shirt to rest on my bare skin.

He'd settled his weight on me and nestled his lower half between my legs, where I definitely didn't want him.

Burying his face in my neck, he breathed in. "I love the way you smell." Although his touch was gentle, his voice was sharp and cold.

He moved suggestively against me.

"Get the fuck off of me," I demanded.

His weight shifted and his mouth moved closer. He dipped down to kiss me.

I twisted my neck, moving my face out of reach. "Get off me. Now." I didn't give him a chance to respond. I bashed my head into his face, striking his nose. He rolled to his feet and I came to mine quickly.

Focused on Cole through narrowed eyes, I snarled out, "Even if Ethan wasn't in the picture, I'd never be with you. I don't like you."

An arrogant, knowing curl lifted the corners of his lips. "You didn't like Ethan, either. Correct?"

How much did he know about us? It felt invasive. It angered me how he took the nuances of our relationship and twisted them. The meticulous studying and conniving fueled my fury. I felt duped as I remembered how nice I'd thought he was, how at moments I'd allowed his words to affect me, considered him misguided rather than calculating and cruel.

"I don't like you," I repeated. The dark taint of anger and hate that hung over the words shocked him as much as it did me. It was ominous and came from a place so dark and wrathful, it made Cole's head tilt slightly as he studied me in a different light. It wasn't dislike—it was pure, raw, undiluted hate.

"Because of Ethan. That's where it comes from. He really has a hold on you, doesn't he?"

"Of course he does, and I have one on him. He's my mate!"

Cole ignored my outburst. "I will continue to challenge him, and eventually I will win. I can assure you, when I do, he won't walk out of that challenge alive."

And Cole wasn't walking out of this one.

I rushed for one of the swords on the wall. Cole and I reached the weapons display within seconds of each other. I had mine first and lunged at him. It whisked past him and grazed his side. I retreated. The room was filled with a series of steel striking steel. Grunts with each movement. My hard swing was met with a blocking circular parry. As the swordplay continued, I wasn't so sure we were just sparring. My strikes were too hard, driven by anger.

Cole had put several feet of distance between us as we caught our breath. We'd been fighting with the swords for over an hour. I had a cut on my leg; he had one on his arm and two long diagonal cuts from the edge of his pelvis up his chest. "'Leave the woman,'" I quietly repeated the abductor's words. "That stuck with me as they were taking Ethan away. Why would they leave me? It wasn't like they were just leaving some random woman, they were leaving a specific woman. Me."

Shocked, he glowered at me, giving me the full force of his Alpha gaze. It was hard as hell to hold, but I was determined to do so. I'd never be submissive to him. His face hardened with defiance as I spoke. His cool gaze fastened on me. "So."

"I don't believe in coincidences. Nor do I believe in convenient injuries. And your injuries were quite convenient. All in places where they can be self-inflicted."

Cool, mocking laughter pulsed through the room. "What a wonderful tale. You think I had everyone abducted and somehow came up with millions of dollars to have people hunt us? Did you come up with that fantastical story yourself or did your mate help you with such an absurd idea?"

My breezy tone matched his: "No, I came up with it myself. It seemed pretty bizarre to me. After all, what Alpha would endanger the lives of others? Who would betray our secrets? Then I remembered how much you prided yourself on knowing so much about this pack. No other pack knew about us lifting the curse on the vampires. But you did. With Sebastian gone, you wouldn't have to challenge him, especially when you couldn't win against Ethan. As you've said before, the beauty of our pack is that we technically have two Alphas."

Cole dismissed my accusations with a roll of his eyes. "Please go on. I'm enjoying this fantasy. It's as entertaining as it is absurd."

Fighting my irritation, I forced myself to concentrate. Taking a cleansing breath, I wrangled control of my emotions. Arrogance brought a smug smile to his face as he dropped his sword and kept it to his side. I pointed mine at his chest. And pressed slightly so he could feel the point of it.

"Put the goddamn sword down!" he demanded.

Ignoring him, I inched forward just a little to pierce his skin. Cole figured I wouldn't kill in cold blood, which had to be why he wasn't trying to defend himself. It was an unethical thing to do, but at that moment I wasn't feeling principled. I was vengeful.

He stepped back from the point of the sword and assumed a defensive stance. "Sky, you can't beat me. But how will things play out if I notify the Council that I was attacked by Ethan's mate? They would assume that it was at his request. You do realize that the Council can strip us of our rank, right?"

"Your wounds weren't like the others'."

"Put the damn sword down. Now!" he bellowed. The Alpha command washed over me, aching in my bones, briefly consuming me. I wavered. It was strong, overwhelming, like being struck into submission. As quickly as it waved over me, it fell from me like discarded clothing. "I'm broken. Those commands don't work on me."

"No," he said, his voice losing all its hostility. "You aren't broken. You know why? Is that what the Midwest Pack tells you? That you're broken?" His features softened, mirroring his voice, and if I hadn't known him for the manipulator that he was, I'd have fallen for it. Been beguiled by his gentle, mesmeric voice, his soothing, kind eyes that draped a person with warmth, his charismatic and appealing features that belied all his perfidy.

"No, they've never told me that. Nor made me feel bad for the changes. You'll grasp for whatever straw you can get a hold of, won't you?" I kept my distance, floated the katana away from him, and let it drop into my hand. "If you took Sebastian's position, the other Alphas would challenge you for the Elite position, knowing you were undeserving." I couldn't hide the contempt.

He chuckled. "Let's say it's true. It's all circumstantial. Do you think they will sanction the murder of an Alpha with the flimsy evidence you have, darling?" The familiarity with which he said *darling* made me want to take his head off right then. "Nothing is going to happen to me. Because I did no such thing. You are tasked with the burden of proving your theory. You don't have it."

His face turned mocking. He was right. We were talking about people's lives and taking them couldn't be handled so casually. I understood that, but my gut was telling me that he was behind it. An intuition that I'd never felt before plagued me. As much as he tried to hide it, his eyes were those of a man who knew more than he was letting on. A person who was guilty and sure he'd never be caught.

"Tell me about your injuries. How did you get them?" I asked.

"Everything was such a blur, I don't quite remember." He smiled and his attention shifted to the ground, where he'd attempted to kiss me. "You didn't dislike that as much as you let on, did you? You're more disgusted by the fact that you felt something, too."

My voice was razor sharp when I asked my questions again. "When did they take you? I want to know everything you can remember, and be specific."

His eyes closed for a moment and I assumed he was trying to get his lies in place. "If I am talented enough to come up with the elaborate plan you think I concocted to betray the packs, don't you think I can come up with a believable story as to how I was taken and sustained my injuries? Come on, Sky, you are better than this."

The sword felt heavy. Not from holding it but from the restrictions I'd placed on myself not to use it. I wanted to hurt the smug Alpha.

"Demetrius and Alexander, why were they taken?"

A spark emerged in his eyes. He'd never admit to his wrong-doing; he was too smart for that. I wasn't expecting a confession, and I was now sure I wasn't going to get one.

His tongue moved slowly over his lips. "Let's say I was the mastermind behind this. Let me help you with your fanciful tale of elaborate collaboration and strategy. Why would a person want Demetrius and Alexander gone and you alive? Hmmm. If I were going to guess, I'd assume it was done by someone who doesn't underestimate your role in this pack and Chris's in the Northern Seethe. Alexander acts without reason and is ruled by his ego and pursuit of pleasure and nothing more. People like that never make good allies. They can't be trusted. They're enslaved by impulse and self-indulgence. Demetrius, although significantly more controlled, and definitely more mature and disciplined, is servant to Chris's desires. He'd manage it better if he'd admit it. Knowing your weaknesses allows you to address them. He has the potential to be a great leader and wonderful ally, but like so many men, he is distracted by his longing for a woman's affections. Whether it is true yearning or not is irrelevant; it compromises his judgment. Chris doesn't suffer such things, which makes her a better leader. She is an ally that most would like to have. She's not the pack's ally, she's your friend. That, among other things, makes you valuable to this pack and her valuable."

He gave me a winsome smile that sickened me.

"If I were involved, that would have been the reason to keep you alive and want Alexander and Demetrius dead. But of course, I'd never do such a thing."

Cole quieted for a moment and inhaled, taking in the sounds and scents. "Your mate and Sebastian are home. I'm sure they'll be disappointed to find out that you didn't get the confession you so desperately needed."

It might have been circumstantial, but too many things were coincidental. I didn't believe for one minute that I was giving Cole too much credit. He was diabolical, a manipulator, and an opportunist. He'd shown the face of an Alpha who only had the pack's well-being at heart while he tugged at the strings of his puppet show, waiting for an opportune time to strike. He wanted to be the Elite Alpha, he wanted the prestige of running the Midwest Pack, and for some reason he wanted me. I was his mate.

Once they were downstairs, Sebastian and Ethan's attention went to Cole.

"I'm guessing, by the gloomy looks on your faces, you two received really bad news. Do you mind sharing?" Cole inquired, darkly amused.

"You should fear for your life!" Ethan snapped, standing just a few feet from him, and in that moment, it was believable that he should. Sebastian stood behind Ethan, his irritation apparent and practiced restraint palpable and explicit on his face.

"You felt concerned enough for your safety while in my house to notify the Council? Really?" Sebastian barked.

Eyes fixed on Sebastian, Cole smiled. "I've always thought the Council was unnecessary and that we were capable of policing ourselves, but over the years as the Midwest's power increased, the secrets that shrouded you all increased, and you seemed to be looked upon as some great influence. A sovereignty that so many follow blindly. Overlooking, or rather tolerating your flaws because you are the Elite. Given what seems like unchecked power and the adulations of a deity. You are a man. A man who is capable of being flawed and having weaknesses." His gaze snapped in Ethan's direction. "Ethan is your fatal weakness. Always has been. The cost of keeping his secrets is your reputation and confidence in your ability to lead without bias."

Sebastian remained silent, his eyes carefully watching Cole.

"The Council is more powerful than you, possessing the ability to strip you of your status of Alpha and Elite if you prove to be a threat to the pack, to other Alphas." Cole made a choking sound that I supposed was a laugh that he'd tried to force out. "You protect Ethan, the Council protects us. You benefit from the protections you extend to Ethan. After all, your pack's strength lies in the fact he is powerful and possesses magic. So does his mate and his brother, who is a blood ally. You would do anything to maintain that status quo, and so would Ethan. Is it so unthinkable that you would poison me, while I was in your home, in your hospital? I've made no secret of my desire for his position and eventually yours." His hauntingly cruel eyes shifted in my direction. "And my desire for Sky. I'm sure none of that sits well with any of you. Would it be beyond what we know of you and what you are capable of to allow me to die of a little accident? An affliction that even Dr. Jeremy couldn't fix? So yes, I feared for my life."

"You know goddamn well we would never do anything like that," Sebastian lashed out.

Cole shrugged nonchalantly as he gave Sebastian a mocking smile. "Do I? No one knows what to expect from a pack that wields as much power as you do. We can't afford to underestimate the lengths you will go to, to protect your pack secrets and maintain your stranglehold on power. We all know power can corrupt the most honorable person and push them to do the unthinkable when they feel at risk of losing it. Sebastian, you have been corrupted. No one would put anything past you, which is why I felt compelled to notify the Council and they so readily addressed it. Do you think those accusations would have been so easily accepted if they were about any other pack?

"If it weren't for them, I would've been falsely accused by Sky and you would have punished me accordingly. How unfair would that be for me?" Although Cole managed to keep his voice even, he couldn't stop a smirk from playing at his lips.

Maintaining his pleasant look, Cole placed the sword on the wall, then straightened his clothes. He lifted his shirt, revealing the small cuts I'd put on him.

"You don't feel safe here? Then leave." Sebastian's deep baritone growl chilled the air as he approached Cole with purpose. Just inches from him, Sebastian took a deep breath and the battle to control his emotions put tense lines in his face as amber flooded his eyes. He stayed planted with his fists balled tightly at his sides.

"Easy," Cole purred, his lips kinked into a miscreant half-smile. He was oddly calm, as if the torrential storm brewing in Sebastian soothed him.

Sebastian's eyes were slits, homing in angrily on Cole. A growl reverberated in Sebastian's chest, and it was obviously sheer will that kept him planted in his spot. I wanted that restraint to break and eased out of the path to give him a clear shot if it did.

Cole sucked in a breath through his teeth, an exaggerated, taunting noise. "You want my head on a platter right now, don't you? Yet, you can't do anything to me, can you? I think the Council is ready to accept that you've ruled with unchecked power for too long. The secrets you kept from everyone except Ethan. The murder of the leader of the Creed, only to replace her with your puppet."

"You don't know Ariel very well. She'll never be anyone's puppet."

"Yet, she's come to your rescue, formed an alliance with your pack. She's in a position of power because Josh got rid of Marcia." He failed to mention that Josh did so after Marcia helped a madman kidnap and perform magical experiments on people—killing many in the process. All because she wanted a way to nullify the were-animals' immunity to magic.

"I didn't orchestrate that. It just happened," Sebastian said.

"You still benefitted from it." Cole pushed the words through clenched teeth. I wasn't sure if he was angry with Sebastian or that his perception was that Sebastian's advantage was pure luck. "The Midwest Pack reigns, and people treat you like a god and you enjoy the spoils of it. Unchecked power and freedom that should have been reined in long ago."

"Is that what you think you are doing, reining me in?" Sebastian moved even closer. He stood just a few inches from Cole, within striking distance.

A maleficent smile coiled Cole's lips as his gaze sharpened on Sebastian. "I seem to remember only one Alpha ever being removed from his position. Am I remembering correctly?"

Sebastian responded with steely silence. His teeth bit into his lips, forcing back words.

"Yes, there was one. About twenty years ago. He was found unfit to lead. They rarely remove anyone from their position, but I wonder how they would feel if I expressed my concern for my life while recovering from injuries in your home? And here I am, barely healed, and you attack me. It probably wouldn't work in your favor that my recovery was hindered by a creature from the dark forest. Hmmm ... who can get in and out of the forest without any problem?" His narrowed eyes shifted to Ethan and then me. At that moment I was thoroughly convinced that Cole wasn't just a manipulating opportunist but possibly a sociopath.

Cole turned his head in Ethan's direction. "The secrets you all keep may protect your pack, but they always cast doubts.

Others admire your position but are distrustful of your process. I guess that's the trade-off."

"What do you want, Cole, my position or Ethan's?"

"You don't see it, do you? Sebastian, you are a true Alpha. You deserve the credit for what you've built. It was hard-earned. At one time I'd have willingly admitted that you were the foundation of the Midwest. A beacon of strength and a testament to its greatness. That was the past. Now you have become an infestation—a termite whittling away at the very core of this pack. All of it could have been avoided. You chose the wrong path. You aren't good for the Midwest Pack, not for any of us. I am the future of this pack, and you are the past. But your talents won't be wasted; I think you will be a good Beta."

The arctic breeze of Sebastian's anger overtook his features and wedged its way into his voice. "I'd leave the pack before I'd be a Beta for you. *But* that's something I will never have to consider. If you are under any illusions that you can fill my shoes, let me set those straight right now. You are quite impressed with yourself and have feelings of grandeur because you were at the top of the game in the minor leagues. Good for you. I'm the majors and so far out of your league, you can only dream of doing what I've successfully done. This pack isn't what it is by accident, as you pointed out. It rose under my leadership but I guarantee it would fall under yours. Even if I were on my death bed, and you were having the best day of your life, I still wouldn't be worried about you being a better leader than I am." He closed the distance between them, coming nose to nose with Cole. "I'm confident enough to say the same about Ethan as well."

It was the first time Cole had felt the power of Sebastian's full rage, the confidence and qualities that gave him his position not only as the Alpha but also the Elite. Cole's ego was clearly battered, and he struggled to regain his fading composure. "You can't hurt me," he blurted out. "Believe me, you will lose your position if you touch me."

Sebastian was past looking as if he wanted to hurt Cole—he wanted him dead, and it was aptly displayed on his face.

"You may want to take my head off, but if you do, you will surely lose your position," Cole reiterated, his tone dropping to a low, soothing rasp.

After several ragged breaths that he struggled to keep even, Sebastian moved back several feet. "When I'm done with you, I think you would have preferred that I'd taken your head off and saved you the misery."

That wasn't enough for me. The threat of future punishment? Cole's immunity from the Council was based on suspicion he'd cast on us. He was the architect of the aspersions and he would benefit from them. Anger rampaged through me and there weren't enough moments of silence, breaths, or calming thoughts to stop it. I had to leave or I'd act on it.

"Ethan," Cole purred as his gaze slipped in my direction. "I enjoyed the day I had with Sky. If we had more time, I do believe I would have gotten what I wanted from her before she—"

Ethan slammed him against the wall, his hand grasped firmly around his neck. Cole struggled for every breath. Eventually it was cut off as the muscles of Ethan's arms strained.

"Ethan, let him go," Sebastian commanded. He kept calling Ethan's name, but he was too far gone. Pushed into a primal rage, he couldn't respond to reason. I knew this was the time I was supposed to step in and talk him into a calm state. I didn't have it in me. Humanity and any empathy for Cole had receded to a place that I couldn't reach. Left in their place was the thirst for revenge. Cole's face was starting to lose color and he clawed at Ethan's hand.

"Ethan! Let him go! Now!" Sebastian demanded in a ringing

growl. His stance changed as he prepared to enforce his command.

I didn't want the strife between Ethan and Sebastian.

"Ethan, please," I said softly. He struggled with finding the serenity he needed to release Cole as gray continued to flood his eyes. He dropped the oxygen-deprived Cole to the ground. I stepped closer, and Ethan pulled me to him and then took a step back. "You smell like him," he whispered.

I expected him to move away, but he moved closer and pressed his lips to my forehead, then he kissed my cheek and finally my lips. His breathing had returned to normal and he was about as calm as he was going to get with Cole present. "Get out of our city," he said as he turned to go up the stairs.

I should have kept my focus ahead and remained at Ethan's side. And I damn sure shouldn't have made the effort to place the katana in its proper place, because if I hadn't, I wouldn't have seen Cole's smile and glow of warped satisfaction. The cruel disregard for the pack and what it stood for, discarded like trash so that he could gain power. He was protected within that shell of cruelty by the Council and the seeds of deception he'd planted. It wasn't fair. They all could have died because of him.

If I'd kept the course, I wouldn't have been treated to the derisive look he gave me. That self-assurance that his acts of duplicity would not be punished. It was a summation of knowing that he was responsible for Ethan almost dying twice, hurting Steven by putting Joan's life in danger, nearly getting the Alphas and Betas killed, and colluding with a number of people because he wanted a position.

He didn't deserve to be an Alpha.

His actions didn't deserve to go unpunished.

He didn't deserve the Council's protection.

He didn't deserve to live.

I struck so fast that he couldn't react. His eyes widened in shock as he looked down at his blood-drenched hands, which rested over the sword I had driven into his stomach. I yanked it out and stabbed it into him again. He dropped to his knees.

I didn't see a wounded man folded over on his knees. I saw him for what he was—a threat. A wild and dangerous person. A rabid animal that needed to be put down. And I had every intention of doing so. I yanked out the sword, reared back, and prepared to take off his head. We survived so many injuries, but nothing—with the exception of Ethos—survived without a head. Cole wasn't going to survive this.

I made a half turn, gathering momentum for the strike that would ensure that Cole would be no more.

"Sky!" Sebastian rushed me, grabbing my arm. I strained against him until he growled. I heard it. I should have responded to it. I couldn't. It was the same blind anger and rage I had for Demetrius, and now it was directed at Cole. I was determined to succeed this time.

Sebastian's hold was strong, and it was like moving against reinforced steel trying to overpower him. His gentle words of reason weren't enough to talk me down. It was force to force as Sebastian worked diligently to protect the life of a person who didn't deserve it.

It took a while before I surrendered my weapon to Sebastian.

Cole dropped to the floor, landing on his back. His eyes looked sunken as life slowly escaped from them. Sebastian knelt next to Cole and cursed under his breath. Through the strain on Sebastian's face, I could see him trying to solve the problem of coming up with a plausible explanation for Cole's death. Weighing the pros and cons of saving him.

With a sigh, Sebastian pulled out a knife sheathed at his leg, ran the blade over his hand, and placed his hand over Cole's injury. Sebastian tensed. The muscles of his back contracted and released as he let out a groan and shifted into his wolf, collapsing next to Cole.

He wasn't saving Cole; he was protecting me. That was the only time I'd felt any regret for Cole. I didn't want Sebastian cleaning up my mess.

"Go get Dr. Jeremy, Sky," Ethan said in a tight voice; his reluctance apparent.

CHAPTER 13

 hen I'd attempted to kill Michaela, I'd gotten a "talking to" that entailed Sebastian taking me to a nice restaurant where we had delicious food and wine while listening to the mesmerizing crooning of a songstress. I fondly remember pie being involved. Try to behead one treacherous Alpha, and things take a different turn. I didn't get any damn pie. Not even a glass of wine. Nothing.

Minutes passed as I watched Sebastian sit and glare at me in silence, then walk and glare at me in silence, and rest against the wall, his arms crossed over his chest, while he glared at me. It had been two hours since the incident with Cole. We were in the final stretch and I relaxed back, watching. Deep amber eyes were ablaze, and he used *fuck* far too casually, often with each measured step.

Finally, he spoke. "What the actual fuck, Sky!" he snapped.

When I tried to answer, he stopped me with a wave of his hands. After several more minutes of pacing, he took a seat and I was treated to his unimpeded attention. Razor-sharp eyes planted on me. Reluctant pride, frustration, and anger played upon his face.

"He's responsible for it," I said in my defense. "I wasn't going to give him a chance to do it again."

"You were about to behead him, Sky!"

"I know. I was there. Like I said, I wasn't going to give him a chance to do it again." I shrugged, seeming more indifferent to brutal violence than I actually was. "The whole not having a head thing would have ensured that."

Sebastian rubbed his hand along the dark shadow of hair growing on his jaw. The next extended breath that he took seemed to relieve him of most of his anger. His voice was even and gentle when he spoke. "I think he was involved, too. *But* what we have is circumstantial—"

I quickly interrupted, listing everything I had on Cole, and my theories.

"Ethan and I put that together as well and it makes sense, but it's circumstantial. Everything Cole has levied against us doesn't look good. You don't think he'll say your attack was to silence him about our wrongdoings? Your actions reinforced that. We are being scrutinized by the Council and need to proceed with caution." He frowned. "If he had died, you would have been guilty of the betrayal as well. And killing an Alpha—" He stopped and blew out a breath. "Sky, don't put me in that position again. Do you understand that if I'd let you do that, it would have been the undoing of this pack? Ethan and I could have lost our positions and your actions would have been considered betrayal of the pack. You understand the penalty for that. You've seen it firsthand."

I had. When Owen had betrayed the pack and sided with the vampires, his punishment was hard and severe. Joan had ripped him apart in front of me.

"I'm sorry." It was a heartfelt apology, because I regretted having put him in such a position, but I wasn't sorry for trying to kill Cole and wasn't entirely sure I wouldn't try to do it again, even with the impending consequences. Logic wasn't overriding my emotions, no matter how much I wanted it to.

"Sky, you are Ethan's mate; your responsibility and actions are taken far more seriously than if you were just a regular pack member. You are going to have to start taking that into consideration."

Blowing out a breath, I really wished there was a mate handbook or something. It wouldn't have changed my mind, but it would have prepared me for what I had to deal with.

Sebastian dismissed me in his typical manner, glancing at the door. *What is his problem with asking people to leave directly?* Did he think looking at the door and giving a person a look that definitely indicated they'd worn out their welcome was more efficient? Or was he economizing his words? How hard and time-consuming was it to say, "You're dismissed," or "Chat with you later"?

When I didn't move fast enough, he instructed, "Close the door behind you."

"Oh, you want me to leave?" I strained to keep the grin from showing.

"Get out."

The door invitation was looking a lot nicer.

I left, to find Winter leaning against the wall, one leg bent back resting against it. Her thin lips furled into a grin. "How was your meeting?"

"Fine. I'm getting a commendation for being the best member in the pack. And there was pie," I shot back while walking past. She quickly fell in pace with me.

"I definitely can see that. You deserve it," she teased. "Especially the pie." She moved with a spring in her step. Most people wouldn't suspect it, but Winter was a gossip. When she wasn't bound by confidentiality, if she had news, she wanted to spill it. She was humming with anticipation to tell whatever information she had.

"For the first time ever, Cole has lost his cool. He is livid."

"He more than deserved it," I said through gritted teeth.

"Your stabbing him isn't what has his undies in a twist. He was just officially issued a challenge."

I stopped walking to look at her. "By who, Ethan?"

Barely able to contain herself, she grinned. "Yep. Ethan just challenged him. The wounds will be healed by tomorrow. Dr. Jeremy wants him to stay for observation, but he wants to leave tomorrow. Don't really blame him, with Assassin Annie ready to take off his head if he even looks at her wrong. He's safer at home. The challenge has been issued and can take place in ten days. Three days to heal and the customary week of waiting time after a near-fatal injury. He can accept the challenge or step down. I suspect he's going to accept."

"I'm not moving to the East. What was Ethan thinking?" I'd changed direction, moving toward Ethan's room, or rather where I felt his presence, which I suspected was in the infirmary. The several inches of height that Winter had on me—mostly leg—made catching up with me easier despite the increased speed I gathered from my indignation. I wasn't moving to the East because Ethan wanted to make a point.

"You don't seriously think that you're moving, do you?" Winter asked incredulously.

Frustrated, I stopped. "The only other option would be for Ethan to lose. Then what's the point?"

She made a sound. "I thought the stories of you not listening during your orientation were jokes and gross exaggeration. Were you drunk during it? Did you not learn anything? Are you just winging it?"

"Yeah, yeah, we all know the stories are true," I said, exasperated. It was the first time I was truly embarrassed about not taking the classes more seriously. They were more than just bureaucratic nonsense or the pack taking themselves "too seriously." "I spent most of it looking at YouTube videos and watching lion cubs learn how to roar and twin toddlers talking their own language. What's your point?"

She rolled her eyes in irritation. "Ethan knows the rules like the back of his hand. How are you two even a couple?" She blew out a frustrated breath. "I don't get you two," she mumbled.

I understood her frustration and annoyance. She loved the rules and considered them essential to the pack. Each year it was getting harder for me to have the same respect and adoration she had for them. Those rules were the reason Cole was alive and in a position to betray us again. A rogue pack would have killed based on suspicion and been done with it. The rational part of me understood and respected the rules for preventing chaos. It was the emotional part that had an antagonistic relationship with them.

"Ethan, as Alpha of the East Pack, can kick Cole out. If no other pack accepts him, which isn't likely to happen, he'll be a lone wolf. He's no longer under our protection. That puts him in a vulnerable position. A *very* vulnerable situation." She frowned. "I can't believe I fell for his 'nice guy' act."

She wasn't the only one who had. Ethan was underestimating Cole, because he'd still have to win the challenge. This wasn't a done deal or a situation that could be easily resolved.

Perched at the door of the infirmary, Ethan seemed quite content with his decision. His lips twitched, restraining the self-satisfied, deviant grin that was threatening to emerge as he watched Cole devolve into his enraged state. Cole definitely didn't like that the tables had been turned on him and failed to mask it. Gavin had molded to the corner, keenly watching as Cole sat on the edge of the bed, glaring at Ethan. Kelly stood between them, defiant and unyielding in her position, fully aware that she was the reason Ethan and Cole weren't trying to tear each other apart. Kelly was aware that she was the best person to do it. A ranked member's interference could easily have been perceived as a challenge in itself. Kelly often forgot that she was a were-animal now—or maybe she hadn't, and just didn't care. As a human, she could stand between two enraged weres, and their desire not to hurt her overrode their desire to hurt each other. It was something she used to her advantage often. Subjugating a human was belittling and frowned upon.

"Ethan, you've made your challenge. It's time for you to leave," she acknowledged, shifting her stance to block his view of Cole.

"Sky's skin is very soft. I enjoyed being on top of her today," Cole purred. "It was only a matter of time before I'd know what her lips tasted like."

Had the blood loss driven him to madness? Ethan was rooted in position, fighting the fury that was brewing in him. Cole was about to win this without lifting a finger by enraging Ethan to the point he'd strike while his opponent was injured. Steven was right about Cole; he was as good a strategist as Sebastian. Moving closer to Ethan, I slipped my hand into his and guided him toward the door.

"She smells like me, doesn't she?" Cole chuckled. "Me lying on top of her. Nestled between her legs—felt natural. Real. Right. It was where I should be." His warm gaze moved in my direction in a languid sweep, taking me in with a renewed interest.

"Cole, that's enough!" Kelly snapped.

It was a hard task getting Ethan out. I wasn't guiding him anymore. My goal was to stop a raging bull—or rather wolf. *Please keep your mouth shut, Cole.* Now in front of Ethan, I was the barrier between them. Pushing him back was out of the question; it felt like I was leaning into a reinforced steel door when I tried.

"Ethan," I whispered his name, soft and entreating. He looked at me for a moment but his eyes quickly went back to

Cole. I had only the image of his wilted body after stabbing him to give me comfort. Ethan had the distorted image of Cole lying on me. I wished the day had gone differently. I should have left instead of trying to get any information out of Cole.

"Ethan"—Gavin's voice was crisp and forceful enough to snap his attention in his direction—"if you attack him while he's injured there will be consequences. You know the moment you attack him after issuing a challenge, he will request that you be restricted from challenging him. Don't do it. Seven days and you can challenge him."

Cole was a snake, and I wanted to stab him again, just to see the shocked and pained look on his face. Looking over my shoulder, I gave him a look. I knew he had to have seen it. I'd mirrored Ethan's anger.

I led Ethan out of the infirmary and down the hall. Distracted for just moments, he regained himself and took the lead, intertwining his fingers with mine. We didn't make it far, just a few feet, before he guided me into a recovery room just two doors away.

He closed the door behind us and pressed his lips against mine. Then he pulled back, taking me in, fixing on my eyes before slowly looking over the rest. I wondered if he knew what I'd thought about moments earlier. He kissed me hungrily. Ravenous and poorly controlled, nipping at my lips, my jaw, and tasting me at the pulse of my neck. He inhaled roughly.

"Today you were—" His words were lost in another passion-filled kiss. I was panting by the time he peeled off my shirt, kissing the exposed skin. Heat coursed over each spot where lips touched. He yanked off his own shirt. Skin to skin, we radiated heat that warmed the room. His feelings were raw and primal. Unfettered need that he desperately needed to quench.

He continued to press kisses along the curves of my body as he lowered himself to remove my pants and underwear. His hands were in constant contact, as if touching me were a necessity. Something he couldn't live without, essential as breath. He stood, unfastening his pants and letting them drop to the floor. He grasped my legs and wrapped them around him as he sheathed himself in me. The door creaked out a steady rhythm as my back slammed into it. Ethan's fingers entwined in my hair. My fingers curled into his skin, pulling him closer to me. Inhaling his scent, the need grew in me, stronger than our physical connection. My mouth watered and my teeth ached. I licked at the pulse of his neck and inhaled again. His aversion from my need to taste him gone, he tilted his head to give me access. The ache heightened, as if my teeth knew they should be fangs instead of slightly longer and sharper than average. Ethan's groan of pleasure filled the room. His fingers curled deep into my thighs as his hips hit a steady and intense rhythm. I drew from him until one need was fulfilled, licking my lips of the rivulets of blood. Ethan's movements became more ardent and intense. He gasped as my nails bit into his back as we reached the heights.

I moaned at the weight of Ethan relaxing against me, pressing me harder into the door. He planted languid kisses on my lips and cheeks before he released his hold on my legs and eased me to standing. We were both panting softly as we gathered our clothes and dressed. Gently, I ran my finger along the bite mark, wishing I had the ability to heal it so that only we'd know. I hated the inquiring looks we got when others saw the bite marks. A reminder of my vampire linkage.

"So, which one got you going, what I did to Cole or the challenge?" I asked, slipping on my shirt.

At the mention of what I did to Cole, raw primal intensity sparkled in his eyes. I watched the beginning of his arousal, which he attempted to hide with his shirt. His tongue slipped lazily along his lips, moistening them.

"That's a very disturbing kink, you know," I chided. "Very weird."

He flashed a half-grin and a hint of color tinted his cheeks. "It's not a kink. I just think you're very sexy."

"It seems like my sexy is only noticeable after I beat up or nearly slay someone." He moved closer and my hand shot out, keeping an arm's length distance between us as I scrutinized an Ethan who looked like he was ready for another round. I straightened my clothing.

"It just heightens it," he admitted, his lips still quirked into a salacious, alluring smile.

"Sounds like a weird kink to me," I said, opening the door and backing out of it. "Come on, we should get out of here."

"*Now* you all want to leave," Winter said from the hallway with a derisive scowl as she looked me over, then Ethan. "I am traumatized by hearing you two and it will be etched in my mind forever. So, you decide to go home *after* the damage is done. I can't unhear any of it." She rolled her eyes and shuddered. The marks on Ethan's neck from my feeding drew her attention. Her lips twisted into a grimace. "I guess I should just go home and wait for the night terrors," she muttered sardonically before she sauntered off.

Face burning with embarrassment, I knew my cheeks and neck were a bright strawberry color. She probably wasn't the only one who'd heard it. Ethan didn't share in my embarrassment or any form of modesty.

A smile crooked his lips.

Cole left the next day. Dr. Jeremy had been obligated to heal him, but he didn't have to be hospitable about it. And he wasn't, nor was anyone in the pack. The speculations about Cole's involvement in the abductions and his reporting of Ethan and Sebastian to the Council made him an untouchable enemy.

Everyone was ready for him to leave and return to the hotel he had been staying at prior to going missing.

Ethan, Sebastian, Winter, and I watched as he left the pack's home. There wasn't any camaraderie, just the shared desire to be rid of him. The departure was made more uncomfortable by interlopers from the Council, sent to ensure Cole's safety. We'd been painted as barbarians who couldn't control our savagery enough to abide by the rules. It was humiliating to do this with an audience who held such low opinions of us.

Cole pressed his hand against the now-healed wound I'd given him as he addressed me. "That thing with you and Ethan was a nice little trick. You were like an animancer—calming the raging beast. You do realize that is what you are to Ethan—a tool to use at his disposal." Then he shifted his attention to Ethan for a moment before returning it to me. "Your purpose in his life has been reduced to nothing more than a caretaker. One that he sleeps with."

Ethan's deep growl and steely glare didn't discourage him from continuing. "Do you ever wonder what becomes of a man who is driven by instinct only? It has to cross your mind whether those instincts—those primal urges that he has very little control over—will lead him to someone else." His low, honeyed tone dripped with concern and sorrow for me.

This cemented what I believed was Cole's lure. His duplicity went unnoticed or ignored because were-animals had a nebulous appeal, a draw that left their prey so captivated they didn't see the danger before them. It wasn't narcissism, but an undeniable self-confidence that enticed people. Cole's magnetism was entrenched in something sordid and indecent. A raw thirst for power at any cost. It lingered behind his kind eyes and artificial smile. The corruption and thirst were there. If I wasn't aware of the snake behind the wolf, I would have missed it. Initially I had.

He scoffed and shook his head. "I'm sure he's shown you

what he is, and yet still you care for him. Noble of you, but selfish of him."

"So, it's a bad thing that Ethan lives by his instincts, which drive him to protect those he loves selflessly?" I said, giving him a chilling, cold look. "I'm not naïve about how intense Ethan is, and if I were to be honest with myself, it's one of the things I'm drawn to the most. Tell me, should I be drawn to a man whose thirst for power is so all-consuming that there isn't a life he won't compromise to obtain it?"

Cole was a spectacle to watch. He was unleashed and accepting of his libertine behavior. Without anything to lose, he had gone all in.

"You think Sebastian doesn't thirst for power? Do you for one moment think his alliances, pack friends, and positioning in the otherworld aren't about power?"

I shrugged. "Perhaps, but he's never aligned himself with anyone who would hurt another were-animal to improve his standing."

Emotion faded from Cole's face, making it hard to read what tactic he'd use next. His voice softened to a whisper. "I will not do a submission fight with Ethan. I will protect my position in the pack with my life."

"As you should. I don't want your betrayal to be punished with a slap on your wrist. I want you humiliated from your loss of position and then penalized with death. A fitting ending for you."

He inhaled a sharp breath before pressing his lips into a stern line, his aplomb shaken as he started to get into the car. The Alpha arrogance was an asset as much as it was a flaw. He needed to redeem himself. To bask in what he'd almost accomplished and how it had been just barely snatched from his grasp.

Instead of getting into his rental car, he stood again, his attention on the pack's home. He eyed it with longing before dropping the same look to me. It had me wondering about the basis of it: was it sexual, or simply longing for what he perceived I could give him?

"The witches, the elves, and the vampires are allies of the Midwest Pack. Do you think that's just to protect the pack or to stroke Sebastian's ego?" he inquired, his brow raised as if he expected an answer.

When a response didn't come, he nodded his head, as if taking my silence as admission of Sebastian's desire to have power. I refused to feel sorry for Cole as he descended into some form of madness. And that was what was happening. It had been initiated by his envy and thirst for power. I couldn't stop imagining him in the East, salivating over everything he perceived Ethan and Sebastian had and he wanted.

Cole no longer put warmth in his eyes or words. He spoke in a sharp, cool, ominous whisper. "You have adopted some of Ethan's arrogance by supporting him in this challenge." He jerked his eyes toward Ethan, who had long dismissed his rantings. "You will lose"—he redirected his attention to me—"and *you* will lose your mate. Are you prepared for that? Don't let my past performance be an indicator of what is to come. I am fighting for more than just my rightful position. No matter how you paint a picture of me, you know I only do what's best for the pack." He clenched his teeth, and it was obvious he knew his last statement was a performance for the Council. He was all in on his lie and defending it to the death. He probably knew there wouldn't be any leniency with a confession at this point.

"I will not be reduced to a lone wolf," he muttered hostilely.

He quickly dropped into the car and drove away.

CHAPTER 14

*C*ole was wrong. I hadn't adopted Ethan's arrogance or self-confidence. It crossed my mind constantly that Ethan could lose. Cole wasn't going to fight to submission; only one of them was going to walk away alive. I wanted to be as confident as Ethan was that it would be him. I wasn't. Ethan said he was a hundred percent but, between the Faeries attempting to kill him and the injuries he'd sustained during his abduction, he'd been through so much. He wasn't the same Ethan who had defeated Cole before, and he'd admitted he'd barely won that challenge.

That was what I was thinking about when I pulled up to Chris's home. Her car was parked out front, which was good. I didn't want to visit Demetrius after our conversation. The entire time that I'd looked for Ethan and the others, people had kept telling me to broaden my views and ignore my narrow beliefs about good and bad, right and wrong, black and white. I had listened to them; right and wrong became indistinguishable, and colors blurred to gray. It felt like I was still living in that mode. My moral core shelved, reducing me to a husk of the former Sky. Or at least I felt that way when I knocked on

Chris's door. I grappled with my feelings and the belief that I was sliding into amorality. She answered before I could knock a second time and didn't look surprised to see me.

A smirk flitted across her lips as I gave her attire a disapproving, scathing look. In direct contrast to the light colors of her home, she was dressed in black from head to toe: black leather pants, scoop-neck shirt, and ankle-length boots. On her right ring finger, she wore what I thought at first glance was an onyx ring, but upon noticing the small diamonds that encircled the black stone, I figured it was a black diamond. More than likely a gift from Demetrius in an effort to buy the affection he wanted from her.

Her eyes narrowed at the downturn of my lips. Without a word, she stepped aside.

"I'm sorry to bother you before the funeral," I said.

She smiled. "I'm not going to a funeral, Bambi."

"Satanic ritual?" I offered with a half-smile.

"You didn't come here to talk about my manner of dress, did you?"

"No, but it distracted me. Since we are ... well, friends?"

"We're not friends, Bambi," she asserted in a cool, wispy voice.

I didn't think we were either or ever would be. I was using the word in the most casual way possible.

"Well, can we at least go shopping as friends, get you something out of the misses' section? We have to move you out of the junior department," I teased with a grin, allowing the banter to lift some of the unease that was weighing me down.

"Of course," she said with a smirk, "if we can return the clothes you got out of the children's section and get you some grown-up wear." She eyed the gray sweater I wore over a burgundy t-shirt that featured an adorable koala, my jeans, and silver slip-on shoes. Granted, the shirt wasn't the most mature outfit in my closet, but I'd woken up that morning in need of something that would lighten my mood, after spending most of the night thinking about the challenge. Who didn't like koalas? I smiled just thinking about them.

"Touché,'" I offered with a wavering smile.

Her gaze homed in on me. "Do you want a drink? You look like you could use one."

"It's twelve o'clock!"

Ignoring me, she went to her kitchen, pulled out two glasses, filled one more than half full with ice and then to the top with bourbon. If that was mine, she should have filled it to the top with ice and added half of a shot of liquor, because that would have been the only way I could drink it.

Returning with the glasses in hand, she took a seat, placed my glass on the table in front of her, and waited patiently for me to speak as I walked the length of the room, trying to gather the courage to ask her to do what I needed. I wasn't sure why I hesitated. A lot of things could be said about Chris, but being judgmental wasn't one of them. Her convoluted and obscure ethics were something I'd never understood, but they allowed her to function as a Hunter and survive in the otherworld. Now those were the very things I appreciated and needed from her.

Asking someone to kill another was hard. That was exactly what I was about to do. I needed Cole dead and I knew that Chris could do it and no one could link it to me. Bile rose at the thought of openly admitting the reason for my visit. Was this what I'd become? I couldn't take a breath big enough. I reviewed all the pros of doing this, which outnumbered the cons significantly. The most substantial one was that Cole couldn't be trusted. I would ensure that Ethan wouldn't have to fight him in a challenge and ultimately save him from death or at the very least more injuries. It could be done so that I wasn't linked to his murder. It wouldn't put Sebastian or my pack in jeopardy. It was a good decision but not an ethical one. The choking feeling of being submerged in a swamp came back and my chest ached as if my heart was trying to rip itself from my body, as though it felt I no longer needed it.

Chris continued to take small sips from her glass, waiting while I built up the courage to start talking.

It was the point of no return. Once I said it, my life had a liminal point. The period before I had an Alpha assassinated and the period after. This wasn't self-defense or a moment of hostility, where I could blame my actions on being overwrought with emotions. This was without doubt a planned act. I'd thought about it extensively for days.

I delayed the inevitable. "How long will you stay here? Eventually Demetrius is going to want you to live with him."

Her shoulders drooped as she breathed out, "I know. But it won't happen until the Presentation ceremony. Those were the terms I set to move in with him." Her face was laden with the heaviness of her concession to Demetrius. She inhaled the drink, reveling in the pseudo escape it allowed her. I didn't think she hated moving in with Demetrius so much as what it represented. It was a piece of her being taken away—her independence, the very essence of Chris. She would mourn that loss like any death. I understood. It was the reason I hadn't sold my home and still kept some of my clothes there. I was committed to Ethan but was having a difficult time giving up my pre-Ethan life.

She sucked in a ragged breath. "I agreed to it. I've made peace with my decision."

Silence overtook the room. I didn't talk about it out of courtesy, because I could see the tension that the conversation caused. I picked up my glass from the table and took a sip. For nearly ten minutes we stood in abject silence, both in an odd contemplation of the series of events that had led us here.

I opened my mouth to speak, and Chris interrupted. "May I say something first?"

Happy for the reprieve, I nodded and took a seat in the chair across from her.

"The rules of the pack are the things I admire about them. There is a code that you live and die by, and it prevents the chaos and anarchy that I see in the other denizens. If there is anything in question, you have books and precedents to refer to; if all else fails, you have a Council and an Elite that are sworn to uphold your rules. It adds honor to the pack. Doesn't stop most of you all from being assholes, but I'll take an asshole with honor and rules any day over the alternative." She stopped, looking expectantly for a cue from me to continue.

I nodded.

"You should understand that nothing is really new—same crap, just a different stink. The pack's process works, but it just takes one act to break the trust in the pack rules. Don't get me wrong, I am very well versed on the creative license you take with interpretation of them when it pertains to people outside your pack. But *within* your pack you handle things with an adherence to the rules that I respect." Leaning back into the cushions of the sofa, she took another long draw from her glass.

"Taking someone's life, even in a preemptive measure, is still murder. You know how I feel about it—I don't care either way. Some things have to be done. But I've grown accustomed to the many shades of gray that color my life. I'm not sure you could live with them. The moment you do it, who and what you are changes. Your life changes. Period. There's no going back. You'll have the demons. I have them. They are an occupational hazard of this job." Giving the thought a dismissive shrug, she took another drink and flashed me a wary half-grin. "I welcome my demons and have become friends with them. They're inter-esting companions. And they do give a person character and a diverse perspective on life and the world—but they aren't for everyone. Most people wither and die under the presence of their demons. Very few flourish. It's good to know how it will affect them."

She knows. How in the hell does she know? Was it that easy to read on my face? If she could see it, could others? My self-loathing quickly turned to panic.

She stood and walked over to me and took my drink. "Whatever you are planning, if in three days you feel the same way"—she walked over to her desk and scribbled something on a piece of paper—"this will be the fee."

I looked down at the paper. Cole's life wasn't worth nearly as much as I'd expected, which was advantageous because I had no idea how I was going to get the amount I'd seen her charge the pack in the past. Some of her fees were close to seven figures. It was still a lot, but significantly less than I'd expected. "You won't pay me but make monthly donations to these places." She took the paper from me and scribbled a few more things on it. One being the YMCA and another a children's home.

"Cole's life isn't worth very much."

She frowned. "If you go through with it, there's nothing I can charge you that will be more than what you will lose." Then she smiled. "Demetrius has more money than he knows what to do with, and I'm content with relieving him of it."

I took another look at the ring. *Yep, it's a black diamond.* The cluster of white diamonds that surrounded it gave off a brilliant glow as the light hit them. Undoubtedly they were flawless.

"A gift from Demetrius?" I asked, examining the gem.

"Of course. Against your suggestion to give me the South, he's decided to endear himself to me, in hopes that I will eventually love him. I won't." She sounded bored, as if his efforts were becoming exhausting.

"You don't hate him." I put enthusiasm behind my words, because that seemed to be important to her. With Chris, emotions were simple: love and hate. Black and white. But her relationship with Demetrius wasn't that defined. It had layers and nuances, even if she chose to deny it.

"No," she said softly, "I don't hate him." For the first time, it looked like it bothered her that she didn't. Was she falling in love with him? That would put a hitch in our plan, but destroying Demetrius had been put on the back burner. And I hated that it had been. I wanted to hate him so hard and vehemently that it consumed me and became a goal I had to achieve.

It was petty, but he deserved it and I wasn't going to fall for his game of redirecting the blame to me. It wasn't my fault that Quell had fallen in love with me and decided that my friendship wasn't enough. My eyes blinked erratically as I fought to keep back the tears that were brimming at the edge of my eyes. I fought them long enough to say goodbye to Chris but wasn't in my car a minute before they fell. It wasn't just sorrow—guilt laced my tears, too, and made them taste bitter.

When Chris came outside, coming to stand a few feet from my door, she frowned at the tear stains. "You won't call me, you won't e-mail me. In three days, I'll drive through your neighborhood, past your house. If your lights are on, I'll know you've made your decision. You'll wait two months before you start your donations, and make sure they are small ones until the fee is paid. I trust that you will do it."

And with that, she spun on her heels and with a flash of movement was back in her home. A sour taste was left in my mouth at how perfunctorily a potential assassination had been handled.

CHAPTER 15

$\mathcal{O}$n the flight to Maryland, I kept looking at the text: "Good job, Bambi." And there was a smiling emoji. I was sure Chris had known I wouldn't go through with it, but I hadn't. On the third day, I sat in front of my house for nearly an hour, contemplating going in and turning on the lights. With a flick of my finger, I could have stopped it. Cole would be dealt with, and I'd know that Ethan would be okay. The people who were still under Cole's spell and considered his life worth mourning, would. All others wouldn't. *I* wouldn't.

Confidence: Josh had it and so did Ethan. I'd stood watching the brothers with morbid disgust as they'd said their departing words, as if Ethan was heading off for a lazy day of relaxation as opposed to fighting another Alpha for his position. Ethan's victory was a given to them. I felt like I'd missed the memo, that I'd been excluded from a miraculous plan that would ensure victory. Whether Ethan had thought I'd follow Josh's example and stay behind didn't matter. I hadn't. At least Josh had a task that would keep him busy, his mind preoccupied by the mystery of what had been used to force them to change. I had chosen to accompany Ethan and Sebastian to Maryland for the challenge.

The East Coast Pack's home was dark brick, three stories tall, and had a small balcony extending from two of the rooms on the top floor. I assumed it was where the Alpha and Beta slept when necessary. A crowd of poplars wrapped around the house and a row of bushes lined a path to the front door. I'd expected their main home to be in New York and was surprised to find that we were going to Maryland. I would have preferred to be in the former, sightseeing, as opposed to witnessing a challenge in the latter. As we made our way to the front door, Ethan gave my hand a squeeze. It didn't calm me, because Ethan losing was a possibility.

As the Alpha of the Midwest Pack and the Elite, Sebastian was required to be there to witness. I suspected that even if he hadn't been, he would have come.

Fallon, Cole's Beta, answered the door, her long, brunette hair pulled back, her face solemn, as if she'd started the mourning process already. Her tone was pensive and rough as she greeted us. At the end of the day, things were going to change. Either Ethan would be a new Alpha who had every intention of handing the reins over to her—essentially making her the Alpha—or she would see another Beta die in front of her. The situation was grim, and there wasn't any pretending otherwise.

"He's downstairs waiting," she said. She started to walk away and stopped, setting her eyes on Ethan, and asked, "You don't plan on remaining Alpha, do you?" She was aware of the relationship that Ethan and Sebastian had, and it was obvious that Ethan wouldn't be away from the Midwest pack and Sebastian for very long.

Ethan shook his head. "This is your home. You deserve an Alpha who—"

"Ethan," Sebastian warned.

It was a discussion we'd had last night and several times this morning. This was one of the few times when Ethan didn't believe that secrecy was the best policy. He thought Fallon should know about Cole's involvement in everyone going missing. But Sebastian had disagreed, reasoning that if Ethan lost, Fallon would have to deal with an Alpha she knew she couldn't trust, whose ultimate goal was to be the Elite.

"I think you will make a good Alpha," Ethan told her. Based on everything that he and Sebastian had said about her, she would. I suspected she never made a challenge because Cole, like most Alphas, wanted them to be to the death. It was hard to wager your life on your ability to best someone. I cringed at the thought. It was something that Ethan was about to do. Fallon, recognizing that Ethan was holding back information, frowned.

"Cole is a good Alpha," she responded, but her words seemed obligatory rather than earnest. As if she were convincing herself of it in case Ethan lost. As we descended the stairs to the pack's basement, the strong, pungent smell of sweat and the metallic odor of blood drifted through the air. The industrial cleanser used didn't help; the potent scents of lemon and chemicals mingled in the air as well. Cole sat in a corner, bare-chested, his gaze cool.

Confidence shrouded him like a heavy coat as he came to his feet, pulling his lips into a tight smile. "Ethan." His eyes barely moved in Ethan's direction before darting to Sebastian as he greeted him with a nod. It lacked the reverence it once had. I suspected he felt betrayed by Sebastian's agreement to this. The irony of Cole feeling betrayed was unsettling. He'd martyred himself and bore the look of someone aggrieved.

"We should get this over with. Shall we?"

My stomach turned. *Someone is going to die; how in the hell are they treating this so casually?*

I opened my mouth to reason with Cole. To either ask him to step down or fight to submission, but his relaxed self-assurance told me that any request would be dismissed. In fact, he'd probably take it as a tacit admission that I didn't think Ethan could win. That wasn't it. I just didn't want my mate to die or be injured again. As a distraction, I looked around the room. The walls were painted a pale green and had a textured finish, I assumed done to hide the imperfections where holes had been patched. The floors were dark and thickly padded.

"Your Beta is here to bear witness, and so am I," Sebastian began in a deep, professional, and authoritative voice. "Ethan, the Beta of the Midwest Pack, has issued a challenge to your position as Alpha of the East Coast Pack. Cole Masterson, do you accept this challenge?"

Cole nodded.

"Do you still hold to the same terms with which the first challenge was made? Will this challenge be to the death?"

Cole smiled, his gaze moving to me, where it stayed as he answered, "The challenge will be to Ethan's death."

I shuddered. Why was he so confident? Both of them were too damn confident, oblivious to the very idea they could lose. It irritated me.

"Sky," Sebastian warned, giving a quick glance at the door, directing me to leave. It was the policy that mates couldn't be present. Ethan had added Josh to his list of people who weren't allowed to watch the challenge. With the exception of a middle-aged African American man who silently molded into the wall, I assumed their pack's physician, I was the only person in the room besides the Alphas and Betas.

"I'm fine with Ethan's mate being here." Cole's grin placed a dark shadow over his face, making him look cruel, maleficent.

Sucking in a ragged breath, Ethan looked in my direction in contemplation.

"The rules are there for a reason," Sebastian said.

"My pack, my rules," Cole quipped back. "I don't mind Sky being here with Ethan to the very end. I find it cruel to offer anything less. She should offer comfort at the end."

Ethan was still mulling it over.

"If you don't want her to see you in your final moments, I understand. She looks like she wants to stay, but you rarely take into consideration what she wants, do you?"

Ethan chuckled at the jab, dismissing Cole's effort to put a wedge between us and cast doubt every chance he had. "It's not that I don't want her here. I don't want her to see the brutality I plan to inflict on you, but it is her call. Sky, sweetheart, do you want to stay or leave?"

Sweetheart? Who is that for, honey, him or me?

"I want to stay."

"Very well," Sebastian said with a nod. He frowned, and I had a feeling it wasn't about me staying but about them skirting the rules. "Sky, you are here as an observer to the challenge. At no point can you intervene. Do you understand?"

That was the reason the mate wasn't allowed to witness the challenge. Admittedly, it would take a great deal of restraint to keep from intervening if Ethan started to lose. I nodded in understanding, but when the pack's physician and Fallon moved closer to me, I knew that my word wasn't enough.

"I will need two iridium cuffs, one for Ethan and one for Skylar," Sebastian instructed Fallon.

Fallon's eyes widened.

Cole chuckled. "You didn't realize that they are both wolves who are able to perform magic, did you? It is something they don't advertise. Both of their mothers were witches, and they both host Faerie spirit shades." He gave me a sly smile before he continued reciting his dossier on us. "Sky is more peculiar than anyone you will ever meet." He studied my eyes for a moment. "Ah, today she doesn't have it, but if you ever encounter her again, study her eyes. She gets a *terait* like a vampire. She doesn't have a natural immunity to vampires entering her home, nor an aversion to silver like the rest of us."

Fallon started out the door, I assumed to get the cuffs, but stopped briefly at the exit to look over her shoulder at me. The pack and I had gotten so used to my peculiarities that I forgot how off-putting they were. The long-forgotten feeling of shame for being an anomaly reared its head.

"Fallon, no need for the iridium cuffs. I'd like to defend my position in animal form," Cole announced. Something didn't feel right about this, and I could sense that Ethan and Sebastian felt the same way. It wasn't unusual for challenges to be done in animal form, but it was peculiar that it was Cole's choice. Perhaps he felt that he'd already lost in human form, so he had nothing to lose.

Ethan barely moved his head in a nod. They quickly removed their clothes and shifted. Ethan's wolf was slightly larger than Cole's longer, sleeker one, which would be able to move faster. Would it make a difference? Both were quick, powerful animals, but it only took seconds—milliseconds—to get the upper hand.

My expectations of what would be said prior to the challenge were more speculation than reality. I'd thought there would be something poetic, a speech about what a challenge means, a soliloquy about virtue and demands. The Alpha was the strength of the pack and core of it, and the position shouldn't be taken lightly. I anticipated a nice statement about what it meant to be an Alpha and responsibility to the pack and themselves. I expected words like *honor, code, duty*, and *pride* to be sprinkled into the dramaturgy. Instead, all I got was Sebastian saying, "The challenge begins." It seemed so insipid and lackluster for something that was so monumental and life-changing. The beginning of someone's end should have been marked with more élan than three drab words.

But that was it. The challenge began.

They rounded each other, baring their teeth, Cole taking a defensive stance, waiting for Ethan to attack. Ethan moved to the right, a quick leap as he tried to take hold of Cole's neck. Cole leapt back and snapped, getting hold of Ethan's flank and taking a plug out of him. Ethan used that moment to claw into Cole's side and his legs, making deep gashes that cut through the skin to reveal fascia and reddened muscle tissue. Cole limped back, his eyes widened as he dealt with the pain. Cole reared back and so did Ethan; they lunged at each other until they were blurs of snapping white teeth, blood-matted fur, and torn skin. They danced back, eyeing each other, assessing the damage, and looking for vulnerabilities. Ethan had claw marks going across his face, Cole's ear was bleeding, and they were both limping.

Moving back to gain more distance, they charged, mouths opened and teeth exposed. The thud of their muscled forms colliding rang in the air. Blood painted the walls and the floor. The combatants were so entangled, it was hard to see who was winning. The slow breaths that I kept taking to remain calm weren't working. My heartbeat was so fast and loud it rang in my ears. Ethan rolled over on Cole, clawing at him and biting, trying to get to Cole's carefully guarded neck. Cole jutted his head up with a powerful blow, snapping Ethan's head back. Ethan choked on the pain. Cole took that opportunity to push Ethan off him and snapped at his neck. His grip didn't hold, but he made a superficial cut.

Heads lowered they glared at each other, baring blood-reddened teeth, fierce savage eyes, and carnal rage. Cole moved back even more and I assumed he was trying to gather the speed to slam into Ethan. He edged more to his right. Running at full speed, he whipped around Ethan, taking to the air in a powerful leap. He wasn't going after Ethan—he was coming after me. My hand shot up to protect my neck, where he'd aimed. His teeth sank into my arm. Pain exploded in me and my eyes blurred from the excruciating ache. I pounded my fist into his nose with sharp, powerful blows until he finally let go. He clawed at me, his nails burning as they ripped into my flesh. His massive body pushed into me, trying to pull me to the ground where he could get another shot at my neck.

I collapsed to the floor as I pounded at the aggressive wolf who was on a mission to get his teeth on my throat. Cole knew he was about to lose his position, and apparently he wouldn't die without doing as much damage as he could first. Kill me, Ethan's mate, leaving him miserable and taking away something he perceived added strength to the pack—another wolf who could perform magic. His claws swiped from one side of my face to the other. Forced into defensive moves, I was reduced to the goal of protecting my neck. I wasn't likely to survive with my throat ripped out. It was hard fighting a person who'd already conceded to death, with the sole goal of destroying everything in his path that he could before the end. He was vicious, desperate, and determined.

My fingers gouged at his eyes. Cole howled but was relentless in his efforts to get to my neck. As he was dragged away, the sound of his nails grating against the floor pierced the large space. Through sweat and tear-blurred vision, I saw Ethan, still in wolf form, with his teeth in Cole's leg, pulling him away. Then he pounced, and using his claws for purchase he moved his way up Cole's back, biting and ripping at flesh at every chance until Cole surrendered, collapsing to the ground. Cole was still breathing. He lifted his eyes to look in my direction, although I doubted he could see anything through the blood that covered his face. Ethan had shifted. The bruises looked worse in human form. I knew the gashes in his leg had to hurt, but he moved fast despite it. Positioning himself over the battered Cole, he placed his hands around his opponent's head and jaw. I turned away, but my gasp couldn't drown out the sound of snapping bone. Ethan collapsed next to Cole.

"Can you change?" Sebastian asked Ethan.

He nodded and melted into his animal form and fell asleep. I didn't bother to take off my clothes, but shifted through them. I winced at how the ripping cloth increased my pain as my body attained wolf form. Positioning myself as close to Ethan as I could, I buried my face in the blood-soaked curve of his neck. When I nestled in closer, a low growl escaped him. He moved slightly to bring his head close to mine.

CHAPTER 16

The next morning, I awoke with Ethan lying next to me, his finger roving languidly over the marks on my face. Last night they had been really bad, and we'd made a point of not drawing attention to ourselves when we returned to the hotel. Claw marks that had been deep gouges in my skin, open, red, and angry-looking, were now healing. The skin had meshed together but was still inflamed-looking and tender. They would be healed in a couple of days. For the second time after a fight with Cole, Ethan was limping. Their doctor looked at his leg but said it wasn't bad enough for him to stitch it. We were spoiled, used to Dr. Jeremy and his plethora of concoctions that healed us faster, often leaving us unmarked. I vowed that once we were home, I would tell him how much we appreciated him—this time without the undertone of acerbity we often used. We recited a speech revering him for his talents on cue when he started to complain about our lack of appreciation for him.

My scars weren't that bad, but Ethan frowned as he gently traced them, as though he thought I'd be disfigured for life. "I can't believe he attacked you."

His voice was laden with anger, self-deprecation, and shame for having allowed it to happen. That was Ethan and Sebastian's biggest flaw. They expected to protect the pack and everyone they loved from everything, and it wasn't possible. They blamed themselves for not anticipating the worse and having a plan in place. No matter how erratic or unlikely the unexpected act was, they castigated themselves for not considering it a possibility. They couldn't protect us from life, but getting them to accept that was useless. It was so ingrained in them that logic had no place in the discussion.

"No one could have anticipated it," I soothed, covering his hand with mine.

He looked hard and dangerous, as if he wished he could break Cole's neck again. He rolled out of bed, still in his boxers, I could see all the marks from the previous day. They'd heal, but he looked like he'd gone through the window of a car and then been hit by that car several times. I was sure I looked bad, but only as if I'd been dragged by the car and the gravel had torn at my skin.

"So when do you turn the pack over to Fallon?" I asked, going over something we'd discussed many times before. It was a well-needed distraction.

"Tomorrow. Technically, Fallon will request to challenge me for the position and I will give it up rather than accept it. The rest is a series of obligatory paperwork and requests for me to return to the Midwest Pack."

"You won't have a rank," I whispered.

"Does it bother you?" he asked.

"Not at all."

"I'll have it back in a week or so, and things will return to normal."

Frowning, I sat up on the edge of the bed, wincing at the pain. Ethan grimaced and sat back down next to me.

"What is normal? Will we ever have normal?" I looked down

at my ring. I bit my lips to keep the words from coming out, but it didn't stop them. "Sometimes I want normal. The real normal and not pack normal. Life without the pack stuff. House, children, waking up with a schedule that doesn't include fighting Faeries, vampires, magic, elves, the dark forest or dealing with fringe packs, otherworld politics, challenges, and people kidnapping us to hunt us."

"Sky." He looked worried. His concern was unbearable. I looked to the floor. His finger crooked under my chin. He lifted it until my eyes met his. "Do you really want to leave the pack?"

I closed my eyes. Seeing the surge of his emotions, a combination of confusion, worry, fear, sorrow, and hurt, was hard. Feeling them was worse. Ethan loved the pack, and I think he felt as if I was asking him to choose. I wasn't. Was I?

Restless, he stood and waited for me to respond.

Leaning into him, I wrapped my arms around his waist, and pressed my cheek against his abdomen. "I was just being hypothetical; I didn't mean it."

He stroked my hair, entwining his fingers in it. Moving out of my embrace, he knelt down and kissed me. Long, hard, and passionately. Panting softly against his lips, I wished I could take it back, but it was out there.

"You meant it. I heard it. All your signs were normal and your voice was level. You meant it, so we need to talk about it."

I scooted back on the bed, away from his touch, which was distracting me. It was entreating, gentle, coaxing me into a direction I was willing to go —but if he wanted to talk, it had to wait. "Okay," I whispered. "Let's talk about it."

He returned to his position next to me on the bed, taking my hand in his. I angled myself so we could see each other.

Licking my lips, I continued, "Yesterday, I watched you prepare to fight someone to death, so that you could get him out of the pack. I spent days before that functioning because I had to, with my heart broken and feeling like the world was crashing down around me, because you were missing and probably going to be killed. I've been attacked and injured so many times that wounds don't even faze me anymore. That should bother me—it used to." My words were just a string of sentences that spilled from me so quickly I didn't catch my breath until I finished. "I've been pulled out of this world, magically hijacked, prepared to perform a forbidden spell to save my pack, killed someone, and watched someone that I cared about be killed in front of me. *Normal* just seems so far from my grasp that it hurts sometimes. I don't need it to always be calm walks in the park and boring days. But I'd like the boring days to outnumber the ones where I'm fighting for either my life, yours, or someone else's I care about."

He nodded slowly, taking in my words with careful consideration. "You think if we leave this, we'll have a normal life?"

Eyes cast down, I looked at our clasped hands. "I was about to have Cole assassinated," I whispered. There was a part of me that was a little ashamed, but it was small. That was what I was most ashamed of. The chastising voice berating me for doing something or even thinking something like that was gone. I closed my eyes, trying to retrieve the feelings, search for that person, and coax her back in my life, but realistically she was gone and I didn't foresee her coming back.

Ethan's face didn't give his emotions away, nor did his voice when he finally spoke. "Chris?" he asked.

"It was a challenge and we knew it was going to be to death. Cole betrayed the pack, turned the Council against us, was trying to get you pushed out of the pack, and was orchestrating a coup of my pack, and he was going to get away with it," I explained.

I searched for something in his face. Oddly, I wanted to see disappointment and maybe even surprise that I would consider such an option. I saw neither. The only person who was clinging to the person I used to be seemed to be me. As he stared at me, I wished I knew what he was thinking. He rubbed his hand over his light beard.

He inched in to me. "You didn't go through with it."

"I couldn't."

He kissed me lightly on the cheek. "Because that's who you are. Parts of you are adapting, but the real Sky is there at the core." We sat in contemplation. Or at least I assumed he was contemplating something. I'd cleared my mind. I wanted to think about nothing for a while.

"Sky, you're a were-animal who hosts a powerful spirit shade and has the ability to perform magic that most haven't seen. You wouldn't have stayed invisible for long. You're right, we've been through a lot of things, but you can't believe a person like you can have a normal life. It's unrealistic." His hand brushed lightly against my face before he planted a kiss on it. "Some things might not have happened, but without this pack, I suspect things would be worse." More weighted silence. I liked the silence now and appreciated how Ethan could do it for hours if given the chance.

"I'm not leaving the pack. *We* aren't leaving the pack," he said firmly.

"I don't want to leave. I love it, but sometimes—"

"You want normal. I get it." His hand ran over the engagement ring. "A wedding is normal," he pointed out.

"There's nothing normal about me getting dressed in a big white gown that makes me look like a fairy-tale princess or mermaid and parading down an aisle to a wedding march while people gawk at me and my overpriced party dress that I will only wear once."

"Overpriced party dress?" he teased. He roared a laugh. "Sky at the core," he whispered to himself.

Playfully, I hit him in the shoulder, and he winced. "Okay, no fairy-tale wedding." He grinned and arched a brow. "A honeymoon is normal."

"I'd like that."

Pleased that he was making some headway, he added, "Maryland's nice. We should stay here for a while. Sightsee or whatever. Do normal stuff."

"Don't you have a pack to run?" I teased.

"Not after I sign the paperwork. It's up to Fallon and however the chain will fall. She'll oversee whoever vies for the position of fifth. We'll stay here for a couple days—see what normal is like." He chuckled. "And ignore Winter's calls. She will not be happy with taking on the role of Beta, and I'm sure she'll feel the need to express those feelings with a lot of choice, colorful words."

He crawled back into the bed and pulled me closer to him. His lips brushed against my ear as he whispered, "I love you."

"I love you, too."

The next morning, I awoke to an empty bed and a note from Ethan telling me he'd be back and that he'd gone to the pack's home. I was about to curl back up in the bed when room service knocked on the door. I opened it and a server pushed in a cart of food.

"Mr. Charleston ordered you breakfast," he offered, responding to my confused look. He uncovered the plate to reveal eggs, bacon, a fruit bowl, and two large stacks of pancakes. Red velvet pancakes. I didn't know those existed.

I smiled. No, I was beaming.

"He said these are your favorite and was quite determined that you have them," he informed me with a half-smile. He didn't demonstrate the level of irritation I'd expect from a person who'd had to deal with a "determined" Ethan. It might have been his professional mask, or Ethan had been charming when he'd needed to be.

"Thank you so much."

As soon as the door closed behind the server, I rushed into the bathroom to brush my teeth. We'd spent most of yesterday in bed and I had more than just bedhead. My hair was a tangled mess of deep waves and curls. I wet it and smoothed it out as best I could in the few minutes I gave myself to tame it. I was in desperate need of caloric refuel.

I did a quick scan of the marks on my face. They looked worse than they felt, but they were healed enough that people wouldn't gawk at us. The bruising was slight, just a light raspberry discoloration. The claw and bite marks were filling in, and I didn't think I'd have scars. Whatever concoction the physician had put on us between eye rolls after taking his third call from Dr. Jeremy had worked.

I was sitting cross-legged on the bed, watching TV and working on the second stack of pancakes, when Ethan walked in.

"I take it you enjoyed breakfast," he surmised, looking at the empty plates.

"I'd visit this hotel for the breakfast alone. I've never had red velvet pancakes. I didn't know that was a thing."

"It is. Not one that this hotel typically makes, and it wasn't on the menu, but I was able to work out something." He flashed a devious half-grin. "I think I have to give the chef our firstborn."

"Deal," I agreed, taking another bite.

Ethan leaned forward with his mouth slightly open, the universal sign for asking for a bite. I shoved another forkful in my mouth. "If I'm giving my first child for this meal, do I have to share?"

He looked at the empty plates. "That was supposed to be for both of us," he pointed out.

I didn't do bashful, and my coy smile wasn't fooling anyone.

"It was going to get cold." I turned the last forkful of pancakes toward him.

"A whole forkful. I must be special."

"Don't you forget it."

He pulled out a small bag of what looked like dried leaves, except their coloring was off: odd teals, gold, and pink. He sniffed, frowned, then shuddered. It took a while for him to settle.

"What is it?"

"I have no idea. We found it in Cole's office. It was in another bag labeled wolfsbane, but this isn't wolfsbane."

"It's usually purple, right?"

He nodded. "And poisonous to humans, not us. The myth is that it prevents shifters from changing. It doesn't. At worse, the noxious scent annoys us. This is different." He frowned.

Moving several feet away from me, he opened the sealed bag against my objections and smelled. Nothing happened. He took out a few leaves and rubbed them against his fingers. Particles kicked up, creating a small cloud. Ethan's nose twitched, then his upper body. Within minutes he was convulsing. Straining to hold on to his human form when the change had been triggered. Turgid muscles bulged from his neck, his face reddened, and perspiration beaded at his temple. He was losing the fight after putting everything in it to win. His body clenched and released a tortured groan before assuming his animal form. He plopped down on his paws and wearily lifted up his head—I assumed to let me know he was okay—before relaxing back on his forelegs.

The massive wolf stayed in the middle of the floor for several minutes before he eased back into his human form. Surrounded by ripped clothing, he remained on the floor for a few minutes before standing.

"You couldn't change back, could you?"

He shook his head. "It's just like it was when we awoke in the room. No one was able to change back." He grabbed his computer and took a seat on the bed. When he opened it, I knew he was about to contact his brother.

"You want to put on some clothes before you do that?" I suggested.

He shrugged, nonchalant. "We've seen each other naked before."

They had. The brothers' biggest similarity was their aversion to clothing. It was a courtesy if they put on boxers. It was weird.

Josh came into view and, like his brother, he didn't have a shirt on, just a bagel in one hand and a cup of coffee in the other.

"You're alive. Thanks for letting me know," Josh said sarcastically.

"Sebastian called you as soon as the challenge was over." Ethan sighed, irritated.

"But *you* didn't! Seriously, how hard would it be to text me, pick up the phone and say, 'hey bro, I'm alive,' or whatever? I bet you let Sky know within minutes."

Ethan's face was a mask of indifference as his brother went on his rant. I smiled. Josh had been at the top of Ethan's priority list all his life. The target of Ethan's obsession to protect. The little brother who was Ethan's world. Despite Josh proclaiming he hated that role, he seemed to have gotten used to it. It was their norm. And now it wasn't. He was having a difficult time adjusting to sharing that space with someone else.

He was putting on a Tony Award–winning theatrical performance of the wronged brother. The affronted one. Now all he had to do was break into a heart-wrenching song that would bring the audience to tears.

Ethan's lips twisted into a scowl. "Are you finished?"

"Yep."

"I'm alive, bro," Ethan shot back with a smirk. "Happy?"

"No, I'm not happy. My brother's an ass."

"Betahole. He's a Betahole," I offered from across the room.

"I guess for the time being he's an Alphahole," I recanted, taking a seat next to Ethan. Based on the look Ethan gave me, he wasn't thrilled with my intervention. Ignoring him, I continued, "You're right, Josh, he should have called. Accept my apology on his behalf."

"Sweet. As a couple you make my brother less of an"—he grinned—"Alphahole."

Ignoring us, Ethan held up the bag. "I need you to come to town and get this. I don't feel comfortable mailing it, and Sebastian's left."

Josh leaned in closer to study it and his smile widened. "Nice. Have you tried it yet?"

"Yeah."

"You think it will make a good edible?"

"What?" Ethan asked. "I'm not going to eat it. It forces me to change to my wolf."

Josh's brows furrowed. "What? It stopped you from changing? That's some weird stuff."

Ethan made a sound of sibling irritation reserved only for Josh. It was a cross between a growl and a groan. "It's not *that*. I found it in Cole's office and it was marked as wolfsbane ..."

"That's not wolfsbane—"

"I know that," Ethan snapped. "It's what they used to make us change when they had us. I don't know what it is. I'm staying here with Sky for a couple of days."

"Pack business?"

Ethan's teeth gripped the bottom of his lip before he let his tongue slide over it, as if he had to taste the words, feel around for them before he actually said them. "No, we're going to stay for a while and sightsee," he admitted quietly.

"Mmmm." Josh directed his attention to me. "So," he started off slowly, "the brain injury—is it severe? I know there are different levels. Which one is he?"

"It's not a brain injury. I just want to spend time with Sky for a few days. Get your ass here by tomorrow," Ethan commanded. He disconnected. I'd heard only "Alpha"—half of what I knew was going to be an overly used sobriquet for his brother.

Ethan's proficiency in planning things bewildered me often, and today was no exception. He'd fully given in to the purpose of the day: we'd gone on a guided tour of the city and two museums and ended the day with a concert in the park.

As the hours had passed, so had his patience for the idiosyncrasies of humans. He'd looked as if he'd been dropped into a foreign land when random strangers stopped us to enlist us as their photographers. I'd done it twice while Ethan stood off to the side, looking annoyingly bewildered. He didn't find the peculiarities of humans amusing and alluring, the way I did. The simplicity of their existence drew me in; Ethan found them insufferable. I was reminded of it at dinner when I decided on a family-style restaurant and Ethan looked like a trapped animal prepared to gnaw off a limb to escape. And I was reminded of his magnetic effect on women and my newly lowered tolerance to them flirting with him.

His lips quirked into a smile that remained for the rest of dinner after a woman used his shoulder to help stabilize her as she stood. Her hand lingered too long, and so did her beckoning smile. Even her friend seemed embarrassed by the blatant display. When she decided to pull that stunt again, a little push of magic drifting between us pushed out a chair. Ethan grabbed it and her, to keep her from hitting the floor. Magic hit his arm, throwing him off-balance. A push of his magic swiftly jabbed in my direction. Then he nudged my foot under the table. "Play nice," he mouthed. He seemed quite satisfied that I wasn't enjoying human interaction so much now, either.

A smirk danced over Ethan's face and remained on it even as

he held my hand and we walked to the hotel. His face suddenly went blank, serious.

He stopped. "You worry about me in this relationship, don't you?"

I wanted to be honest with him, so I considered the question for a long time. My thoughts meandered to the numerous times Cole had attempted to cast doubt on my relationship with Ethan. I recounted how I felt, the irritation that plagued me because I'd allowed Cole to get into my head. But why? Did I question Ethan's ability to be faithful? Ethan's impassive expression fell to concern, the longer it took me to answer.

Finally, I shook my head. "No. But I'm not used to feeling ... any of it. Women looked at you before, now it bothers me. It irritates me that women fawn over you. And I feel the irritation intensely. I'm not used to feeling that way. I don't like it."

The amused grin returned, and I wasn't any fonder of it than I'd been in the restaurant. "You're not used to feeling jealous." He showed his finger with the wedding band he had purchased for himself; then another finger ran along the band of my ring. "I guess the wedding band isn't the attention repellent I thought it would be. Jealous Sky is kind of cute ... scarier and an abuser of magic, but cute."

We walked in silence for a long time. It was comfortable, or so I thought until Ethan abruptly stopped, his sharp, gray eyes holding mine with intensity. "It was like having a craving that couldn't be satisfied," he admitted softly before he continued walking. "You know you want something but you don't know what. And you keep searching for that one person who fits— who satisfies completely. There are women who come close, but it's not exactly what your body is craving."

My hand tightened around his, knowing how difficult it was to confess this to me. Knowing that the walls he'd built around him, that had made up his very existence, were faltering and at risk of collapsing—for me. In silence, I continued to listen.

"Then you find the perfect fit—that one person who satisfies a longing you've had so long you accepted that it would be part of your life forever. Like a curse that can't be lifted." He sighed. "The person is like a decadent food that you know you shouldn't indulge in because there are consequences."

Should I be flattered?

"Maybe it will lead to high cholesterol and be your physical undoing—a tragic death from an embolism."

This isn't flattering at all. "In this story, I'm the embolism-causing treat? I do not come off good in that story."

Ethan laughed, a deep, throaty one that I didn't know he had in him. "Sort of. You make me vulnerable. It's difficult feeling this way," he admitted. "Superficial relationships are easy. I didn't try hard and didn't care." He shrugged. "I need you to trust me and know that I'd never do anything to hurt you."

I nodded. "For the record, I was annoyed that she saw that you arrived with me, wore a ring, was talking to me and didn't care. It's a little uncomfortable that women are so drawn to you."

"I'm a very attractive man."

"Oh, I forgot, I'm dealing with the arrogant brother," I countered, comically scowling at the smile.

His fingers stroked my hand at a steady rhythm. A glint of amusement was still deeply seated in his steely eyes.

"I have a mirror, Sky."

"You're absolutely right. You're breathtaking, and people are going to look when you walk in a room. It's such a horrid burden you must bear. How have you lived your life like this? Causing eruptions of swoons when you walk into a room. Your life must be tragic. You're right, you *are* too pretty. We're going to have to disfigure you. Since we heal so fast, it's going to be brutal. Sorry, buddy, but that pretty face is going to have to go. How are we going to do it? Sledgehammer to the face?"

"We aren't disfiguring my face. You'll have to deal with it the same way I deal with advances toward you. *But* I need you to make a promise to me," he said seriously.

"What's that?"

"Magic. Let's never use it against each other, okay?"

"Why?" I asked. The shift in his mood concerned me. He seemed genuinely bothered by the idea.

He shrugged. "I don't know. It seems wrong for us to use it against each other. It made me feel disconnected from you."

Although he didn't fully explain it, I understood. "We're were-animals first—we share that commonality, with more depth and similarities. It's our bond and what joins us. Our magic"—I searched for the right word—"I know it's a part of us, but somehow it still seems foreign and unnatural."

Giving me a half-grin, he nodded. "Yes, I guess that's it."

"Okay, I promise never to use magic against you. Just women who seem to forget what a damn wedding ring means. She was all over you. You couldn't have been more obvious showing her the ring."

"I know. She deserved to fall flat on her face. You showed her," he mocked.

"Your sarcasm is neither warranted nor appreciated."

"Of course, dear," he replied, his tone laden with condescension—which made me regret my promise not to use magic against him, because I'd have loved to give him a magical shove.

Our conversation came to an abrupt stop when we entered the hotel's lobby and saw his brother perched on a stool in the restaurant's bar with a glass in hand. London was next to him, nursing a drink and eating a plate of appetizers.

"I'm proud of you," I joked with Ethan when we were just a few feet from his brother.

"For what?"

"Going out and just hanging out with people."

"You realize I deal with people regularly and don't have some odd aversion to them."

"You deal with people on your terms and are actually paid to be stubborn, cantankerous, and … well, let's just say 'confident.' It's your wheelhouse. But relaxing, hanging around with strangers, and not having a schedule and just taking it easy isn't your thing."

"And he's not fond of humans, either," Josh added, swiveling his stool to his brother and flashing him a grin so wide it showed almost all of his pearly whites. I wasn't surprised to see a colorful picture curling up his neck, as he'd been released from his promise to Claudia to abstain from getting tattoos. I assumed he'd had more added to an existing one.

Ethan glared at him. "I'm not very fond of you right now."

"Of course not. The hierarchy is: were-animals, people who can use magic … and way down here"—Josh lowered his hand close to the ground—"humans."

"They don't bother me," he snapped back, giving his brother a look. "Have you found anything?" He made it obvious he was changing the subject from his subpar social skills.

When the bartender handed Josh the check, he gave it to Ethan. "You got this, right?"

"Of course," Ethan said absently, looking at the new ink marks inching around his brother's neck, an extension of a tattoo hidden by his shirt. His skin still blushed from the fresh art. Ethan's brows rose. "Claudia said no more."

"She released me from it," Josh said brightly, as if he'd been relieved of a prison sentence.

Ethan's lips twisted, scanning the exposed art on his brother's arm, probably imagining the ones that were concealed, and the studded earrings in his lobe and at the top of his ear. He waved his brother on. They both threw back their drinks and followed us to the elevator. Once it shut Ethan said firmly, "No more."

London's eye roll mirrored mine. This wasn't going to end amicably.

Josh scoffed at the command. And then glowered—a challenge. They'd just devolved from two men with jobs and responsibilities to children bickering over the most frivolous things.

Here we go.

Josh took the more adult route. "Whatever." Which was sibling speak for "you aren't the boss of me." To drive in his point, sparks of magic skipped and danced along his fingertips, becoming more erratic as the elevator ascended.

Amusement kicked up the corners of Ethan's lips and I could tell he was deciding whether to escalate the situation or squash it. Passive-aggressive taunting was something they'd made into a sport—an Olympic event in which each one was aiming for gold. Telling each other how much they loved each other was just too pedantic for the powerful wolf and witch. Instead they'd reduced their emotions to juvenile antics, an overly circuitous way of saying, "I love you and what happens in your life matters."

Ethan's eyes followed the spasmodic movement of Josh's magic.

Ethan shrugged. "It's just a suggestion. You like getting them; I don't want you to run out of places to display them. If you slow down, that's less likely."

"Okay," Josh agreed reluctantly.

This was a good behavior sticker moment. I needed to get some gold stars to give to them. Instead of taking the easy resolution at face value and being pleased that they'd handled their disagreement amicably, they looked at each other like hostage negotiators waiting for the deal to go bad. The eye rolls passing between London and me were hard enough to cause fits of nystagmus. Perhaps she could see it in my face or was feeling the same way about the dueling brothers.

London smiled and gold bounced off her fingers, hints of glittery magic, as she formed a star in the air. I choked on my laughter as she quickly waved it away when the brothers looked in her direction. Stolid, she just looked back at them, eyebrows raised as if to ask, "What are you looking at?"

Both of them studied us. Heat brushed along my cheeks as I suppressed my laughter. Eyes narrowed suspiciously on us, and then they turned their attention back to each other, wearing slightly hostile looks as they had before.

"Let me see it," Josh urged once we were in the hotel room. Ethan pulled the bag out of his luggage.

"You couldn't stop the change?"

Ethan shook his head in response.

Josh hissed out a breath. "This is bad, really bad."

"I know. I have no idea what it is."

London moved in to study the contents of the bag. "It was in Cole's office, right?" she asked.

"Yes," Ethan offered.

"What's the relationship with the elves here?" she asked.

"Why?" I asked.

After several moments of consideration, Ethan urged, "Just say it." We had laid out most of our secrets to the witches. There wasn't any more censorship. It was refreshing to have that type of relationship with someone other than the pack.

"I don't want to be indelicate, but the were-animals are the weakest link in the otherworld." She punctuated her words with a weak, apologetic smile. Then she studied the contents of the bag again. "If someone sees one of us perform magic, it's easy to dismiss it as their eyes playing tricks on them. They see a person shift to an animal, there's no question about that. The Red Blood want to expose you all. But have they mentioned anyone else? They aren't even worried about vampires—who can live for an eternity. It's shifting to animals that seems to defy nature so much they seek to destroy those who do it. And if you all are outed, the otherworld could be rid of you." Again, we were treated to a remorseful smile.

She held up her hands in surrender. "There are many who don't feel that way, but with the situation with Steven and everything that has occurred that has been linked to you all, there is unrest." She sighed. "Even the witches are being pressured to distance ourselves." Frowning, she looked at Ethan and me. "And your mating has caused an uproar like I've never seen before."

It was the second time someone had mentioned my mating with Ethan as if it were a horrific, cataclysmic event that was bound to destroy the world as they knew it. It was obvious that London wasn't just speculating.

She tapped the bag. "If this was something that could be easily found in nature, don't you think it would have been stumbled upon?" When she ran her fingers through her hair, it made a cascade of pastel colors show from the strands underneath, which disappeared as dark brown hair spilled back over them. "The Red Blood have been working diligently to out you all. Following you, waiting to catch you changing. You think Dexter wouldn't have discovered this stuff? The only explanation is that it has been created. We haven't seen anything like this, but who has been known to create harmful things and tuck them away until they need them?"

Ethan sighed and cursed under his breath. If Cole had possession of a sample, he'd gotten it from the elves. The question was which ones had helped him.

Ethan pulled out his phone and called Fallon.

CHAPTER 17

$\mathcal{I}$t was never a question of doubt when you were dealing with a Makellos, the self-proclaimed elite and pure elf. They wore that arrogance like a gilded crown, and imperiousness wafted off them like a fragrance. Fallon was able to secure a meeting with them in less than two hours, but the moment we walked through the doors of the large brick home that was an homage to their idea of self-importance, I regretted it. The extended walkway that led to the home displayed manicured bushes and flowers that I wasn't familiar with. Bronze statues placed in the yard looked remarkably like our two hosts in front of us—so settled in their self-importance they felt a need to immortalize it with statues.

At home we only had to deal with arrogant looks of contempt from Liam; now we had two pairs of eyes looking at us with derision. They belonged to Dalia and Gregoire, our aforementioned hosts. From the gentle way that Gregoire had escorted Dalia into the room, I assumed they were a couple.

Several braids wove through her auburn hair to keep it away from her face, drawing attention to the unique characteristics of her features. A rich sepia-colored, heart-shaped face with an overly angular nose, full lips, and round, bright, expressive eyes. She was striking, and I was sure she told herself that often.

Gregoire's presence was consuming, and so was his broad and stout build. His square features made the forced smile that curved his lips in greeting seem harsh. Just a little shy of six feet, he towered over Dalia, who was just barely over five feet in heels. Based on their aristocratic countenances I figured his pearl-gray tailored suit and her classic-lined burgundy slacks and lace-trimmed silk shirt were typical and not special for the meeting. With the exception of Ethan—who had on his version of business casual, brown slacks and tailored beige shirt—we all had settled on jeans. We didn't appear to be attending the same event.

Gregoire lifted a brow in irritation as the silence stretched. Ethan's face remained stoic, but I knew he was debating how to address the issue at hand.

"You called this meeting, Ethan. I assume it's not to introduce yourself as the new Alpha, so I'd prefer if we get on with it," Gregoire commented in a brassy voice tinged with annoyance.

My eyes, along with Ethan's and Josh's, slipped to a room off in the distance and the small cadre of military-dressed people there: three women, three men, standing side-by-side with stern looks of concentration as uniform as their clothing. The barely contained magic wasn't hard to miss and made Josh stand taller, his eyes narrowed, hands at his side, in a subtle defensive position. Preparing to respond if necessary.

Dalia, noticing Josh's change in demeanor, smiled.

"Do you know what this is?" Ethan asked, apparently deciding on the direct approach.

"*Mond*," Gregoire asserted, nonchalantly glancing at the bag. "It's a wonderful little plant that we've been dabbling with for years. It's taken a lot of trial and error but I'm quite happy with the result. I'd like it to be stronger, but it serves its purpose. Is there anything else I can help you with, Alpha?" The latter sounded like a curse rather than Ethan's new title.

An odd glint shimmered over Ethan's eyes. Shock. He didn't expect Gregoire to be so forthcoming. "Do you have more of it?"

"Of course we do."

"Darling, we *had* more of it. It's been dispersed among the masses," Dalia purred, displaying obvious amusement with the situation. They were quite the pair.

"Who did you *disperse* it to?" Ethan asked.

Gregoire paced dramatically, his head tilted back slightly, as he tapped on his jutting chin, in thought. "There was a very enthusiastic witch, I believe his name was Sean, Sand ..."

"Samuel, dear. His name was Samuel."

"Oh, yes. How could I forget him? He was quite enthusiastic in his agenda. He despises magic in this world, but he seems to find 'beasts who present themselves as men' even more offensive. Rumor has it that you've thwarted his plans." Amusement played along the strong planes of his face. "He was not at all happy with that and quite vocal about you siccing the new witches on him. Who, in turn, unleashed a rogue fae on him. He was livid just retelling the course of events."

"The 'beasts' do manage to rub people the wrong way, don't they?" Dalia mocked.

Pretty much like you are doing now.

I didn't hide my irritation nor the dark thoughts that accompanied it. I bared my teeth, and the smile slipped from Dalia's face. Her schadenfreude wasn't appreciated, especially since she and her counterpart were the root of it.

Ethan waited patiently. Shackled emotions made his face expressionless, but his eyes were steely as he kept them fixed on Gregoire, waiting for him to continue to determine the extent of the damage.

"There was another witch, Rayna. I remember her because I

haven't seen fiery rage like that in years. It was white hot, vengeful, and oddly not directed at the were-animals, who tend to have their little snouts in everyone's business. If only someone took a rolled-up paper and whacked them to remind them where they belong." He sighed heavily. "Alas, it never happened. Oddly, Rayna's anger was directed at the were-animals' little witch. What a plot twist."

Gregoire's smile widened, exposing all his teeth. An accusatory gaze shifted from us to Josh. "You killed the members of the Creed and it went unpunished."

"It went unpunished because it was justified," Josh rebutted.

Gregoire huffed out a dark laugh, sizing Josh up. If he knew as much as he let on about us, he would know not to underestimate Josh.

Gregoire's stance was cautious, keeping his distance from the powerful witch whose control on his temper was wavering. Josh's eyes clouded over, dulling their bright cerulean to a dusky blue. Magic radiated off of him like a current.

"Ah, you have adopted the ways of the were-animals. Jury and executioner. Well, it seems as if Rayna is seeking her own justice."

"Mond won't affect me," Josh pointed out.

"Hurt the brother, hurt the witch," Dalia whispered from her new position several feet away, closer to the wall and farther away from Josh, who was becoming noticeably agitated. Muscles along his arms contracted and relaxed as he attempted to calm himself. Dalia was stating the obvious. Anyone who knew the brothers knew they could hurt one by injuring the other. They were each other's Achilles' heel.

"Then the humans found out about us." Gregoire chuckled, seeming giddy as he confessed. "Well, they didn't so much find out about us as much as we contacted them and told them of our little plant and that the very thing that could force were-animals to change could be theirs for free. Oh, they were elated."

"You are hurting yourself. When we are outed, then people will believe in the impossible. If humans can shift to animals, what's to prevent the masses from believing in those who can perform magic? As usual the elves are shortsighted and foolish."

"Are we? If the rumors are correct, you and your peculiar mate are responsible for the vampires' ability to blend seamlessly with humans. No more aversion to light. If they manage their appetites, no one will discover what they are. And as for those of us who possess magic, we will use self-control. We will never be discovered while they are dealing with the abominations that are you all. 'The beasts who present themselves as men.'" Gregoire's smile widened as he looked to Dalia. "I rather like that description. What about you, love?"

"It's quite fitting," she said, her voice heavy with mockery.

Ethan closed the distance between him and Gregoire. The men in the other room shifted and in unison moved closer to us but still kept enough distance to seem unobtrusive.

"You know a great deal about us—which is good. At least you aren't going into this war unaware of what you've gotten yourself and the people who aid you into. I will be merciless in my retribution."

"Are you ever merciful? That animalistic behavior is what got you into this." He beckoned to one of the men, who grabbed a computer off a side table, opened it, and turned the screen to us. None of us bothered to look at it. We already knew what it was. Steven's infamous video. The violence of that moment played in the background as Gregoire continued, "Perhaps if you all had practiced some mercy and discretion this wouldn't be happening."

"We had handled it. You've exacerbated the situation!"

"No, you didn't handle it. The humans, the Red Blood, aren't handled. You will be the sacrifice to keep the others hidden. Once they can prove Steven is a were-animal, that video demonstrates how dangerous you can be. There are so many were-animals that we will continue to go unnoticed. Resources and time will be directed at containing the beasts who hide behind a human shell."

The obvious betrayal of another denizen of the otherworld brought a deep growl to Ethan's chest. I wondered how Cole tied into this. "How did Cole get it?"

"He helped us test it," Gregoire admitted. "A sample of it was all he requested."

"I doubt he knew your plans. There's no way he would have helped," Fallon spoke up. Her tone was low and measured, but her face reflected a recognition of betrayal. The spark of hope that Cole had been a better person than his actions had demonstrated was slowly fading. I could imagine how painful it had to be to find out the person who'd been responsible for protecting your pack had been working against it. And for what? Power.

Cole's plan took form, and I didn't need anyone to elaborate. Everything always circled back to Ethan and Sebastian and what was the best way to make others lose trust in them: to be seen by humans indiscreetly changing in public—and therefore outing us. They'd fall from leadership quickly, and Cole would replace them. Those unable to see past the iniquity of his charismatic ways and alluring Alpha presence would fall for him. He'd use the elves to get what he wanted. I didn't know if this was plan A or B.

Gregoire's interest flowed among us all, and a satisfied look skated across his face. He shrugged. "Cole had proven to be of no use to us. He never used it. Such a shame; he seemed like he had been determined to do so. I was curious as to what he'd planned to do." Deviance replaced amusement on his face. "Since you are the Alpha now ... it doesn't matter."

Ethan was so calm, I knew a category five storm was in play. It happened faster than I expected. One look at Josh, and a powerful blast of magic floored the security team. They were ready for action, but they weren't prepared. People had heard the rumors but were always unaware of the full extent of Josh's power.

Coal black smothered his blue eyes as he called on strong magic that tossed the men back, pinning them against a wall. The six struggled against it, trying to loosen themselves. Their mouths started to move, to perform invocations, but Josh was faster, capturing their words and rendering them silent.

Josh's face strained with concentration as he shattered the windows. Shards of glass stopped just inches from the elves, up against the wall. Fallon had darted toward Dalia, pinning her, but her hold was replaced by London's. Shocked into silence—more so by the violence against her than the magic—Dalia glared, her mouth gaping open. She was clearly used to her actions not being challenged—it was obvious she'd expected this meeting to go very differently. Part of me had, too, until they'd backed us into a corner, leaving us with limited options.

"You are going to take me to the garden," Ethan instructed Gregoire.

"Were you not listening to me? There's nothing there."

"I'd like to see for myself."

"Let her go!" Gregoire demanded.

"She will be let go and unharmed, along with the others, as long as you take me to the garden."

"I will not take you anywhere until—" His voice cut off as Ethan's palm pressed into his chest, pushing him back into the wall. Secured against it, he struggled to get out of Ethan's hold. Anger and resentment ghosted over his face. Ire flickered in his eyes but quickly faded into indignation and self-satisfaction. Stone-cold eyes leveled in Ethan's direction made it apparent that he'd acquiesced to martyrdom. He was willing to sacrifice his life for the ultimate goal—making us pay for whatever sin he felt we were guilty of. I'd seen the look so often that it meant nothing to me. This abnegation was nothing more than an empty self-sacrifice.

"Your death will mean nothing," I whispered into the silence. "I know you believe it will be an epic stance that will lead to you being hailed as a hero in historical accounts. It won't. This is foolish and without merit. Though you see us as the enemy, everyone else doesn't. The story will be framed by the ones who live to tell it. You will not fare well in it."

With a great deal of reluctance, Gregoire took us to Elysian. Ethan emptied one of the coffee cups from the car and handed it to me. The earth split, revealing the elves' hidden exotic land. The peculiar animals roaming about, the vibrant hues of green on the trees, the glistening deep blues of manmade ponds placed throughout the space were beautiful and breathtaking. Gregoire seemed to be seeing the world through the eyes of a visitor rather than a person who had probably seen it a hundred times. My appreciation brought a faint, short-lived smile to his lips before he turned it into a frown. Ethan and I looked around, and I followed him as he went to a small area of disturbed dirt. He ran his fingers through the fertile soil and then sniffed them. He held them out to me; the scent of the Mond still clung to them. The plants had been removed from this patch.

"Do you have more?" Ethan asked Gregoire.

"No, it's served its purpose. It is out of our hands."

"How did you make it?"

Gregoire's lips pursed together. He seemed to be resolved to this ending poorly for him and wouldn't do anything to ease it.

"Cup, please." I handed it to Ethan and he put a handful of dirt in it. Then he returned his sights to the dirt. His mouth moved slowly and the hum of peculiar magic swirled between us, coating the air with power I'd only felt when he killed the Faeries. A nimbus of magic inched throughout the area. This wasn't the magic that was used on the Faeries; it was similar to the kind Claudia used. It held the dankness of death and unfurled off Ethan and bolted into the ground. Magic pulled the life from the dirt, replacing it with death. Fertile earth no longer existed. Gregoire's mouth dropped open.

Elysian was soaked in gloom, the land now fallow, destroyed by Ethan's magic. The area that was once verdant and lively, with flowering trees and exotic fruits hanging from vines, looked drastically different. Gregoire gave the area a long, mournful look. It was apparent he was pondering whether his martyrdom was worth it.

We left Gregoire in the middle of Elysian, in a state of hate-filled awe. It was the first time since we'd encountered him that he seemed anything but casually arrogant. It was hard not to gawk at Ethan as we drove back to Gregoire's home to get Josh and London.

"We will have to return home," Ethan said, frowning. "We're going to miss the play."

"What play?"

"*The Lion King*. I got us tickets to see it Friday in New York."

My nose crinkled when my brows pinched together in confusion. "Why did you pick *The Lion King*? I've mentioned *Hamilton* a dozen times."

"You keep singing the soundtrack to *The Lion King*. I've heard you hum 'The Circle of Life' at least seven times," he said, looking as confused by my dismay as I was by his theatrical choice.

Heat crept up my neck and I flushed. I knew my cheeks were bright red. "The Presentation," I mumbled softly, providing my embarrassed answer.

Ethan still looked confused. "Chris's Presentation?"

I nodded sheepishly.

His face was pinched in a peculiar blend of bewilderment, amusement, and shock. It was as if he had a threshold for considering someone peculiar and I'd crossed it without much

effort. He spoke slowly—very slowly—trying to make sense of things himself. "You hear that the most powerful vampire in the world will be presenting a new Mistress to the otherworld. His partner, the woman who will wield as much power and influence as he does and could change the dynamics of the world we know, and 'The Circle of Life' plays in your head and you imagine him a lion—
"

"Mufasa," I interjected.

He swallowed hard and pushed the name through clenched teeth: "Mufasa is Demetrius, and I'm assuming Chris is the lion cub—"

"Simba."

Ethan squeezed the bridge of his nose with two fingers and glanced in my direction. It looked like he was fighting a smile or maybe another scoff. "Okay, Chris is Simba and she's being lifted up and presented to the other denizens like the cub? That's what comes to your mind when you think of the Presentation?" He sounded incredulous by the time he finished. His lips parted in awe.

Ethan was rendered speechless. I had his full attention. As fast as he was driving, I wished he would've diverted some of that focus to the street. His lips twitched at a smile that he wouldn't give in to, before finally returning his attention to the road.

"Oh, come on. You want me to believe it didn't cross your mind once?"

Shaking his head, he laughed. "Sky, you are a *very* unique woman."

"Why do I have a feeling you're not using *unique* in a flattering way?"

"How should I describe a woman whose mind goes to *The Lion King* and Mufasa presenting his offspring, Simba, to the animal kingdom to describe a vampire ceremony?"

"Of course it sounds silly when you put that tone with it!" I countered. "Everything sounds silly with that level of condescension in it."

"You're right, love, it's very much the same thing. I can definitely see why you think of *The Lion King* when you hear 'Presentation.' That's a reasonable thing to think of. It's practically the same thing," he said in fake concession.

That's worse than the unique *comment, Mr. Alpha.*

"Your sarcasm is neither needed nor appreciated," I said.

He simply chuckled.

CHAPTER 18

our pages later I realized I'd skimmed through the book of spells and hadn't analyzed them as I should have been doing. I didn't know how Josh continued to work under the burden of stress. Maybe it fueled him. I kept thinking about our visit to Elysian. Had Gregoire told other elves how to make the Mond, and if so, had they attempted to do so? Flashes of Liam's smug face answered the question for me. If he'd had the opportunity to do it, he would have. I hoped he hadn't.

My thoughts went to Samuel and his possible role in the Mond being distributed and used against us. The witch who wanted to get rid of magic by any means necessary had resurfaced. His last failure had only made him rethink his plan, not abandon it.

I sighed into my cup of coffee, fondly remembering the two days Ethan and I had had of a somewhat normal life. Ethan was right, were-animals who hosted spirit shades and were part of the Midwest Pack weren't going to have normal lives. This was our normal. The concession tasted bitter, but the acceptance unburdened me from the expectations I'd had of eventually experiencing a mundane human life. Now we were back to the place we'd started. The mountain of paperwork was quickly done to restore Ethan's position as Beta. Winter was quite proactive in making sure everything was expedited quickly— making no secret of how much she disliked her transitional role as Beta.

David's distinctive rap at the door reminded me that I might not have "normal," but I did have Trent and David, and that was better than normal. "Hey, Peaches, you didn't run off and get married, did you?" David rushed by toting a large basket that he promptly took to the kitchen and placed on the kitchen counter once I moved aside to let him in.

I see we've circled back to fruits again.

"Married?" I held the door open, waiting for Trent, who was leaning into the trunk of their SUV. "Why would you think I got married?"

"You went MIA for, like, a week. We couldn't get ahold of you, so we figured you'd eloped." The hitch in his voice told me that was just one of his conclusions. I was sure the others were grimmer.

I flashed a large smile. "Nope, I'm not married, still mated."

Rolling his eyes, he went to the door and waved Trent forward, then turned around and gave me a big hug. We were still entwined in the hug when Trent walked in, his long, wiry arms wrapped around three garment bags. He laid them over the arm of the sofa, and moments later I was entangled in a peculiar three-person hug. Trent pressed into my back, wrapping his deceptively strong arms around me. David's hug tightened as he pressed his cheek against mine. The hug was as weird as it was the first time they'd done it, and I hated that it was now our thing. I wanted a new thing.

"We missed you, Peaches," David said and kissed me lightly on the cheek. *Peaches.* I definitely wanted *that* to be a new thing. I'd lost the nickname battle years before, but I clung to the hope that I'd be just Sky.

Untangling from the three-person hug, they followed me to the kitchen, where I went straight to what was obviously my full-moon basket, which made me forgive him for all the pastries, cuddly animals, and other cutesy names he called me. My attention quickly moved from the garment bags to the basket. I could do without the weird cheeses; I didn't like them nearly as much. Thankfully there wasn't any fruit. Fruit basket —what had he been thinking that month? Unless it was dipped in caramel or chocolate I couldn't care less about it. Seeing the Belgian chocolate, I opened it and stuffed a piece in my mouth before directing my attention back to the garment bags.

"Suits?" I asked. David and Trent felt I should be a part of their shopping excursions. I loved suits, and men in suits were fun to look at, in small doses. Trent giving me his full-on fashion show as he turned their home or any available hallway into a catwalk was a big dose of Trent. A very big dose. He lived by the motto "go big or go home," and he was always big. It brought a smile to my lips.

"Of course not. They're wedding dresses—"

I was about to interrupt him when he held up his hand in protest. "I know. I know. You aren't going to have a wedding, just some tacky little shindig, but my dear, must I tell you for the hundredth time"—he dramatically grabbed my ring finger —"you don't buy a woman a ring like this to amble down to a courthouse or participate in whatever little downtrodden hoedown you all plan to have. A ring like this is to be enjoyed by the masses. It needs to be celebrated with a beautiful dress, a flower girl, and lovely people dressed in lovely clothes. You, my dear," he drawled, "are doing this ring a disservice."

"I wasn't aware the ring had feelings. I'll make a point to send it an apology," I snidely shot back.

He gave me a look of derision.

I sighed. "I'm pretty sure no one cares about my ring or to see me walk down the aisle dressed like a fairy-tale princess."

"What's wrong with being a princess for a day, kitten?" David asked haughtily.

Kitten. Dammit. We're back to that one. I preferred being called fruit.

"You promised you would think about it," David reminded me before I could protest.

"Just try them on. You can wear one to the courthouse or wherever. Please," Trent added. His soft, entreating eyes had me doing what I usually did with him—giving in.

"Fine, I'll try on one, but I'm not going to put on a fashion show," I huffed, giving him a stern look.

"Of course, just one." Trent looked down at the ring. "It's so beautiful. I can't believe you don't want a wedding. I thought everyone wanted a wedding."

"No, not everyone. We're mated; the wedding is just a formality."

Trent rolled his eyes, and with a sweeping move of his hand dismissed that idea. He and David had a hard time grasping the mating concept of our relationship.

"Well in the non-supernatural world, we like to make that commitment to each other in front of our friends and loved ones, instead of biting each other in the privacy of our homes," David said as I followed them into the living room.

Looking around the room, Trent frowned. "Where's tall, hot, and broody? I mean your *mate?*"

"He's not here."

"Wonderful, we won't break tradition by having him see you in the dress." Taking me by the arms, he coaxed me upstairs to the bedroom. They both had the same look of awe they'd had the first time I'd given them a tour of it. While I found Ethan's home overwhelming and excessive in every way, David and Trent loved it. David pushed open the double doors leading to our room and sighed.

"*This* is a bedroom," he said. Ethan's room—*our* room—was

three times the size of the one in my house. The furniture was dark wood. The bedding was recently changed from dark grays and deep hues of blue to a lighter neutral beige with hints of pale blue and mauve. I wasn't sure why—I didn't mind the gray.

Trent and David's interest in the dresses was quickly replaced by their fascination with the closet. The differences in Ethan's and my personalities were seen in the closet. Ethan's suits were grouped together based on color. Shirts and ties were given the same treatment, aligned from light to dark and solid colors separated from patterns. For years, I'd lived my life not knowing the various shades of black, but Ethan did, and his slacks were aligned accordingly. Shoes were shelved in order based on style and color. Trent and David didn't seem to be as amused as I'd been when I first realized that Ethan hung up his jeans and t-shirts.

A frown of sheer mockery curled my lips at the large, smoke-gray ottoman in the middle of the closet. Did the decorator think Ethan was going to get fatigued in the middle of dressing and be too tired to go to his bedroom and have a seat? More absurd was a closet big enough for an ottoman that size.

My side of the closet didn't impress my friends as much. Mostly pants, dress shirts, and a few dresses that were recently purchased since I'd started seeing Ethan. They hung neatly, but I hadn't grouped them by color, length, season, or all the other elements Ethan used to organize his clothing. My clothes weren't on the floor or tossed over the chair placed in the corner of the closet, so to me it was neat enough. I still hadn't figured out the purpose of that chair. Did picking out an outfit require enough contemplation that a person needed to have a seat?

Appraising the differences between our sides of the closet, I attempted to see it from the perspective of an outsider. Someone who would just peek in—how would they view us?

"I wonder if this is how serial killers' closets look?" I mused aloud, my gaze moving between the two sides of the closet. David did the same, one arm crossed over his chest, the other elbow resting on it, allowing his hand to cradle his chin.

"Definitely," he finally admitted, after giving it careful thought. He walked to my side of the closet. "Only a true sociopath would hang her sweater over a hanger like this," he chastised, swapping out a wire hanger for a padded one. His lips twisted in a playful grin. "Clearly"—he waved his hand over my side of the closet—"someone who sets up their closet like this should be on some type of government watch list."

He and David wandered into the bathroom. I didn't bother to follow them. I suspected it had been purely left up to the designer and builder. Ethan enjoyed the spa shower, but unless I was in it with him he didn't seem very interested. And I was positive he'd never used the whirlpool tub or lounged in the sitting area. It was for aesthetics only. Beautiful but impractical.

"Why haven't you moved in already?" David asked. "This place is gorgeous."

"I do live here," I pointed out. Almost in unison they cast me skeptical smirks.

"You sort of live here. Honey, you spend just as much time at your house as you do here."

"I'm still moving. It takes time."

Turning away from them to walk to the bed, I ignored their disapproving glowers and opened the garment bags. There were three dresses, very different in style.

"Since you will only commit to trying on just one, try this one," Trent said, pulling out a pearl white mermaid dress with a sweetheart neckline and narrow off-the-shoulder sleeves. Intricate embroidery and frosted lace overlay the body of the dress, which pooled out at the bottom in layers of satin and lace.

"Which royal wedding were you preparing for when you decided on this one?" My fingers ran over the intricate details of the lace.

"Oh, hush, it's a beautiful dress you will look absolutely wonderful in. Try it on," he insisted and pushed it in my direction.

Giving it a once-over, I took it and started for the bathroom to change.

"Yeah, because seeing you in your underwear is going to irreparably damage us," David quipped. Ignoring him, I marched into the bathroom. They weren't as bad as most were-animals, who didn't have a problem with nudity at all and often had to be coerced into dressing. Joan had once said that most of them wouldn't think anything of walking down a major highway naked, and that was the truth. Ethan subscribed to that belief, and it was fine now that we spent most of the time at his home, where we were surrounded by stretches of trees, with neighbors hundreds of feet away.

"It's strapless. I'll have to take off my bra." I made a face, and said over my shoulder, "I don't let just anyone see my tatas."

"Yeah, just you, Ethan, and the other people who are present when you all celebrate the full moon," David pointed out derisively.

"Whatever." I slammed the door and quickly undressed and slipped on the dress. I took a look at myself in the mirror, unable to recognize the person in front of me. I had changed. My life had changed. Ethan's mark was on my shoulder. I stood looking at myself in the mirror—the new Sky, unrecognizable from the person I'd been years before. Old memories and pain that I'd buried deep resurfaced. I thought of my mother.

Tears welled in my eyes and I tried to blink them away. I took a seat to gather myself. I didn't want to cry since I'd done enough of it over the years to last a lifetime, but I gave myself the time I needed to miss her. I lost the fight, and the tears spilled as I wondered if what I had become would have made her proud. I was so different. For several minutes, I sat taking slow easy breaths, until the pain and sorrow became just a dull ache. I knew that feeling too well. After that ache, there was a reprieve from it all. I waited. It took longer than usual.

I took a deep breath, brushed the tears away, and walked out of the bathroom.

"You look beautiful!" Trent exclaimed.

"Kitten," David cooed, and then covered his mouth, awestruck. He gave me another long, lingering look. "If planning a wedding is too much, we'll do it. Let us do it. It'll be our gift to you. All you have to do is say yea or nay. Period. Nothing else. I promise." He seemed wistful as he waited for me to answer. He and Trent had had a small private event for their union. I wondered if they were living vicariously through me or if this was indeed a gift they wanted to give me, knowing that if I didn't have one, I'd regret it in the future.

"Please," Trent whined as he stood next to David, both giving me puppy-dog hopeful looks that I wasn't prepared for.

I sighed. "We already decided against a wedding."

"I think it's a good idea," Ethan said quietly, as he softly walked into the room, startling all of us. I was drawn to him in a crowd of people. In a city, I seemed to be able to locate him, but somehow he was still able to sneak up on me. Getting him a bell didn't seem like such an outlandish idea.

Trent lunged in front of me as if his coltish, thin body could block Ethan's view of me in the wedding dress.

"Trent," Ethan voiced a poorly suppressed warning. Trent stood taller, persistent in his goal. Ethan's cool, gunmetal gaze narrowed on him, and he reluctantly conceded.

Ethan's eyes roved languidly over me and then the dress. He moved closer until he was just inches away from me, seeming to have forgotten about David and Trent. His finger lightly trailed over my shoulder, a gentle brush that left heat in its wake. When he reached the lace his fingers traced the intricate pattern before continuing their journey down my arm. His other hand rested around my waist, and his fingers curled into my back.

He pressed light kisses along the line of my jaw and my shoulder. Featherlike pressure warmed every spot that it touched. Pulling me closer into him, he covered my lips with his. His tongue entwined with mine and explored my mouth, commanding. His fingers laced in my hair as he pulled me deeper into the kiss. I fisted his shirt, hungry for more, oblivious to everyone except Ethan. I quickly became complicit with our exhibition, making Trent and David voyeurs. Before it could escalate any further, Trent's face pressed into the limited space between us. He was close—too close. If he were any closer, he'd become part of a peculiar three-way. We pulled away with a start, surprised by the invasion.

"So, wedding or no wedding?" Trent asked, crowding us, his eyes bright with anticipatory excitement. His eyes fixed on Ethan, and I waited for Ethan to voice his opinion.

"Do you want to do this?" Ethan asked me. "Because I do."

Trent was vibrating with eagerness, in contrast to David, who remained composed and expectant waiting for my response, since the final decision had been deferred to me. I said nothing but ushered Ethan down the hall—and had to promptly stop Trent, who had decided to follow.

Out of earshot, I looked over my shoulder to make sure Trent hadn't trailed us. Trent had been pressed so close to us, his scent traveled with me, making me think he was near.

"Are you sure?" I asked.

Ethan stepped back and gave me a long, lingering look, taking in my face, traveling down my exposed neck and shoulders to the bodice of the dress, until it had moved over every part of me and the dress. His eyes were intense as he nodded. "I'm sure I want to marry you."

"That's sweet. But are you *sure* you want to give Trent and David full rein in our lives as they plan a wedding? I don't think we are prepared for this—for *them*."

"I'm prepared to marry you," he echoed, pulling me to him

and kissing me hungrily as his fingers clawed at the fabric, drawing it up until it slipped up my leg.

I nipped at his lips in protest. "There are people behind us," I reminded.

"So," he purred, achingly close. His lips hovered over mine, and warm tentative fingers pressed into the curves of the dress. "They'll leave."

Most people would leave—not them. David and Trent would grab snacks, pull up a chair, and start voicing their suggestions and offering commentary: "Wow, that's bigger than I thought it would be, nice, Ethan. Good for you, Sky." "Ugh, that's not a sexy sound—are you enjoying it?" "Wow, that's pretty vanilla sex. You should get the Kama Sutra." "Sky, don't make that face. No one wants to see that." "Spank it."

I put some distance between us and shuddered at the thought of them watching us. "No, they won't."

That distance was quickly lost as he attempted to kiss me again. I backed away. "Stop it. What's with you?"

"You look gorgeous."

I looked down at the dress and the unbridled lust in Ethan's eyes. I could see every salacious thought he had in the lascivious way he looked at me.

"Is it the dress? Please don't tell me this is a *thing*, too."

His tongue slid across his lips. "It's not a 'thing.' I love the way you look in it."

Freak.

I looked over my shoulder. Trent and David were in the hallway looking like meerkats as they waited for an answer.

"So, what's the answer?" Trent shouted, forgetting he didn't need to shout to be heard. He started walking toward us.

"Stop. Leave us alone," Ethan commanded.

"Broody and rude. You got yourself a good one, Sky," Trent mumbled sarcastically, turning around. "Being gorgeous can only get you so far, you have to have a personality, too, you know," he grumbled, as he leaned against the wall. He crossed his arms and glared at Ethan.

They weren't as afraid of Ethan's bark as they once were. They knew that as humans, unless they were a direct threat, they would be handled differently—more kindly. As Kelly had, they weren't above exploiting it at times.

"What do you want to do?" Ethan asked me.

"They agreed to do everything so it would be simple for us. But you know how it is. They might plan it, but they are a lot. At times over the top. It'll be beautiful—"

"But it will be intense for a while working with them," he finished.

I nodded.

After several moments of quiet consideration, I looked over my shoulder to see them waiting in anticipation.

"You have a month. That's it," Ethan informed them.

"We only need twenty-one days," Trent shot back confidently.

"No, thirty days is good," David said, giving Trent a look.

But I was sure they could do it in twenty-one days. When I'd shown them the ring, their eyes had glazed over as if they were entranced, but I knew they weren't. They'd been planning the wedding in their heads. I'd never forget how they looked when I told them I wasn't having a wedding. Their expressions moved between sorrow, disgust, and derision. As if I'd told them I had five days to live and planned on spending that time punching babies, knocking geriatrics down, and throat-punching strangers for the hell of it.

Now there was going to be a wedding, and they were beaming. Ethan's hand rested at my waist until Trent smacked it away. Ethan's first response was shock. Then a growl reverberated in his chest.

"Paws off the dress—we have to return this one." He nudged Ethan over as both he and David started talking. I watched the mocking smile flourish over Ethan's face as he backed away and David and Trent tugged on my dress as if trying to determine how it needed to be adjusted.

"You can't wear this one, it's already been seen. But don't worry, Kitten, we'll get something just as striking. In a couple days we'll have more specifics. Fitting, dresses, venue and all that, and menu." I was in a dissociative state as they discussed variations of white and cream. Asked me questions about music, food, and possible locations. I nodded my head periodically, not really sure of what I agreed to. I wanted so desperately to wipe the look of amusement off Ethan's face. Before I could come up with anything, Trent looked in Ethan's direction. "Don't go too far, mister, we want to discuss colors and tuxedos with you, too. I don't see you in just a typical tuxedo; we'll need to go over some options. I'm assuming Josh will be the best man. Well, set up things with him. And you'll have to tell us what plan to give the wedding party."

Ethan's mocking smile vanished and mine widened. My cheeks were starting to ache from the wide grin fixed on my face. Ethan backed away and gave the dress, David, and Trent a once-over and turned around and left. Unless he planned on leaving the house, he wasn't going to avoid them.

"When do you think we can get Winter and Kelly in to look at dresses?" Trent asked. I shrugged. Trent and David looked at me with the same twist in their mouths and assertive gazes.

"There's no time like the present to ask them," Trent said, as they continued to lead me toward the bedroom. David grabbed his phone, scrolled through his contacts, and called. "Hello, Kelly, love." *She gets "love" and I get called pastry, fruit, and small animals. How is that fair?*

"Sky would like to talk to you," he said. Then he lowered his voice and crooned, "It's pretty exciting." He was giddy. David didn't do giddy, and it was contagious, melting away my apprehension. It didn't eliminate the concerns I had about Trent and

David becoming overzealous. A wedding—it didn't seem so daunting.

Kelly's voice was bright with anticipation, and I wasn't sure if it was because of David or just Kelly being overly enthusiastic, something she was most of the time. Her jovial personality was infectious.

"Yes, Sky?" I could imagine her, bright smile exposing her teeth as she bounced happily while seated on the sofa. I could even picture Gavin, sitting next to her, narrowed eyes fixed as he remained in his perpetual state of broodiness, unaffected by her mood. As if he'd been inoculated against it.

"Ethan and I decided to have a wedding—"

"Yes," she blurted.

I had to take a few steps back because Trent and David were crowding me.

"You didn't let me finish."

"You want me to be a bridesmaid, right? Am I right?"

"I would like that."

"I'd love to!" Her enthusiasm matched Trent and David's, and I was thankful she was somewhere else. "I'm so excited for you. If there's anything I can do for you—or Gavin—"

"Just Kelly," Gavin interjected, which Kelly quickly chided him for, urging him to be nice. Her voice was muffled, so I assumed she was doing what we'd seen them do, resting her face in the crook of his neck. Flashes of Winter rolling her eyes and snidely commenting about them being more annoying than me and Steven made me laugh. They were cavity-inducing— that was what Winter would say. Each time they walked past, she mentioned needing to make an appointment with her dentist.

"She agreed," I told David, who promptly took the phone and told her the plan to narrow down the dresses and that he'd keep her updated.

I didn't expect calling Winter would go as easily but she managed to make it worse than even I could imagine. "So why are you having a wedding?" "I thought you weren't going to have one." "Is this because you want to wear a big fluffy dress?" "Who's planning it?" "*Really*, that's going to be fun. Seriously, if you want to be tortured, I can do that." When I reminded her that they were standing next to me, she reminded me she knew because David's number came up on her caller ID. "Did they put you up to this because they want to look at wedding dresses? Tell them no. How annoying do you think they are going to be? On a scale of one to ten, I'm giving it a hard eleven."

It was the last comment that had David grabbing the phone. "Look, little swan," he started out addressing her by the name they'd given her. "That's enough of that out of you. You're going to do this, and that's that. Once we have a dress, we will let you know."

"We're thinking about pink and ruffles," Trent added, squeezing his face in next to David's to speak into the phone. "You'll wear it and like it."

"Really. Would you like to place a wager on that?"

Trent grabbed the phone from David. "Look missy, we are not going to let you ruin our—"

"You mean, *her*, right?" Winter corrected, snidely.

"No, I mean ours. I'm treating this like it's mine, and if you ruin it by being prickly you will feel my wrath." It was a great threat but ineffectual, coming from Trent. His voice was always kind, too soft, and even with an edge it wasn't hard enough. Him adjusting his hair in my mirror while fidgeting with the tubes of lip gloss on the dresser didn't exactly scream *bringer-of-wrath.*

"You're going to be annoying with this, aren't you?" Winter groaned.

"If you make this hard on Sky, yes. I have the ability to be the most annoying person ever, when I put my mind to it," he asserted proudly.

Weird thing to be proud about.

Winter's voice was cloying. "How will I ever know the difference?"

"You want to test it?" he challenged. There was a long silence and then she asked to speak to me.

"I would love to be part of this glorious union," she said in an overly sugary voice. "I imagine it's going to be sunshine and bunnies and the most fun you will ever have in your life. I don't think it's going to be like hitching a ride on the crazy train at all. I look forward to the show."

I laughed. "Thank you, Winter."

Before she could hang up, Trent told her he'd see her on Thursday.

My brows rose, intrigued. "Thursday?"

"Yes, we see her on Thursdays."

"Why?" My gaze bounced between the two of them. They shot each other furtive glances as if they were reminding each other they were sworn to secrecy. I wracked my brain trying to figure out what they might do on Thursdays with Winter. Not just *a* Thursday but a weekly thing. I decided it was to watch several daytime TV shows that she was embarrassed to tell people she enjoyed. She could watch with them and discuss them without judgment. That was the beauty of David and Trent. They were life, fun, and pure human indulgence, without judgment.

CHAPTER 19

*E*than hadn't left but had slipped into his office, where he'd been since we agreed to have a wedding. I didn't feel the strong presence of his magic around the door, but it was locked. I knocked.

"Are you alone?" he asked in a gruff voice. I had been tugged, poked, and treated to a number of celebratory hugs that had made David's and Trent's scents and mine indistinguishable.

"Yes, they went home. It's hard to feel welcome when someone, in no uncertain terms, tells them to go away."

The door opened. "You were right, they are going to be a handful, and I'd answered their questions already."

"You came here to hide from them?"

"I'm not hiding, but they're your friends .…" His face twisted as his voice trailed off, but there was still a hint of anger and frustration that weighted his words. He'd taken a gentler route with Trent and David because they were my friends, but Ethan wasn't above escorting them out of the house, either. I suspected his irritation was directed at something else. When he stepped aside and I saw books and papers scattered about on the desk, I knew it was.

"Liam hasn't been able to make the Mond, but it's not for lack of trying," Ethan offered, returning to his seat. No matter how he tried, he couldn't get the frown to relax. "Sebastian thinks we should just come out."

"And you don't?"

He shook his head. "Gregoire said Samuel, another witch, and humans were given the Mond. I'm going to assume the humans are the Red Blood. The witch, Rayna, one of Marcia's acolytes."

Scowling, I felt perplexed that she'd had any. Marcia was cruel and adhered to antiquated beliefs and practices that were inhumane. She'd been barbaric, and no matter what beliefs she held, favoring infanticide because a child might be a potential threat made her a monster in my eyes and deserving of her fate. How could she have followers? But I knew there was a small group of people who were purists, and nothing superseded that attitude. That tenet blurred ethical lines, put blinders on their thinking, and led them to do deplorable things. While I saw her as an antihero, those who believed in her cause saw her as a martyr for the purity of magic.

"She had followers who mourned her," Ethan said. He stood and looked over the rows of books, pulling some from the shelves and placing them on the desk among the others. He exhaled a frustrated breath.

"There's no way we'll be able to get a hold of all the Mond," he admitted. He wore the defeat heavily in his scowl. The thick, dark feeling of despair overtook the room.

"You're looking for a spell?"

"One that will nullify it."

To distract myself, I browsed the shelves, my fingers sliding over the bindings of the books that were at arm level. *Spell. Another spell.* Perhaps the witches were right; we didn't really respect magic the way we should. It was our go-to for any problem. I battled with the conundrum I felt. We needed to do it but magic had a penalty. Global magic, more drastic consequences. What would they be if we nullified the effect of the Mond on us?

"Have you found a spell?" I asked.

He shook his head. "Josh is better at creating spells than I am." Hearing the tightness in his voice, I looked and saw a slight blush on his cheeks. Ethan was so used to being good at things he was embarrassed when he wasn't.

"They seem complex. It took nine witches working together to come up with one to remove Josh's curse."

Ethan blew out a breath. "I think we're going to need those nine witches again," he admitted.

I was reminded of Nia, one of the members of the Creed, and how she had expounded about our role in the Faeries coming back and chastised us about our lack of deference for magic. How we used it without discipline or regard for potential consequences. In the eyes of the witches, we played into the narrative that were-animals shouldn't have access to magic.

Absently, I had moved over to the only information in the house that the witches hadn't combed over when they were helping Josh. A dark cabinet that had a built-in lock. Ethan's refusal to open it had led to a tense, pseudo-polite exchange between him and Ariel. She'd conceded, but I wasn't planning to.

"What's in here?" I tugged at the locked door.

Without looking up from the book in front of him, he said tersely, "Nothing."

Before I could comment further, Ethan grabbed his notebook and extended it in my direction. "Do you mind looking over these spells and telling me what you think?"

My lips twitched at Ethan's efforts to deter me. He was a master of sleight of hand and distractions, skills honed from his need for privacy and desire to protect his secrets and Josh's safety.

"I will, once I see what's in the cabinet."

Sensing my tenacity, he sighed heavily. "It's nothing of importance to you."

"If it's important to you, it's important to me," I argued.

"Sky," he asserted, power in his voice. That tone made me stand up taller, feel the command, and question whether it could be ignored. I ignored it. It was just as ineffectual as it was when Cole had used it. I could hear it, feel the primordial and preternatural strength behind it, and yet, it meant nothing. Once again, I found myself comparing the changes that had come over me.

"It's really nothing."

"Then you won't mind showing me nothing. I'm sure I'd lose interest in nothing," I quipped back.

His jaw tensed with the same anxiety and frustration it had when he'd allowed the witches into his office. Ethan had two, one on the other side of the house that had his law books and business information, which he kept open, and this one, which he had locked down with not only a key but a ward as well. One so strong that even Josh wasn't able to break it.

"It's personal. My personal things," he asserted, his voice tight, as he struggled with the words. I realized that Ethan existed with barriers and they had become such a part of him that removing them chipped away at who he was. I debated whether to pursue it. Would Ethan, totally exposed, be the same Ethan?

"We can't have secrets, Ethan. I know that's how you survived and what you had to do. But I'm your mate. We are as one and you can't keep things from me. I tell you everything about me."

"Eventually," he pointed out. I knew he was talking about me attempting to hire Chris to assassinate Cole. I hadn't told him about it; I'd confessed it.

I smiled. "You're right. I don't want any secrets between us.

I'd like to know what's in there but if you're not ready, I understand."

Taking a seat in the chair next to him, I started looking over the list of spells that he'd compiled and stacked the corresponding books with them in order. Unlike Josh, whose lists were scribbling and shorthand of the books that the spell had come from, Ethan had the spells arranged alphabetically according to the corresponding books.

As I read over the first spell, I could feel the heaviness of Ethan's gaze on me. I looked up to meet the peculiar blue-gray eyes of the man whose animal half hadn't quite receded to the background.

"I love you," he said. Each time he said he loved me, it was as if it were a new discovery. Him charting a territory so unfamiliar that he proceeded with caution.

"I love you, too."

His movements had lost some of their grace, now heavy and slow as he made his way to the small cabinet, took out the key, and unlocked it. He pulled out a weathered book, its binding worn and the Latin words on it faded. He continued to pull out things: a box, a small chain bracelet that I thought was silver until I felt the weight of it and confirmed it was iridium.

With a half-smile, he admitted, "I wore it instead of the iridium injections."

This treasure trove was a window into Ethan's childhood, his past, his life. I felt like an archeologist discovering the artifacts of an unknown tribe. The findings kept coming: a photo album, a tattered notebook with unfamiliar writing on it, a medallion similar to the piece that Josh had tossed at Marcia's feet and the one Ariel had offered to Josh a couple of months ago.

"Are these your family things?"

He nodded. "This was my mother's"—he picked up the medallion—"before they cursed her." His lips pressed into a line.

Remaining cautious, I just listened as parts of his life that he'd kept secured behind wards, locks, distractions, and walls were laid out in front of me.

"I like having actual pictures," he admitted, looking fondly at a woman with honey-colored hair pulled back off her face into a relaxed ponytail. Her grayish blue eyes simultaneously exhibited Ethan's intensity and Josh's mischievousness, like it was a trick of the camera, allowing the viewer to see the many facets of her personality.

Another picture with his mother and Claudia, their faces brightened by smiles. Claudia's vibrant, whimsical smile was alight with a carefreeness that enthralled me. The broker of fine art didn't seem capable of joviality; her smile and mannerisms were refined and mirth bridled. I gawked at the picture as if I was being introduced to a doppelgänger.

Noticing my interest in the unfamiliar Claudia, Ethan said with a wry smile, "She changed after the curse."

"What happened?" I knew that Ethan's mother did a *rever tempore*, a forbidden spell that led to her being cursed. It was to help Claudia, but I didn't know with what.

"Claudia made a vampire," he said abruptly.

"She can make vampires! Is that why Demetrius shows her such reverence? Because she's a Messor, a combination of Faerie and vampire?"

"He's unaware of what she is. His 'reverence' isn't because he knows what she is, it's because he doesn't. It's equivalent to us sensing an Alpha among us. You might not be able to put your finger on it, but you know there is power." He smirked. "You're the only one I know who senses it and ignores it."

"I sensed it when I met you and Sebastian," I retorted.

His nose and mouth crinkled into a mocking scowl. "Really, and that's how you responded?"

"Meh, you weren't so special."

Ethan laughed, a deep rumble that I suspected came from an

uncomfortable place rather than from true levity. His version of a nervous laugh. He was giving me more pieces to the puzzle that was his life, his history, his existence.

"Claudia created a vampire?" I asked, redirecting him to the story.

He shook his head. "Based on what my mother said, it wasn't a vampire. Not like the ones we were used to. Claudia didn't know that was going to happen. She found a nearly dead man who'd been drained and discarded. She knew what she was and thought she could save his life by changing him. Making a vampire is easier than making a were-animal. The transition is easier, too. Claudia waited until the heart slowed and fed him her blood. She did everything she was supposed to do." He stood and paced the floor, running his fingers through his hair.

"It wasn't like a regular vampire, was it?" I guessed.

"No. It was ravenous like a new vampire, but even they can be reasoned with and controlled by their creator. He behaved as if he wasn't linked to her. A savage animal that ran rabid throughout the city. Leaving a trail of bodies."

Leaning back, he continued recounting the incident, most likely from tales his mother probably had told him numerous times to explain her reason for doing the spell that led to Josh being cursed. "She's part Faerie, and they are difficult to kill. A stake through the heart wouldn't work, and this thing moved so fast that they couldn't contain him—or kill him. Magic didn't work against him. She'd created something that should be feared. She didn't have a lot of options and couldn't go to the Creed."

I understood why: it would have fed into their biases about hybrids and interspecies mating, because no one knew what the results would be. After all, both Ethan and I could perform magic because our mothers were witches. It was theorized that were-animal magic would suppress witch's magic, but there were always anomalies.

"The only way to stop him was to do the *rever tempore?*" I asked.

"Yes, and my mother never told Marcia and the others why she did it. And for that reason, she was punished. She couldn't say what Claudia had created, because it would have been their mission to find a way to destroy her because of it."

This led to Ethan's mother being punished with a curse that doomed Josh to death at eighteen. In order to save him, Ethan had to get access to more magic without the witches finding out. "Who found the shade for you?"

"Claudia. She knew we'd need magic stronger than the group of witches that performed it, and my mother's magic had been restricted as part of her punishment."

"That was extreme," I said, understanding his distrust of and displeasure with Marcia and the Creed.

"Marcia and the others were always looking for a reason to restrict my mother's magic. Her skills and abilities surpassed theirs tenfold, and they had a problem with that."

"Your mother wasn't able to help you with the spell?"

"She did; she made the spell that we used. But I had to perform it. It was a witch's spell so it was a combination of her magic and the Faerie's that made me strong enough to perform it."

Taking hold of the worn book with the faded letters on the binding, I opened it to discover that it not only contained printed spells but also some handwritten ones in the back. A lot of handwritten ones. His mom had been just as gifted and prolific at making spells as Josh, if not better. All her spells, like Josh's, were written in Latin but translated into English. I would have liked Ethan's mother. Josh wasn't pretentious or traditional in any way, except when it came to magic, which he always preferred to be in the language of the original spell, usually Latin. He reasoned that a spell could be translated incorrectly. And that was true, but I still liked to have an idea what I was saying.

"Your mother found a way around a curse. Do you think maybe there's a spell in here to nullify the effect of the Mond on us? Something that can act as a workaround?"

Hopeful, Ethan took a seat next to me and we started going through it.

It was a good thought, but none of the spells in Ethan and Josh's mother's books seemed as though they would help nullify the effect of the Mond. But there were three potential spells that could have been used on Josh to circumvent the curse. There were healing spells, shifting spells, and a number of others that I didn't think were possible, including some that dabbled in necromancy. Reading through the spell book, I could see why the members of the Creed were jealous of her, and it made me wonder if it was merely envy that fueled their decision to restrict her magic—or fear of what she was capable of. Josh's magic didn't seem so impressive once I knew the source of it.

I had gone through the book, and so had Josh and London. Which was why Nia, London, and Josh were gathered in the pack's library, combing through our impressive collection of works.

Nia's gaze swept over the library, something she periodically did during her research. "You all have far more books than we have. Books that we thought were lost," she drawled out slowly. Far too many for a group that had just one witch as a blood ally. Nia's assessment shifted to Ethan and then Sebastian, who'd stepped into the room for the third time. I knew why—he was looking for Ariel. "It seems odd that we have to come here to research it instead of our own library. After all, we are witches."

"Josh is a witch," Ethan pointed out.

"True. But since we are here, perhaps—" She stopped and it was obvious she was trying to find the right words to say that Josh might not be enough. "The Midwest Pack seems to be in need of skills beyond his personal reach. I am confident he will obtain them with our assistance. Providing that assistance would be easier if he'd accept our mark." The mark wasn't an actual one, but the emblem they all carried as a show of their fealty to the Creed. Ariel had offered it to Josh twice. After he'd thrown it at Marcia's feet as a sign that he'd rejected them, he seemed hesitant to accept it again. I understood, but I had a feeling their patience with him was growing thin and our alliance wasn't as beneficial to them as it had proven to be to us. One witch was an asset, nine was a force to reckon with.

"Perhaps you are right," Sebastian said. "About the books. I can't make Josh's decision for him but maybe we can work out a deal with the books. I'll have to discuss it with Ariel and Josh."

Nia's face brightened. I scrutinized Sebastian's words; he'd discuss it with Ariel and Josh, but would it be on his deathbed ninety years from now?

She must have sensed duplicity as well. "I'm sure Ariel would appreciate it. Perhaps I'll take these two as an act of good faith. If you find two others that are more suited for us, we can work out a trade."

"Nia," London said, giving her a look. "Rude."

"I'm not trying to be rude. I enjoy working with you all. The dilemmas you get yourself into definitely stretch our magical muscles, and you're sleeping with Josh, good for you." She directed the latter to London. "It's fine that you want to help your boyfriend—so be it. But us being called in to help you all so often makes this alliance seem very one-sided. It just seems like it would be a nice sign of appreciation to at least offer us something. After all, how does finding an inoculation from whatever you all were poisoned with affect us?"

London's eyes widened at Nia's response but she didn't

say anything, and I had an inkling that London felt the same. She might have been Josh's girlfriend—or whatever they were calling whatever was going on between them—but she was a witch first and part of the Creed, responsible for the health and safety of the witches in the same way that ranked were-animals were for the pack, and that took precedence.

Sebastian's gaze shifted to Josh and then back to Nia, or mini Ariel, because it was quite reminiscent of something she would say. I wouldn't have put it past Ariel to plant that idea in Nia's mind and even coach her on the talking points. Because of her tumultuous and reluctant relationship with us, Nia wouldn't mind addressing it.

"Let me think about it," Sebastian repeated, his tone firmer than before, leaving no room for further debate.

It was a cue that Nia either missed or ignored. "Well, I really hope you can do that within the hour. I'm getting tired, and I think a shot of knowledge from books with spells over a hundred years old might be the little perk I need."

Although amber streaked over his eyes for a moment, Sebastian's smile showed admiration and appreciation.

Dear lord, don't let him have the hots for her *now.* I didn't get Sebastian; the more adversarial a person was, the more intrigued he became. It reminded me of Winter. Ethan wasn't immune to it, either, pursuing Chris romantically after she'd shot him.

"Point noted." He left without any further discussion.

Sebastian was seated behind his desk by the time I got to his office. Since he hadn't closed the door all the way, I took that as an invitation to enter.

It wasn't.

His brows lifted and he regarded me with belabored interest.

"Did you need something, Sky?" he asked as I took a seat in the chair in front of his desk.

"Yes, I need you to put on your Alpha big-boy pants and fix whatever the hell is going on between you and Ariel."

It was a proud moment for me when he stammered out an "I'm sorry" before reasserting his composed façade.

"You came into the library because you smelled Ariel. I do, too; it's the sweater Nia's wearing. It's Ariel's. I've seen her wear it before."

I wasn't convinced that Ariel hadn't loaned it to Nia. Had her wear it, or at the very least bring it to have Sebastian scent her, only to be disappointed. He and Ariel deserved each other and I wasn't sure if that was a good thing. There were too many strategic maneuvers and games for my liking.

"We need to figure out a way to inoculate us against the Mond. Josh and London haven't been able to do it. When you asked for assistance, she sent two, Nia and London, out of their eight." I paused to let it sink in. "Do you think two of the Creed are better than eight?"

"London and Nia are quite gifted," he acknowledged.

"And when Josh was warded against the Faeries to keep him alive, do you think it would have been as effective with two? Ariel created the spell—the spell that saved his life. We need her. And even if we don't need them all, isn't it better to have too many than not enough?"

He took hold of a pen and rotated it over his fingers, closely studying it. "She's being stubborn and pulling a power play; I will not bend to it."

"Because you're not being stubborn at all," I mumbled sarcastically.

"Did you say something? I think I missed it."

Fine, Mr. Alpha, I'll play your game. "I said, 'because you're not being stubborn at all.' It was sarcasm. You're being needlessly stubborn, and whether she's making a power play or not, a good leader knows when to ask for help." I repeated the very thing that he'd said to her. "We need her help."

"I asked for help. I will not entertain her jealousy."

I sighed heavily. "You're not entertaining her jealousy. You were wrong."

His head jerked slightly. I was sure he hadn't lived this long without being told he was wrong at some point.

Welcome to the real world. People are wrong—often. You are wrong—now.

"If she's uncomfortable with the way I handle relationships with my Alphas, that's her problem, not mine."

"It's not your relationship with *your* Alphas that are in question here. It's your relationship with Joan. If I see you interacting with Ethan like that, I'm going to be a little jealous."

Sebastian grinned and relaxed. As relaxed as a person like Sebastian could ever be. Surely he couldn't believe that people were oblivious to the strange intimacy in their interaction. Touches and looks that were solely theirs. It was as if they shared a secret, a history, or something. I couldn't quite figure it out.

"I have no idea what's going on with you and Ariel, but if you two aren't on the same page, there's more to lose than a night of kiss and tickle."

His brows hiked upwards, amused. "'Kiss and tickle'?"

"I don't claim to know what goes on between you two when you have your 'meetings.' It seems to involve expensive wine, well-prepared dinners, push-up bras, and sexy undies, but it can't interfere with your obligations. You are going to have to put your ego on a shelf and address this. And that's all it is. Your ego. Don't make it more complicated than what it is," I advised.

The pen had stopped dancing and was balanced on one extended finger, while his gaze stayed fixed on me. I was preparing for verbal sparring and being harangued about the number of boundaries I'd crossed and codes of propriety that

I'd broken. Instead he blew out a breath. "You're right," he admitted.

My victory dance was going to have to wait. I hoped I would at least be out of his line of sight before it started. It wasn't going to be pretty or rhythmic. Just my arms flailing and my neck bobbing and my body moving like a spastic puppet's. He let the pen drop to the table.

"I'll address it."

"Good." I eased back in the chair and clasped my fingers over my stomach, ready to bask in my moment of superiority.

"Is there more?" he asked evenly.

Of course there was more. I was basking. I expected something more than his brown eyes shifting periodically to the door. There should have been a speech or something to mark the moment. He should have monologued about how my wisdom and diplomacy had saved the pack. He was a better man for knowing me. How at first, he was lost and my wisdom had led him to the path of victory. Or something along those lines. It didn't have to be a soliloquy.

"Not really." But I was on a roll. I'd just told him to shelve his ego, put his Alpha pants on, and do the right thing, but I was ready to push the envelope even more.

"I don't know anything about you. No one does," I said.

His steely gaze was unwavering as he said, "That's not by accident."

I'm just going to ignore that.

"So"—I leaned forward to the desk, resting my chin casually atop my clasped hands—"what is the deal with you and Joan? I've always imagined a blissful night of passion. She travels with Steven to bring him down for the summer. He's off somewhere —perhaps resting after a long day of being mentored by you— and you two are in the living room talking about the day and that turns into something more."

Sebastian's face was blank, stone blank, giving me no cues as to whether I was even remotely close.

I made another futile attempt. "Was it more? A real relationship? Years of on-again, off-again, and then you two realized it just couldn't work? Two heartbroken people who wanted a relationship to last but just couldn't make it work?"

Nothing. Sebastian was a solid block of emotionless ice, with the exception of the brown that was slowly eclipsing to amber. Wavering between the two colors.

"Was it just a kiss?" And I went on with another spiel that involved a long passionate kiss, them yearning for more but allowing pragmatism to mess things up.

Sebastian cast a look at the door. "Close the door behind you when you leave," he instructed, tersely.

"Of course I will. Now back to Joan." I was about to start on more scenarios that I'd been holding on to when he hit me with arctic, steely silence. Responding to his defensive posturing, I tried to defuse the situation. "Come on, Sebastian, we are having a moment. Let's do this!"

His face crinkled into a glower of dismay. "*Moment?* We are having a moment?"

"Yes, I've set you on the right path with Ariel. I've counseled you and we've shared a friendship moment. It's time for you to spill. I wonder if my imagination is anything like the reality."

"I'm sure most stories are less dramatic than the ones you've invented," he offered in a cool, placid voice. "Nothing you can come up with will be as scandalous as what I've heard said about us."

I studied him with renewed interest, a curiosity that needed to be sated. "I bet it's probably more romantic. You two walking in the meadow, close but not hand in hand, *yet*"—my eyebrows arched as I studied his stolid expression—"discussing how amazing Steven is, which is the truth, and you realize you don't want to discuss Steven. You kiss her and you sense she wants the same thing. You make passionate love, right there in the meadow. Then you two lie there, basking in the warmth of the day, enjoying the post-sex euphoria. Am I even close?"

Eyes narrowed, he leaned in, his baritone voice deep and foreboding. Peeking through was the wolf ready to strike. "Like I said, far more dramatic than anything that is real." Amber rolled over his eyes. A nonverbal warning. "In a minute you are going to be on the other side of the door. Will you walk out or …" He left the rest to my imagination. He looked as menacing as his words, his voice husky and ominous. "Pick your poison, Sky."

"Geez, I was just chatting with you. If you wanted me to leave, all you had to do was ask," I said in a light, airy voice, feigning a precocious innocence.

"Are you still pretending that Sebastian looking at the door isn't an invitation to leave? Why do you make it so hard on yourself?" asked Steven's familiar voice.

I'd like to say I handled seeing him with a certain level of dignity befitting a Beta's mate, with a poise that would make anyone proud, instead of letting out a high-pitched squeal before running at him. There wasn't anything dignified about my greeting as I ran at him and hugged him. I slammed into him so hard, he expelled an exaggerated cough. "I can't breathe," he teased.

"You're fine. You can go six minutes without oxygen," I informed him, keeping my hold on him. Giving in to it, he returned the hug and rested his chin on top of my head. I gave him several sharp pecks on his cheek.

He winced. "Six minutes, huh? Good information to know. Do you plan on depriving me of oxygen for five more minutes?"

I pulled away. His hair had grown out, and it was a little unruly from doing what he was doing at the moment, running his fingers through it. The light shadow of a beard never achieved what he wanted, to look more mature and camouflage his cherubic features. Just a few days back in the South, and his drawl was a little more pronounced. That gentle lilt that made everything seem so polite and sweet. Whatever was going through his mind aged him and chiseled away at his ethereal beauty.

"What's wrong?"

His lips lifted in a small smile and I knew whatever he was about to tell me wasn't going to be the truth. It was the confidence he gave me when the world was aflame and he was trying to protect me from it. "Nothing."

There was a long, strained silence between us. It felt so wrong, like it wasn't Steven but some random guy that looked like him, moved like him, and spoke like him but couldn't duplicate the connection we had. I frowned.

"Stop." He flicked my lip lightly. Another thing the stranger before me had duplicated that Steven and I used to do to get each other to smile.

The constant silence between us was becoming annoying. But I was afraid if real words were spoken, I'd hear something I didn't want to.

"Have you eaten?"

I shook my head.

"Let's go get"—he looked at his phone—"a late lunch, early dinner."

Steven looked surprised and crestfallen when I declined. If we didn't talk, then it wouldn't happen. It was illogical, but I grasped at it for all it was worth. I didn't want to have this dinner or have the talk. I knew it was the talk I was regretting. The one where he told me that he was leaving. He couldn't leave. I just couldn't handle it.

With a wry smile he said, "Sky, let's grab something to eat."

This wasn't a casual dinner, something we'd shared many times before. I could feel it in our clumsy interaction, the heaviness in his voice, and his posture—his hands shoved in the pockets of his jeans while he shifted from side to side. He had something to tell me, and I knew it wasn't good. The juvenile part of me took over, the part that wanted to believe that if I didn't hear it, it wouldn't happen. I wasn't above sprinting away from him with my hands clamped to my ears, screaming at the top of my lungs so I'd never hear a word he said.

The Sky that had to do the mature thing agreed, with a half-hearted nod. I knew he was going to tell me he was moving back to the South. I followed him out of the house, deflated.

CHAPTER 20

*S*teven put down his drink, tea with so much sugar in it
that undissolved particles floated at the bottom. My
teeth ached each time he took a sip.

"You're having a wedding," he said, bemused.

"How did you know?" I asked, shocked, since we'd agreed to
it just twenty-four hours ago.

"David called me to ask me ... no, *tell* me I'm in the bridal
party. I'll be walking you down the aisle, and apparently Sebastian is officiating the ceremony." He chuckled, probably
wondering, as I was, whether they had asked our Alpha or just
appointed him. I brushed that idea aside. Of course they hadn't
asked; Sebastian would receive an impromptu visit from them
with instructions on where he could be ordained, along with a
copy of the script. Several variations of the scene unfolded and
brought a smile to my face.

"I hope Sebastian doesn't bite them," I said, laughing.

"Even if he does, I don't think it will stop them."

The server brought my chocolate cake, his Texas fries, and a
bowl of jalapeños. Steven unceremoniously dumped the latter
on the pile of fries, melted cheese, and chunks of bacon.

"You want some?" he asked, nudging the plate in my direction.

"No, I don't want any of your pepper fries. And you can't have any of my cake," I said in anticipation of his fork making its way onto my plate. That was another one of our things. If one of us offered the other food, it was a tacit agreement that the other would do the same. The problem with the arrangement was that, most of the time, I didn't want any of his weird concoctions, which were always the worst variations of whatever was on the menu.

"I don't want your cake," he shot back. "You look like a feral animal—I might lose a hand if I come near it."

I made a deep guttural sound in an attempt to sound like a rabid animal.

Steven's familiar laughter just made my heart ache more, knowing that the times I would hear it in person were coming to an end. "You sound like a snarling teacup puppy. Like you are going to attack the hell out of my ankles," he teased. "You still don't have the menacing look down." His flashed over his face. I'd seen it before and never liked what I'd seen afterward. I was sure others regretted seeing it. The difference from his usual sweet cherubic appearance was unsettling.

I was just about to tell him how much I was going to miss him when he blurted, "Taylor will be transferring to this pack."

"What?" I asked, confused.

"Taylor, the were-cheetah from the Southern Pack—"

"I know who she is ... but is that why we're here, so you can tell me that Taylor is moving to our pack?" I didn't want to seem callous, but I didn't care. "You're staying?"

He nodded. "Of course."

Shoving a forkful of cake in my mouth, I was still confused. It wasn't that I was complaining about having dinner with Steven; I wasn't. I was expecting him to tell me more than the woman I'd walked in on him, well, let's just say naked-sparring with, was transferring to the Midwest.

"Why are you telling me this?"

He ran his hand through his ginger waves. "Ethan made me … he didn't really make me … it's just that … Sky, you really need to find a way to control your anxiety. It makes everyone crazy, and number one on that list is Ethan. Quinn and the Worgen pack can't deal with it yet. They're new and aren't used to filtering such dominance. You have to be aware of it. Taylor will need to learn as well."

"And Ethan?"

Steven started to roll his eyes in annoyance and stopped mid-response. "Ethan can bear your emotions just fine. You being unhappy seems to send him into a fu— freaking spiral. Apparently, Ethan can't bear for Princess Sky to be discontented." That time he completed his exasperated eye roll.

I scoffed. "That's not it. I give you my word. That's not it at all. He's fine with me being unhappy and irritated and gets great pleasure in being the source of it. He digs his heels in on the weirdest things."

I told him about the ring incident.

"He wouldn't put on the ring?" he asked incredulously.

I nodded. "Just out of pure defiance. How hard was it for him to just put the ring on my finger? He was so resolute you would have thought I'd asked for his kidney."

"How hard was it for you to put the ring on yourself?" Steven asked with a smirk.

"I didn't want to!"

"Yeah, he's the stubborn one picking unnecessary battles." Steven laughed. "You two are hilarious. You make him more lighthearted." He downed his brown sugar water and pushed the empty glass to the middle of the table so the server could see it when she returned.

"I don't think you are using that word right," I rebutted.

He chuckled. "I'm using it right. He's more comfortable. Maybe he feels he can relax, now that he's not working so hard to hide how he feels about you. Or just fighting it period. It had to be exhausting." His lips hitched into a mirthless smile and he shrugged. "We all could see it. He wasn't fooling anyone with the incessant meetings and obvious info-gathering inquiries about our interactions and the progression of our relationship for the sake of the 'pack's health.' Something he had never been concerned about with anyone else and their so-called 'close' relationship."

That was the segue I needed. "What's the deal with your mother and Sebastian?"

A cool, blank look became his mask. "Sebastian and my mother? Nothing."

"*Nothing?* The special treatment he gives her. The touches. The gentleness that he has with her that he has with no one else."

"He's gentle with you," he retorted defensively.

"I was injured. He thought I was dying."

"And so was my mother." He flushed, and I quickly realized I needed to change the subject. Whatever it was, I was still speaking of his mother and asking him to give me scandalous information about her and Sebastian. Someone that he had an oddly paternal relationship with.

"Whose idea was it for Taylor to transfer?" I asked, scooping another forkful of cake into my mouth. The traces of his embarrassment with the topic eased from his face, replaced by pride.

"Mine. Mom's a great mentor for her, but since the incident with Ethos, Taylor is just guilt-ridden, blaming herself for my mom getting hurt. It's just not good for either one. She likes it here in the Midwest. She has friends from college here, and I think we'll be a good fit."

"And, she has you?"

Giving me a noncommittal shrug, he responded drily, "Yeah,

we get along fine. She's tough and quick. I like sparring with her —she challenges me."

"Yeah, you do," I mumbled with a wily smile. "Naked sparring."

"You're never going to let me live that down, are you? We were just practicing, trying to release some pent-up energy—it just happens. It happens more frequently than you think."

My mouth twisted in doubt. I didn't care how many times people wanted me to believe that kicking, punching, and fighting someone to the point the person submitted was an aphrodisiac. It was a strange perversion that Ethan, Winter, and apparently Steven had. *Weirdos.*

I couldn't believe how I felt, knowing Steven was staying. There was still a nagging feeling that he would leave eventually, but for now, he was staying. Things were different since I'd mated with Ethan. I didn't care about all the rules of propriety— he did. Steven liked the pack's rules. In a way, there was comfort in the structure. In all the chaos, there were still the pack rules.

Ethan looked up from his papers when I walked in and smiled at the carryout bags.

"Dinner for me?" he asked.

I nodded. "Of course." But I figured he'd already eaten. Dinner with Steven had taken a long time—five hours. Once I put the food away, I plopped down in the seat next to Ethan.

His nostrils flared. He leaned into me, inhaled, and frowned. "Tell me, when you and Steven are together are you engaged in some weird Tantric hug-fest? You smell like him. It's like you two are one." He attempted to make his statement light and lively, but there was an undercurrent of steel and tinges of jealousy.

I stroked his cheek. "It was just a hug. He won't come near

me. You all have successfully indoctrinated him in all the pack's rules and heightened his sensitivity to impropriety. We don't sit on the same side of the booth anymore."

"That's good, because that's just odd for anyone to do if there's a seat available across from each other." His lips quirked. "Winter's right, you two are pretty peculiar."

"What's weird is me having to get a crown, because apparently I'm the pack's 'princess' and you can't bear for me to feel any form of discomfort, pain, or denial in any way," I said in a dramatic, haughty voice. "Interesting. That's going to be a full-time job, protecting me from life."

His brows furrowed. "What?"

"You told Steven he needed to tell me what was going on with Taylor's transfer."

Ethan chuckled, amused. "I live for the day that you feel some discomfort from Steven and my brother. The day when you ask them to do something and they actually say no. I'd like a front-row seat for that monumental event. Sky denied. Price-less. But it will never happen because they can't bear to see the face. Steven hadn't made a decision and it bothered you. You didn't know if he was coming back and that's where your anxiety was coming from. It wasn't fair to you or the pack. He'd hold off and try to never tell you because he didn't want to see the face. If he wasn't coming back, you needed to know so you could deal with it. Steven leaving would trigger a grieving process for you."

There was a long stretch of silence as he studied me. "Steven may eventually leave this pack—you know that, right?"

I swallowed a ragged breath but couldn't answer—didn't want to answer.

"He'll be an Alpha one day and I don't want him to be reluctant to do what he needs to because he can't bear to see the face. It's not fair."

"The face—my face." I would rather discuss anything other

than the inevitability of Steven leaving. More changes that seemed to be coming far too fast. I would never want him to decline doing something he wanted for me. But for the life of me, I couldn't imagine why anyone would want the position of Alpha.

Ethan leaned in and kissed me on the tip of the nose. "The face: doe eyes that look like someone just kicked a puppy, demolished a world, broke your heart a thousand times over. Then there's the little puffs you make with your lips. When you finish, a small pout remains, making you look like you'll never know happiness again. I took a vaccine; it doesn't affect me. For a while, I was convinced that you had the power to compel."

"You couldn't have thought that, because it didn't work on you," I objected, pointing out our many less than favorable interactions. There was no way he thought I had the power to compel.

"Exactly." He shrugged. "Then I realized it's just Josh and Steven." He chuckled wryly. "They are Sky weak, or maybe they don't know how to deal with a person like you. It is quite complex. How do you deal with Sky? You never know what supernatural miscreant she'll bring home to fix. A person whose filter is so broken, it doesn't stop her from telling her Alpha to put his 'big-boy Alpha pants on.'"

"You heard about that?" I said with a prim, innocent smile.

"Yeah, I heard about it. And I heard about your inquiry regarding his relationship with Joan."

"So there was a relationship. Do tell?" I turned on the sofa, legs crossed, waiting for more detail.

Ethan returned to looking at his notes. "What did Sebastian tell you about it?"

"He told me to get out of his office, and he wasn't very polite about it," I said in a huff.

"Did your superpower fail you?" he mocked, keeping his focus on the paper. It was a list of spells and at that moment he reminded me of Josh with the intense way he studied them. He didn't have to say it, I knew they weren't right. They'd probably spent most of the day testing them.

"I think Ariel and the other witches need to get involved. This can't be handled lightly."

"I didn't say you were wrong about telling Sebastian what he needed to do, I just can't believe you said it that way." He suppressed the laughter so much, it was reduced to a deep rumble in his chest.

"Sometimes you just have to shoot from the hip." I was feeling especially confident, wearing a large, cocky smile full of bravado. I took out my air guns and fired off a couple of shots.

Ethan tossed the notebook on the table. "Nice." He leaned forward, kissed my cheek, and warm breath breezed against my skin. More soft kisses trailed down my neck, which he followed with little nips. In a graceful, sweeping move he turned on the sofa, legs outstretched, and my back pressed against his chest. The warm kisses continued. I sighed into him, gentle moans escaping at the languid presses of his lips against my skin. He nibbled on the lobe of my ear. I moaned softly.

"The listing realtor that I recommend is named Megan Franks. She'll be e-mailing you the contract. Let me know if you'd like to use someone else. The movers are scheduled next week Friday. Plenty of time for us to pack up your things." Again, his lips pressed against me. "Take a look around the house and see where you'd like to put some of your things."

I scrambled and turned to face him, wondering how we got to this place. A wolfish grin flitted across his lips as he took a few shots with his own air guns in an exaggerated mockery of mine just minutes ago.

"Movers? Realtors? What's going on?"

"Yes, movers. Realtors. We're mated and will be married in less than a month. What exactly are your plans? Do you plan to live here and your place?"

Silent, I took a look around his house, taking in his dark, comfortable furniture, stainless steel appliances, crown molding, granite counters, and expensive-looking art. Hues of brown, tan, and rich chocolate and occasional complements of beige colored the vast space—my home could have fit in two of the rooms. What would I bring from my house that would match his furniture and not disrupt the meticulous décor that his decorator had established?

Were we going to change out my bed for his? After sleeping in his bed, which made me feel like I was being cradled in fluffy cushions and swaddled in satin, I didn't even want to nap in my old bed again. Ethan studied me, his amusement becoming concern as he looked around the house as if he was trying to see it from my perspective.

"We can redecorate and it can be a combination of our styles."

"I love your home."

"*Our* home," he corrected. "Then what's the problem, Sky?"

My attention moved from studying the house to studying him. His face defaulted to impassive, but not before I got a glimpse of the pain.

"I have a chair, I want it. I usually read on it. And I need to bring all my blankets because"—I grabbed the one folded and draped over the back of the sofa—"these are so nice and luxurious I'd feel terrible if I spilled something on them and damaged them. Mine already have stains." I wasn't sure who to blame for them, Steven or me.

I leaned forward, kissed him lightly on the lips, and then rested my forehead against his. "I adore our home—and the fact you are a neat freak so I don't have to lift a finger. It has nothing to do with you. It's another chapter in my life. I seem to be zooming past them all so fast, I find myself digging my heels in, trying to slow things down. I want to live here, with you. I'll have all my things moved in by next week, and I'll contact Megan tomorrow."

He sprinkled me with more light kisses. "Please tell me all your sexy nightwear is still at your house. Because I saw footed pj's yesterday."

"I have so many more of them to bring here," I teased. "So. Many. More. You've seen my sexy clothes. I wore them for you last night."

"The pink tank top with the unicorn and glitter and lime green shorts?" he asked, incredulous.

"It was hot, right?" I asked, my voice tight, forcing back the laugh.

"So hot," he agreed sardonically.

CHAPTER 21

The next evening, I stacked filled boxes in the corner. Winter and I looked at my other two helpers, Trent and David, seated on the sofa, glasses of red wine in their hands and laptops on their laps. Packing my things was better than watching Nia, London, and Josh try spells to nullify the Mond—which failed, one after the other. Since they hadn't been sent more help by Ariel, I assumed that nothing had changed.

"No guys, don't worry about us, we got this. You just sit there with your wine and watch us work," Winter said, placing another large box near the door.

"That's exactly what we plan on doing. We have twenty-five days to plan a wedding, and some of the people involved aren't doing their part," Trent said, directing a sharp, accusatory look in her direction.

With his third glass of wine in hand, he was becoming increasingly mouthy and courageous without his basic filters, which led him to call Sebastian. Sebastian's annoyed, deep baritone resounded over the speaker.

"Did you not receive my e-mails, texts, and voice mails?" Trent asked in a huff.

"Yes, I received them all," Sebastian responded drily.

"I see, and you decided I was just sending them for fun? Get it together. Have you done the paperwork so you can officiate the wedding?"

"Yes, I've officiated a wedding before," Sebastian informed him. His tone held a hint of annoyance and the practiced patience that he'd adopted to handle David and Trent.

"Wonderful." Trent ticked it off his list. "I'm assuming you are ordained as well?"

"Yes."

"Registered with the court?" Trent asked.

"No, it's not required."

"It is as of last year, so do it next week. Just send me an e-mail or text to let me know when the task is complete."

Winter snorted and turned away to keep from laughing. The deep, resounding growl made it sound like Sebastian was in the room with us. Trent made a face, took a long drink from his glass, and kicked his legs up on the table.

"Are you happy with yourself now?" Trent drawled. "I look forward to getting your e-mail." He scanned his to-do list. "After I have that, all I will need is your ceremony script. I can help you with that if you'd like."

"Of course. Is there anything else I can do? It's not like I have a pack to deal with." Sebastian's tone, melodious and saccharine, was filled with strong notes of sarcasm that Trent chose to ignore despite the warning look David gave him.

He was in a state of alcoholic bliss where sarcasm, self-preservation, and tact didn't exist. Floating on his planning-and-wine high, he thanked Sebastian for being a team player.

Returning to his list, he surveyed it, making marks and annotations. "No, that will be all." Trent's tone was breezy with defiance, ignoring the sarcasm-drenched tone of the Alpha.

Trent was ready to take on another battle and looked at

Winter before standing and walking toward her. Brows raised, he pointed his finger at her. "What about you?"

"I got the damn dress!" she muttered, grabbing two boxes and taking them to her car. I had a feeling she wasn't going to return until our helpers were gone. Trent knew it, too, because he walked to the door, leaned out of it, and called out, "Don't forget the shoes." He went back to his spot on the sofa and made another mark on his list.

Two hours later, I plopped on the sofa, taking an inventory of it all. Almost everything was packed up, and in a few days, the house would be empty. There were a few boxes in one corner that I was taking to Ethan's. I had a substantial donation pile: I'd felt the tug of Trent and David's collective look of censure when they'd gone through my boxes, frowning at clothes I was taking that they deemed unacceptable. Making subtle suggestions about me tossing my cute t-shirts and sleepwear.

Sitting cross-legged on the sofa that would be picked up later that day for donation, the realization hit me— I wouldn't have a place. It felt like another chapter of my life was passing and I was on to a new one. Mated and married Sky.

Answering a light knock at the door, I was surprised to see Chris. Her focus went straight to the boxes in the room. Breezily allowing her gaze to run over them, she made a face. I assumed this was a reminder of the pending changes in her life, too. After the Presentation ceremony she'd be expected to move in with Demetrius, the man she "didn't hate."

"Hi," I finally said, pulling her attention from the boxes.

With a frail smile, she handed me a velvet crimson-colored envelope with so many embroidered fancy curls and sweeping lines it was hard to imagine my name was hidden within them. I broke the custom seal. *Come on, Sky, you can do this without comment or mocking.* But I couldn't. I rolled my eyes dramatically as I shifted my weight to give Trent and David a better view of the envelope; instead of mocking it, they were intrigued.

Inside, on thick vellum, was more elaborate script, written in soft gold and inviting me to attend the Presentation of Christina Rose Leigh. I said her name softly to myself. A delicate name seemed unfitting for such a Presentation. Christina Rose Leigh wasn't the Mistress to a man that she "didn't hate," whose life would change in thirty days when she became the Mistress of the North, to be either revered or hated by the masses. Her vacant, dismal stare made me feel as if she felt the same way.

This couldn't have been the life Christina Rose Leigh's parents saw for her, but it was doubtful I had the one my mother had planned for me, either.

"It's not during your wedding, it's after," she fumbled out. My eyes narrowed in inquiry, wondering how she knew I was getting married and the date. Her gaze shot in Trent and David's direction. I gave them a disapproving look and they flushed.

"I'm not coming to your wedding." Nervously she wiped her hand on her pants. "I just feel … I don't think it would be appropriate," she explained.

Dammit, they had *invited her.* Again, I shot them a stern scowl. Ethan would have a mantrum if she came, but that wasn't my biggest concern—that would be Demetrius. In a month, she would be introduced to the world as the new Mistress, and they would be a couple. If she attended, he'd probably be her plus-one. I didn't want Demetrius at my wedding, and I didn't want to attend the Presentation because he was the host.

Sensing my apprehension, she swallowed several times. I could feel her looking at me as I studied the invitation. I glanced up. She was fidgeting. I didn't think I'd ever seen her nervous.

"Sebastian and Ethan will be there. It's normal for the head of every denizen to be present. I figured Ethan would bring you … but … I … I'd really like you to come."

It was more than a simple invitation, it was a gentle entreaty. She inhaled an unneeded breath, displaying her difficulty with truly acclimating to her vampirism.

"Everyone will be there. It's social protocol. But I wasn't sure if you would come with Ethan or he'd come alone." Chris was blabbering. It shocked me.

Nervously, she chewed on her bottom lip, and there was a hint of a glow to her nose and cheeks. Like the vampire's version of a blush.

"Of course. I'd love to come," I said.

At my acceptance, the nosey duo had inched their way over, admiring the invitation and Chris, who was dressed in a different vampire-y outfit. She might not have truly adjusted to being a vampire, but she dressed like the star of a campy vampire flick. Her short-sleeve peplum shirt with a plunging neckline was made of soft burgundy leather. Her jeans were bound so tightly to her body I imagined her inhaling, hopping around and, just to get them on, doing a gymnastic program that would have taken home at the very least a silver medal. Tall boots that couldn't possibly be comfortable completed the ensemble. I noticed on one of her fingers a black, expensive-looking band with a unique multicolored stone in it.

Trent felt that once he knew a person's name, a little thing like personal space was unwarranted. He took hold of her hand and admired the ring with interest.

His invasion and lack of adherence to social norms on personal space usually shocked people into compliance, and Chris wasn't an exception. Eyes narrowed, she watched him while he examined the ring.

"This is a natural alexandrite, isn't it?" he breathed out in amazement, leaning in more to examine it.

Both he and David were in awe of the ring. Based on the state of admiration and fascination it put them in, I knew it wasn't a little stone that had been purchased at a mall jewelry store. And if it was a gift from Demetrius, it was undoubtedly very expensive and one of a kind.

"It's an apology," Chris admitted casually.

Studying it, Trent asked, "What exactly did Demetrius have to atone for with such a gift? It must have been quite an event." He took another look at the large stone on her finger.

She shrugged. "He was apologizing for making me stab him," she said casually. Too casually for someone admitting to an assault. That shocked the smile off Trent's face. Was it a perverse dark joke with the intention to shock, or a disturbing confession? Her face didn't give a clue, but I knew it was the latter. Demetrius and Chris had a dysfunctional, volatile relationship that would send normal people running in the opposite direction. I recalled how disturbing it was to see the lust and warped display of adoration that had overtaken Demetrius's onyx eyes when Chris had held a knife to his throat.

Demetrius, in all his depravity, was drawn to her explosive responses. It was highly likely that she'd stabbed him and he'd rewarded her reaction—or rather overreaction—with an expensive ring.

Trent was still wide-eyed, and when she smiled and bared her fangs I thought he'd scuttle away, as a normal person would when faced with the confession of a felony and fangs. But not my enamored, enthralled guests. He and David both stepped back and gave her another once-over that renewed their fascination with the future Mistress of the North.

No, you don't smile at the woman who just said she stabbed her lover. You run. Run like hell. Run like a hatchet-wielding psycho is after you.

But they didn't. Instead they pulled on their amiable smiles and continued to look yearningly at the invitation.

"So, this event, is it just for ... can humans come? It seems like it would be okay for us to come, since we already know everything," Trent wheedled.

"We'll sign a nondisclosure agreement," David added.

That wasn't how this worked. That wasn't how any of this worked. Panic slammed into my chest. Did they think the otherworld was a business, with PR people and NDAs? Had they not been paying attention over the past few years?

"Well ..." Chris looked at me as if she was trying to gauge what I wanted. Apparently my "hell no" look needed some work. She frowned. "Traditionally just the garden attend—"

"But you don't seem like a traditional type of woman," David flatteringly reminded her. He flashed her his brightest smile, ingratiating but confident, appealing to the little narcissist that he believed lurked in everyone. "I see a trendsetter. A woman who plays by her own rules."

Chris wasn't falling for the flattery, and the unyielding smirk on her face aptly demonstrated that. "You seem like the type of man whose smooth talk and adulation probably ensure he's never denied anything he wants." She moved closer, exposing the edges of her fangs. "I'm the type of woman who loves denying men like you."

"We give you our word, you will not have to worry about us," David promised, more beguiled than before.

They were relentless. Trent and David weren't drawn just to the vampires' mystery and seduction, but to the promise of an extravagant gala that only they could deliver. The velvet-enclosed invitation, written in what I was starting to believe was real gold, was just the precursor to an experience they weren't likely to deny themselves. Trent ran his fingers over the smooth envelope.

"Sky needs us there," he assured.

"No, I don't!" I blurted.

"Yes, you do. Ethan and Sebastian will be there doing the whole supernatural diplomacy thing. Rubbing elbows with others, spending the night mingling, and you'll be alone. But we will have your back. We'll be there for you, someone to talk to. If we aren't there, who will you talk to?"

I'll talk to the dust on the walls.

Amused by the effort, Chris watched Trent and David plead their case, their minds whirring for every possible argument to ensure them a spot at the vampire celebration.

"I'll leave it to Sky. If she would like to bring you two, then you are more than welcome to attend."

With a sly smile, she left. It would have been better if she'd said no. But since the address was on the invitation, I wasn't positive they wouldn't just show up, and she knew that, too.

"Will you at least think about it?" David begged.

"Sure," I said, with no intention of giving it a second thought.

"Promise?" Trent urged. "Real thought. There's no way anyone would touch us with the big bad wolves present. A man who buys a woman a thirty-thousand-dollar ring for stabbing him, sends invitations like that, and has an event at the McCallister Mansion isn't going to have a party without ensuring it will be safe. This is upscale on a level I'll never have the chance to see again. Please don't take this from me," he beseeched, with a twinge of harrowing sorrow, as if he'd been left bereft of something vital to life.

It was a freaking party, not breath, water, or food—the actual things he needed to survive—but the way he looked, those things were trivial. The Presentation was the breath of life for him.

Saying no was going to be so hard.

CHAPTER 22

"*A*nd then they made me feel like I was being unreasonable for not wanting them to hang out with vampires. Like they couldn't understand that dressing in fancy gowns and nice menswear doesn't change the fact that they are vampires!" I was complaining to Ethan, stopping only to take sips from my martini. It had been two days since Chris's invitation, and Ethan had heard this at least four times. He let me vent without a response. But this time he was distracted by the witches on the dance floor. They were dealing with the energy from the failed spells that they had been working on all morning. Those not on the dance floor were perched on stools at the pack's bar, finding comfort or anxiety relief at the bottom of a glass.

London was drowning herself in the hypnotic beats of the music as she danced. Her hips and arms rhythmically moved with the music. Her body whipped, gyrated, and spun, throwing off the five failed spells they'd tried. Josh watched her from a few feet away, periodically taking sips of a gold liquid in his glass, doing a poorer job of brushing off the failure. Steven stood close to the stage, sullen and tired-looking from volunteering to be the subject of the spells and changing multiple times in succession.

Nia was probably somewhere in a chair at home, curled up with the two books that Josh had agreed to give the Creed. One look at the greedy interest she'd displayed as she perused the books and I knew she'd be spending the night getting more acquainted with the information in them.

Winter was at a table in the corner shooing away her third male suitor of the night. What about her fixed scowl and I-don't-want-to-be-bothered glare would make anyone even consider approaching her? She hadn't given the last guy even a chance before she said, "Go away."

"BE NICE," I texted her.

She responded by multitasking, using her middle finger to scratch the tip of her nose while letting me know what she thought of my request.

Ethan turned from watching them to me. Leaning in, he pressed his lips to my forehead, stubble from his chin grazing my skin. "It has to be hard to have someone want to go into danger while you try desperately to stop them," he commented quietly, placing light kisses on my temple, my cheek, my lips. His long fingers splayed over my waist, pulling me to him. "I can only imagine the challenge of seeing the potential for danger and having that person totally ignore it." Another kiss, an attempt to soften his censuring words that were intertwined with his brand of sarcasm and snark.

I stepped back and narrowed my eyes on him. "It's not the same thing." I jutted out my jaw defiantly.

"Really," he drawled haughtily. "Please, Sky, tell me how different it is?" His gunmetal eyes smoldered with smug bewilderment. I knew that look: ready and set for the debate. The litigant—armed with enough evidence to bury me. It was easy to forget his legal background until I was about to argue with him.

Disgusted, I growled my displeasure while rolling my eyes. Ethan bent down, nipped at my ear, and whispered, "Did I just win?"

"No," I snapped. "I'm right because I am."

"Ah, yes. The 'I'm right because I am' argument. It's one of your most insurmountable defenses."

"You're neither funny nor clever," I huffed, rolling my eyes and directing my attention to the performance in front of me. And it was indeed a performance.

Kelly was at the opposite end of the dance floor from London. Kelly was a prism, absorbing the music and becoming one with its rhythmic beats. Formally trained in dance, she was a sight to watch. Her lithe, sinuous, and graceful movements were a physical expression of the music, something that defied simple dancing. Gavin was out on the floor reluctantly moving with her. While dancing he lost the fluidity that commanded his movement in human and animal form. He was disjointed and stiff. And as mesmerizing as it was to watch Kelly dance, it was more entertaining to watch him lumber and twitch his way through each song. Onlookers probably wondered if it was the beginning of a neurological event. Gavin was enjoying Kelly, but not the activity.

"I believe Kelly can get people to do anything," I said, hopping onto my chair and spinning to face my drink to take a sip.

Ethan glanced down at his buzzing phone. "I wonder if Kelly can get David and Trent to leave me alone?" he grumbled.

"What do they want now?"

"I told them I owned a tux, but apparently since one person in this damn city has seen me in it, one who won't be at the wedding, I can't possibly wear it again." He took a long draw from his glass, Scotch neat, and signaled the bartender to bring another. "You think they're being a pain to you? They're pains in my ass."

"The polite thing to say is they are enthusiastic and determined."

He shrugged. "They are enthusiastic and determined to be pains in the ass."

I was a little smug, watching him deal with the same frustration I'd been feeling for the past few days. He'd never looked so beleaguered before. His phone buzzed again, and he growled at it. Relieving him of his trauma, I looked at the phone to see picture after picture of tuxes. "I like this one. It'll look good on you."

A hubristic smile slowly unfolded.

"If you say 'everything looks good on me,' I won't run interference and you will be dealing with Trent and David yourself," I threatened.

His lips twitched at the effort to wipe away the smile. He positioned himself as if he was allowing me to get a full look at him. He *was* very good-looking—something he knew and didn't need reinforced. "I don't really think I need to say it, now do I?"

I rolled my eyes and returned the message, then read the response that came just seconds later. "You have to have it fitted. He said he'll text you the time and day."

"Of course he will. And then he'll keep texting until I reply."

I guessed he was rethinking handing over the reins to our overly enthusiastic planners.

His face became pensive, and I knew he wasn't thinking about anything regarding the wedding. Four spells had failed to inoculate us. The Mond had been dispersed among three people who hated us and were set on destroying us. But how would they use it? Would Samuel use it to get the Clostra? Would he out us using the Mond or try to remove magic from the world, including taking away our ability to control our animal form? Ethan was convinced that would kill us. I wasn't, but either way, we'd be human. Years ago, that would have been ideal; now it seemed like losing a part of me. Reducing me to half a person, rendering me incomplete.

I could feel Ethan's eyes on me, and I attempted to unburden myself.

"They already have a location for the wedding," he said. I knew he was redirecting me to something less tragic than the place that my mind had wondered to.

What about the other witch, Marcia's advocate—her acolyte, Rayna? What was her game plan? Was it to just out us in retaliation? Did she believe that what the humans would have in store for us would be worse than anything she could subject us to?

"They also have the flowers and a caterer," Ethan said, interrupting my thoughts.

"David texted me about it already."

"Based on the invoice, I'm assuming each person involved is a graduate of Le Cordon Bleu," Ethan complained, taking another sip from his glass. I smiled at the French accent, his pronunciation indicative of the numerous languages that he spoke.

David and Trent had expensive tastes, and they'd thrown caution to the wind since someone else was footing the bill.

"I can't believe they got so much done in such a short time." It was impressive, but I couldn't say I was surprised. I expected it from them because I knew the moment I'd shown them the ring, they had picked out a dress, location, and at the very least flowers.

"Where are we going to honeymoon?" Ethan asked absently, intently studying the room.

Honeymoon? With the way things were going, I considered it a leap just to have a wedding without incident. Taking on a honeymoon with everything that was going on was inconceivable. I didn't want to leave only to return to a disaster.

His expression changed. Noticeably tensing, he put his glass down on the bar.

"What's the matter?" I asked.

He made a face as he scanned the room. "In the past eight minutes there has been an influx of people that I don't recognize. Something's off. They don't really fit in here. Do you smell it?" He inhaled again.

I shook my head and breathed in deeply, picking up the strong scent of alcohol, which was expected. One of the draws of the bar was the stronger drinks. Were-animals also attracted people in a nebulous way that couldn't be described in simple words. Even if human patrons couldn't see or convey the enigmatic draw, it was there. A unique dynamism that enthralled and enticed. There was something primal that spoke to a person and a raw sexuality that led to the seduction of the club. The mixture led people to believe they were going to have a night like no other. And Josh played a part in the bar's appeal that extended past the magic he wielded. Or perhaps his charisma and magic were so entwined that they ensnared people in a way that couldn't be described.

Taking another whiff of the air, I smelled musky cologne, perfume, alcohol, and pheromones. The scents of fruity drinks and juices also soaked the air. Another sniff and I got a hint of metal, grapefruit, and juniper. It was faint, interlaced with the other scents; if Ethan hadn't said something, I'd have attributed it to the cologne.

Again, Ethan scrutinized the room, and his eyes landed on a cluster of people off in the corner to the left. "New faces."

We had a new band and they had a large following. The new faces didn't bother me.

"I don't think that's a big—" I stopped abruptly as I watched the scene unfold, my mind trying to grasp what was happening and how to react. Ethan and I moved at the same time, but it was too late; nothing could be done. My heart raced as several people moved toward the other were-animals. Dust was released and it kicked up in the air. At the potent smell I stopped, grabbed several napkins off a table and covered my mouth.

It was too late for the others. People screamed as chaos unfolded before them. Gavin fell first, his body convulsing with spastic movements and his eyes flooding with green. A man just a few feet away smiled, his phone aimed as he waited for Gavin to change. Steven ran for Josh's office and others followed his lead. Kelly tugged Gavin to his feet.

London's eyes were wide, taking in the scene. They bounced over the room, seeing exactly what I was seeing—people wondering why a small group of people in the club had gone into convulsions while others ran, looking pained. Two people wearing cruel smiles and holding up phones jumped into the path of several were-animals seeking safety, trying to avoid being exposed. London's lips moved fervently, then she flicked her hand, and a small fire ignited the napkins she'd dropped in the middle of the floor.

People screamed "fire" and rushed for the door. A bartender grabbed a fire extinguisher and put out the small fire in the middle of the floor. Josh touched a few of the chairs, igniting the wood. As other fires flared throughout the club, the occupants raced for the exits.

Familiar magic pulsed through the air as the sprinklers came on, drenching everything and dampening the various smells in the room. Sirens screeched as fire trucks approached the building. Ethan and I headed toward Josh's office, and Josh and London moved toward the door for damage control. I followed the powerful stream of magic that was retreating out the door, following the crowd. *Samuel.*

The smell of fear was just as strong as the magic. Wet from the sprinklers, I navigated the crowd, being shuffled and slammed by others rushing out the door, until I was outside. I eased around the corner, through the narrow path between the buildings, where the magic was so strong it overpowered the air.

"Samuel, show yourself," I demanded.

A strong arm clasped me tightly around the waist and pulled me into a muscled chest. "As you wish," he whispered against the nape of my neck.

CHAPTER 23

$\mathcal{I}$ didn't wait for the world to stop spinning or my stomach to settle. Once I had the sensation of ground firmly under my feet, I spun around and put my hand to the chest of the person holding me and pushed magic through him. It was indiscriminate, powerful magic—unexpected.

Samuel was pushed back as though he'd had a bungee cord strapped to his back that had been stretched too far. A kaleidoscope of emotions flared over his face, and his mouth was an O as his arms windmilled. He choked out a grunt as he plowed into the ground. He quickly came to his feet and erected a protective field. I thrust more magic at him, battering it. Still wide-eyed, he stood confidently behind his bastion of protection. Eyes narrowed, I approached, studying it, giving myself a moment to pore through the various spells in my mind and the defensive magic I had available.

Samuel's frustration at what had happened was palpable as I stalked around the circular defense that enclosed him. His eyes were laser-focused on me, studying me with poorly suppressed disgust and umbrage.

"We need to talk," he eased out through clenched teeth.

MCKENZIE HUNTER

I tapped on the barrier, sending a little spark of magic that made the wall waver violently. I knew it wasn't enough to break it, but he stiffened at the waves that made his magical cocoon spastic.

"You've given in to the magic, haven't you? A beast that presents itself as a woman now has magic." It was what he didn't say that mattered. *Abomination.* He considered me an abomination.

"What do you plan to do with the Mond?" I asked, positioning myself directly in front of him. Ethan had slipped out of my own protective field with ease. I figured if he could slip out of one, I could slip in. Samuel was going to tell me how to get the Mond so we could destroy it.

Death. I could be death. I pressed the palm of my hand against the barrier, feeling its liveliness, its existence, on my skin. Concentrating, I drew out what made it come to life and stopped its metaphorical heart. My hands slipped through. Magic slammed into my side, battering against my ribs. I stumbled to the side. I was hit again by something that felt like hellfire. Clenching my teeth, I bit back the pain as I was tossed to the ground.

Pinned to the ground, I tried to shift as a woman moved into my line of sight. I could tell she had experience with magic—dark shadows of it consumed her deep brown eyes. Despite the dim light given off by the moon, I could still see a hint of a glow on her peach-colored skin. A pleasing oval face was hardened by a deep-seated scowl. Even the faint lines around her mouth looked angry and embittered. This had to be Rayna.

"I told you to be careful with her," Rayna snapped, her eyes narrowing on me as I struggled against her magical restraint. "I have no idea what you witnessed when you met her, but she can't be underestimated. Her or the other one."

I assumed the other one was Ethan.

"I was prepared. She reacted faster than I anticipated,"

260

Samuel said, coming to my right, snapping the iridium cuffs he had in his hand on me. Freed from the magic, I stood as best I could, with my hands firmly secured in front of me.

"Then that means you weren't prepared," she snapped.

If looks had the power to kill both of them would be annihilated. They were fuzzy bodies through the slits in my eyes. "Samuel"—then I directed my attention to the other witch —"Rayna."

"You've done your homework," she said, smirking.

"More than you've done yours," I spouted back. I just couldn't believe that anyone would align themselves with Samuel, knowing his ultimate goal was to rid the world of magic.

"What don't I know? That he's a magic-phobe?" She harrumphed, obviously finding his tenet as ridiculous and foolishly naïve as I had. "He's a proponent of this utopia where all the bad things that exist because of magic will go poof and the world will be right as rain." She rolled her eyes, hard. It had to be painful.

Samuel's face was pinched so tight it forced the skin to stretch over bone. Rayna had aligned herself with him out of necessity, not shared beliefs. The pack made strange bedfellows out of people. We were supernatural magnets, forcing opposites to attract. Unifying people for one goal—to "tame" wild were-animals that didn't respect magic or the guidelines of the otherworld.

"You're part of the pack, so I will assume you know their history and that of the Faeries as well as anyone," Rayna started slowly, wandering in front of me as if she was a professor about to give a rudimentary lecture.

She finally stopped and leveled a cool gaze on me. I studied her. It wasn't anger that cascaded over her features, it was frustration and disgust. It wasn't just directed at me. I suspected she hated aligning herself with Samuel, and it was because of me she had to do so.

"You need to remove the were-animals' ability to change. Get the Clostra, find the spell, and make it happen." I didn't respond because I could sense she wasn't finished. "Your magic and whatever magic your mate has needs to be removed or restricted. There isn't any question that you two have been the cause of what has happened over the past year. It reeks of behavior that can only be attributed to were-animals."

She stood in front of me, imperiously delivering her sentence. Her arrogance shattered any possibility of me trying to negotiate and handle this amicably.

I derisively mirrored the look of umbrage and disdain she was giving me. "I didn't realize we had been found guilty of a crime. Please go on. Tell me why I need to commit genocide, because removing our ability to change will kill us—"

"Nonsense. That's just an excuse you all use. Defaulting to the ridiculous notion that it is intertwined with who you are so intricately it can't be separated. That's false."

"Even if it is true, would it be so bad?" Samuel deliberated. We both shot him angry, quelling looks for different reasons. It was clear that Rayna felt she was the lead on this after the fall of the original Creed. After all, she'd descended off her high horse to work with him. A lowly witch who didn't have any affiliation. I supposed the witch camp was now divided into followers of the original rule and the new rule; the deference given a camp depended on your beliefs. New Creed seemed to be team were-animal and lenient toward abnormalities. Old Creed were okay with our annihilation and would do anything to maintain the purity of magic.

"The Mond is an indicator that it's not true. You all can't change back. It's your human side that recognizes you don't want to be in that form, yet it can't take control because it doesn't have control," she said confidently.

I shrugged. "Fine. I was trying to do this amicably, as opposed to telling you what to do with your order. Now I'm forced to be rude. Take your commands, write them ever so neatly on a piece of paper—no, use a scroll. Can you still buy scrolls? Well, if you can, put them on one, and ... well, no need for me to be crass. You know where I want you to put it." I bared my teeth in a smile.

"I have absolutely no desire or need for this to be handled amicably." She jerked her head in Samuel's direction. "He's the one with the idealistic view of this situation." Again, she rolled her eyes. "'Give them a chance.' 'Sky will do the right thing.' 'She's sensible. She sees the world differently.'" She made a juvenile face of disgust and mockery that I would have found funny in any other situation. She thought so little of me, of him. She didn't want this to be conciliatory, and negotiation wasn't an option. It was a command that she expected to be followed.

Her smile sparked frustration that had evolved into anger that I was sure would become a blazing conflagration that would consume the two people in front of me. It would be as painful and torturous as any death by fire. It would not be the smoke that smothered out the light of life. There was no way that my face hadn't gone primal, my eyes predaceous and vicious, because the emotions were so strong it was hard for me to control them. It wasn't because I lacked control, but my patience had been fatigued beyond repair. Instead of strengthening for constant use, it was withering, buckling under the constant assault of people wanting to judge us, kill us, betray us. Strained by constantly dealing with people who dealt with us by way of ultimatums. Overloaded by people wanting me to betray the people I loved.

They saw the look, because I couldn't hide it and wouldn't have even if I could. I contemplated changing and letting my wolf handle them, but iridium was a tough metal and I wasn't positive I could change without injury. I thought too hard about risking the injury for the payoff of getting my teeth buried deep in Rayna's neck.

The ravenous violence I felt was obviously displayed on my face, because Rayna quickly went for a gun that she had concealed in the back of her pants, and Samuel reached for a knife sheathed at his ankle. Guns and knives looked peculiar to me. They were such human weapons. Used by those that didn't have teeth, claws, and magic. I frowned.

"I hate guns," Rayna admitted. "I'd prefer to use magic, but if you shift, I'm left at a disadvantage."

This moment should have been intense, and I should have been more focused on the weapons pointed at me than my "I finally have a rep" fist pump. They didn't want me dead. If that was the case, this scenario would have played out differently. I relaxed noticeably but refused to give them any other displays of concession.

Rayna kept her gun trained on me. "You don't like guns, either?"

I didn't answer.

"You'll have to get used to them, because once you are exposed, that's what the humans will use to manage you all. Guns and their plethora of weapons and the network of denizens who want you all to pay will work around the clock to make the were-animals look like a threat. All we have to do is expose a few. Then they'll wait for the full moon, Mercury, the eclipse, until they find you all. But they won't need that help, because we'll give them a list and help them find all of the were-animals. What happened today at the bar is just the beginning."

We had made alliances with people who had different agendas. Those hadn't been witches at the bar; I was sure they were members of the Red Blood.

"You think magic wielders will be exempt," I pointed out. "They will come for us first and you all next."

"How will they prove it? Even the vampires will be hard to

detect. Thanks to the were-animals' past doings—and we do know it's because of you and Ethan—the vampires don't have daylight aversion. No more of the vulnerabilities they once had. Fangs can be capped if they so choose. But the call to change can't be stopped. With a little nudge, discovery is inevitable."

"You can stop it, Sky," Samuel gingerly appealed to me, his voice a direct contrast to her hard, terse one.

I listened while wondering who was in this cadre of subversives whose goal was simply to get rid of us. Without a doubt, I knew one person who was part of it—Abigail.

"There's nothing to lose. It's the same situation either way. But at least you can control the outcome. The Faeries had been dormant for ages and then they reappeared," Samuel provided.

"They're dead." *Most of them.* I knew they weren't all dead. There was one masquerading as my cousin. But she wasn't among those who wanted to ascend to power. They hadn't come for the protected objects.

"So I hear. But it doesn't erase your role in their emergence or the insurmountable number of things you all have done." Rayna frowned. "Were-animals and magic," she grumbled.

I stared at her in defiance, prepared for the recurring speech about how we didn't respect magic. Were-animals with the ability to perform magic were an abomination. The sky was falling, and surely the were-animals had looked at it wrong and caused it. I'd accept that we'd done our share of shortsighted things, but we'd cleaned them up, dealt with the aftermath.

I extended my arms, cuing her to remove the cuffs. "I'm assuming we are done here. Release me."

Frowning, she eased toward me with caution. Samuel sheathed his knife and magic looped around his fingers, ready to be discharged. *Damn, my rep is badass. This is Sebastian-and-Ethan level of preparedness.*

The grimace still on her face, she moved even closer. "Then you two mated." This was the same level of censure Mason had displayed. Did a newsletter go out when it happened? Did they start their secret group then? Were they expecting our offspring to be shapeshifting Faeries who sucked out the souls of strangers while doing vampire stunts, using the fire from a dormant dragon gene to bake a cake, and employing Godzilla powers to level the city? What the hell did they think Ethan and I were going to produce? Why did they fear our union? It not only infuriated me, it made me a little scared.

Sensing Rayna's careful assessment of me, I kept my expression blank.

"You have five days to comply." In a swift and practiced move, she removed the cuffs and then both were gone.

I started walking west, toward the tug of Ethan's heightened anxiety. My heart pounded in my chest so erratically I finally pulled out the phone and called him. "I'm fine," I said as soon as he answered.

"Good," he said as he exhaled a ragged breath.

"I guess I'll see you in a little while," I said, about to disconnect, when he stopped me.

"Don't hang up. Just stay on."

Really?

"Okay." Walking on the side of the road, my chest was still tight—something that should have resolved. "Ethan, are you okay?"

"No," he admitted, a whispered confession that stopped me in my tracks. Even with the wafer of light from the moon, everything seemed black, bleak. It was because of Ethan's confession. It was watching the foundation waver and knowing the building was just minutes from crashing.

"We were almost exposed today. The witches aren't able to find a spell to inoculate us, and it's just a matter of time before we are publicly outed. We were lucky today; London thought quickly, but I'm just waiting to see if anyone got enough for it to make people speculate. And—" he broke off with a deep sigh.

"You know Samuel is involved?"

"Of course he's involved. We have to fix this some way. We can't let them win."

When Ethan arrived, I got into the car. He leaned in and kissed me once on the lips, then on the forehead, before resting his against mine. "You're okay," he breathed.

"They're more afraid of me than I'll ever be of them." I settled into the soft leather. The building was crumbling and I could feel it in the way Ethan grasped my hand, too hard, as if he feared I'd be snatched away again. It didn't loosen until I said his name.

Josh's office wasn't small, but the menagerie of animals in it made it look diminutive. Kelly and Gavin were tucked in the corner, Gavin's massive panther lying over hers. A coyote curled behind the door, and two wolves, a leopard, a hyena, and an ocelot covered the rest of the floor. All of them resting after being forced into a change. Trying to recover the energy from the fight they'd lost.

"Can you change back?" Ethan asked loudly enough to jerk them out of their lethargic state. Steven was the first to try; he twitched a couple of times, but gave up the fight and plopped back on his paws.

Ethan started toward him, I assumed to help him change back, but I touched his arm to stop them. "Let's see if they can."

Everyone was stuck in their form. Josh was at his computer, scouring the Internet, trying to find out anything about the night. Two of the three phones had been retrieved, but the other person had disappeared. I wondered if he'd had magical help from Rayna, who had shown up after Samuel. I kept speculating on how many alliances had been formed, and who was part of this conventicle.

Josh split his attention between his computer and his phone

as he texted. "Quinn has a list and pictures of the Red Blood; hopefully we can identify them."

But identifying them wasn't enough. They needed to be stopped, and Ethan's sharpened gaze showed he was thinking the same thing. I cursed Gregoire again, wishing Ethan could destroy the land once more.

Nearly forty minutes had passed when Gavin melted into his form, triggering Kelly to do the same. Next, Steven shifted and then the others.

London peeked her head in first and, seeing a group of unabashedly naked people, put her fingers to work to change that. Everyone was soon clothed and looking fatigued.

Josh took a seat on the desk across from London, who was seated at the desk I usually used during work. "We need to figure out a way to inoculate you all against it," he said.

CHAPTER 24

*S*ebastian stared into the palm of his hand, which had just a quarter-sized amount of the Mond in it. It looked so innocuous, and he had the same look as everyone had upon seeing it. How could something that looked so benign be so dangerous?

Ariel studied him and then the list of spells the others had tried over the past few days. Seeing her walk into the library earlier had been a relief, even though there was underlying tension between her and Sebastian. Before, it was undeniable attraction; now it seemed like there was something unresolved. They exchanged furtive glances, and whatever was swapped between the two of them obviously wasn't enough to repair it.

Fighting the urge to pull him aside and ask what had happened, I focused on the help they were giving us. Ariel was talented and within an hour of being with us had come up with three more potential spells. Then there was the nuclear option that she only touched on briefly—Sebastian had quashed it at the mere mention of the outcome—taking away our ability to change except during the full moon, Mercury rising, or a solar eclipse. As far as Sebastian was concerned, it was moot, not even an option.

Ariel frowned and sighed, scanning the paper in front of her. "This one is the strongest of the ones we've tried."

She approached him slowly, knife and small bowl with the other ingredients in hand. He followed her out of the library into the living room, where there was more space. They'd learned the hard way, after several mishaps and violent changes, that more room was needed.

Placing the bowl on the table, she took his empty hand, her eyes fixed on him the entire time as she pricked his finger. Blood welled. She grabbed the bowl and placed several droplets of it in the bowl. "If this works on you, then we can do a global spell and it should inoculate the others. If it doesn't—"

"Then we keep looking," he interjected, refusing to consider the nuclear option.

"Sebastian," she said with quiet understanding, seeing the stress that choice placed on him. Our lives would be irreparably changed. It would weaken our defenses as much as the Mond had. Changing into our animal half protected us from magic, gave us another weapon in our arsenal. It wasn't an option that would be taken lightly.

"Okay, this will work." Her words understandably lacked confidence after a series of failures.

Invoking the spell, she nodded at him and blew the Mond into his face. Nothing. I was momentarily fooled into thinking it was a success until his body stiffened, his eyes flooded a deep amber, and he lurched sporadically until he collapsed onto the floor. His eyes closed and the rapid beating of his heart slowed. He panted as perspiration pooled on his forehead. At the sound of the noise, Ethan and Winter came into the room. Winter's eyes widened when Sebastian convulsed on the floor.

"Stop it," she demanded in an icy voice.

"There's nothing for me to stop," Ariel responded in a low,

calming voice, carefully watching Winter, who was on the brink of losing control. Ethan stopped her when she started to move toward the witch.

"You need to stop it now," she ordered Ariel.

"Winter, if I could do something, I would. I can't stop his change."

Sebastian was indeed changing. It was rough and forceful. It jolted and I heard the bones snap as they prepared to assume the new form. Hair ripped through his skin, and he howled in pain. For several moments we had to watch, helpless to stop his explosive change. The spastic movements were accompanied by the nauseating sounds of his organs repositioning, preparing for the change.

The large wolf sprawled on the floor, panting. Sweat-matted fur clung to his body. Winter moved to his side and sat next to him, gently running her fingers along the flank of his body. Her eyes were like galvanized steel at Ariel's approach, stopping her in her tracks.

Reflexively erecting a protective field around herself and holding her hands up, Ariel said, "I didn't do this to him."

"I know," Winter whispered, watching Sebastian's chest rise in inconsistent measures in time with his ragged breaths.

Winter hissed, a cold hard sound, when I inched forward and then immediately whispered an apology at my surprise. Her desire to protect her Alpha at his weakest overruled her logic. She closed her eyes and took several long, controlled breaths until her rigid posture relaxed. We kept our distance while we waited for him to change.

Half an hour later, Sebastian was sprawled on the floor, naked, covered in a light sheen of perspiration. A change that was usually graceful had been far from fluid. His body had jerked and twitched, aggressively tossing off his wolf form and forcefully taking on the human one. The struggle showed on his distressed body as he lay in the middle of the room. When he pushed to his elbow, Ariel waved her hand to clothe him. Having had his fill of being the recipient of magic, he lifted his hand to stop her.

"I'm fine," he said, pushing to stand and shaking his head at Ethan, who had stepped forward to help him. Silently Sebastian walked away, and for the first time since I'd known him, he looked burdened by his position as the Alpha. Beleaguered by the decision he had to make. We would have to take the final option and prevent our ability to change, other than when we were called to do so.

The Alphas arrived at the pack's house within hours of Sebastian calling the meeting, their faces pensive, as if they knew what it was about. Ethan said they hadn't been given specifics, but Sebastian had called an emergency meeting of all the Alphas and even the head of the extension packs. Ethan stood next to Sebastian, and as the room filled, everyone kept a cautious eye on them. Their stoic faces revealed nothing, but their eyes gave them away. They struggled to silence their animals, who were railing to get out—to protect.

It wasn't primal or predaceous but mournful. The way I suspected they would be when they were taking their final breaths, aware the end was near. My heart was breaking for them. I'd feel it, too. I would miss my wolf; over the years I had bonded with her. She protected me and I valued her; now we'd be separated except for once a month. I reminisced over the short but vital moments I had shared with her. Tears stung my eyes, and I blinked them away.

"Sky"—Ethan leaned in to whisper in my ear—"do you need to take a moment?" I looked at the crowd and realized all eyes had moved to me. I hadn't perfected my mask and the room became suffocating with a rise of panic and anxiety. It was at that moment that I understood why Sebastian had told me it was important to keep my emotions in check. They stifled the room, filling it with a dank, acrid smell. I wanted to open a window, run outside, change into my wolf, sprint through the woods, and be overtaken by the smells of oak, dirt, grass, and crisp fresh air.

Their intense looks in my direction were only interrupted when London, Josh, and Ariel entered the room. Interlopers—witches. It heightened the turbulent emotions at play and confirmed the seriousness of the situation.

Sebastian kept his voice even, his emotionless mask firmly in place as he explained the situation. The other Alphas and their Betas weren't able to hide their emotions. Horror, anger, and frustration coursed over their faces.

"Why can't we just find the Mond and destroy it?" asked the Alpha from the West Coast.

"It's not possible. There was too much distributed among Samuel, Rayna, and the Red Blood. There's no way of guaranteeing we'll get it all," Sebastian said in a tight voice. I suspected he was finding it difficult to remain diplomatic and understanding when he was being challenged on his process.

"The options we have are either to come out or give up our ability to change on our own," Joan said in a low voice.

A heavy, protracted silence consumed the room as everyone mulled over the options. It wasn't too long ago that we were faced with a similar situation. Except there had been a sliver of hope that coming out wouldn't be an option.

"Will coming out be so bad?" Fallon asked. Her eyes brightened with a naïve hopefulness that made me realize she was the optimist of the group. Unlike the others, who held humans at low or often no regard, she believed in humanity.

She moved to the middle of the room, looking each person in the eyes, making sure she had their undivided attention. "We are the unknown to most people; but, there are some humans who are aware of our existence. Those people will come forward on our behalf. We've all dealt with humans and they lived, so they know we aren't monsters."

The West Coast Alpha scoffed and waved off her defense with a flick of his hand.

"That's not helpful, Kyle," Joan chided him.

His mahogany eyes roved over her slowly, assessing. Alphas were analytical, but also used to being in total control. Being around Sebastian was the only time they had to relinquish command, and the struggle with it was obvious. Kyle's eyes moved from Joan to Sebastian, who didn't hide his displeasure with Kyle's snide response.

"That was rude and unnecessary, Kyle. But it is being foolishly optimistic to think humans will come forward on our behalf. That people won't fear us," Sebastian responded.

"Or that you won't cause strife in the otherworld," Ariel said. She remained confident and cool under the weight of the hostile gazes that were pinned on her, attempting to quell her, which she ignored. "Coming out is a terrible decision if you have other options, and you do have other options. It's not ideal but your anonymity will be preserved."

Confusion flashed over Sebastian's face. It was quickly masked by his cool guise, but not before Ariel noticed it.

"I'm with you, Sebastian," she said, turning for a moment to look at Joan. "I told you last night that I will support any decision."

The award for pettiness goes to ... drumroll ... Ariel.

"We appreciate your help and your role in helping us deal with this matter, but it is still a pack concern. I'd appreciate it if you would take that into consideration." Leave it to Joan to find a diplomatic way of telling someone to shut up and stay out of pack business.

As polite as it was, Ariel didn't get the hint—or chose to ignore it. "It is your business, but contrary to what Rayna believes, the humans won't stop. Once you expose yourselves, their imaginations will go rampant. All the stories they speculated about or marked off as fantasy will have merit. They will pursue those things. Logic won't rule their actions, paranoia will. People who aren't of the otherworld will be accused, and life will change and turn upside-down." Ariel paused to take several breaths, because the urgency of the situation had spilled into her words. That her emotions were getting the best of her seemed as unexpected to her as it was to us.

"I understand your hesitation to do this because it can't be reversed, but being able to control your animal in the manner that you do now is fairly new. You all will adapt." Ariel directed her statement to Joan. "To save your son, I think it was an option. And I agreed, but honestly, I was confident that a way to protect him without having to expose your existence would be found." She then addressed Sebastian. "I agreed in front of the others because it needed to be done. I know how the were-animals are seen and your enemies are just waiting for a reason to turn against the pack. Honestly, you've made it hard not to hate you."

The room was too tense. The smell of fear was potent and reeked.

"The elves created the Mond, so it only exists because of their magic, right?" Kyle said, hopeful.

"Yes, and in order to make it ineffective, the elves associated with Gregoire and his bloodline would have to die. Like witches', elven magic doesn't die with the person, but is passed down to their descendant. Innocents would be paying for the sins of another. Being penalized for something that they probably wouldn't have done. Not all of the elves are against us. I know you would never suggest genocide or containment for the actions of a few, right?" Josh asked, scrutinizing the West Coast Alpha with searing blue eyes.

Kyle was honest enough not to deny it, but wise enough to

be embarrassed by it. It was a reminder of how irrational fear and self-preservation warp people. It was that fear that drove the witches to commit infanticide and was the force behind the paranoia about me mating with Ethan.

"Can their magic be stopped?" Fallon asked. "If you are able to take away their magic, can't that nullify the Mond?"

Ariel started to speak but quickly stopped and considered it. "I don't know," she admitted. She looked at London and Josh in speculation, seemingly just as hopeful as Fallon was. "We had been trying to inoculate against it; we never considered removing the magic from it."

All eyes had turned to the witches, and they felt the pressure. It was our last hope. Sebastian and Ethan remained impassive.

"We don't know if it will work," Ariel cautioned. "If it doesn't …"

"We know," Sebastian intoned. "We use the final resort." He gave them all a look, no longer accepting their feedback but taking advantage of his role as the Elite. Making a decision on behalf of the pack.

"To counter elf magic, we'll need an elf."

"I can do it. I can mirror their magic," I volunteered. "I've done it before."

"Mirroring their magic isn't the same. We will need the blood and magic of an elf. A Makellos elf. The stronger the better. Gregoire was a Makellos?" London asked, already going to work on the spell. She used magical script. The moment the idea hit, she started sketching out a spell, while Josh stepped back and watched. He wore a look similar to his brother's: admiration and intrigue.

I understood the fascination. London made magic into a mesmeric display that could be put to notes and played with the passion of any artist. Various hues of orange and green marked the air, creating an invocation. She moved her hand like a conductor, striking the air with sharp, quick movements. Then she stopped.

"Are you all going to watch me or find an elf? I have the easy part—you getting an elf to agree to help is going to be the difficult part."

Ariel blanched and then London made a face, realizing she'd misspoken. Attentive to the work in front of her, London ignored Sebastian's inquiring eyes.

"Why will I have a hard time getting a Makellos elf? Gideon is one," Sebastian queried, directing his question to Ariel.

Ariel glowered. "Then go get him," she suggested in a level voice.

"You seem to think I'll have a problem doing that."

She let out a heavy sigh and continued to look at London's work. "It's not my information to tell."

"Can I have a moment?" He nodded his head toward his office.

She turned to face him, her face stern, her voice stringent. "No. We are working, and there's nothing we can discuss in your office that can't be said here." She squared her shoulders and locked eyes with him. "Being allies with this pack is hard. Period. It puts a target on us and taints our reputation. I've accepted it as the consequences. Not only do I see the value of an alliance with you all, I respect and admire the dedication that you all have for the safety and health of the pack." Her tone had lost the empathy it possessed before and was now professionally bland. She moved closer to Sebastian.

He closed up the fraction of space she'd left between them. The intensity of their looks mirrored each other's and, if they had an existing romantic relationship, they'd shrugged off whatever friendliness or intimacy it had forged. They were two leaders establishing boundaries, or challenging them. Ariel continued, "But make no mistake, I see you. I see all of you. And sometimes the pack is just as reckless and cruel as the other races. I don't think it's just about power but self-preservation as well. And with all your posturing and power plays, at the core of it, you are the most vulnerable. The easiest to be found out. But I don't agree with all your tactics. Let me be very clear about that. I didn't agree with the elves' rule to contain dark elves, although I understood the fear. I didn't agree with the witches' fear and the cruelty with which they dealt with were-animals who showed magical ability. And I definitely don't agree with some of the things that were suggested here today, by your Alphas." Kyle received a castigating look.

"I have responsibilities to my witches, as you do to your people. So, if you want to find out if something has changed between you and Gideon, I suggest you ask him. I will not get between you and him on that. If you can get an elf, you need to do it quickly. Each moment that passes increases the likelihood of you being exposed." She returned her attention to what London was working on and turned her back to Sebastian. "If it can't be achieved today, I expect the other option to be performed immediately."

"The witches' help in this matter has been appreciated, but it is a good practice to know where you stand when making commands about what we do. You don't have that power," Sebastian reminded her.

Ariel kept her focus on the invocation in front of us. Her voice remained cool when she said, "You're right. But I've made my opinion known. This is a last-ditch effort and I hope it works—I do—but if you decide not to pick the other option, you've made your choice. A reckless choice that will put us in danger as well." She craned her neck to look at him over her shoulder. "I will remember that selfishness."

They needed a time-out. Their conversation had been reduced to poorly veiled threats and political posturing and was going to escalate quickly without intervention.

"If we have limited time, it's probably best that you get

Gideon," Joan said softly, breaking the hard stare Sebastian had on Ariel.

"You're right. I need to handle this."

"Yeah, *she's* right," Ariel mumbled under her breath. She'd been around us enough to know that even a whisper could be heard—she didn't care.

"I'm sorry, I missed that," Sebastian said, his voice softer than expected and tinged with amusement.

"No, you didn't," she asserted.

Sebastian did the amicable thing and left without preamble or pushing the issue. The tension was left unexplored but, considering the look on Joan's face, she seemed to believe she was the source of it. I wasn't sure if it was a good idea that she stayed behind. It was a delicate dance, navigating the political minefield we were negotiating. Showing up at Gideon's home with four Alphas might have been considered an act of aggression. I wasn't sure I, Ethan, Sebastian, and Winter would be any better. Winter's relationship with Abigail was tumultuous, and I didn't see Abigail succumbing to the old feelings she'd once had for Winter, especially since her efforts to rekindle their romance had been met with contention.

Our arrival didn't go unnoticed. The sky darkened and crackled as we drove into the parking area. Small droplets of water thumped against the car window. Once we were parked, the rain came down harder. By the time we got out of the car, it was a torrential storm. We weren't welcome.

Wind howled, blasting us aggressively, making our journey up the sidewalk feel like an uphill climb. The door opened as soon as we ambled up the steps. Soaked and cold, we stepped into Gideon's government residence. He'd always taken his position as leader casually, and it was surprising to see uniformed guards standing at attention, aligned side by side. Like Liam's. With a sharp flex of a finger, one of them directed us to follow them. They didn't seem worried about the trail of water we were leaving. We walked past the living room, several rooms that looked like offices, and another that was a tribute to their history. Portraits and framed documents covered the walls.

In silence, we were directed to a massive room at the back of the building. A wooden table took up the back of the room. A floor-to-ceiling window overlooked a garden with exotic plants and flowering trees, similar to the ones in Elysian. It was hard to appreciate it when I was drenched and painfully aware of the coolness of my body. Ethan moved closer, but even he couldn't give off enough heat to warm me.

"That was a hell of a welcome," I said softly.

"Yeah. I don't think we're welcome here anymore," Sebastian acknowledged, looking around the room, scrutinizing a long wooden desk at the opposite end of the room. Exquisite carvings decorated it and the arms and legs of the high-backed, patterned-silk chairs behind it. Sebastian frowned at the furniture, which looked like it was fit for royalty and ready for judgment of anyone who stood in front of it.

An eerie feeling nagged at me. Sebastian looked at his watch and frowned. We'd been waiting for fifteen minutes. Our patience thinned. Sebastian let out a long, irritated breath and started for the door. The click of heels on the floor stopped him from advancing.

Abigail walked into the room, moving in silence past us to the ostentatious desk. While Gideon didn't seem to enjoy the theatrics and formality that came with his position, his sister certainly did.

She took a seat and waited for us to position ourselves in front of her. No one moved; instead, Sebastian gave her a defiant smirk. "I need to speak with Gideon."

"I know you feel that the world is at your beck and call. I'm here to ensure you that it is not. My brother is coming eventually. He's handling other problems that have arisen." She shot Ethan a sharp look and then returned her attention to Sebastian.

She grew silent, drumming her nails along the desk, creating the only sound in the room as we waited for Gideon. Her cold, accusing eyes seared through us, only softening when they landed on Winter with what seemed like longing. I couldn't help but wonder if she regretted having made Winter a pawn in her game and ruining any chances she had of rekindling the relationship. They were embroiled in a moment, their faces presenting vastly different emotions. Winter's was raw and contemptuous. Abigail pulled her gaze from her when she was met with the vertical slit eyes of a snake preparing to strike.

"Unexpected guests," Gideon acknowledged reticently. His face displayed his irritation as he took a seat next to his sister. No matter how many times I'd seen them together, the strong similarities between the fraternal twins were always off-putting, and I found myself preoccupied with trying to determine the perfect description for them: handsome-pretty, angelic, androgynous, peculiar? Their striking narrow features, aquiline noses, and platinum hair gave them an ethereal appearance. The stormy coolness of their eyes, which could be attributed to them being elemental elves, struck me as odd. It made them seem unapproachable and aloof.

"You made that painfully clear," Sebastian pointed out, exasperated. The day of debate and hard decisions didn't show in his face but had put a tinge of ire in his tone. One that the elves didn't appreciate.

"I'm sorry I can't be more accommodating to the very people who destroyed Elysian. Are you here to apologize?"

Sebastian, laughing at Gideon's question, didn't set the foundation for amicable dialogue, and his refusal to stand in front of the desk where the elves were positioned was just another move in the struggle for dominance. The posturing, the subtle acts to undermine people, the need to subjugate were reasons I hated the politics of the otherworld. The weariness and practiced actions between everyone seemed to indicate they were getting tired.

"We need to borrow your magic," Sebastian said, without prelude. Time was ticking, there wasn't any other way to broach it.

Gideon snorted, his brow furrowed, his mouth cruelly set. "I've repaid my debt to you tenfold. We are no longer able to provide unconditional assistance. You ensured that when you allowed your Beta to destroy our land. And instead of an apology, you have the audacity to request more favors. Your arrogance is showing."

"And so is yours," Sebastian retorted. "I'm not here to ask for a favor, I'm here to give you the opportunity to right a wrong."

Really! That's the angle you're going with? Damn, talk about getting people to see the reality you want them to see. This is magician-style sleight of hand. Go on, Alpha-Wizard.

Gideon jumped to his feet; leaning over the table, he scrutinized Sebastian. "Right a wrong! Are you serious? You destroyed Elysian. The grounds are fallow and it will be years before anything can be grown from the soil. Ethan made sure of that, and you feel that I have something to right?"

"Yes."

I dropped my eyes because them widening at Sebastian's response wouldn't have been missed.

Sebastian moved from his position at the side to stand directly in front of them, changing the intended dynamics in which they were sitting in judgment of him. His powerful presence overwhelmed the room, as did his deeply sonorous voice as he presented his argument. "Your land being destroyed was the doing of your people. Before you even ask, if the situation was reversed, would I be obligated to right a wrong? The answer is yes. But here is where we are quite different. Everyone judges us for our perceived carelessness and lack of respect for magic and the rules. Where is your judgment? The sole purpose of the Mond is to force us to change. What purpose does that serve other than to have control over us?" His attention skated over to Abigail, who, unlike her brother, was unmoved by his words. "Gideon, you might not have known of this, but your sister did. There has to be some accountability for this."

Gideon's frown eased and he closed his eyes for a moment, pressing his fingers to the bridge of his nose. "I didn't agree with its creation," he admitted.

"I know you wouldn't have, but as the leader of the elves you have an obligation to help me fix it. I will not mince words; I would not be here if I didn't need you. I realize I've come to you for a debt that has been satisfied. But as I am culpable for the actions of those under my rule and even of lone were-animals— because I pride myself in making sure they aren't causing trouble—I hold you to the same standard."

Abigail leaned in to her brother and whispered something in his ear. Forever the voice of contention and portent of potential destruction. The naysayer who seemed to be angling for a power grab using her best weapon—manipulation of her brother. His face crinkled into a frown. He rested his chin against his clasped hands and pondered whatever she'd said to him. His tense gaze moved from Sebastian to me and Ethan, where it stayed with considerable contemplation. Satisfied with whatever seed she'd planted, Abigail relaxed back in her chair, looking impish in her smugness.

"It is my understanding that there have been failings in an effort to contain Ethan's and Sky's magic?" he started off slowly, choosing his words with precision. "They are quite the force, don't you think? Magic so strong that it's summoned the

Faeries. So virulent and uncontrollable that it can't be contained by powerful witches—or so the rumors have suggested. I'm inclined to believe them. People are concerned with the level of power and destruction you will have at your fingertips with a pair of weres who can do great damage. Ethan and Sky's union has caused a lot of concern, and I'm sure you are aware of that."

"And yet whatever goes on between them has nothing to do with you," Sebastian interjected, inserting a hint of a threat for him to drop it.

"It does. Unfortunately, as much as we like to believe we can live independent of one another without the actions of others affecting us, it isn't true, now is it?" Abigail blurted. "You all doing forbidden magic affected us all because it awakened the Faeries. How many years had they been dormant? Then Sky joins your pack—the world as we know it changes. We deal with people like Samuel ... rumors swirl about the mad witch who wants to get rid of magic. And if we map it back—his actions, the fervency of them, the potential for his scheme to be made possible—who do we find entangled in it? Your little wolf! Shall I go on with my list? Because it is quite extensive."

"You can read from whatever goddamn list you'd like, it doesn't change a thing. Whatever goes on with me and Sky isn't your business, nor will it ever be," Ethan objected.

"Fine, then we have no more business with you," Gideon said, and he and his sister sat back in their chairs. The rhythmic sounds of the booted feet of their guards hitting hard against the floor sounded like stampeding horses.

A wave of Josh's hands and the door shut and a silver translucent barrier enclosed us all, protecting us from the guard and penning Gideon and Abigail in.

"We need your magic to undo the Mond. I'm not asking. Don't make me force you." Sebastian was no longer a man standing before them but a feral animal being held back by a tendril of restraint that was threatening to snap at any moment.

"I won't list your number of transgressions. Gregoire put us in this situation and you will get us out of it or so help me—"

"Enough with your threats," Gideon snarled.

"If only it were." Sebastian looked at his watch. "We are running out of time. Send your guards away and come with us."

Moving as one, they stood and crossed their arms in defiance. It was their desperate effort and refusal to give in that left me curious as to what they were really after.

"What do you want from us?" I asked softly, knowing the others were driven too far over the edge to be able to compromise. We needed them to be amiable and not dragged away kicking and screaming, forced to help. I didn't want to deal with the aftermath of the latter.

Abigail answered, "You all have the protected objects in your possession—they have been the source of a great deal of problems and it has been proven that you cannot be trusted with them. In exchange for our help, we want them. All of them."

Before I could answer with my own declination, Sebastian did. "No. You penalizing us with that is equivalent to me wanting retribution for the sleeper that we found on your brother"—he shot her an accusatory look—"that eventually infected Kelly. Or making you continue to pay for our help in recovering your creatures that escaped from the dark forest, or for Mason putting together a group of mercenaries to put us down like rabid animals. *Or* the fact that I believe you had something to do with my abduction," he hissed acridly. "I'm feeling really fucking vengeful about that. No, you don't get any protective objects. You will get one thing and one thing only, the promise that I won't hold you accountable for those things. End our alliance, fine. But know that if you ever need us, we will not be available to you. Ever."

Taking in those words, Gideon seemed to be looking at his sister with a new perspective, as if he was seeing her and her illicit involvement in things for the first time. Questioning her stories and how they lined up with what was the truth. There was a flash of panic in her face, as if she'd pushed Sebastian to the point of telling about her part in her brother's assassination attempt.

Seeing Gideon's resolve faltering, Sebastian continued. His voice was still determined but lacked the wrathful acuity it formerly had. "You know how it works. We can't stop the change when exposed to the Mond. Eventually we will be discovered by humans. Before when this was a possibility I promised to protect everyone from it, and I accepted it was our actions that caused it. Now it's the elves' actions that have put us in this predicament—do you think that protection still stands? We will be at a disadvantage if you decline to help us, but I will ensure that it is indeed a Pyrrhic victory for you."

Way to go for subtlety. Why not just say, "I plan to rain down hell on you"?

Gideon swallowed, his face a mask of neutrality as he pondered his options. The Midwest Pack, even with all the demands that came with being allied with them, was a far better friend than enemy. Gideon waved his hand at the exit; my heart skipped. I tried not to let the feeling of hopelessness show on my face.

"We'll follow you out," Gideon informed Sebastian.

"Where are you going?" Sebastian inquired when Abigail headed for the opposite direction of the front door.

"I need a jacket. Or have we been stripped of all our autonomy and have to get your permission to address our basic needs?" Violet eyes bore into her brother with contention—she obviously saw his acquiescence as submission, not a compromise to protect the elves. Her displeasure with the situation was redirected back to Sebastian.

"We'll wait for you in the car," Sebastian informed her, scrutinizing her departure as she walked away.

We waited for a long time. Nearly twenty minutes, and

Sebastian and Ethan were fidgeting with irritation. This wasn't just Abigail retrieving a jacket—it was a statement of defiance. Her demonstrating that her participation was done under duress. When she emerged, she had on an entirely different outfit. Her shirt and slacks were several shades darker than her eyes, giving her a dramatic, portentous appearance, worn with a darker, woven, waist-length jacket. Her glower and the restrained steps she took as she approached the chauffeured car indicated that she and Gideon were not willing participants but hostages.

CHAPTER 25

*S*pace was needed to perform the spell. Gideon and Abigail eased into the wall, their expressions contradictory as if they were watching two very different stories unfold. His stance was stolid, but his violet eyes were inquisitive as he watched the witches line up ingredients necessary for the spell. Abigail's face was austere. Like me, she seemed interested in the unfamiliar were-animal in the room.

Responding to my curiosity, Joan moved next to me and said, "We have to represent all the families to ensure immunity of everyone." She nodded her head toward the tall woman with warm, honey-colored skin and emotive dark eyes, who stood so erect it looked uncomfortable. She was taking in everyone in the room, reminding me of Ethan's perusal of every space he went into. It wasn't just a scan; it was an inventory, an evaluation. Thorough but done quickly. Of the new arrivals, she seemed the most cynical.

"That's Cheyenne. You'll rarely see her. Part of the pack in name only," Joan said. "She's equidae, a Friesian." Beguiled by the visitor, she continued in a low, bemused whisper, "A war horse."

That was a given. She didn't seem like a horse you'd go up to with an apple without expecting a good kick.

Ariel looked impatiently at the spell ingredients, the paper next to it, and the door.

"He'll be here. He had to be tracked down."

Before I could ask who "he" was, the door swung open and a massive man that I'd seen briefly years ago when I'd first met the pack strode in. It was Dakota, a bear. Ursidae, the final family we needed. Ariel swallowed, like everyone else who wasn't familiar with him. He lived in the woods and, preferring his animal form over his human one, was called out of his preferred dwelling only when needed. As he approached, it was obvious by his heavy steps and unintentionally imposing presence that his human form was used so infrequently that it felt foreign to him. His dark, scalp-short hair made him seem even more menacing, but when he looked at Joan, his lips curled into a meek smile. His voice was a smooth, deep baritone, surprisingly mellow as he spoke to her. I figured it was the only time it sounded that way. Joan had a way of calming those around her.

"I took a plane to get here but plan to use other forms of travel to return home."

Joan smiled and gave him a gentle, appreciative and comforting touch as he moved past her.

Usually confident and controlled around Sebastian and the rest of the pack, Ariel seemed edgy. Perhaps she had the same concern as the rest of us: this was our final hope. If this failed, then we didn't have any other options. The pack would be irreparably damaged and the fragile relationship we had with the others would be severed.

She handed a knife to Sebastian and then to Abigail, who didn't move to take it. Giving his sister a sharp look that she promptly returned, Gideon took hold of the knife. "Let's just get this over with and then we go home," he told her sternly. Abigail seemed rooted in her insolence, unable to let go of Gideon's perceived betrayal by agreeing to help. She was so manipulative, I wasn't sure if it was a countermove to reflect the anger and frustration he'd shown with her earlier. No longer blinded by their sibling bond, he seemed to have gotten clarity in regards to his sister and was willing to look past the rose-tinted veil that had obscured the intent of many of her acts and caused him to overlook a lot of her behaviors in the past.

Blood was drawn from each family and placed in a separate bowl from the elves'. Waves of strong magic pulsed through the room as the Creed and Josh said the incantation. Even Ethan sucked in a rough breath, feeling the summation of strong magic that teetered on the line between natural and something different. All the witches' eyes were coal black as they called on magic so strong they held on to each other for support. Blood rose from each bowl and coagulated into long crimson lines. Parallel to each other, the lines would inch closer and then repel. The witches focused on the gathered blood, more fervent words spilling from their mouths. Voracious commands of magic continued, and without preamble Ariel broke from the spell. Waving her hand in Abigail's direction, she slammed her into the wall, hard enough that cracks spread from where the elf's body was fixed. "Keep the spell going," Ariel instructed as she quickly moved to Abigail. "Don't break it, or we'll have to start over." The blood rods shimmied closer and rebounded away. Certain lines in the spell promoted affinity, and I could see the rods attempt to blend, as I assumed they needed to do to complete the spell.

Ariel busied herself with searching Abigail, quickly running hands up her legs, torso, and shoulders until she came to her left arm, covered by a large sleeve. Ariel yanked up the sleeve to reveal a wrapped bracelet that coiled up the length of her arm, little spikes embedded into her flesh. As Ariel studied the contraption, I could see the dilemma coursing through her mind. She battled with taking the brutal approach, ripping it off, or unlatching it. Jaws clenched, Ariel continued to examine the brace and then she pressed it; spikes unclamped, and the device fell from Abigail's arm to the floor. Ariel kicked it out of reach before pulling back her magic and letting Abigail fall to the floor.

Quickly finding the rhythm of the incantation, she rejoined the spell. The rods inched together, unraveling enough to form threads that meshed and interlinked until they formed what looked like a DNA helix. The witches invoked another spell and it disappeared. Remnants of crimson and magic lingered in the air.

London grabbed a handful of the Mond. "Who do we test?" she asked.

"Probably best to check us all," Sebastian said. One by one, she huffed it into their faces—without provoking a reaction.

While it was being tested, Abigail attempted to slip away, dour and disappointed; Gideon looked as if he was leaving with her out of an innate loyalty as opposed to a willed action. A rigid scowl cast a dark shadow over his pleasing features, and his violet eyes were alight with so many emotions they were hard to read.

"What was that?" Sebastian asked, looking at the discarded bracelet.

"Spitze," Abigail said, jaw set, unrepentant as she picked it up on the way out the door. I was surprised when I saw Joan move for her; I'd expected it to be Sebastian. He called Joan's name softly, to stop her. A look passed between Gideon and Sebastian. I wasn't sure what it meant, but obviously, Gideon didn't see Abigail's acquisition as a threat.

Once Abigail and Gideon were gone, Joan looked to the witches for an explanation.

"It neutralizes blood. It makes it undetectable as elven, which is why the spell wasn't working," Ariel offered in a stiff voice. She still hadn't warmed to Joan and was handling her with a professional aloofness. Sensing it, Joan stopped her questioning, but it was with great effort. I wasn't sure if it was diplomacy or Joan's desire not to disrupt the fragility of the relationship between the witches and were-animals—or rather Ariel and Sebastian.

∽

Three days after the spell was done, Ethan was settling back down on the sofa after receiving a short and sweet video message from Quinn. "You are going to love what I sent you."

At my approach toward the sofa, Ethan looked up from his book and grimaced at the bowl of ice cream, topped with cookies, caramel, and fudge, and the apple in my other hand.

"We had dinner half an hour ago," he pointed out.

I stopped, face twisted and brow furrowed as I scanned the room.

"What's the matter?" he asked, scooting over so I could sit closer and view the screen.

"I was just looking for the judgment-free zone. Is it over there?" I jerked my chin in the direction of the woefully out of place chair that I'd brought from my place. It had been quiet for the past four days since we'd disabled the Mond, and we'd used the time to move me completely out of my home. My cranberry-colored microfiber chair looked out of place among his expensive-looking cognac-colored leather sofas, woven patterned accent chair, and deep mahogany tables. I'd be the first to admit it looked downright tacky. His furniture, sleek and comfortable, looked new despite daily use. The chair in the corner looked comfortably worn and didn't complement anything, including the art on the walls.

My lips quivered as I fought the smile threatening to emerge. Ethan hated the chair, and each time he walked into his great room, his eyes seem to purposely skip over the area. I'd draped a multicolored comforter over it, and my Kindle and a stack of paperbacks sat on the small table placed next to it. When he couldn't avoid looking at it, tension overtook his body. He'd glowered at the space but suffered in silence. I planned to get another chair, something that would match the décor better, but I was being petty. Marking my territory and trying to make his home mine.

As if he'd read my mind, he suggested, "We can move."

I scoffed and licked at the melting ice cream. "I just moved in here. I'm not moving again."

"Fine. The house can be decorated again."

Appraising the house, I made a face at the idea of doing that, too. I loved Ethan's home and if I ignored the serial-killer type organization and attention to detail, I appreciated it. Most of all, I enjoyed the beautiful sculptures, unique canvases, and various tableaux of wildlife. The display made me feel like I was in Claudia's gallery. The presence was the same. The dark furniture mixed effortlessly with neutral browns, tans, and eggshell. His home had a casual, modern elegance that I hadn't mastered. He probably hadn't, either, since he'd had it decorated rather than doing it himself. The place was as comforting as Ethan had become to me.

"What are we going to love?" I asked, licking the melting ice cream off my spoon.

"Don't know yet." He opened Quinn's e-mail and played the video attached. An average-height woman dressed in leggings, an oversized thin sweater, and flats navigated through a crowd of people. I wasn't sure what we were going to love about her. She moved through the busy streets near the art district. Her movements were graceful and fluid enough to mark her as a dancer. Then she looked up, the sharp, primal intelligence of the were-animal displayed in her russet brown eyes. Oblivious to a camera on her, she continued to walk, her gaze cautiously sweeping over the surrounding area. Her eyes sharpened and she took in a deep breath. Just as she frowned, as if recognizing a familiar scent, a person passing her tossed herbs in her face. The woman wailed so loudly, you would have thought it was acid and not herbs that would only incite fits of sneezing. But it had the desired effect: people came to a halt, watching her, and the person with the camera zoomed in on her.

"What did you do to her?" another woman asked, her voice rough and angry.

"Don't let him get away," a male voice ordered. And then began the bustling of the crowd: people asking if she was okay and her wiping the dust from her face as she sneezed and looked frightened. "Why would they do this?"

The camera stayed on her expectantly for several moments, getting nothing but a woman having a sneezing fit as a result of the Mond being tossed on her.

Someone asked if it was a prank, and another person, irate, pointed out it wasn't much of a prank if it was one. The were-animal continued to wipe her face and dust the herbs from her shirt, repeating, "I'm okay. It just startled me. It came out of nowhere." Her voice was soft, which only angered others who didn't find the "prank" funny. The video ended just after the woman's tepid gaze turned to face the camera, a flash of cold, predaceous ire overtaking her eyes for just a second. The cameraman, if he knew what to look for, could not deny she was a were-animal, he just couldn't prove it. Hadn't proven it. Once again the Red Blood had failed to prove it. If it was up to the perturbed crowd, local law enforcement would get involved. What would their defense be? "Officer, it was supposed to change her into an animal."

Ethan grinned as he closed the laptop.

"Why would they keep that when it only makes them look bad? Reinforcing that they are nut cases. They believe a magical dust will change humans to animals or that people who shift to animals exist."

"I'm sure Quinn acquired it before they could delete it," Ethan asserted matter-of-factly.

"How did he get it?"

"I don't know, and I like it that way."

"Good, plausible deniability. That's exactly what you need. When the federal officers come for you, the lie detector won't snitch on you," I teased.

"I can beat it," he supplied smugly.

"Don't be proud of that!" I chided, reminded of the pride he held in getting people to see the reality he wanted them to believe.

A deep chuckle reverberated in his chest as he turned lengthwise on the sofa, and I slid against him, resting my back against his chest.

"Sure, I'll remember not to be proud of it."

"The woman in the video—who is she?"

"Her name's Alexandria, and she's a jackal."

"You saw how well she handled it. Very in control of her other half," I acknowledged.

"Yes, Sebastian noticed that about her a few years ago. She's been living as a loner for nearly five years."

"Have you all approached her to join the pack?" My enthusiasm heightened at the idea of someone who didn't identify so closely with her animal, abating it for her humanity. She had control because it was secondary in her life. There for protection only. "Who asked her? You or Sebastian? Did you use your subtle threats that, believe it or not, are more of a deterrent? You know, the whole 'if you become a threat to the pack we'll treat you like all threats'?"

"We do know how to behave and can be quite charming when we need to be."

"I didn't see any of that charm when you were recruiting me."

"You weren't going to get any from me—I didn't want you in the pack," he reminded me.

That made me think of what Steven had said about Ethan being happier now that he wasn't denying his feelings for me. It made me forgive his efforts to keep me out of the pack and his inhospitality.

I placed the apple on my lap and started on my ice cream. When I twisted to give him a spoonful, he declined, as he did every night. He pushed my hair back and kissed me on the neck, wrapped his arms around me, and rested his hands on my stomach.

The comfortable silence was interrupted by his phone buzzing. He ignored it. Then it buzzed again. His chest vibrated with a growl of irritation. It kept on buzzing.

"You're going to have to answer it eventually, or they're going to come over," I told him.

He snatched the phone up. "What!" he barked.

"Good evening to you, too, Mr. Broody. You didn't respond to my calendar invite," David informed Ethan in a professional voice with notes of irritation. When he dealt with Ethan it was as if he was being polite during a hostile takeover. In many ways he was. Ethan didn't like relinquishing control. David and Trent were just as big control freaks as Ethan, only in a more reserved manner.

"Fine. You will be there tomorrow at three?"

I turned to look at Ethan's face, now strained. Pulses of gunmetal surfaced over his eyes. "Yes," he pushed through clenched teeth.

"I've sent over the invoices for the violinist, rental of the arboretum, and the photographer."

"They've been handled." His words were so strained, they sounded bestial. "I didn't realize you got Annie Leibovitz to take pictures. I'm impressed."

"You know it's not Annie, and if you have a problem with the cost, take it up with Claudia. She recommended the photographer, and after seeing her portfolio, I see why. She's fabulous. Once all those invoices are taken care of, just send me screen grabs or copies."

"If I say I'm going to do something, no need to worry—it will be done."

"Then say you'll send the screenshots or copies and the conversation can end," David said in a cloying voice, an attempt to ease Ethan's frustration while still keeping control. This was painful to watch, and I could see Ethan remembering my warning. "I told you so" was at the tip of my tongue, so I shoved a large spoonful of ice cream in my mouth and kept shoving until I no longer had the desire. Or rather until Ethan was finished talking—he hung up.

"Ethan," I said softly. He was rigid with irritation. I put my bowl down and lay back on him; his racing heart and ragged breathing slowed. He wrapped his arm around me, pulling me closer. His fingers clasped over my stomach.

"We should have just gone to a justice of the peace," he admitted. I knew that admission that I was right didn't taste like chicken. Probably like dirt and grass, with a hint of compost.

"In three weeks it will be over. You won't have to hear anything about flowers, food, photographers, or any of it," I assured him, my fingers gently stroking his hand. "Really, all we are doing is either rejecting or accepting their decisions. We have it easy."

"Really? Easy. They contact us at least five times a day. My e-mail is full of pictures and invoices and invites. When did we agree to a reception?"

I sighed heavily, feeling empathy for Ethan. Relaxing the reins on situations and relinquishing control wasn't hard for me; he was struggling with it. Admitting defeat in arguments didn't sit well with him. He'd clearly lost the argument about a reception. When David and Trent had "explained" that it didn't make sense to not have one, since the arboretum had a venue for it, maybe they'd pushed him into a fugue state.

"It's right there on the grounds. Guests can walk to the hall. It's a three-minute drive!" David had asserted.

"What do you plan to do, 'Hey, thanks for coming to my wedding, now go away'?" Trent had added, unaware that for Ethan, that was a reasonable alternative.

It was one of the many times I'd found myself taking on the role of the negotiator, beast whisperer, calmer of riled wedding planners, and voice of reason. I still felt the ache I'd had at the look of betrayal on Ethan's face when I'd agreed with them. "It'll be short, right guys?"

"Two hours at the most. We'll kick them out ourselves if we have to," they'd promised.

Ethan hadn't technically agreed but had turned and taken off his clothes before he'd headed for the back door. I'd had to redirect Trent and David, who'd been distracted by the view of a naked Ethan walking away. "Get back to work," I'd snapped.

"Every time I think you can do better, he does that. You *can't* do better."

"Gee, thanks."

Refocusing on the present and not a discussion from two days ago, I turned around to face Ethan, reminding him, "It's just two hours. And then—"

"We leave," he said, relieved.

I smiled. "We leave."

He leaned in and pressed a light kiss to my bottom lip. "Where are we going for a honeymoon? You haven't committed to anything."

"Portugal is out of the question." I hated that it was, but I didn't want Ethan to feel guilty. He had pack obligations.

"We can go," he said.

"Ethan, the Presentation ceremony is five days after the wedding. We can't leave the country. You have to go—it's your responsibility." I made a face. "Besides your prickly personality, I knew what I was getting with your role as the Beta." Ethan frowned at the lie. Okay, I didn't exactly know, but I was starting to realize and accept it. Things weren't going to be normal for me. His Beta obligations affected our plans.

Returning to my rapidly melting ice cream, I picked up the bowl and apple, not wanting to see his face when I said, "*And,* I promised Chris I'd go." I picked up my bowl and returned to my position, leaning back against his chest. I took a bite of the apple and put a spoonful of ice cream in my mouth.

"I really don't like this burgeoning friendship between you and my ex."

"We aren't friends."

He had stiffened but his thumb stroking against my stomach was gentle, a featherlike, soothing touch.

"She asked me."

"And you could have said no."

"But I didn't." After a long moment of weighted silence, I added in quietly, "I couldn't." I thought about how nervous she'd looked asking. As if asking me to the Presentation was scarier than becoming the Mistress of the most powerful and ruthless vampire Seethe. I'd never be able to explain the feeling of obligation that I felt. Her moment of vulnerability had evoked something in me. We weren't friends and would never be. Something in me felt a kinship and commonality that was unexplainable, and I felt confident that if I asked her to attend something like a Presentation, she would.

The quiet didn't seem heavy, just contemplative. I thought about the complexity of my relationship with Chris and I wasn't sure what Ethan was thinking of, but his hold on me tightened.

"Then you'll be there to babysit Trent and David."

I'd turned again to face him, on my knees, and reared back on my feet, determined eyes fixed on his. "There is no way in hell they are going to that vampire prom."

Resting back, he clasped his fingers behind his head, enjoying my reaction too much. "Do they know the day of the Presentation?" Taunting delight punctuated each word.

I nodded.

"I'm assuming they know the time and location as well, correct?"

"They saw the invitation." I was curt in my response because I knew where he was going with his line of questioning.

"Hmmm," he breathed out. "And you are under some illusion that they won't show up?"

"If I tell them they can't—then they won't," I said confidently.

"Ah, yes. You would think people would respond when you request that they not do something for their own good. After all, you're just trying to protect them and they should accept it and follow your directions ..." A roguish smile flitted along his lips and I definitely wanted to take my fingers and force it off his face. "I once knew this woman; she was so tenacious and spirited. I would tell her to stay away from Tre'ases, and guess what? She didn't. She'd been warned no less than five times to stop playing with vampires and I swear she set up weekly play-dates with them. She was a very rare wolf who could do wondrous things with magic, so she was advised to use it sparingly, so she practiced it daily with a tattooed renegade witch who had an aversion to following basic rules. I seem to remember telling the precocious, beautiful, doe-eyed brunette not to go to Logan's. I'm sure if I searched my phone, I can find the old texts. Hmmm. I can't remember if she listened, but my gut is telling me she didn't."

"She sounds terrible. What ever happened to that trou-blemaker?"

"She's still around. Now she's on the opposite side of a similar situation. Karma is a joyous thing. The naïveté with which she's handling things is quite entertaining. She's so cute."

Making his voice a high, annoying falsetto he repeated my words: "'If I tell them they can't—they won't.'"

"You think they'll show up even if I ask them not to?"

"Definitely."

I thought about my options for a moment, and they were all along the lines of things I'd had done to me that I hadn't liked. There was a wrenching feeling of guilt as I thought of all the criticisms and judgments I'd lobbed at Ethan and Sebastian on how they had handled things with me, and now I was considering doing the same.

"You aren't thinking about locking them in a room on the night of it, are you?" He reminded me of the time Sebastian had locked me in his room after I'd fed Quell for the first time, afraid that with the ability to call me, the vampire would possibly kill me.

"Yeah," I admitted, ashamed.

"Let them go. David was right. There's no way Demetrius or Chris will allow them to be harmed. Not because Demetrius has any code of honor to protect them, but hurting them would surely cause chaos at this absurd event."

I rolled my eyes. "This vampire prom is going to be obscenely over the top."

"Agreed." Ethan stood and went into his other office and came back with his computer. "We have to find a honeymoon destination."

CHAPTER 26

*C*laudia opened the door dressed as if we were having a business rather than a casual meeting. Merlot-colored suit, with a chemise underneath and her signature pearls and complementing gloves that never looked pretentious. If anyone else wore the latter, it would elicit a strong eye roll. She had her hair pulled back, and her smile looked brighter, genial. It was a very different appearance from the waning one she'd had when I'd seen her last, after the Faeries attacked and I'd seen exactly what she was.

More aware of the power of her touch, I should have been wary, maybe even afraid. There was an ease that existed between us, and I briefly entertained the idea that it might be part of her magic. Ethan thought that I was able to compel people; would it be unthinkable for Claudia to have that ability? Her smile faded as she looked at me, and I knew my concerns must be displayed on my face. Pushing the thoughts aside, I focused on her home. The plants destroyed by her on my last visit were replaced by vibrant greenery that made the room seem relaxing.

"Thank you for coming, Sky." She leaned in and placed an air kiss on each side of my face. "We'll have drinks in the tea room."

Yeah, because it's so normal to have a room dedicated to tea.

I followed her through the living room to a small area set off from it and overlooking a small garden. Near the bay window was a table with a tea set on it. A printed silk settee was on the opposite side, complementing the pearl-colored walls. Claudia's tea room was the embodiment of her: refined, beautiful, warm, and elegant. The nonessential room was very essential for her. Chamomile, lavender, and low notes of vanilla and spearmint hung in the air.

"I wasn't sure if you'd had lunch already, so I prepared sandwiches and desserts." I didn't get too excited about the prospect of her sandwiches because I knew from experience they were finger foods. Often things that I wouldn't consider sandwiches: cucumber, cream cheese, and vegetable, or her version of chicken salad thinly spread on bread. I remembered her look of abhorrence when I'd crammed several of them together and shoved them in my piehole. Her head had tilted, brow slightly furrowed, and a little wrinkle had formed around her lips as she'd gawked at the savagery before her.

As I slid into the chair, I wasn't surprised by the tray of cucumber sandwiches and shortbread cookies. It was as if she didn't have a godson who was a were-animal or hadn't remembered that I was one. Forcing a smile, I ate one of her fake sandwiches.

"I'm so happy to hear about the wedding," she said, after she'd poured the tea and prepared each cup to our liking. Or rather her liking. She studied me and smiled. I had on my visit-Claudia clothing. Gray slacks, cashmere sweater, flats, and dainty silver necklace. Too polite to ever comment on anyone's style of dress, she would comment often how she missed some aspects of the days when people dressed for dinner. Even Josh dressed when he had dinner with her. I was sure he had the

"Claudia" section in his closet. It was probably the only time he'd wear a button-down or slacks.

Leaning in, she took my hand. "It looks even better than it did in the store. I told Ethan this was a good fit for you."

I extended my fingers to get another look at the ring, seeing it with renewed eyes. "I love it. It's beautiful."

The warmth of her smile made me feel like she was welcoming me into her heart, her family. "He's yours and you're his," she whispered reverently.

Don't roll your eyes, I commanded myself. I never understood her need to see us as possessions. Seeing the lack of understanding in my face, she elaborated. "People take care of the things they consider theirs. A pack means nothing until the member claims it. Then it has a place in your heart, a desire to protect it, care for it, strengthen it. How did things change for you when you stopped saying you were part of the pack and referred to it as 'my pack'?" She took a sip from her cup.

She knew the answer. I'd become dogmatic about protecting it. Protecting us. I fought for it, risked my life for it, and killed for it. I sucked in a sharp breath.

"I know you will protect Ethan as you would your pack," she insisted. There was confidence in her words but apprehension in the purse of her lips and her now tepid voice.

"I don't think Ethan needs protection."

A soft, gentle laugh emanated from her. It was a nervous sound. "There's more than physical protection. I've watched Ethan all my life and the parade of women he's had." The frown deepened. "Relationships that had no more depth or value than a penny." She stopped and considered me for a moment. There was a slight relaxing in her hinged moue. "People think he's callous and cold." She shrugged as she wrinkled her nose. "Perhaps he is at times. It is his way. I believe he said you called it being a 'Betahole'"—her accent hit each syllable, making it sound far less insulting than intended—"yes, yes, that's what he said you call him."

Flushed, she smiled, amused by the word. I couldn't believe he would disclose that to her.

"He can be a Betahole at times." She paused at the "hole," obviously finding it distasteful. "It allows him to be proficient in his job. He does love others, and when someone has his heart, that person is everything to him. Josh has trouble with how Ethan shows it for him." I could hear the maternal adoration she had for them in her voice. "They are so different. Same level of love, just very different in execution. Don't you think?"

"Yes, they are *very* different."

She looked down into her cup with consideration. The silence stretched for minutes as she fell into deep contemplation. "Ethan's history and experiences are so different from yours, which is why you two complement each other. At the risk of being hyperbolic and citing overused platitudes: you two make a whole. Now that he's experienced ..." she trailed off. The tenderness she felt for him was undeniable. It dawned on me that Cole's attempts to put a wedge between us may not have gotten to me, but they had led to insecurities in Ethan. Could he possibly think that because I didn't have as much experience as him, I would leave—cheat? Guilt burdened me as I considered Quell and how Ethan felt about him.

"I love Ethan," I said. "I don't think it will change or that I would be happy with anyone else but him. I don't need to experience other people to know that. I don't worry about Ethan, and he doesn't worry about me."

Relief put a wide smile on her face. I was still puzzled by her concern and slightly slighted. "What is so alluring and charming about you is that you don't see it—how people migrate toward you. It is quite understandable why Ethan suspected it was intertwined with your magic." Her face twisted into something that was a combination of a frown and a snarl, and then she continued: "Cole." He'd elicited strong defensive urges in her. Protective anger wafted off her and reminded me of the cool way she'd looked at him and how she'd siphoned life from a plant; I was sure she could turn that power on something—someone—else.

Calm down, mamma bear.

"Cole," she pushed his name through clenched teeth. "There will be others like him. Men who will find you intriguing, be compelled by you. A peculiar connection. Like Sebastian has for you."

I glowered, disgusted at the idea. Claudia quickly added, "Not romantically. But he is delicate with you."

She was using that word *so* wrong. I needed to carry a summary of how delicate Sebastian had been with me: choking me, locking me in a cage, and most recently, threatening to toss me out of his office. *Yeah, he's so delicate with me. If he was any more delicate, I'd be in a body cast.*

"You will pique a lot of interest, and not just because of who you are mated to. Your relationship will be tested in so many ways." Apparently saddened by the thought, she frowned. "And the community isn't very happy about your union. They're afraid."

"I know, and I still don't understand it. It's not even us that they are afraid of, it's the potential for offspring. What exactly has them so fearful?"

"Something that can't be contained. Like the Faeries. We all have weaknesses and can be controlled to some degree by magic. Wards and protective fields are the only things that work against you in animal form. Witch and shapeshifter unions have always been frowned upon because of the unpredictability of the offspring and their powers. You both host spirit shades and by all logic, it shouldn't have an effect on your child. Magic is so imprecise, however, that having concern about it isn't unwarranted."

Sipping tea that had to be cold by now, she withdrew into her thoughts. Her thin lips curled into a faint, docile smile. "Have you found any of the protected objects that were taken by the Faeries?"

"No, Josh and the witches are looking for them. We still have the Clostra, but that's it."

"Rayna's supporters have grown. There is dissent among the witches. Some have left Ariel to follow Rayna, who has vowed to protect them from the likes of the 'ruthless and irresponsible were-animals.'" She shook her head. "She is aggressively looking for the Aufero—to punish those who have refused to follow her. She is worse than Marcia."

The heavy sigh that I let out truly expressed my mood. I couldn't deal with someone worse than Marcia. I wasn't sure there could be anyone worse.

I looked up from my weird vegetable sandwich to find Claudia's sympathetic eyes. "Honeymoon. Have you all decided on a place?"

"Ethan wanted to go to Portugal, but we only have five days before we have to be back for an event. So we are going to Hawaii." It seemed so traditional and expected. I didn't want traditional and typical, and yet everything about our wedding seemed just that.

"Ah, yes, the Presentation. I will be there as well." She might have attempted to sound annoyed, but I think she was looking forward to the extravagant beauty and pageantry of the event. She looked at her watch. "Oh, I always enjoy your company far too much. You have somewhere to be in an hour."

"I'm meeting the planners to pick out the final dress."

Standing, she took a look at the empty platter she'd put out. I'd devoured the food and she took it as me liking it. I was just hungry, so I'd accepted her partially sugared cookies and vegetable sandwiches.

"Before you go, I have something for you." Quickly she left

and then returned with a dark-wood framed piece that matched the frames of the art in our home. Confirming that she was responsible for the pieces.

"Abstract expressionism," I whispered.

Her face brightened with delight and pride. "I knew you'd know."

"You made this?"

She nodded. The colors, emotions, and symbolism that caught my eye reminded me of the painting that I'd fallen in love with. Although I knew she was the artist and the boys in the picture were Josh and Ethan, she'd never confirmed it. The colors of this work were warm, not as vivid as her other art. Shapes looked like wolves to me. Through the swirls of colliding colors I saw a face—no, faces. Three. And more animals in it. Or images that made me think of my pack.

"I love it," I said with awed reverence. I wasn't being polite; it was beautiful.

"You see a lot in it, don't you?"

I nodded. Her smile widened. "That's what I love about you and your interpretations. You always say that they are simple and inexpert, but your insight is unique, seeing things in art that others don't see. It's refreshing."

"Will you go with me to look at dresses?" I blurted out. I didn't want the time with her today to end. If I were to be honest, her hand on my shoulder, the warmth and endearment I felt, genuine acceptance—I didn't want it to end.

She made a sound of surprise. Genuine surprise. And when she clutched her pearls I had to bite my cheeks to keep from laughing. I think I had just seen Claudia's version of her happy dance.

~

Claudia didn't need any introduction; when she walked into the bridal shop, David instantly recognized her. Not as Ethan's godmother but for her art gallery. Trent was enamored by Claudia and as she declined the offer of white wine in lieu of tea, I stood next to him, seeing her the way he did. He scanned her and smiled approvingly. He did a double take at the gloves and flashed a smile. They didn't look peculiar on her. Claudia's appearance nudged that part of him that adored classic elegance. That side that loved Katharine Hepburn and old movies and secretly adored a time when people were more formal and clothes a statement. Claudia was the embodiment of it.

They seemed entranced as she sat with her tea.

"That's not three dresses." I pointed to the rack of potential dresses.

"No, there are nine."

"I said three."

"They're similar; pick the three you want and try those on," David said, waving his hand dismissively at the display.

Claudia rose from her chair and moved to each dress, giving it a long appraisal, then me, and then the dress again. She separated out three. "I think these would work well for you, dear," she advised gently. "Although I'd really like you to give these two a try as well. I think they will look good. But it is your decision."

I groaned. Managed, that's exactly what was happening. It was what happened to Josh, to Ethan, and now to me. I didn't have a problem barking my dissatisfaction at David and Trent, because they would snap right back. Then we'd verbally spar until someone conceded. Nothing like that would happen with Claudia. She'd look hurt and I'd feel horrible.

I nodded and asked Trent and David to help me bring the five dresses into the dressing room. The beauty of by-appointment-only shopping was the privacy. I tried on each dress and walked out into the sitting area to show Claudia. Instead of giving an opinion, she asked what I thought.

It was the fifth dress that invoked silent appreciation. Claudia didn't have to ask my opinion, because I knew it was on my face. It was a soft champagne color with floral lace appliqués over the bodice, floor-length, understated tiers of satin and silk organza. I sighed, looking at my reflection in the mirror: it was the very thing I'd said I didn't want in a dress but was what I ended up loving. I felt like a hypocrite.

"Look who doesn't have a problem looking like a princess," Trent teased, adding to my apprehension.

I winced, loathing being a cliché in the fairy-tale ballroom gown of lace, silk, and satin. I looked back at my second choice. Claudia eased up behind me and slipped off my ponytail holder; when my hair fell, she gathered it and held it pinned up.

"You look beautiful. Do you plan on getting married again?" she asked earnestly.

"No."

"Then why not get the dress you want and be happy, rather than subject yourself to some arbitrary restriction of what you can or can't wear? If you want to wear a dress like this, then wear it. You love it, I know you do, so get it."

I loved it.

She let my hair fall and took my hand and patted it and looked shocked and amused when I held on to it. Claudia stood next to me, while I looked in the mirror, holding my hand in the most maternal way, and it made my heart ache. This wedding was making me emotional, and I could understand why. Perhaps it was the human part of me. I was getting married to the man I loved.

"This is the dress," Claudia assured me, while Trent and David were empathic with their approval.

I chose the dress.

CHAPTER 27

*W*ith the wedding at one, of course my day started at seven in the morning, when David knocked on the door with a team of people for makeup and hair. Because the day before the wedding I wasn't supposed to sleep with Ethan, per David's declaration, I was in a hotel near the wedding venue. Then from the hotel, to a small tent near the wedding, because heaven forbid Ethan got a glance of me before the wedding; apparently the world as we knew it would come to an end, birds would plummet to the ground, the sky would bleed, and geriatrics would collapse out of wheelchairs. I just reminded myself that we were in the final stretch. I'd had enough of my favorite people slash wedding planners to last several weeks.

Steven poked his head into the tent before stepping in. His ginger curls were coiffed, a result of what his mother had been doing to him when David had rushed me past them to my little hideaway.

"Here you are!" he said, his smile broad and dimples deepening in his cheeks. His granite-colored suit was beautifully complemented by a mauve handkerchief and patterned tie of mauve, gray, and cream. It matched the flowers and the inter-woven flowers and stones in my headband.

"I'm not hard to find; after all, it's a tent in the middle of an arboretum." I gave David a scathing look. "A tent I'm sure he didn't have permission to erect."

"It's a yurt, and they didn't say I couldn't." David sniffed, slighted.

"Of course they didn't," I said. "There's always a loophole. I hope it serves as a good defense when they try to ban you from ever reserving here again," I teased.

He made a sound of irritation as he darted a look over his shoulder at Kelly, who was soothing a disheartened and disgruntled Gavin, who continued to complain that he hadn't agreed to do this. He reminded her that she was the one who'd decided to assist, not him. Her full lips spread in a beguiling, calming smile.

"You are part of everything. I couldn't imagine walking down the aisle with anyone else but you," she soothed, kissing him on the cheek. It worked—in a manner that it only did with Kelly. He still contested his participation in the "froufrou" event out of principle—taking an obligatory stand like Ethan did with so many random and inconsequential things. Finding it amus-ing, Kelly crossed her arms and listened to his complaints with a placating smile.

"They're so funny together," Steven mused, watching them. I noticed it was the same way he looked at me and Ethan. We were an unlikely couple, but I didn't think we were as dissimilar as Kelly and Gavin. I didn't get them, which was the beauty of their relationship—it just worked.

"Are you ready?" Steven asked, when David left to referee the dispute starting between Winter and Trent, who was trying to remove another one of the many weapons she'd thought was appropriate for my wedding.

Steadfast, Trent had his hand out, waiting for her to hand over the knife she had sheathed at her thigh.

"It's a wedding, woman. Seriously, how do you live your life? Where are you hanging out that you need to be armed at all times?"

"I like to be prepared."

"For what? Do you plan on slicing the bouquet if it comes in your direction? Or do you think the caterer is going to forget their cutlery and be in need of yours? Knife. Please." He extended his hand, as defiance and determination overtook his features.

"No," Winter asserted, just as determined. I couldn't help but wonder if she really thought nothing was going to be said about the dagger she'd brought or the sword she had sheathed to her back, which Trent and David had wrangled from her.

"I let you do this to me"—she jabbed her finger in the direction of her hair, interwoven twists, braids, and hair overlays sweeping into an updo that was quite flattering but nothing she would ever do to herself. "And this ridiculous dress. I'm not giving in to any more of your demands." I swallowed my laugh.

Trent gasped and stepped back, his hand to his chest, being more theatrical than usual, looking as injured as he would have been if she'd turned the knife on him. Winter rolled her eyes and slapped the hilt of the sheathed knife into his hand. "Fine, the dress isn't ridiculous. It's quite nice," she breathed out drily. Trent took care in picking dresses and had settled on an A-line, and a sweetheart neckline. Wispy and flowing chiffon and silk, cinched at the waist by a satin sash. If it wasn't for the mauve coloring, it would have made a beautiful wedding dress.

"And you look absolutely beautiful in it."

She rolled her eyes again, then lifted her dress to expose the lower half of the calf, where another knife was stored. Pulling it from the sheath, she handed over what I suspected was the final

313

weapon in her arsenal. It was the closest thing he'd get to an apology.

"It's Sky and Ethan's wedding—I think we all should be armed. No telling what's going to happen."

With a dismissive wave, Trent said, "Almost everyone in attendance has claws, fangs, or magic. I think we'll be fine."

I hadn't even thought about it, but it was the mating that seemed to be the problem. A wedding wouldn't change anything. I had to believe that and hope no one would ruin it just for the hell of it. I hoped I was right.

David looked everyone over again and nodded his head in approval. They lined up: Gavin with Kelly, Winter with Trent. Steven bent his arm for me to take as they headed out. I hesitated—too long. So long that Steven took it and placed it around his arm.

"You're not getting cold feet, are you?"

"No, I love Ethan. We're mated and live together. And as nerve-wracking as David and Trent made this, I want to do it. This just seems like the final step. The final change in my life. The mating is recognized by the otherworld, and the marriage will be accepted by the human world." In that moment my life replayed and I dropped my hand from Steven's arm and took his hands into mine. "Thank you," I whispered.

"What?" he questioned, shocked and confused.

"I don't think I've ever thanked you for all that you've done. You were my first real friend. The best introduction to the pack. A person who I loved like you were really related to me—my brother. I love you and thank you for that."

Unable to hold eye contact, Steven looked away, his cheeks ruddy. "I … we … nothing to thank me for," he fumbled out. "I love you, too. You've always been more than a friend. … You're my family, too. …" He sighed an exasperated breath. His fingers nervously ran through his hair, disheveling it and undoing his mother's grooming. "We should head out or David's going to come back. He's kind of demanding and an ass when it comes to this wedding."

I grinned. "You should thank me for preventing you from living your life in filth. You really need to get better about cleaning. That's the only thing I would change about you. You're a pig," I teased, hooking my arm through his as we went out of the yurt.

"If it's any consolation, it's the one thing my mother would change about me, too. She made me sleep in the barn for three nights: 'If you want to live like an animal, then you can go sleep with them.'"

I laughed because it was a threat I'd made to him as well.

Our delayed presence earned us a dirty look from David.

"He's a wedding tyrant," Steven mumbled.

Claudia was right. I planned never to do it again. The arboretum seemed fitting, my pack seated where they were surrounded by trees, nature, and air scented by flowers, oak, and poplars. The aisles were lined by Ipomoea alba, moonflower, and large bouquets of them were placed at each side of the entrance.

Sebastian stood just outside the decorated gazebo, dressed in charcoal gray. His deep brown eyes looked relaxed and warm as I approached, my arm slipped through Steven's. Ethan held my attention. It had been thirty-seven hours since I'd seen him.

A dove-gray tuxedo brought out the blue of his eyes. I garnered the full intensity of his gaze as he saw me for the first time in the wedding dress—quite different than the other one he'd seen. His eyes were vivid and compelling, as if the wolf half had receded far back, allowing him to enjoy this wholly human moment. Standing relaxed, he watched me with hypnotic attention as I walked toward him. I didn't care that all eyes were on me as I walked down the aisle, slow rhythmic movements in time with the classical rendition of the "Wedding March" performed by a violinist and cellist.

The ever-present human part of me saw this as the final process of our mating. This was the joining that she understood. She found comfort in Sebastian's speech joining two people who loved each other in matrimony.

Ethan cleared his throat as he looked past me. Drawing his eyes back to me, he gave a faint smile. "I never thought I'd be here," he admitted softly. "Not here and especially not with you."

This better get nicer really quick.

Recognizing how it sounded, he shook his head and moved closer. In that moment, it seemed like the world around us disappeared. It was just Ethan and me, talking. Speaking words of love with the reverence and dedication of a pledge.

"I didn't think I'd be here and I didn't think it would be with you, but I'm happy it is. I can't imagine anyone else I'd rather spend the rest of my life with. Our life together won't be easy." The realization eclipsed his face. He moved even closer, his voice dropping to a faint whisper. "And we'll never have the normal that you want, but we'll have each other and we'll create our normal. I can't think of anything better than experiencing life with someone who makes it infinitely better. I love you, Skylar Brooks, in a way that I never thought I could. In a way I never thought I could love anyone. I plan to do so until I take my last breath. To make our normal the best it can be, for us."

He bent down, his forehead pressed against mine. His warm breath brushed against my lips as he spoke. "It was a bumpy ride getting here, but I am here—with you. And there isn't any place I'd rather be—ever." His voice dropped to an emotional whisper. "You are my forever."

It felt like it was just us. Our forever and our moment. I blinked back tears. Ethan leaned down farther to kiss the lone one that slipped past.

"I guess I can't just say 'ditto,'" I said in a hushed, shaky voice.

He chuckled.

The speech I had memorized was long forgotten. It seemed so manufactured, inauthentic and polished—the opposite of what Ethan and I had. It was complicated, with peaks and valleys, and roughened edges. It wasn't necessarily pretty, but we'd created something we adored despite its flaws. He and I had become us.

"I love you, Ethan, and everything about us—even the things that drive me crazy. You're right, it took us a while to get here, but it was the journey that made us what we are. It grounded it into something that is real—that is truly us—and nothing else compares. I am so happy to have my forever start now with you. Until I take my last breath, I love you."

"I love you, too, Sky." We stayed close, still unaware of the people around us witnessing this exchange. It wasn't until Sebastian cleared his throat that we remembered we weren't alone. We stepped back into our original positions and allowed Sebastian to close the ceremony.

While everyone headed to the reception conveniently located on the grounds, Ethan took my hand and guided me to the car, parked away from everyone, near a large oak tree. He'd had his share of interaction with people and between the photographer, the driver—whom he'd sent home—and the caterers, he needed a reprieve. I needed one, too. Fingers intertwined with mine, he walked to the car with purpose and helped me in, folding and twisting the voluminous material inside. Ethan watched everyone from the rearview mirror.

"Let's leave," he suggested, shifting his gaze to me. His voice was rough and breezy with a sensual undertone to it.

"And not go to the reception?" I asked, stunned.

"It's just a party. Let them eat, drink, and have a great time."

"Without the bride and groom?" I asked in disbelief.

He turned toward me, and his tongue moved languidly over his lips. He leaned over and pressed his lips against mine. A sensual caressing of my lips, nothing like the chaste kiss he'd given me during the wedding or the cool, restrained one he'd done for the pictures. In fact, those were rigid and apathetic as he struggled with dealing with the demanding and annoying photographer, who kept taking pictures. Pictures I knew would be placed in an album that might never be opened again. But it was traditional and what we were supposed to do. Twisting and contorting who we were into tradition and "normalcy" was getting tiring. It was a harsh realization that, after all the lectures about what was "wrong," "traditions," and "purity of magic," there were similar values, views, and restraints in the human world.

Ethan's strong, commanding fingers pulled me closer to him. His lips moved to my jaw, lustful and wanton, planting satin kisses over my bare skin. Long, deft fingers played along the edges of the corset near my breast, sending a shiver through me.

"We go to the hotel, order room service, spend the rest of the night there"—he nipped at the bottom of my lips before kissing me—"leave the next morning for the honeymoon." He'd moved his hand from the nape of my neck and through the layers of fabric up my thigh until he felt the lace edge of the stocking and the decorative clip holding it up. A deep growl reverberated in his chest, and he looked at the dress again. His intense gaze moved from the edge of the skirt, over the bundles of gathered satin and the lace overlay of the corset to my breast.

I pulled away and put as much space as I could between us in his new sporty acquisition, a Spyker C8 Preliator, a reward for getting through the wedding. An expensive treat that had Steven, Josh, and David having car-gasms over it. I just didn't get it.

"We go to the hotel and ..." The suggestion lingered, and the way he was looking at me, my mind went to places it shouldn't have.

"What do you have on under there?"

There wasn't any way I was showing him, but if reason failed, I'd tell him how I'd acquired the sexy ensemble, which involved Trent sweeping me away to a lingerie store and putting various scanty outfits in front of me until we'd agreed on one that could be easily concealed under the dress. But I couldn't un-see Trent giving me tips on the art of seduction. "Ethan's seen me in a t-shirt and shorts. Those seduction efforts seem to work just fine," I'd reminded him, and once again was rewarded with a disapproving eye roll.

I'd thought he was going to have a conniption fit at the mere suggestion of me wearing my typical nightwear on my wedding night. Just thinking of the past month and the preparation for it, skipping the reception didn't seem like such a terrible idea.

Seeing the contemplation on my face, Ethan's brows rose. "So, we're going to leave ..."

"No," I responded, firmly enough to dissuade him from any more effort to convince me. "We go to the hotel and then what, spend the next three hours with Trent and David knocking at our door? Because they aren't going to go away. We go to the reception, make an appearance, eat food, toast, have wedding cake, and then escape."

I coughed out a laugh at Ethan's sulky face. It took years away from him and made it difficult to remember that vicious wolf that lurked behind the moue of displeasure.

Trent and David let out a collective sigh of relief when we entered the large banquet hall, hand in hand. We had agreed to the reception but the plans had become a heatedly contested debate and, surprisingly, I was the one who'd required arbitration. David and Trent had wanted traditional, with us seated at an extravagant table with the wedding party. I hadn't wanted any of it. Ethan's prowess as an attorney had been on full display during the debate. I was used to being the one handling the situation and talking Ethan into playing nice with Trent and David, so this turn of events had left me flustered. It was just supposed to be an after-event party, with food, drinks, friends, and family.

Moonflowers were placed at the center of each table in glass vases with the image of two wolves wrapped around the bases. I looked over at David and he winked and smiled. The room was too big for the number of guests, but the increased space allowed for a large dance floor, the open bar, and the DJ.

At the edge of the dance floor was the cake—simple vanilla because, as I was reminded, red velvet wasn't a flavor that everyone liked. During dinner came the toast: Josh telling a room of people he was glad we ended up together before we ended up killing each other. Based on the applause and laughter, it was a mutual opinion. But he went on to say how happy he was that his brother had found someone who clearly made him happy.

Sebastian's commanding presence overtook the room as he stood with a genuine smile of happiness and addressed us. He raised his glass and spoke earnestly. "You two were the bane of my existence," he started off slowly.

"Bane of my existence"? What type of speech is this? I know you are aware of what they are. They're like your rants, but nice.

His smile faded slightly but there was a spark of enjoyment in his amber eyes as his gaze settled on Ethan, who was showing his dissatisfaction with how long the reception was. My new husband had a passable hitch in his lips that could pass for a smile.

"Your differences complement each other despite the battles, the eye rolls, frustrations"—he gave Ethan a look—"and constant assertions that 'the brunette is going to be the downfall of this pack.' And here we are. I don't think I'm alone in saying that I didn't see this coming—but I'm glad it did. It's a completed circle," he said softly. Ethan took my hand; it seemed like a sweet gesture until he gave me the "after the speeches we are leaving" squeeze.

I curled my hand around his and my nails bit into his skin. *No, it's our reception!*

The toasts continued, or I assumed they were toasts; after Winter's I started to think they didn't know the difference between a toast and a roast and fought the desire to tell them that a toast was the nice one. Ethan and I sat as they toasted—or roasted—us getting together and seemed relieved that we ended as a couple rather than two corpses, taking their last breaths as they strangled each other. I didn't think we were that bad.

Ethan continued to smile, something that would have seemed believable to and even considered charming by any other audience. Instead, as we moved through the small crowd, thanking people for coming, Josh gave his brother an assessing look and smirked. "That looks sincere."

"It's been a long day," he admitted.

"And we are going," I said, clasping his hand in mine.

We left.

Ethan's warm fingers were interlaced with mine as he opened the door to the hotel. A different hotel than the one I'd gotten dressed in earlier that morning. Our suitcases were in the corner. He released my hand and stepped back, taking me in. His eyes eased over me in slow, languorous sweeps.

"You look beautiful," he breathed out, giving me another perusing look.

I looked down at the dress, studying it anew. My lips quirked into a grin. "I feel like I should be in an amusement park, taking pictures with small kids."

"No, it's beautiful. You're beautiful. Mrs. Skylar Brooks-Charleston?" he asked softly, faintly amused. Moving closer, he carefully removed my headband and then the tie securing my updo. My hair fell, and he ran his fingers through it as he kissed me.

His satin-soft touch was a contrast to the ravenous way he'd looked at me just moments ago. He explored my mouth, slowly and attentively. Heat inched over me at the gentle touch of his hand cradling my face as he kissed me again. His tongue traced lightly along my lips. Each time Ethan kissed me, I was reminded of how decadent his kisses were. The sensual softness of his lips, the languid but primal way they pressed against mine. An unsated hunger he seemed desperate to soothe. Lacing my fingers through his hair, I gave in to the comfort of knowing he would be the only man I'd ever kiss again. Stepping back, he loosened his tie and removed it, watching me the whole time.

His heavy, fixed gaze seemed unable or unwilling to look anywhere else. The suit jacket and shirt soon followed. Naked from the waist up, he glided toward me, giving me another kiss —hungry and voracious—and I panted softly against his lips before he pulled away.

A vulpine look coursed over his face. "I'd like to see what you have under the dress," he whispered.

I nodded once and turned my back to him, exposing the zipper. Taking the invitation, he moved closer to me. He pushed my hair away and kissed me lightly on the nape, then along the curve of my neck. I shuddered as his nails grazed along my bare skin before caressing it. Deft fingers slid the zipper down and then he gave the dress a little tug and it slipped from me and pooled at my feet. I stepped out of it and turned to face him. He exhaled an indulgent breath and held it for what seemed like forever. A deep rumble reverberated in his chest with his exhalation.

His gaze lingered. "This is a far cry from t-shirt and shorts."

He took in the lace-trimmed stockings, the garter belt with a little bow on it, the panties—smaller than anything I'd ever worn before—the pearl-colored lace corset. He lightly brushed the skin over the swell of my breasts before placing a kiss at every spot his fingers had caressed. I closed the very small space between us until I could feel him against me. His breath was warm and rough against my ear, seemingly torn between being there, touching me, roving his eyes over me, and removing the lingerie. He knelt down, pressing his lips against the bare skin around the clips holding up my stockings and leaving trails of warmth from his lingering tongue. His fingers stayed in contact with me as he moved upward, nails lightly grazing, hands caressing as he took his time unlacing the corset.

Once he had it loosened, he gave it a little tug and it dropped to the ground. He cupped my butt, lifted me, and carried me to the bed. In haste, he removed the remainder of his clothes. Each touch and kiss that roved over my body felt like erotic reverence. I clawed at the sheets as he kissed and tasted every inch of my body. Panting with desire, I shuddered when he finally sheathed himself in me.

His movements were slow, rhythmic, and controlled, a distinct difference to the fierce way he looked at me, the fervor of his kisses, and the passion in his fingers as they dug into my skin. He whispered my name, my full new name with his, over and over again, like an oath or prayer. The mating satisfied the wolf, the marriage the man.

The floor-to-ceiling window gave us an unobstructed view of the beach and the clear turquoise water. Palm trees and large, aromatic flowers peeked out from the sides of the hotel. The scent of fruit and chocolate from the basket left in our room filled the air. I wanted to joke about this being ostentatious and clearly a waste of money. And complain about the semiprivate plane with just two other passengers, I assumed a couple, on it. They clearly didn't want to be bothered or make any friends. They didn't care why we were going to Hawaii, and Ethan didn't care why they were. I was curious, but their "your side of the plane is that way" look quashed my curiosity quickly. Ethan was pleased by their incivility; it unsettled me.

"This is amazing," I said to Ethan when he embraced me from behind.

"It's not Portugal, but we'll have a great time." The tinge of disappointment in his voice bothered me. He wasn't disappointed that we were in Hawaii but that he couldn't give me the honeymoon he thought I wanted.

"It's beautiful, Ethan. A perfect beginning," I said turning to face him. *Come on, you're always assessing my vitals. Do it now!* I didn't have to coax him to do it; he smiled. "And we won't miss the vampire prom—"

"Presentation, Sky."

"Whatever. They are going to be dressed in their finest attire —you saw the invitation"—I rolled my eyes at the image of it that popped into my head—"and it's going to be the most extravagant, ridiculous soiree I'll ever witness in my life. I am positive of that."

Ethan chuckled and moved toward his bag, pulled out his swim trunks, and stripped and dressed. I did the same, slipping into my bikini.

Lips curled into a sly smile, Ethan eyed my white cover-up, its thin crocheted design along the waist exposing my stomach, and tugged at the tie revealing my swimsuit. My tiny swimsuit.

"When we change with the pack, you spend most of your time crouched over, hiding your 'lady goods,' but you're okay with your barely there bikini," he teased.

"It's the beach. Of course, I'm fine with it. Standing in the middle of the forest naked is odd, and you can't convince me otherwise. You just like being naked. Oh, so I won't have to say it again, just because it is a semiprivate area doesn't mean you don't have to wear clothing. People can see you."

Ethan smirked and moistened his lips, and I knew he was about to hit me with his brand of arrogance and say something about no one complaining. "Just. Don't. Do. It," I responded preemptively. "No one wants to see your ass, no matter how nice you think it is."

"You think it is."

I rolled my eyes, grabbed my small tote, and tossed stuff into it: towel, sunblock, my Kindle. Ethan slipped his Kindle in, too. His phone he turned off and stored in a drawer. "Are you sure you want to do that?"

Without hesitation, he nodded. "For five days—it's just the two of us. Winter can handle anything that happens. I'll just deal with her litany of complaints when I return. For years, I was concerned about her eventually challenging me—I'm not anymore. Apparently, I have to do too much. 'You know how I feel about Sebastian, but I don't need to talk to him every day. That's just weird.'" Ethan ended with a poor rendering of Winter's voice.

I followed suit and put my phone away. "Okay, just the two of us."

CHAPTER 28

*E*than kept his promise. For five days it was just us, without any outside interruption. I was quickly jolted back to the real world once on the plane, as his annoyance heightened at his ignored video chat requests to his brother. Before the plane took off, he called Josh.

"Why aren't you picking up your video call?" he snapped as soon as Josh answered the phone.

"I answered your text," Josh responded breezily, which he knew would fuel Ethan's agitation.

"I texted you because you didn't answer the chat. I texted you to answer the damn call."

"I'm quite aware of what your texts said, Ethan," Josh continued, relaxed and aloof, and I could imagine the smirk as he needled his brother. "So, what's up, bro?"

"Don't 'bro' me. We will be taking off in a few minutes. I need you to answer your video. I want to see your face."

"No."

"No?"

"No, that's weird and so random. What's wrong with you? You want to see my face? You see it all the time, it hasn't changed."

"Is everything okay?"

"Yes. Everything is fine, just like I texted."

"I can hear it in your voice. I need to see your face. I can tell when you're not being honest with me."

"The world didn't fall apart because you left for five days. Have a safe flight."

Josh ended the call, and I slipped the phone from Ethan's hand before he crushed it. Slumping back in the deep leather seat, he scrubbed his hand over the light beard that had formed from the missed shaves over the past five days. The light tickle of the hairs didn't bother me anymore, and I loved the way it made him look. He was going to shave it the first chance he had, but casual clothes, mussed hair, and a light shadow beard that brought out defined cheeks and intense, emotive eyes made honeymoon/vacation Ethan even more appealing.

I placed my hand on his leg. "We'll stop by his house as soon as we land."

I was absolutely positive it was the plan anyway, but I preferred suggesting it as my idea as opposed to him playing into the role of overprotective brother. It wouldn't fool Josh, so I wasn't sure why I even bothered.

Josh looked expectant and smug, leaning against the frame of his front door as we pulled into the driveway. Poking at the irritated wolf in the only way a sibling could. A devilish grin spread over his face.

"Rayna has the Aufero," he informed us once we were in the house.

"That's not something you thought you should tell me?" Ethan derided.

"What exactly could you have done about Rayna getting the Aufero? We've been looking for it for weeks. She got to it first."

Josh was attempting to sound calm, but there was a concerned catch in his voice. "You couldn't have done anything about it while in Hawaii. You needed to enjoy your honeymoon."

Ethan's hostility faded and he nodded at his brother and gave him a small smile. "Thanks."

Come on. Hug it out. This is one of those hug-it-out moments.

It was wishful thinking. They had drifted from the moment to action mode. Ready to divide and conquer the situation.

"She's approached Ariel." Josh shoved his hands in his pockets to keep from biting his nail beds and showing his concern.

"About what?"

"Their hand in helping you all, the were-animals. She expressed her concern that Ariel is doing a disservice to the witches' reputation."

"Is she strong enough to use the Aufero to strip them of their power?"

Josh took in a sharp breath, trying to tamp down his growing fear and keep his voice steady. "*Us.* You know once she comes for them, I'll be next."

"Does she have the other objects?"

"I think she has them all," he admitted. There was a long, strained silence. "She's not going to stop until she has everyone turned against us—the were-animals."

The complexity of Josh's situation reared its head. He wasn't a were but considered himself one as much as a witch. He was the pack.

Minutes later we were going over the dossier that Ethan, I suspected with the help of Quinn, had compiled that had Rayna's last four addresses. We traveled to the only one that was in the city in Josh's Jeep. From the rearview mirror, I could see

Ethan perusing all the information he had on her, looking up from the information in thought.

"What triggered it?" he said aloud with deep consideration as he looked out the window. There were more layers to her return. Could it be the return of the Faeries? Or that the clandestine veil the pack had stayed behind for so many years had been pulled back, and what they saw of us warranted her carrying on Marcia's legacy of disgust and hate toward us? Or was it as hazy and obtuse as Ethan and I mating? Had the potential of offspring made her fully accept Marcia's flawed vision?

The lights were off, and we didn't hear any activity inside the home. Ethan nudged the door with his shoulder, breaking the lock. The lights were off—we turned them on. It was better to have them on and go through the house like we were expected guests rather than snoop around with a flashlight. If a neighbor happened to see us, it was less likely they'd consider us intruders. After all, who'd be so bold as to walk around a house as if they belonged there when they didn't?

There was nothing inside except an opened journal revealing a written account of were-animals. Their true form— before magic and evolution made us what we were today. There were horrid accounts of our existence and misdeeds as scavengers and animals who walked on two legs like men but looked like beasts. Animalistic features, elongated snouts, large teeth, gray/brown fur covering every inch of our bodies. Long claws on our hind legs that dug into the ground for purchase, aiding in balance to maintain our upright position. Our speech was unintelligible, hindered by our primordial form.

I decided not to read further. I'd experienced our history firsthand. Rayna had made her point: we were just those things to her and would never be anything more. With the crimes she had assigned to us, she wasn't willing to see us as anything more.

I breathed in deeply; hidden behind the residual magic, amber, sulfur, and tannin was a very familiar smell—Liam.

Elysian was our next stop. Using the same power words we'd used before to obtain entrance, we waited for the barrier to open to us. Instead, it held, bucking and pulsing as the others struggled to keep the doors closed to us. After several unsuccessful attempts, Liam emerged, blocking the small opening that he'd used.

His haughtiness was on full display. He looked down his aquiline nose at us.

"Is there a reason you are here?" he asked with bored annoyance.

"We need to speak with Rayna," Ethan explained to him, the sharp edges of his words inferring that we knew he was hiding her.

"You think she's here?" His brows arched. It was baffling how such a small movement could be so powerfully expressive. "Go away. You're wasting my time. But for the sake of amusement, let's say she's here—what do you want with her?"

"She has something of ours that we want returned."

Liam made a bemused sound, sporting the same annoying brow arch. "Does she have something that is yours or something you *think* should be yours? Because possession is ownership. I can't imagine with your *colorful* retrieval tactics and"—his lips pursed derisively—"ways that anyone would have anything that you considered rightfully yours."

"It's mine and I want it back. In fact, I want them all back. They aren't rightfully hers," Ethan challenged.

"And yet she has them," Liam rebutted ruefully.

"We need entry to speak to her." The slight rumble in Ethan's voice wasn't missed by Liam, who stood taller, his regal appearance a peacock's display of his title of Makellos, the elite among the elves. The purest of their kind.

"I do not wish to be part of your battles, but whether or not she's here is not really of your concern. If she were, I'd not allow you entrance to speak with her. Nothing you have presented has warranted it." His gaze sharpened. "Unlike Gideon, I will not buckle under the demands of your pack, and I'm fully prepared to fight for the privacy of Elysian. Our guests will remain unharmed and unharassed. But I am not a man without a moral compass. If I believed you were missing an object you indeed owned, I'd ensure that it was returned to you. After all, I am a man who honors and respects the rules." An implication that we didn't. "But until you have more evidence, I cannot be of help."

"She threatened me. We need to make sure that she's not in a position to follow through with it," I said.

Making an annoyed sound, he dismissed my accusation with a wave of his hand. "Posturing and threats among the denizens are so typical, they're essentially greetings." He waved indifferently and his tone was flippant: "'Hi, I plan to destroy you,' 'Good evening, tonight I will bathe in your blood,' 'I'm going to wear your head as a charm.' It's so"—he inhaled a breath and exhaled it in one word—"exhausting. I'm going to suggest you file away her words as just that, words. She hasn't acted on them, and you of all people know how often threats are used and not enforced."

"We've never made one that we didn't follow through on," I pointed out.

"Of course." He gave us another castigating look of disgust. "Well, most do it out of anger and frustration. More so when dealing with the likes of you. It does take a toll on a person, as it is doing with me now. To be honest, I'm quite bored with it all. I've been reduced to only responding to attempts. Has an attempt been made on your life, Skylar Brooks Charleston?" he asked. It was a special talent, his way of saying a name with the same tone of one finding animal poo on his shoes.

"No," I answered.

"If she acts on those words, then I won't offer her safety, but I will not stand by and allow you to steal from her. If it were indeed yours, you'd have it in your possession."

"Then know this: if one of the objects she has is used to hurt others, you allowed it to happen and will be held just as accountable as she is. These are not just words that I've spoken on a whim. I mean it," Ethan warned.

Liam's nostrils flared as he lifted his nose in that snooty way that was becoming increasingly annoying with each moment I spent with him.

"Well, of course. You are nothing if not consistent." His lips pressed into a line, his gaze roaming slowly over each of us, the most attention placed on me and Ethan. His voice was too small and wistful, briefly reminding me of Demetrius the time he'd shown the other side of himself, something more linked to humanity than anything I'd seen before. "I preferred what you were before to what you are now. Then we could see the were-animal. It's too far removed now." He eyed us again, this time focusing on Josh. "Were-animals and magic don't mix well. There was a reason you were made that way." With that, he slipped back behind the invisible wall. A wall that held steady at our attempt to reopen it. We could have used more magic and torn at the hole, but Ethan seemed reluctant.

"Just let it be for now," he said. Responding to our surprise at his suggestion, he said, "The picture." It seemed that even Ethan was tired of us being depicted as creatures not far removed from our ancestors. "It gives her more credence and proof. If we tear open the barrier and she hasn't actually made an attack, she'll continue to win people over and make allies of those who otherwise would remain neutral. We take away that power and make her look like the aggressor by doing nothing. If she stays quiet, great. If not, then we respond with force."

CHAPTER 29

*D*avid, Trent, and I all stood wide-eyed in awe at the display before us. The extravagant, ostentatious pageantry was a manifestation of how Demetrius saw the vampires and the lengths to which he'd go to curry favor with Chris and get her to return the feelings he obviously had for her. The large, stylishly decorated ballroom had high ceilings, marble floors, and exotic statues flanking the entranceway. Exquisite star-shaped chandeliers had been dimmed and gave off a moonlight glow to set the midnight mood.

The ballroom was filled with vampires, some of whom I knew. There were far more that I didn't. This was more than just a small party to show off Demetrius's shiny new mistress, it was an exhibition of a change in order. Chris would be the Mistress of the Northern Seethe. Once the most infamous Hunter of the otherworld, she was now the Mistress of the largest and most powerful Seethe.

A small band in the corner played gentle soothing melodies that blended seamlessly with the chatter of the attendees. Most of the conversations were murmurs but others were just loud enough for me to glean the main topic—Chris. A few people believed that it was too soon; others wondered what had taken him so long, aware of Demetrius and Michaela's polyamorous relationship. Many thought it had been destined to fail and had expected that one of his lovers would quickly take her place.

Ethan kept a protective hand pressed against my back. I had a cautious eye on Trent and David, who were being quickly taken in by the spectacle and grandiosity of the party. Even the pristine hosts—I suspected members of Demetrius's garden, dressed in tailored designer suits, both the men and the women —left them in a state of amazement. It wasn't as if they weren't used to nice parties and exorbitant galas; David worked as a publicity agent for several high-profile clients and Trent had a successful business as an events coordinator. The lavishness of the vampires seemed to exceed their expectations. Beautiful people were dressed in formal wear that was as lovely as they were. They took sips of champagne, which was very pleasing and undoubtedly very expensive. Hints of crisp peaches and light tones of honey lingered on my palate.

I'd opted for a floor-length, strapless silver gown, the darker-hued embroidery complementing Ethan's dark gray suit. It was a last-minute purchase, since I wasn't able to fit into my original dress and the other dresses in my closet were too snug. Too much eating and not enough exercising over the past month and the honeymoon had made it worse. Light cast a pleasant shimmer over my new husband's appearance, defining his attractive rugged looks and deep bluish-gray eyes that sharpened as they traveled over the room.

"This is so over the top even for them," Ethan acknowledged as he looked at the floor-to-ceiling windows that formed the back wall, offering an unobstructed view of a light show outside among sculpted fountains.

"Look at that," I suggested, tipping my head to the far end of the room where there was an ice sculpture of a winged woman, an angel I suspected, standing in the middle of an opening flower, extending her arms in offering as if presenting a gift. That was the closest thing to the famous scene in *The Lion King* that I was going to get. But the image of Chris being held up to the overdressed crowd in presentation made me chuckle.

"This is amazing," Trent mused. His attention bounced between the two people in the corners, dangling from the aerial lyra. A man in one corner, a woman in the other. Scantily dressed, they were grace in motion. Lithe and sensual, they moved with ease to the slow swing of the music. I could see Trent's fascination with them. There was something enchanting and commanding about their performance.

I did another scan of the room and had to clench my teeth down hard on my tongue to censor the many snarky and judgmental things waiting to be said. This was absurdly and unapologetically pretentious. It was Demetrius on steroids. If I hadn't already disliked him, this fiasco would have easily shoved me in that direction.

Ethan's fingers pressed even harder into me as I noted the entrance of the vampire who'd just walked in. Confidence and profound arrogance cascaded off the planes of his sharp jawline and supple bow lips, which curved into a grin at the room and showed his fangs. His eyes were midnight onyx, the sign of a well-fed vampire. He ran a hand through soft waves of gilded hair that seemed too light for his dark eyes, even with the thick-lined pale lashes. He stopped just a few feet from the entrance, looking over the room, seemingly posing to allow others to get a good look at him. Dressed in a navy suit, he wore no tie, and the handkerchief in his pocket was various hues of vibrant blue and green. In a room full of dark suits, he stood out, which was obviously his point. Before Ethan could tell me, I'd already guessed—Alexander.

As his gaze moved around the room, his disdain for some of the attendees, mainly Ethan and Sebastian, was apparent. They seemed equally unhappy with his presence.

I split my attention between him and the several vampires who seemed very interested in David and Trent. It was the incessant attention that made me realize there were no other humans present, with the exception of the band. Allowing my friends to come had been a bad idea.

"They'll be fine," Ethan assured me, sensing my discomfort. "I suspect more humans will show up for dinner and the entertainment." My stomach turned. It wasn't the dinner part—I took blood from Ethan more often than I or he cared to admit, so I couldn't be turned off by that. It was the entertainment that left me perplexed. The vampires' "garden" of people who willingly allowed themselves to be used by them in any manner they saw fit bothered me, and squelching the urge to protect people who foolishly didn't feel any need to be guarded was difficult for me. I was all too familiar with the lure of the vampires; on a different level it existed with were-animals, too. Something tenuous, raw, and ineffable spoke to people on a primal level and left them bewildered by the allure they felt. I tried to transfer that understanding to the vampires—I couldn't. With the exception of Quell, and on a very peculiar level Sable, I didn't like any of them. Images of Chris popped into my head. I liked her. Chris was a vampire—it seemed more real now standing in a room of people who were celebrating that and her ascension to Mistress.

The luscious, fragrant smells of exotic flowers, wine, perfume, and cologne overwhelmed the room, but based on the scowl firmly fixed on his face, Ethan couldn't get past the scent of vampire. Sebastian, who was on the other side of the room looking just as disgusted by the overzealous display, was the powerful image of primal beauty and looked as if he belonged in a place filled with beautiful people. Ariel, who'd come with him, smiled as if she had read my thoughts. Her white, flowing goddess dress with a long slit contrasted with his black suit. What was her deal with white? I made a mental note to ask her.

Perhaps she considered herself the person who always wore the white hat, especially when she was chastising us over our misuse of magic. Her hair was worn back from her oval face, showcasing dangling diamond earrings.

Gideon and Abigail completed the show of leaders from the otherworld. The fraternal twins had dressed to complement each other and their peculiar violet eyes. Gideon's wine-colored suit flattered her deep taupe sweetheart ballgown. The lower half of the gown had a delicate embroidery overlay. She looked sweet and affable in it, belying the cruelty of her nature; it was the most deceptive dress in the room. The contempt I had for her and the dress must have shown, because her smile faded once her eyes turned to me. I yanked my gaze from her because I knew I could easily spend the night glaring.

Ethan was the first to notice Claudia as she entered the room, elegantly dressed in a modest tulle dress with appliqués that matched the pattern of her gloves. Hair pulled back in a stylish bun and a small flourish of flowers, her expression remained neutral as she took in the room. Unlike me, she managed to look at the over-the-top Presentation without letting her thoughts be expressed on her face.

Finding us in the crowd, she greeted all four of us and, despite Trent and David's fascination with the extravagant Presentation before us, her simple appeal spoke to them. It was a different appreciation for what she offered, and it seemed to be the consensus of many people in the room. Her supernatural identity remaining a mystery to most—she was often regarded as a fae—she commanded unusual deference. Ethan stood next to her, where I assumed he'd stay the rest of the evening.

"Enjoy yourselves. I'm here to make the obligatory appearance, but once I greet Chris and Demetrius, I will be leaving."

She excused herself to mingle with the guests, and we returned to our position across the room.

My attention returned to where it should have been, on the

vampires. I reactively assumed a protective stance when a woman eased her way across the room, gliding with the grace of a dancer. She smiled at Trent, showing the edges of her fangs. He returned the smile. He wasn't intrigued by her grace and beauty but rather by her couture silk dress, which melted over the lines of her body. At that moment I realized that David and Trent's awe wasn't fascination with the luxury of the gala but rather what it represented: a time when people were formal. When people dressed for dinner, and wore layers of clothing. No matter what fueled the appreciation, it was still a vampire ball and he had the attention of one. *Move along, lady, there's nothing here for you.*

"Hello." Her voice was velvet-smooth and inviting, just like her smile and dark, warm eyes.

Trent had received the talk before we'd arrived. It was probably similar to the kind a parent delivers to avoid having a child lured away with the promise of candy. Five glasses of champagne later, I knew his walls of protection were paper thin.

"You may be the most beautiful person here," she cooed, her eyes moving over him in appreciation. She reminded me of Michaela but, except for the dark hair, there weren't any physical similarities.

She dangled the candy, a compliment that made him blush, and he was about to take a big chunk out of it.

"Please, you must dance with me," she said, extending her arm. Without a second of thought, he was about to grab it. This was such a bad idea.

Grabbing his arm, I tugged him out of her reach and hissed, "You do realize David's here."

"Yes, *Mother*, I realize that. She asked me to dance, not to have sex with her in the middle of the room. And I promise if you let me go, I'll be a good boy." Easing his arm away from my hold, he moved toward the vampire and let her guide him onto the dance floor.

As one of my *children* escaped me, because apparently I'd assumed the role of the nagging parent, I realized I'd lost sight of the other. David had been ensnared by a couple on the other side of the room. Their arms were interlinked as they spoke to him, and he seemed to have forgotten that healthy fear he'd had of everything vampires were capable of. His light laughter made me tense.

He looked in my direction and caught my disapproving look. His smile fell for just a moment before they said something else that brought another curl to his lips.

"Calm down, they're fine," Ethan instructed in a gentle, coaxing voice. How wound up was I that the king of overreaction and overprotection was instructing me to calm down? Was I that bad? I must have been, because I hadn't realized he'd taken my champagne glass from me. "I was afraid you were going to break it. Then we'd have something to worry about."

He leaned in, pressing his lips to my cheek before whispering in my ear, "You don't have anything to worry about. Just enjoy the night."

"Give it to me!" I commanded, extending my hands. When he didn't immediately fill them, I patted his chest and pockets.

Confused, he asked, "What? Give you what?"

"Drugs. Whatever you've taken, I want some, too. And if you had some of those fun brownies your brother's so fond of and didn't share, I'm going to be really upset with you," I teased.

The levity of his laughter relaxed me some, but not enough to keep my eyes off Trent and David. At least they heeded my warning and made sure not to hold the enticing vampires' gazes for an extended period of time. Trent moved along the floor with the honey-complexioned vampire, dancing with a grace and ease that made them seem like they belonged in a different era. Trent looked so stylish and poised, no one would believe he sometimes sat on his sofa, a wineglass in hand, yelling at the housewife of whatever city to "tell that cow ..." or "yank out her extensions." The refined person in front of me would do no such thing. David and Trent were social chameleons, and I loved that about them. They'd adapted relatively well to me being a wolf, the pack, and a world full of dark things that did more than bump in the night.

Ethan's ease bothered me. A man that could be bothered by the wind blowing too hard was draped in a calm, easy awareness. I was convinced he adopted such calmness just to annoy me. I was the erratic person on edge, tensing every time someone looked in Trent's or David's direction or moved within five feet of them. Ethan enjoyed every moment of my heightened awareness and the predator in me being alert and ready to act at any moment. His lips curving ever so slightly as he watched me out of the corner of his eye confirmed it.

Voice lowered to just a whisper, he said, "You don't have to worry, because any bad behavior would reflect on Demetrius and would be penalized harshly. Do you think he would prepare such an extravagant event only to have it ruined by a fight? You think the vampires aren't aware that they are our humans?"

"*Our humans,*" I repeated, frowning.

Ethan sighed heavily. "Do you think they refer to them any other way? That means something to them. While they are friends to our pack, they are nothing more than 'our humans' to the vampires, which gives them just a slightly higher standing than other humans." Vampires didn't think much of humans and considered them nothing but currency to be exchanged and bargained with or objects to be used for food, salacious acts, or both.

The band stopped playing, and everyone stilled and turned to Demetrius, who personified midnight: dark tailored tuxedo, blue/black hair that gleamed under the light, which cast a dark shadow over strong features. His self-satisfaction added a hint of a glow to him. Chris had her arm linked through his, her eyes moving around the room. It looked as if she had to suppress an eye roll at the Presentation—or maybe I was deflecting.

She looked undeniably, stereotypically, and seductively vampy. She'd poured herself into a long, garnet strapless gown that plunged in the front, making it obvious taping techniques had been used to keep it in place. It hugged her toasted-almond–colored body like a second skin. A network of thin straps laced up the back. The dim light reflected off a ring that made my wedding ring pale in comparison. Hers could have given birth to mine. It was ornamental and brazen, like the solitaire stone that hung from what I suspected was a platinum chain. Her dark brown hair was swept away from her face and tucked behind her ears, displaying earrings that matched the necklace. Chris was right, Demetrius had more money than he knew what to do with. And yet he still couldn't buy the one thing he wanted—Chris's true affections.

For thirty minutes I watched Demetrius and Chris address the crowd, waiting for the Presentation. I expected theatrics: perhaps a marching band, a town crier, a person dropping from the ceiling to perform an over-the-top aerial ribbon routine, or a melodious tenor serenading the guests. My imagination went wild, and yet I don't think it could ever match what Demetrius had planned for the evening.

Demetrius's attention was abruptly pulled from the guest he was communicating with as Alexander approached him. They chatted for a few minutes before Demetrius clapped his hands once, and from each corner of the room, a woman in a flowing, shimmering gold dress, a crown of flowers adorning her head, emerged holding golden chimes, on which she played a unique melody while the band played quietly in the background. It would have been enjoyable if I wasn't preoccupied with rolling my eyes and wondering at what point gagging wouldn't be considered rude. Taking Chris's hand in his, Demetrius led her to the center of the room once the chime introduction had finished.

Demetrius nodded in the direction of the band's conductor, and the players packed up their things and filed out in a line with the same practiced elegance as they had played, taking with them the aerialists and a few of the servers. I assumed the other humans who remained were part of the Seethe's garden.

Demetrius's deep, smooth voice rose above the crowd: "Thank you all"—he looked over the room in one sweeping move—"for joining me in this momentous event as I present to you Christina Rose Leigh, my partner, consort, and the new Mistress of the North. This marks a new era, one that I'm sure we will be proud to be a part of."

Was she becoming the Mistress of the vampires or being crowned a queen?

Alexander snorted and wasn't deterred by Demetrius's cold, chastising gaze. Easing slowly toward the center of the room, he said, "It *is* a new era. The one where the North will fall from greatness because you've decided to take a paramour that is so common and a very undiscerning choice. Even if you ignore that she attempted to kill me, should we ignore the fact that the new Mistress of the North used to warm the bed of the Beta of the Midwest Pack? Is this what you've been reduced to, taking the discards of a cur?"

Chris remained stoic, skilled at ignoring insults and allowing them to roll off her as if she were Teflon. I wasn't sure if it was something she'd learned to do as part of her job as a Hunter or if she didn't think highly enough of most people to care what they thought of her. Whether she was offended or not, I was offended on her behalf.

Alexander had positioned himself in front of her, although he continued to address Demetrius. "Have you no shame? Must your people be subjected to having"—he sneered at Chris and then shot Ethan a disparaging look—"the were-animal's cast-off as a Mistress?"

Chris's lips curled into a mirthless, disparaging smile that mirrored the one Alexander was giving her. "If he should have shame for anything it should be for allowing a poorly controlled Neanderthal such as yourself to have control over the South. You shouldn't be responsible for the care of your own life, let alone hundreds." She stood taller, straightening her spine until she looked rigid, an iron bar that could withstand anything. "I make no secret of my past, because it is what has made me who I am today. But *you?* You have plenty of things you should be ashamed of because they have not made you a better person, just more abhorrent. I tried to kill you because, although minimal, we do have rules of engagement when it comes to those in our use." I thought calling them a garden was bad enough. She made it sound worse—or rather called it for what it was.

"You had drugged that poor woman and were doing cruel things to her. If I had my way, I would have done even crueler things to you. But you are Demetrius's, and I will not fault him for the fondness he has for you. It does seem that he is blinded by the love he has for his imbecilic progeny. Where most fathers would harbor nothing but shame and regret, he still manages to show pride and adoration for someone who is clearly undeserving of it. While you cast aspersions in my direction, know that you can never think any less of me than I think of you."

Alexander started to respond but stopped when Demetrius held up a hand. His sire's face wore a combination of pain, betrayal, and overt confusion. The mélange of emotions made him look vulnerable. Demetrius could be hurt—and he was. "You have been in my city for days, have fed with me, been entertained by me, and have spoken with me about all the inane things you could think of, but it is *now* that you've chosen to express your concerns with my choice?"

Indignant, Alexander spat out his words with virulence.

"How should I have handled it? You held no regard for us by choosing, *this!* And I am to answer to her as my equal."

"As your superior." Demetrius gave Alexander a well-deserved look of reproach. "I created you, and the South was a gift. One that you didn't earn or ascend to. And yet, this is how you reward my generosity."

"Demetrius." Chris's tone was gently firm and chastising. "You can't be surprised by this behavior. He is handling this in the manner he's handled most things: without any reason, strategy, or propriety. I understand and respect the love you have for him. But do not expect him to be anything more than a disappointment. I've dealt with him only a fraction of the time you have, and because I am not blinded by emotions, I see him for the maladroit that he is. You continue to waste time trying to make him something I can assure you he will never be. Though created by you, he will never meet your expectations or your greatness. He is indeed a waste."

Directing her attention to Demetrius, sympathy and affection resonated in her voice and her features like I'd never seen before. If she was putting on a performance as the doting new Mistress, she'd succeeded, and most of the crowd was looking at Alexander with the same disapproval and disparagement that she was subjecting him to.

Vampires couldn't blush, but his cheeks had an odd glow to them. He was pale and fuming with contempt. Still focused on Demetrius, Chris didn't see Alexander stepping forward to backhand her, sending her back several feet. He lunged at her, and my yelping her name came too late. He slammed her into the wall. Hoisting her up by her neck, he slapped her again. She whimpered, defenseless, sagging into his hold. Ethan grabbed me when I started toward her. Wrenching my hand from his hold, I started forward again, preparing to slip off my shoes and use the heels as stakes. They were long enough. I'd made sure of that.

Ethan's hold on me tightened. "This is not your concern. Let it play out."

"'Let it play out,'" I hissed through clenched teeth. "This isn't a childhood fight on a playground over a toy. He will kill her."

"Sky, I'm not going to let you go." His arms were a steel girdle around me. "Let. It. Play. Out."

I was fuming more than Alexander. I watched in forced patience.

Lacking an appropriate weapon, Alexander decided to use his fangs like a knife and went for Chris's neck. Demetrius was on him in a flash, ripping him away and tossing him back into the middle of the room. His fury radiated like a fiery, devastating storm that would level a major city in a matter of minutes. His quick, sharp, vicious movements were a reminder of how he'd become the Master of the North and why he was as feared as he was revered. He plunged a stake into Alexander, who had a look of wide-eyed betrayal. Years of being favored and doing whatever he liked with impunity left him bewildered that when he was finally punished, it was with his life.

Demetrius watched in silence, his face devoid of emotions, as his progeny went through a slow and painful reversion. He took his eyes away from the scene only to give a cautious glance to the crowd, as if he was warning them not to stop it by feeding him.

The process seemed to take longer than I'd ever seen, due to the intensity and absurdity of there being an audience as Demetrius committed prolicide. Once he was standing in front of a pile of ashes, he looked over the crowd. A swell of emotions, possibly sorrow, pain, anger, frustration, regret, and entitlement, converged into something that made him seem despotic.

"Does anyone have anything else to say?" he asked in a tight, cool voice.

Weighted silence filled the room for several uncomfortable minutes. "Very well, let's continue with our celebration."

From the corner, Ariel's fingers circled the air in sharp, precise movements as she whispered a spell. The ash came together in a pile, whirling around in a cyclonic spiral and levitating in the air until the empty champagne glass she'd moved with another wave of her hand was under it. The ash-filled glass lingered in front of Demetrius until he took hold of it. With a nod of appreciation, he took it into his hand. Sorrow overtook his features for a fraction of a moment as he looked at the glass that now held the ashes of the Master of the South and his beloved progeny.

I will not feel sorry for Demetrius. Empathy reared its head, and for a moment, once again, I found myself reluctantly feeling sorrow for him. It was short-lived when he gave a nod of his head, and his uniformed garden ushered in a cluster of humans dressed in clothes that were formal but tailored to expose necks, wrists, and thighs. Given the salacious display of veins, they were going to be used for entertainment and hors d'oeuvres. I looked for Trent and David, who had moved to the other side of the room and, despite the violent ordeal earlier, were still being entertained by two male vampires. They were enthralled, but not magically. Unlike the other vampires, who were fixated on the new arrivals, appraising them as if in an art gallery preparing to purchase or bid, the vampire duo's interest was firmly fixed on Trent and David. As I made my way over to them, I had every intention of disrupting it.

Geniality was harder than I expected, since I knew the vampires' intentions weren't good. It was confirmed the moment I got close: my body hummed and vibrated as if I were entering dangerous territory and needed to be alert. The dagger-sharp looks that the vampires gave me made it clear that I'd become an obstacle to their plans.

"I'm sorry to interrupt," I said in an overly saccharine voice.

"Gentleman," I entreated David and Trent, "it's getting late and it looks like the night is geared toward the vampires." I let my gaze drift to the gaggle of humans being ogled, touched, and inspected, hoping that Trent and David could draw their attention from the men long enough to take in what was going on.

One of the vampires stepped forward, bowing his head in acknowledgment. "I'm Vincent, and you are?" he asked, his voice smooth, intoxicating, and musical.

"Sky." My voice sounded rough and hard compared to his.

Taking my hand, he kissed it. "It is a pleasure to meet you. I noticed you earlier and your attempts to help the new Mistress. It is greatly appreciated. I'm forever in your debt." Keeping a light hold on my hand, he directed his attention to his partner. "This is Ashton."

He reminded me of Quell, and I was struck by the same feelings I'd had when I first met him, spending my introduction looking for the flaws. Finding any was going to take more time than I had. As I sized up Ashton and Vincent, I knew most people didn't stand a chance against their allure, and my infatuated friends weren't making any secret of it. Trent had a desire to taste vampire blood again and wasn't above doing an exchange, and the defenses that David had earlier seemed to be wavering.

"No problem. I just tried to warn her. But it wasn't enough. It's a pleasure meeting you." I slipped between David and Trent, hooking my arms around theirs. "It's getting late, and you know my saying—I leave with the people who brought me," I said, my attempt at levity, while fighting the urge to scream, "Stranger danger!"

"And you are. He's at the door waiting for you. Tall, sexy, and broody as usual," Trent shot back, glancing at the door where Ethan stood.

Seeing the other leaders of the various sects preparing to leave, I knew the night was about to move into vampire entertainment. Fake smile still plastered on my face, I gave them both a little nudge. "I came with three men, I'm leaving with three. Besides, we're your ride," I reminded him.

"If that's a problem, we will make sure they get home. And make sure they are safely tucked in." Vincent flashed a smile, making me think I was going to be the first person to ever reject him after seeing it.

I'm sure you will, but I'm going to bet it won't be before you've had a taste.

"No, I don't want to intrude on your evening. Enjoy the festivities." With a firmer nudge from me, they reluctantly followed my lead out the door.

"I don't think I've ever met more intriguing people. They are over a hundred years old. So many wonderful stories," David said, his voice full of delight. It was obvious that his interest was strictly in the stories that the vampires had to tell. I wasn't totally sure that Trent shared it.

"Yes, but I can assure you that their interest in you was more than just another person to tell their entertaining stories to."

"Life has to be hard for you to be so cynical and on alert even during such a nice party." Trent had just said something that I'd thought about Sebastian and Ethan so many times. Guilt warmed my cheeks. But I'd seen so much that I couldn't see the world with rose-colored glasses and naïve optimism.

"You are human. They see you as entertainment only. What you were being treated to was seduction into being just that. It is easy to be enthralled by it and not see it for what it is."

"Your relationship with Quell didn't happen by seduction," Trent pointed out. It was as if the wound of his death was reopened, and it happened every time someone mentioned his name. I wondered when it would stop.

"No, we were friends." My voice quivered.

"I don't doubt that they were interesting and they were probably interested in you as well, but that would not override

348

their desire to feed from you. You two would present a challenge, far more exciting than the willing participants they traipsed in. Whether you realize it or not, you were being hunted. Their Master was just killed and they are in a new town. I doubt much care would be given. Not everyone respects your affiliation with our pack. Or perhaps they'd be willing to take the risk to have you. Flattering, but won't mean a thing if you are dead. Sky saved your lives," Ethan offered, his voice cool and even.

The blood drained from their faces. Once again I was filled with guilt for bringing them into this world and pondered if there was a way to make them forget it all. A spell or something. But that would make it worse. I believed forcing a person to operate in the dark left them more unsafe. I'd been on the other side of that darkness and wouldn't do it to them.

They had the same solemn looks on their faces when we dropped them off at their home. "You scared them," I said once they were inside. Trent was at the window, assessing his surroundings, probably with his sword in hand. It wouldn't do him any good; despite his training with Winter, he was more of a danger to himself than others. I was opposed to Winter's "strike first and ask questions later" approach to protecting themselves.

"They need to be afraid. Fear might motivate them to be safer. I don't want them to die." For Ethan, that was equivalent to confessing he cared for them. He'd never say it. They would never hear it, and just saying that much probably left a dank taste in his mouth.

He kept looking in his rearview mirror as he drove away. When their home was no longer in view, he pulled out his phone and made a call.

"Are you busy?" he asked Winter when she answered.

"What did Sky do and how bad is it?"

"I'm right here," I said, knowing she'd be able to hear me.

"I stand by my question," was her brazen assertion.

Ethan laughed. "It's not Sky, but it's Sky-adjacent."

"David and Trent?"

"Yeah. The Presentation didn't go as smoothly as expected and the Southern vampires no longer have a Master. He wasn't much, but his erratic behavior did help some. I have a feeling they are going to have a lot of fun in our city and leave a mess to clean up. I don't want David and Trent to get caught up in that. They piqued the interest of two old vampires. I don't think they are going to leave without having that interest satisfied."

"Okay, I'm going over there, but I'm going to kick Trent's ass if he tries to 'find the woman behind the scowl' and give me one of his dumbass makeovers. I don't like people touching my hair."

"Don't scowl, 'black swan,'" he joked. Winter said something rude and he laughed. I still didn't quite understand the camaraderie that existed between them, but it was a different relationship than either had with any other pack member. He said they understood each other, and I still had no idea what that meant. "Winter, things are a little fragile. If any vampires show up, please try diplomacy first."

"I will. I'm going to show them all types of diplomacy. Diplomacy will be seeping out of all the cuts on their body." She hung up, and I shook my head.

Ethan smiled. "I didn't see what happened today coming," he admitted.

Still irked by him stopping me from intervening, I had to work to keep the anger out of my voice. "I think Alexander was underestimated. You saw how quickly he overtook Chris. With all the rumors and things said about him, I didn't expect him to be so powerful."

Ethan's brows pinched together and he frowned. "Powerful? Why do you think that?"

"He overtook Chris so quickly." I turned to face him, now

displaying the same anger and frustration that I'd had to fetter at the party. "Why did you stop me? He could have killed her."

"I stopped you because it needed to play out the way Chris intended. She goaded him into attacking her." His eyes moved from the road to me, taking in my response to the information before continuing. "Chris allowed him to overtake her. Alexander didn't stand much of a chance against her when she was human. Now that she's a vampire, he had no chance in hell."

His lips quirked into a smile in response to my shocked look. "When he attacked her, she didn't look at him, she watched the crowd. The Northern vampires who moved to protect her are the ones who have accepted her position and can be trusted. Those who did nothing will be watched and are possibly enemies. In her position, I would have done the same thing."

He chuckled, and a look of admiration moved along the planes of his face. "Most people would have missed that and will perceive her as weak. That will give her an advantage, because those who haven't accepted her position and want to remedy it will be surprised. It's an excellent strategy. People often dismissed her success as a Hunter as luck. It's always good to have those who might be opponents underestimate your abilities."

Feeling foolish and misled, I frowned. I never would have thought of doing that. "Is there a class about this or something? If so, I need to take it."

"Sweetheart, if there were a class, you would spend most of it looking at videos on YouTube. I can't imagine how many videos of cute animals there are on there to distract you."

I should have been more discreet about doing it during the pack classes, because everyone kept bringing it up.

"Do you think the visiting vampires are going to start trouble?"

"Some will, to test Demetrius. I'm sure there are some that cared deeply for Alexander and, although they would never directly challenge Demetrius, they will do things to make his life hell. One way is to visit and leave a mess in their wake for him to clean up." The last words held a rumble of anger.

"The witches," I blurted. "Sebastian took Ariel with him. I'm sure they know who you are and her display of magic revealed her ability." Not that they didn't know who she was the moment she walked in.

"I don't think they would go after the witches. Vampires and witches have had an amiable relationship for many years. It's the relationship with vampires and were-animals that's strained and fragile. ..."

"Vincent and Ashton's interest in David and Trent is just to start trouble?"

"I'm not sure. Although Vincent claimed to be appreciative of your effort to save Chris, he didn't move to prevent Alexander from attacking her. There could be a number of reasons: fear of Alexander's retaliation if he'd lived, the desire for him to fail and die, making the Master's position open, or just indifference."

"You heard what he said from across the room." Each time I was faced with Ethan's heightened senses it made mine seem subpar in comparison.

"I read lips, too," he offered. "And I wasn't happy with him kissing you."

"On the hand?"

"Still didn't like it."

Ethan's phone rang before I could comment. It was Winter. "This isn't going to be handled diplomatically. There are more than just two here. There are seven. Two of them came together. Two annoyingly fancy ones I suspect are the vampires you were worried about. There are others and they aren't formally dressed. Maybe visitors that just started trouble."

"No, it's doubtful. Alexander had been here several days. I suspect they are newly created by him and have heard of his death," Ethan pondered. "They are going to try to start a war between us. With Alexander dead, control falls to Demetrius until another Master is appointed. Their behavior is a reflection on Demetrius. We'll be there in a few."

Ethan turned the car around and continued to drive while making a string of calls warning others of his suspicions.

Josh was the first person he called; Ethan was obviously relieved once he knew he was safe. The question was, would he remain that way? The threat was worse now; because of us, the vampires were no longer restricted by daylight. The fact they hadn't attacked didn't mean they wouldn't.

I hated the political maneuvering, posturing, and people using others as tools in efforts to get revenge. If they had a problem with Demetrius, they should take it up with him.

Ethan's unfettered emotions crowded the interior of the car, and I wondered if he was thinking the same thing.

When we came to a main street, Ethan didn't move immediately once the light changed, seemingly debating which way to go. Right would take him to David's, left to his brother's. The decision was hard for me as well. But at least Josh had magic. Powerful magic that he was extremely skilled with and had successfully used against vampires before. Winter was skilled beyond most expectations, but dealing with seven vampires, even if most of them were newly created, was going to be difficult. Ethan must have made the same assessment, because he drove toward David's home.

CHAPTER 30

e waited in the car when we pulled into David and Trent's driveway. Winter was to the right of a group of vampires, watching inquisitively what was playing out. Although vampires were able to walk in the day, they preferred the cloak of night, which at the moment worked out well because most of the neighbors were in bed and wouldn't witness what looked like a vampire standoff. Ashton and Vincent stood in front of five vampires who weren't as well dressed. Not poorly dressed in the eccentric way of Sable, but as if they weren't cared for. Ethan was right, these were newbies and pretty much orphaned.

Had Alexander planned to take them with them and help control them, or just make them and leave them to start trouble in the city? What happened in situations like that? Did they become Demetrius's problem? Demetrius wouldn't be able to spend time with Chris if he was trying to clean up behind newbie vampires that weren't created by him or his Seethe.

David stood at his door, shotgun in hand, aiming for the vampires. He seemed just as confused as I was as to who were the good guys and who were the bad—or were they all bad guys? Why had Vincent and Ashton come to their home? For a late-night meal?

Get in the house. Unable to convey those thoughts with my eyes, I slipped off my heels and slowly ambled to them.

"Get in the house. They can't pass the threshold without being invited," I said.

That's when I saw the face Trent made from behind David. "You invited them in already, didn't you?" I said, exasperated.

He nodded. "Just Ashton and Vincent. They were here before the others came."

I cursed under my breath but made sure I didn't show my irritation. It wasn't his fault. Trent saw them as interesting guests, not the walking death that they were. And maybe Ashton and Vincent found Trent and David equally intriguing and wanted nothing more than a friendship. The problem was that if they wanted more, my friends weren't equipped to defend themselves. My mind drifted to the first time David found out what I was and the days that followed when I explained everything to him. I would never be able to wash away the look of sympathy he gave me when he found out I was a werewolf and that of incredulity when he was informed of the other things that went bump in the night.

One of the vampires was no longer listening to Vincent, who seemed to be attempting to reason with them. Two seemed to stand down at his command, but there were two that seemed distracted. The youngest of the latter was splitting his attention between me and the gun that David had pointed in their direction.

Winter's patience had thinned, and it was starting to show. She didn't know who she should be going after. When it came to vampires, she would have been fine with taking them all on, but she was following our lead. Without the specifics of what happened at the Presentation, she was proceeding with caution.

The young vampire made his move, lunging through the air at a speed like that of a bullet, making it difficult for David to train his gun on him. He didn't go for David; swooping around him, he crashed into Trent. His hand went around Trent's mouth. He wrenched his head to the side and started to latch on to his neck. The only thing holding him back was the grip I had on a hank of his hair. He writhed and jerked, trying to get out of my hold. I tossed him back. His eyes widened and he leaned forward, inhaled, and moved back, hissing at me.

Trent was trying to make it to his feet. Then his eyes widened as he looked forward. The other one of the unmanageable two was moving toward him. Winter caught him midflight, an arrow from the crossbow in her hand piercing his heart from the back. Before he could get very far, there was nothing but ashes left.

Ethan kept a watchful eye on the remaining three and averted his eyes for a second when a bright red Audi R8 convertible drove up. Chris, not bothering to properly park what I assumed was another gift from Demetrius, stepped out. Vincent and Ashton's focus moved from the vampires to her.

"We have this handled," Ashton said, dismissing her with a roll of his eyes.

Chris was casually dressed in jeans and a pale blue t-shirt, a stark contrast to how she looked just two hours ago. I was wrong; the ring wasn't ornamental—or at least not to her, because she still had it on. Was it a reminder to others about her status as the Mistress? I didn't remember Michaela having one. But then again, Demetrius hadn't tried to purchase his previous Mistress's affections. Perhaps she'd put her ring away, along with some of the feelings she'd had for Demetrius. Their polyamorous relationship was something I had great difficulty understanding. I couldn't see how they could have loved each other and be involved in one, yet they'd confessed it quite often.

I shrugged off the thoughts.

"You should be with Demetrius, not here dealing with this."

"True. Yet, *this* is now my responsibility." She looked at the newbie vampire that I still had by the hair; Winter, who looked like her thirst for violence against vampires hadn't begun to be sated; and the three remaining vampires.

"Which ones are yours?" Chris asked, softly addressing Ashton.

His lips tightened. "We had every intention of taking them with us. We weren't going to leave them behind."

"That's not the question I asked. Which ones are yours?" she commanded.

"These three," he said, referring to the ones that he and Vincent were trying to get to comply.

"Neither one of you are strong enough to be creating vampires." For a brief moment she closed her eyes. I figured she was trying to decide what to do with them. She seemed to be grappling with the decision.

Chris's severe gaze bobbed between Ashton and Vincent and then to the barely controlled vampires.

"You will bring them to our house, where you will stay until they exhibit control that I am satisfied with."

"We were planning to leave tomorrow," Vincent said, squaring his shoulders in a display of defiance.

"Those *were* your plans before you decided to create vampires and let them loose in my city. There are new rules of engagement …" her words trailed off. Alexander's death didn't need to be relived. "Your plans have changed. Alexander allowed things that won't be accepted any longer."

Vincent dropped the look of geniality and replaced it with one of ire. "Alexander's way worked and we were happy to follow him." He moved closer to her, obviously an attempt to intimidate. She looked bored.

If I could hear the subtext in what he meant, I knew she could. *Not you. We will never follow you.*

"Gather your newbie vamps"—her gaze shifted to the one I was holding—"and the ones that Alexander created and left, and come to the house. I expect you to be there within the hour." She turned her back on him, which was a mistake in itself. Nothing said you were considered innocuous and nonthreatening more than having someone turn their back on you. It was a subtle and powerful statement. Chris had slipped into her role as if it were a glove—her birthright. Before she got in the car she said, "You can choose to ignore me, but I assure you it will be the biggest mistake in what will become your very short life."

And with that, she drove off. I could tell by the change in their stances that they struggled with feelings of anger and embarrassment. Anger Vincent wanted to direct at Chris was released on the vampire in my grip. The older vampire grabbed him by the shirt and tossed him into a car. The others followed without needing more incentive.

I stared at the cheese, chocolate, and bread platter placed on David and Trent's coffee table, along with four glasses of wine. Soft rock spilled from the speakers in the corner of the room. David and Trent hadn't decided on the position they were taking on inviting the vampires over. They were waffling between embarrassment, obstinacy, defiance, and repudiation.

"You asked them over?" I asked, making my words a rough growl as I looked over the room. "What did I tell you?"

David committed to an emotion and went with defiance. "Look, I know there are some bad vampires, just like there are horrible weres, but I don't appreciate being treated like a child. I can pick my friends just fine."

Ethan took a long, ragged breath, his jaw clenched so tightly, I feared it would lock. Instead of reacting on his impulse, he moved back, turning slightly to me. "Handle this, Sky," he urged through gritted teeth, his fingers pressed along the bridge of his nose. My ability to do so amicably was teetering. Civility dwindled as the misguided hosts stood taller with an air of defiance that irritated me. Having been in their position myself, I knew that being forbidden elicited something that couldn't be described as anything other than juvenile. It was the inherent dislike of being stripped of autonomy and free will. I got it, but the instinct to protect them was so strong, I was just seconds from locking them in a cage until they came to their senses. They weren't were-animals and subjected to our questionable rules and practices—what I wanted to do to them was illegal. Abduction. The fact that potentially committing a felony didn't deter me as much as it should have bothered me.

I blew out a breath and softened my voice as much as I could. "Vampires are intriguing. The lure is undeniable—"

"It's not the lure of vampires. It's Vincent and Ashton. They are different," Trent interjected.

My teeth embedded in my lips, pushing back my words because they were only going to make things worse. I wanted to call them naïve, tell them how stupid their actions were, and yell at them for behaving like they had a death wish. Several beats of silence passed and I spoke again when I was composed. "Fine, they might be good—there are plenty of good vampires."

Ethan scoffed, and I shot him a look. "I told you guys to be careful."

"We were careful. You saw them—they handled it and would have handled it just fine if you all hadn't intervened." David's voice was level and professional, which made his argument more cogent. He wasn't coming from an emotional place. His decision wasn't a result of him succumbing to simplistic urges. "Quell was a good person—not a vampire." I flinched at him invoking Quell's memory for this argument. "And Chris doesn't seem that bad. Let's be honest, if we were staying away from scary supernaturals"—his gaze flicked in Ethan's direction —"you two wouldn't be in our lives."

I couldn't argue against the defense he'd made. "Okay, but I need you two to be more careful."

David looked at the shotgun placed by the door, the sword housed in the umbrella stand, just like it used to be in my home and in Winter's. "We are."

"You handled that just great," Ethan muttered, irritated, once we were near his car. I stopped abruptly and glared at him. Angry that I wasn't able to change David's mind, I felt an abundance of pent-up anger, frustration, and fear. Emotions were spinning like a cyclone in me, and now they were ready to be unleashed.

"What did you say to me?" I snapped.

Ethan, just as irate about the situation, repeated himself with the same tone. Virulence colored his words as he met my challenge.

The fuse was lit. I stomped toward him, fiery with rage, and his look of defiance—the Alpha stare—only made things worse.

"You think that's the way I wanted it to end up? If you knew all the horrible things that went through my mind, what I was willing to do to keep them safe, you wouldn't dare talk to me that way," I spat out angrily.

I blinked back tears of rage and frustration. He jerked his eyes from me. He took several long, controlled breaths before his gunmetal eyes turned back to me and then dropped to the ring. I remembered when he'd proposed he'd said it was a reminder of the depth of his love for me. His attention was focused on it. Fixed in that moment. The tension slowly eased from his face. Clearing the distance between us, he gently took my face in his hands. He inhaled my scent, then pressed his lips to my forehead. They remained against my skin.

His breath warmed me as he spoke. "If something happens to them, it will devastate you. I don't want to see that happen."

I didn't want to have it happen, either, but we didn't have a lot of options. "They're not as careless as we think they are. Things might not have happened the way you would have liked, but it was handled."

"Yeah." Ethan was noncommittal and bland with his response. He didn't believe what I'd said any more than I did. He stepped back and extended his hand, and I took it, holding it tightly for the few feet we had left to get into the car.

He grabbed his phone and made a call as soon as he started driving.

"This can't be good," Josh said groggily when he answered the phone.

"Can you go to Trent and David's and put a ward around the house?"

"Does it have to be now?"

"Yes. I'd like one as soon as possible."

"Okay, give me half an hour."

CHAPTER 31

"You need to come get your humans." Demetrius's command was cold, callous, and indifferent. He rattled off the address and hung up the phone before I could repeat it back to him. My heart pounded. Ethan remained calm as he approached me. I knew it was for me—so he could help me achieve it, too. Scared and unfocused, tears welled and I couldn't stop the images of Trent and David being injured or worse.

Ethan embraced me from behind, his breathing gentle, slow, calming. Ensorcelled in his warmth, I felt my heart rate slow in pace with his. My breaths were no longer short, shallow pants but longer—allowing me to focus. After several moments, I allowed myself to relax against him. At least I could approach this with a clear head, without being guided by my emotions.

It had been five days since our last run-in with the vampires, and Trent and David's interest in them seemed to have waned. When I'd attempted to discuss Vincent and Ashton, the flicker of interest they'd had at the Presentation and that night at their house wasn't there. Had I missed the signs?

I was shrouded in guilt I couldn't shake off as we drove up

the driveway of a small, abandoned-looking stone home. The lawn was unkempt, the garden in desperate need of weeding, and one of the windows was boarded up. The gray stone was covered in dirt, and moss crept along it. Weeds grew out of cracks in the driveway. We parked behind Demetrius's car.

The moon was obscured by large poplars whose crowded branches allowed very little light to slip through as we made our way to the front door. The scents of wine, fruity body sprays, perfume, and cologne were faint in the air, all but overwhelmed by the smell of blood. My heart pounded harder as I followed trickles of blood that left a trail leading into the house. Walking through the darkened house, which was bigger on the inside than it had appeared, I wondered what condition I would find Trent and David in.

Light whimpering was faint in the air; occasionally there was a thud and someone groaned. Reluctantly, I tried to get a lock on their scent. Ethan's hand splayed on my back, urging me forward. We stopped nearly involuntarily when we saw a menacing-looking Demetrius in one room. The deep hues of his clothes were just as portentous as the malicious cast on his face, as he held Ashton off the ground by his neck. Ashton clawed at his relentless hold.

"Was this your plan?" Demetrius derided angrily, dropping the battered Ashton to the ground and then grabbing him by the scruff of his neck like a pup to face the onlooking vamps, who were wide-eyed and fearful at the sight of an enraged Demetrius. "Did you and Vincent really think you could over-take me with these new vamps?" Ashton's head started to drop and Demetrius wrenched it up, forcing him to look at his error.

"What the fuck were you thinking?" Demetrius criticized.

Finding their courage, several of the new vamps presented looks of determination, squared their shoulders, and took a step toward Demetrius in an effort to save their creator. Demetrius pinned them with a cold stare that promised a brutal end. "He is your creator; I am your Master. Who do you fear the most?" He drew back his lips, exposing red-stained teeth that had obviously been used as weapons at some point.

Ashton and Vincent were creating an army of new vampires. *Please don't let Trent and David be part of it.* I moved quickly through the house following their scents, checking the rooms with closed doors, in case my scenting of them was off. Ethan moved past me, taking a left down a long hall, and I ran to catch up with him. Throwing open the last door we found David, cradling a pallid, unconscious Trent in his arms. His head lolled to the side, and I could see the bite marks. David looked at me with teary red eyes as he pulled Trent closer to him. He started to sob uncontrollably.

I stopped cold. Breathing didn't come easily, and I had to force out each breath. My eyes burned with unshed tears. Mouth dry, I couldn't speak or move. Rooted in my position, all I could do was gape at Trent. An unmoving, pale, blood-drained Trent.

"He still has a heartbeat," Ethan said after a few moments of silence. I didn't hear it. Trent looked dead. I had already started the grieving.

"It's really weak, but it's there. We have to get him to Dr. Jeremy." Ethan moved quickly, taking Trent from David and rushing toward the door. Glass shattered and by the time we were outside, we saw Ashton running from Demetrius. In a flash of movement, Demetrius caught up with him. He yanked him back by the shirt and threw him to the ground. The group of young vamps, suddenly emboldened, charged at the Master. We wound our way through the bodies being tossed about. Pounded flesh, groans of pain, and hard thuds resounded. Chris drove up, blocking us in. Seeing Trent in Ethan's arms, she backed out and moved the car and quickly got out.

Crossbow in hand, she diverted just a fraction of her attention toward us as she watched Demetrius.

"Is he alive?" Her voice was brusque but there was concern in her eyes.

I nodded.

"Hurry up and get him out of here," she said, moving toward Demetrius. Ashton was still on the ground; several of the other vampires had been tossed aside, either injured or unmoving in states of reversion. Demetrius was too distracted to notice that Vincent had moved behind him, and turned in time for his heart to receive the stake that had been aimed at his back.

Chris drew in a shocked breath. Becoming a bullet of violence, she shot Vincent, and he dropped to the ground next to a dying Demetrius. His reversion was taking place much faster than Demetrius's, a sign of the difference in their ages. Ashton wailed at the loss of his lover and met the same fate, the result of an arrow from Chris's crossbow, as soon as he came to his feet.

As we began to drive off, I watched Chris kneel down next to Demetrius, her movements slow, mournful, and measured. She dropped her head, and moments later her shoulders shook, lifting up and down in jerky movements. She was crying. Chris was crying over Demetrius's impending death. My mouth dropped open, and as Ethan backed out of the driveway, I jumped out.

"Get them to Dr. Jeremy, I'll meet you there," I instructed.

"Sky, get back in the car. Now!"

"Just go. Please."

I ran toward Chris and Demetrius. Noticing me, she attempted to discreetly wipe the tears from her eyes. Tears. I knew that me gawking at her like I'd seen a four-headed camel wasn't helping. As I neared her, she was unable to hold my gaze. If she were human, she would have been flushed from embarrassment.

"I won't be able to find someone to feed him in time to save him." Her words rang true and not as a performance for

Demetrius. If it were, she deserved an award. The wariness and sorrow that clung to them were fooling me as well. He was dying, and the vampires who were in any shape to leave had scurried away at the sight of her. Vincent and Ashton were nearly gone, their bodies in the late stages of reversion. Demetrius didn't fight death the way I thought he would. Instead he rested against Chris, his deteriorating body unmoving. Long, dexterous fingers were the only functioning part of him, and they clung to Chris's hand. I cursed when I felt tears welling in my eyes when the only time he moved his lips was to press a kiss to her hand. Chris's face was moist from tears. She screwed her eyes tight to prevent them, but they trailed down her cheeks.

Aren't you going to beg me to save your life? Make a bargain of riches beyond my imagination to spare your life. Plead and promise to live a life of servitude. Something.

I found myself angry at them for not doing it. Him for not bargaining for his life and Chris for not doing it on his behalf. These messed-up whackadoodles deserved each other. Warped, sadistic, or masochistic, I had no freaking idea. I'd have to see whatever the hell they were in the DSM-V and, if nothing fit, make it a life goal to have someone add the Chris/Demetrius affliction to it.

Fingers placed firmly on Chris's chin, I made her look at me. Eyes reddened and moist from crying, she was unable to hold my gaze. *Ask me?* I knew she was holding fast to the promise she'd made to me. She'd let Demetrius die and sentence herself to a life of misery out of the obligation she'd made to me.

Woman, you have a problem.

Knowing it, I couldn't drop my eyes from the hardened woman who couldn't maintain that facade under the insurmountable pain. Her mask had fallen and her weaknesses were exposed, and I couldn't be the person who didn't help stop the pain. I'd probably live to regret helping Demetrius but I knew I would regret not easing her pain when I had the ability to do so.

When I shoved my arm in front of his mouth, Chris made a soft sound of surprise. Demetrius showed the same disbelieving look. His eyes widened as his lips parted. He hesitated before taking hold of my arm. Tentatively he inched toward it as if his life wasn't depending on taking the blood—my blood, the only thing keeping him from real death. Timidly, he sank his teeth into my flesh, watching me with suspicion. I realized that he was anticipating me taunting him with my blood. Giving him a taste and snatching it away to prolong his death, to be cruel. It was something he'd do. Then I actually considered it. I was helping someone stay alive who would think to do such a thing. It was the glistening in Chris's eyes that kept me from doing it. She cried—real tears. Real mourning. I wasn't so far removed from humanity that it didn't affect me. I dropped my gaze to the ground to keep from looking at her with renewed fascination, but it didn't last. I was staring at her like a child on her first visit to the circus.

"Please stop." Chris's request was barely audible. It had to be humbling to be looked at with wonder for showing a normal emotion that so many had displayed before. As if she wasn't privy to such things.

"I'm sorry," I whispered.

I didn't have to stop Demetrius; he did it on his own. He wasn't at full strength but was no longer in reversion.

Without me asking, Chris jerked her head in the direction of the car. "The keys are in the car." When I looked at Demetrius, she gave me a faint smile. "I'll call someone to bring him more." Her mouth opened several times to say something but I was pressed for time and couldn't wait for her to work through her peculiar emotions and feelings that I knew were just as mystifying to her as they were to me.

CHAPTER 32

The tidal wave of emotions eased in me when I walked through the door of the pack's house. Ethan's hair was disheveled from what he was doing at the moment, pushing his hands through it. Shirt wrinkled from carrying Trent, he hadn't bothered to straighten it. He stood in the middle of the room, frozen, his face unreadable, which triggered my panic. He blew out a breath. Weary and downtrodden. Sensing my panic, he said, "He should be fine. There was a significant amount of blood loss, but Dr. Jeremy is confident he'll be okay."

I exhaled forcefully, letting go of the breath I'd been holding since I'd entered the house. Ethan's face hadn't left mine, an audit of my appearance. He frowned. "You Skyed it, didn't you?" he said in a rough exhalation.

I wasn't sure how I felt about being a verb. When you Skyed it, was it a good thing or a bad thing? His indecipherable appearance didn't help, either.

He moved closer, his eyes still pinned on me. "Demetrius is alive, isn't he?"

I nodded, slowly.

"Skyed," he repeated with a dark, mirthless chuckle. He

moved to me, hugged me—hard. I had to pry myself from his hold. Reading his emotions was hard. It wasn't anger—something else. Resolve. He'd accepted that things were going to be Skyed. If only I could figure out if Skying was synonymous with screwing things up. I hated being a verb.

"Did you see her face?" I whispered. It kept replaying in my head. Chris had cried over Demetrius. It was hard grasping it. How hard had it been for her to feel the tears, to shed them, to have someone see her do it?

"Yes, which is why I knew he'd be alive." He took my hand and led me to the hallway outside of the infirmary, where David was standing, watching through the window whatever Dr. Jeremy was doing. Red-eyed and fatigued, he attempted a smile, his lips lifting slightly.

Ethan maneuvered me between him and David as if he needed a buffer. Noticing it, David stood tall, chin lifted, a poorly timed display of confidence that he shouldn't have. I was confident. I was a hundred percent confident I was the only thing standing between Ethan and a release of that repressed frustration he'd been refraining from revealing. I'd seen it peek through when we'd found them. Ethan had suppressed it. He looked like he didn't want to do that any longer. Instead, he distracted himself by watching Dr. Jeremy monitor the machine that Trent was hooked up to and Kelly the PICC line. Periodically she would stop to rub the patient's arm. He was sedated and it was clearly just comforting her. Dr. Jeremy made a face— vaguely similar to what Ethan had given me. Was she Kelly-ing things?

"They said they just wanted to talk."

"Don't talk," Ethan fired.

David swallowed but continued, "They were nice, I never—"

He stopped when he found himself face-to-face with Ethan, no longer confident that Ethan wouldn't hurt a human—I wasn't so sure, either. "What part of that fucking command did you not understand?"

"I am not part of this pack, you don't command me to do a damn thing," David challenged.

Thank you, David. As if Mr. Wolfie isn't pissed enough.

He'd nudged the ravenous wolf awake. Eyes galvanized to cold gunmetal, my mate was haplessly teetering on the line between beast and man. David saw it. Eyes wide, he let his pride foolishly rule his behavior and glared at Ethan.

"Then don't take it as a command; it's a threat. Don't open your mouth again. Nice or not, the damn ward was put in place for a reason. To protect you two. The only way it could be dropped is with the keyword that we have and you all had. You let them in." Ethan jabbed his finger at the door. "So whatever happened to him is on you. He could have died. How in the hell do you think that would have made Sky feel?"

David started to answer, but good sense and the look on Ethan's face quelled him. I could see the realization that the "hurt no humans" rule was slipping, and Ethan looked at him as if he were the biggest threat known to the pack.

I slipped between them and spoke softly. "David's been through enough today. Let it go." I nudged Ethan's hip and he turned. "You know you can stay here. Just pick a room. We'll be back tomorrow, and if you need anything Kelly will help you. She won't go home." Not because she couldn't. She wouldn't.

Just as we started out the door, Winter charged in, walking with purpose. "How did they get past the ward?" she asked the moment David was in her line of sight.

I sighed heavily. In one move, I had my hand on her, guiding her right back out the door she'd come in. "No. You're not going to yell at him, too. He realizes what he did was wrong. Please don't kick him while he's down."

"Trent is okay, right?" she whispered. "When Kelly called me, she told me he was going to be okay." Winter attempted to keep the emotion out of her voice, but it betrayed her. A wistful sorrow lingered on the last words.

"He should be okay. If you go in there you can't yell at David. I'm sure he's feeling like crap. He doesn't need more from you two." I shot Ethan a disapproving look. Defiant as usual, he returned the look. I could give him a long lecture about it and he'd still stand by his actions.

Winter nodded. She took several long breaths and closed her eyes, trying to get a handle on emotions that I thought she wasn't used to feeling and grappling with the fragility of caring for humans who were so easily broken. The confluence of that and how she felt about Trent's injuries was starting to show on her face.

"Okay," she said. She relaxed her frown and made her way back in David's direction.

CHAPTER 33

$\mathcal{D}$r. Jeremy had called to tell us that he'd be releasing Trent the next day. Ethan listened to the conversation from his position on the sofa, flipping aimlessly through the book he was reading. The nearly inaudible sound of the turning of the pages was the only noise in the room and had been since last night, when Ethan had said in no uncertain terms that he had no intention of apologizing to David.

In the kitchen, I kept looking over my plate, glaring at Ethan. I harrumphed, knowing he could hear me but was refusing to acknowledge it. A casual smirk lifted the corners of his lips as he relaxed back on the sofa, legs propped on the ottoman, dressed—as usual—as though he had somewhere to be: a light-gray shirt that brought out the gunmetal coloring of his recessed wolf and grayish-blue slacks that mirrored his eyes.

I was reduced to snorting and huffing while shoving muffin in my mouth and occasionally drinking a glass of milk. I wasn't opposed to milk but I preferred coffee with breakfast. The milk was a better pairing with the blood-rare steak, eggs, and side of red velvet muffins Ethan had prepared for breakfast. I hadn't been in a rush to have breakfast, to sit at the table with him, and had spent most of the morning in the bedroom.

I was content with stewing in my anger for a few more hours. All I had to do was load the memory of David's fear-stricken face for a few more minutes of self-righteous ire.

After I directed a particularly loud sound of irritation at my husband, he put down his book and donned the most saccharine smile I'd ever seen him give anyone.

"Sweetheart, if you're not going to speak to me, can you find a way of doing it a little quieter?" His cloying, bright voice was a direct contrast to his normal deep and effortlessly sexy one. It was more irritating than if he'd just continued to ignore me.

He rose slowly, a graceful wave of movement, still sporting the sugary smile that looked ridiculous on him. But I found a gleam of joy in the situation. As much as I hated seeing it, I was sure he hated doing it twice as much. He went to the fridge and pulled out a carton of milk and refilled my glass.

"Do you like the almond milk?" he asked.

"I'm not speaking to you."

"Yes, dear, and you are doing an exceptional job with it, too."

He laughed, breaking character, at my hard glare that folded my face in, wrinkled my brow, and pinched my lips. I had to look like a petulant child about to throw a tantrum—but I had every right to be angry.

"I know that's your pissed-off face, and perhaps I should have told you this years ago, but your face is too round and your features too soft to pull off that look. It's not intimidating, and to give you an idea of how innocuous it is, Gavin refers to it as your 'angry doll face.'"

I growled.

"That's more like it. Now, that's intimidating," he teased. He quivered dramatically. A charismatic wafer of a smile lingered over his lips. I didn't care how handsome and adorable he looked, I wasn't in a forgiving mood.

"How could you have spoken to him like that! You scared him!" I snapped.

"Good. Maybe enough that they'll be more careful next time," he countered, remnants of the same anger he'd shown David inching into his voice.

He started to fill the glass. "I want coffee instead."

"We've been drinking a lot of coffee lately. Let's try milk for a while." And in effort to show solidarity, he poured himself a glass. "This silent treatment you're giving me; how long do you plan for it to last?"

When I remained silent, he sighed. Inching close to me, he pressed his forehead against mine, his fingers brushing away wild strands of my curly hair that had slipped from the messy knot on top of my head. When he attempted to kiss me, I moved back a few inches and gave him a quelling look that he ignored. A quick peck on my forehead, and he shifted back. "What happens now, Sky?"

"You apologize." *Damn, do you need a social graces class or something!*

"What exactly do I have to apologize for?"

"I don't know, maybe you can apologize for the new flavor of Lays. What do you think you should apologize for: yelling at him, threatening him? You scared him."

"Good. Then I may have saved their lives." There were hints of concern behind the coolness of his voice.

Ethan's face was set, and I knew it would be a debate I wouldn't win. When he thought he was right, he was unyielding.

"You could have handled that differently," I admonished softly.

He shook his head. I knew that resolute look—I'd seen it enough. "I'm not sure I could have. You can be upset with me if you want; I will accept that and deal with it. Sometimes you have to be cruel to be kind. I'm trying to keep them safe, instill in them the need for caution. If they die, they won't have to deal with your sorrow—I will."

I blew out a breath. I was at a loss about how to deal with Trent and his vampire curiosity and David's obliviousness to the true dangers. Were they truly clueless?

"I still think you should apologize."

Ethan considered it for as long as I think was possible for him and said, "No." His expression was pained and he pinched the bridge of his nose before he dropped his head in annoyance.

"Answer the door; I believe it's for you," he huffed out.

Oh look, the wolf is going to blow the house down.

"They never came before," he grumbled. I knew who "they" were. Vampires.

I answered the door to find Demetrius, as healthy and vibrant as a vampire could be. He had to have been fed often to recover. His eyes were reverent, and his sudden bow at my presence was pious. Uncomfortable, I grimaced and put a few more feet between us. The heaviness of his gaze was hard to hold.

"Demetrius," I whispered, and it was then that he blinked. Just once.

He sniffed and handed me a black velvet envelope. Did he have stacks of envelopes from the haughty and ostentatious market? It was so beautiful that I couldn't help but run my thumb over it before breaking his seal that closed it. By the time I'd slipped the heavy paper from it, he was gone. I looked down at the bright white paper, and on it was his full name in script, signed in blood.

I knew it had meaning. Profound meaning. He had to have passed Edible Arrangements, a bookstore—I liked books—a store where he could have gotten a gift card or something. I'd even accept a t-shirt that said, "I saved the Master of the Northern Seethe and all I got was this t-shirt and a weird velvet-encased letter."

Ethan looked over my shoulder at the paper and made a surprised sound.

"What?" I asked, turning to look at him. Brow furrowed, he looked at the paper with grave surprise. Again, he made a sound of disbelief.

"I take it this is a big deal," I said, lifting up the blood-signed paper.

"It's a promissory note. Equivalent to him saying he will protect your life with his blood and life."

"Okay, it's a nice gesture but—"

"No vampire has ever given one to anyone who wasn't another vampire. It's so untraditional—like if we made a witch the Alpha of our pack. That's how unlikely it is to happen."

I slipped the paper back in the envelope and took a few seconds to align the seal, unreasonably more fascinated by it than what it held. "Cool."

"Cool?"

"Yeah, cool. Now let's talk about this apology."

Ethan and I were at a stalemate. He was determined not to issue an apology to David, and I had been hinting how "nice" it would be if he would. It would be appreciated. David and Trent would see him in a different light and not as the big, bad, broody wolf. Problem was, Ethan was content with never being considered nice; "big, bad, broody wolf" was his brand, one he'd worked years to develop. He had no intention of rebranding. Ever.

His gaze traveled over the room. "Obviously, I'm not 'big, bad, and broody' enough." Our home looked as if we'd had a housewarming and needed to figure out where to put the gifts from people who obviously hadn't looked at the registry.

The vampires visited in droves. Some offered a simple reverent thanks. Others brought tokens of their appreciation: wine, chocolates, an iPad, first-edition books, crystal stemware.

Not one of the gifts was particularly weird in itself, but watching a vampire shove it toward me with heartfelt gratitude was off-putting. They were just random gifts. Then there was Sable's—a guinea pig. That was goddamn weird no matter how it was spun. A guinea pig.

Sable had arrived dressed in pink from head to toe, including poorly applied hair extensions. Her black eyes still seemed lost, wanting. I saw Quell in them each time I looked at her.

I looked at the guinea pig running around in the cage. What could have inspired her to give me the little chubby rodent? "This is weird," I finally admitted to Ethan. I had played it cool because one of us had to be the calm one who rolled with the wave of oddity like an experienced surfer. Ethan wasn't about to assume that role for any reason.

"Just the guinea pig is weird? Not the slew of vampires coming to our house? Do you know how many vampires visited this home before you moved in?"

"Five," I blurted out in a lively voice, hoping to ease some of his frustration. "No, six … two … seven. Final answer —three."

"None. Vampires never came to my home. You move in and it becomes vampire central."

"That would make a great bar name. Let's get a sign and charge a cover," I teased.

He growled, a deep, rolling rumble that reminded me of a thunderstorm. He dropped his head in disgust and said, "Another one." Having had his fill of vampire visitors, he went upstairs. I was proud he'd lasted this long.

This arrival wasn't any visitor, it was Chris. I'd heard the click of her heels before Ethan had announced we had another guest. Chris's steps were always used as an announcement because she seemingly floated on air, moving without a whisper of sound when she needed to. This was better than a knock. It was the herald saying, "I announce to you—Chris, Mistress of the North."

I opened the door before she could knock. She scanned the room behind me, taking in the gifts. "I see that the Seethe are showing their appreciation," she surmised.

Glancing over my shoulder, I gave the scene another once-over. "Yeah. It's so strange."

"Strange?" she asked, brow furrowed as she extended her hands out the door. Was she requesting I join her for a walk? She probably didn't want to run into Mr. McBroody.

Once we started walking the trail outside the house, I knew it was something else. She wanted to enjoy Ethan's backyard. It was beautiful. The verdant landscape was vibrant and entrancing. The sounds of the small creatures that lived deep in the forest added to the natural symphony of soothing sounds. For a long time, I'd assumed that it was magic—and maybe it was, but I couldn't detect it. The rich variations of green with earth brown interwoven and hints of color from flowers that seemed to show up to break up the monotone made Ethan's home tranquil, inviting, therapeutic.

After several moments of silence, Chris asked, "Why is it strange that the Seethe is appreciative of you saving Demetrius's life?"

That's easy. He's a sadistic jerk. I can't believe people like him, let alone care whether or not he lives. I kept those thoughts to myself and said with practiced diplomacy, "Because he's not often kind." *And by "not often" I'm sure the number of times he has been can be counted on one hand.*

Chris nodded slowly, considering my answer thoughtfully. "If Sebastian died, do you think people would wonder how a person like him could be mourned?"

A replay of the highlights of Sebastian's interactions with others, including him nearly forcing the witches to leave for their protection, seemed cruel from the perspective of an onlooker. His tactics, no doubt, would be perceived as manipulative and the behavior of a narcissist. Alpha confidence seen as unabashed arrogance. The protection of his pack at all costs easily considered reckless, selfish, and shortsighted.

"I suppose they wouldn't, but we see more sides to him that others might not, or choose to ignore."

"And you don't think we see that in Demetrius?"

Including you. "I think you're right ..." I started, carefully aware of how delicate the topic of her feelings and her reaction to his near-death was. "I think he should stay the leader for a while. His hold is too strong. I have no doubt that you would be a great Mistress of the Seethe, but earning their loyalty to follow you the way they do him will take time. We should put a hold on our plans."

She lifted her chin and squared her shoulders, showing overstated confidence and indifference. "He deserved a better death —that's all," she said in defense of her behavior, aware of what I was doing. "It wasn't a death worthy of someone like him."

Really! You were crying because he deserved a better death? Is that seriously what you want to believe? Fine, if we are just throwing around nonsensical statements: I think Santa Claus would be epic at slam poetry.

"Well, now he lives so that one day he can meet a death worthy of him." I was surprised I was able to keep the insolence and skepticism out of my voice. I wondered if it showed on my face. It was really hard not to give away such a blatant lie.

"Quell?"

The breath I exhaled at the sound of his name was sharp. Emotions slammed into me hard enough to leave me winded. It felt like she'd punched me rather than just said a name. I took several steps back until my back was against a large oak tree, then slid into a sitting position.

"I don't know if avenging his life is my right," I admitted softly. "I did love him—but not the right type of love."

Chris's eyes widened. Although she didn't say it, her face spoke volumes. "What's happening?" it asked.

She retreated, looking like she was being ambushed by a cadre of assassins rather than a woman readying to spill her guts. To have a real conversation. I suspected she would have preferred the ambush. She and Winter hated each other because they were similar. This was a reaction I'd expect from Winter, but Chris could occasionally offer some empathy. Winter had none when it came to vampires.

Believe me, you're the last person I want to have this conversation with, but you're here. And this is about to happen. "He asked me to kill him—but I couldn't."

"I know," Chris whispered.

"I never would have. He was tired of this life and ready to move on, but I couldn't do it. I don't know if I loved him too much or too little. He was clearly unhappy." My eyes dropped to the ground and my forehead rested on the heel of one hand. I clawed at the ground with the other, massaging the dirt as a distraction.

"As long as Ethan was in the picture, I'd never love him the way that he wanted. Even if Ethan wasn't, I'm not sure I could have loved him the way that he wanted—or needed to be by me."

Tears burned at the edges of my eyes and I blinked them back. After several moments of silence, Chris knelt down in front of me. "Faking that you love someone the way they want is cruel. It seems like the right thing to do—and really, it's just the easy thing to do. It would have led to you hating him and that would have been a sentence worse than any death. The story didn't end the way you wanted it to, but it ended the only way it could have without you doing Quell and yourself a disservice."

Chris stood and I knew our talk was over. Slowly she backed away from me, treating my emotions like a deadly weapon and my discussion like an act of aggression. I doubted she even realized she had her hands slightly raised as if she was negotiating with someone to put down their arms and leave her in peace.

I knew she didn't want to walk back to the house with me, and I really needed a few more cleansing moments outside. I'd probably change and go for a run.

"Chris," I called after her when she was a few feet away. "There's a guinea pig at our house; can you do something with it? Sable gave it to me."

Chris's shoulders sagged as she blew out an exasperated breath. "She's so fucking weird," she mumbled under her breath.

"Yeah, she is. A guinea pig. Why a guinea pig?"

Chris's back was to me as she started slowly toward the house. "She likes them and is always suggesting them to others. It's as desirable as feeding from a rat, but she considers it a delicacy. For some reason she thinks you are Peruvian. *Cuy*—guinea pig—is a staple in Peru. I've corrected her several times about her misinformation, but in her mind, the dozens of people who've told her otherwise are wrong. I'll just regift it to her. She'll be very happy."

She stopped and turned. Frowning, she said, "Gavin was really good for her. I know he's with Kelly, but ..." She just sighed. Gavin and Sable's situation was similar to mine and Quell's—she realized it the moment she said it. Giving me a wry smile, she turned and continued toward the house.

CHAPTER 34

*T*he next day, vampire gifts were the last thing on my mind. After calling Trent and David and not receiving a response, I was trying to convince Ethan to show some goodwill and apologize.

It was my third attempt of the day. "Maybe you should call them to check on them. While you have them on the phone, maybe you can apologize," I offered casually, as if it was just an afterthought, sitting on the table in front of him.

His face was twisted in defiance. "I'm not going to check on them or apologize to David, because I think they're okay," he said, rising to his feet and heading for the door. He'd opened it before anyone could ring or knock to reveal Trent and David, standing there with a basket. My brow furrowed. "I heard their car," he offered as explanation.

The scent of apples, blueberries, confectioners' sugar, and vanilla floated from the basket. Noticing my attention, David smiled, walked into the house, and handed the small basket to me and a bakery box of cupcakes. "Cupcake for my cupcake," he said, giving me a peck on the cheek. He was handing me a box of cupcakes—I didn't really care what he called me.

Trent was all grin, so wide that it overtook his narrow face. It made me suspicious. They were both humming with energy, and their increased heart rates were distracting. I opened the bakery box and took out a cupcake, keeping a suspicious eye on them as I ate.

His hands twisting together nervously as if he was rubbing lotion on them, Trent shifted his weight from side to side. He wasn't just humming with energy, he was excited. David looked like he had gossip he couldn't wait to spill. I'd seen that look from time to time when he'd had something on some of the residents of our neighborhood.

Ethan watched them with caution as they noticeably gathered their thoughts, preparing to hit us with something. I had no idea what to expect, and their silence allowed my mind to run wild with all the possibilities, the most disturbing being that they'd decided to move away. Responding as if they'd delivered the news already, my heart raced and my breathing changed noticeably. I was almost panting.

Ethan eased next to me; his arm dropped to his side. He took the hand not holding the cupcake. It wasn't calming enough. My voice was steadier than I felt. "What brings you by?" I finally asked.

David's smile broadened. "We've decided we want to be wolves," he blurted.

"*He* wants to be a wolf. I want to be a jaguar," Trent added, like he was a petulant child picking something off of a kids' menu as opposed to a life-changing thing. "Maybe a bear, but before I decide, I have some questions."

"And I want to be a unicorn," I spouted back.

Both of their faces twisted in confusion.

Ethan moved away from me and directly in front of them, commanding their undivided attention. "We don't have a jaguar in our pack. There is one in the South, but if you are turned, it's better to be done by someone in this pack. I also strongly recommend both of you be changed to wolves. Either me, Sebastian, or Sky can do it," he responded in a professionally stoic voice. As if he was reading the rights and restrictions of a contract and not telling them that they were about to go through the most painful thing in their lives and be irreparably changed.

"The first couple of days will be difficult for you. Similar to the way you felt when you took vampire blood. Also, you will have a bond with whoever changes you—it will be odd at first, but you will quickly adjust to it."

Why was he even entertaining this? Feeling a fog come over me, I stood motionless with cupcake in hand while they discussed this, as if they were deciding something as frivolous as what movie to choose.

"No," I said softly. They all looked at me, but when I didn't elaborate Ethan continued. He gave what seemed like a mini orientation, a small "welcome to were-animal life."

"No!" The command erupted from me. A cloak of darkness consumed me and I felt like I'd sunk into an abyss of despair and lost control of the world I once knew. Trent and David weren't in the otherworld. They were my comfort zone, my link to humanity, and in one single day, hour, minute—that was no longer the case. I felt ill and unable to keep my composure. I felt frantic, like I was fighting for the life I'd once known, the one I liked. I clung to it because it was the only thing that offered any familiar connection to my old life. I was part of a pack, hosted a Faerie spirit shade, no longer housemates with Steven, was mated and married, lived in a house totally unlike my small, cozy one, and was living without Quell. I'd be damned if I didn't fight for the final morsel of my former life. "Stop talking to them! Stop acting like this is going to happen!" I shouted at Ethan. "No! Just no!"

I had their attention, but not because I was shouting at them like a banshee. I was shaking uncontrollably. This couldn't be happening.

Voice gentle and soft, Ethan said, "Sky, it won't change things—"

"It changes everything. How can you agree to this? This will change them. They won't be human anymore. We can't take that away from them. Not in such a trite way. We're asking them to give up too much."

"You all didn't ask, we did. It's what we want." David's sobering response hit home. We hadn't asked, they had. This was their decision.

"You're making a mistake," I asserted. "A big one."

"I know you think we are entering this foolishly, but we aren't. It's been something we've been considering for a while. More so since we nearly died by that vampire attack. This is our life now, what we deal with. Isn't it better that we are prepared?" David debated.

"I won't do it! Or have anything to do with it." I turned to Ethan and demanded, "You won't, either. You will not do this."

"I'm sorry, Sky."

I was a spectator in a show that I didn't want to see. Feeling helpless to change the ending, unable to do anything about the plot other than watch. I felt sick. I tossed the cupcake aside and ran for the bathroom. I made it in time to lose everything I'd eaten. Nauseated, I stayed there for a few minutes, blinking away tears that brimmed at the edges of my eyes.

This was too much to deal with. Instead of returning to the kitchen with Ethan, David, and Trent, I went to his bedroom—our bedroom—and sat on the bed.

"Feel better?" Ethan asked softly, coming into the room.

"Are they still here?"

He shook his head. "No, they went home." He inhaled a breath and released it slowly. "But they will be at the pack's home tomorrow with Dr. Jeremy for the change." He took a seat next to me.

"If a doctor needs to be present for something, it can't be safe. Do they know that?"

"They're healthy; there shouldn't be any problems." As soon as he took my hand, I pulled it away. I crossed my arms over my chest.

"Tell them no. If you tell them you don't think it's a good idea, I know they will listen. They'll just think I'm overly cautious or sentimental."

"I'm not going to tell them that, because you are. There won't be any complications with their change. And they will be more equipped to protect themselves than they are now."

"Do they know they have to change during the full moon?"

"Yes."

"Vampires have killed were-animals before. Just changing them isn't going to make them immune to that."

"We'll make sure they can take care of themselves. Sky, no matter how they presented it, I don't think they came to this decision lightly. They've seen us change, they understand a lot of the pack's dynamics, and they aren't afraid. They aren't making this decision out of fear. Although I wouldn't care if they were, I know you would."

As Ethan gave his little spiel, I kept shaking my head. His lips pressed into a thin line.

He sighed. "This is one of the times that will create difficulty between us. I'm not your husband or your mate when I make this decision. I'm the Beta of the pack, tasked with keeping friends of the pack safe. People who achieved that privilege because of you. It's going to happen, and I'd prefer you be on board for it and to do it."

I considered it as long as I was capable of before the thought of it made me ill, and once again I was in the bathroom.

Ethan placed a cool towel over my face, then leaned against the sink.

"At least give them a week. Can you do that? They know it's going to happen. Before, it was just speculation. Let them live a week with the certainty."

He nodded in agreement. "Sky, you know it's not going to change anything."

"I know, but at least it will give me time to come to terms with it."

I hated the haughty look of self-assurance Ethan gave me when I told him we should get an objective opinion and suggested Sebastian.

"Of course," he said aloofly. At least he made an effort to look beleaguered by the suggestion. His tells were minuscule, but if you studied him long enough they were decipherable. He pulled his lips in ever so slightly when his emotions were insincere, like they were at the moment. He gave in to my request because he was confident that I would fail.

I'll show you. Too bad my petulant response was said out loud as I headed for the door.

"Of course you will." The look on his face matched his voice.

I didn't care how long the shot was, I had to do whatever I could to stop this mad train that was careening toward destruction.

I was positive Sebastian knew why I wanted to meet, but he behaved as if he was clueless, resting back in his chair, his hands clasped behind his head. Brown eyes rested on me as he waited for me to speak.

"I'm sure you've heard about David and Trent," I started out.

"What about them? Them hosting a pair of vampires at their

home, the newbie vampires showing up there, or the display of force Chris had to show to get everyone to leave?"

"Keep going, I know you know more," I said, cocking a brow. It was a pack matter, and I was sure, as soon as Ethan knew I was okay after my third bout of sickness over the situation, that he was on the phone with Sebastian.

Sebastian's aplomb pricked at my irritation as he remained eased back in his chair. His lips rested casually in a lazy smirk. "Why don't you tell me; perhaps it can give me a little more insight in this early morning visit." His eyes flicked to the clock. It wasn't that early, just a little after ten. I wasn't due at work with Josh until later that afternoon.

"Trent and David want to be changed into wolves. ... Well, Trent wants to be a jaguar"—I rolled my eyes at that—"but David wants to be a wolf. I think it's a terrible idea."

Nodding, he asked, "Have you discussed your concerns with Ethan?"

"You know I have. We aren't going to pretend for one moment that it hasn't been discussed at length during your late-night lovefests."

"Lovefest?" His grin widened and his eyes sparked with amusement.

It might not have been a lovefest, but it wasn't until I lived with Ethan that I realized how much they spoke to each other.

"Ethan thinks it's a good idea. It's not. If we change them, they become part of *this* pack?"

He nodded. "By default. It is unusual after being changed to decide to be part of another pack. We've had one request, a transfer, but that was because they wanted to relocate."

Sebastian cared about the health of the pack. That was always his priority. "I don't think they will be a good addition and could prove to be problematic."

The amused grin had become such a fixture on his face that I was losing confidence in my argument and my chances to persuade him. "This pack is about rules, regulation, order, and conformity. And pack propriety is important. David's obstinate. He's the most stubborn person I know, and I think following the pack laws would be difficult for him. Trent is impulsive and rebellious. He does whatever the hell he wants. That guy's a real wild card. That's not what this pack is about. They will be a pain in your ass."

"Stubborn, obstinate, impulsive, rebellious, wild card, and does whatever the hell they want. My god! Whatever would I do with a person like that in my pack?" he said with mocking drama.

Everyone's a freaking comedian.

He came to his feet, a prelude to his invitation for me to leave his office. "I suppose I will just address them as Sky #2 and Sky #3."

No one thinks you're funny. "Exactly. You have me, you don't need another. Let alone two more."

Instead of going to the door and opening it and giving me his less than subtle invitation to use it, he sat on the edge of the desk just a few inches from me. "You want to protect them and I understand that, but denying them this isn't protecting them, it's leaving them vulnerable. No one coerced them. In fact, I debated whether to offer it. They're not going anywhere. They are in your life, in this world—give them the means to protect themselves. Believe me, there is more security and influence that goes with them being part of this pack as opposed to friends of it."

The final, solitary line straddling the world and the other-world had broken. My delectably human friends would no longer be that. I didn't have any more arguments or excuses as to why we shouldn't change them.

I looked up from the floor, where my eyes had drifted, to find Sebastian evaluating me. "What else is going on, Sky?" He seemed worried, and I couldn't help but suspect that I looked as bad as I felt.

"Things are more different than I ever imagined."

"They always will be." With that, he went to the door and opened it. "I don't think David and Trent need more time; they've called me three times already." The last part of his sentence failed to hide his irritation. I smiled; Sebastian was putting on a brave face. He wouldn't be so arrogant when he had to convince Trent the Midwest Pack didn't need a team shirt to show unity, have a league in the community softball games, or whatever team-spirited thing he'd come up with. The idea brought out a smile of satisfaction.

"We'll start the process tomorrow. Are you okay with doing it, or would you prefer me or Ethan to?"

"I can do it."

He rested his hand on my shoulder. "Rest assured, your relationship with them will continue to be absurdly inappropriate, as it is with Steven. Things won't change."

They wouldn't understand. It wasn't just my relationship with them I was worried about. They were the final link, that beacon and reminder of the brevity and fragility of human life. Once you crossed over, it was hard not to feel removed from it and have the same appreciation for it. After the change, Trent and David wouldn't be the same. They wouldn't be *my* David and Trent. They would be were-animals: David and Trent who happened to be my friends.

My world had changed.

David and Trent seemed oddly relaxed, despite being minutes from life becoming totally different. Feeling everything more intensely, learning to ignore all the sounds and smells that were more pronounced and heightened and, because they wouldn't be used to it, distracting. I wondered if their attraction to each other would heighten the way Kelly's had to Gavin. Those two couldn't keep their hands off of each other, and at any given moment, in any room, a poor unsuspecting soul might walk in on them.

As I stood on the precipice of things, I could no longer attribute the fluttering in my stomach, anxiety, or nausea to just them. I was late. A week late. It took up a lot of space in my head, crowding out some of my apprehensions about the situation. Could I be pregnant? No, I wasn't pregnant. I couldn't be. If I were ... My heart raced and my head pounded. If I were, what would happen with Maya? Her resurfacing came to my mind, when she'd used me to cast a spell on my own pack that would have killed them. What would she do to my child? Every possible scenario raged through my brain until I bent over and hyperventilated.

Ethan was quickly at my side, concerned. His brows inched together as he cradled my face. "Sky, are you okay?"

My mouth opened to tell him, but I changed my mind. *I'm not pregnant. It has to be the stress of everything.* I inhaled deeply and nodded.

"Fine, just last-minute jitters." I directed my attention to David and Trent. "Are you ready?"

They were more than ready. They had stripped out of their clothes to their underwear—before anyone told them to, I might add.

"You can keep your clothes on until after the bite," I informed them.

"I thought we'd be forced into a change," David said.

"Once the serum is in your system and works its way through it, then the change will be initiated. But you'll have time to undress. You should feel it once it starts," I informed them.

They looked at each other and shrugged. "We're half-dressed. Might as well get it over with." They removed their briefs and were naked—unabashedly naked. Naked as the day they were born. Naked and unashamed and standing in the middle of the pack's infirmary, all smiles, as if it were the most normal thing to do.

Great, I had to worry about two more people being naked all the time. Now they would have an excuse. "The wolf needed to be free," or "It hurts when we tear through our clothes when we change."

I went to one of the recovery rooms to undress. When I changed into my wolf this time, I was acutely aware of the process of my body taking on its wolf form. How it elongated, stretching my ligaments to the point they felt like they were going to snap. Did it hurt? Not really, it was just uncomfortable. The pain came when my organs shifted to prepare for the new form. I'd gotten used to the feeling, and it was equivalent to my monthly cramps. Fur pushing its way through my skin and sheathing my body wasn't painful. The skin seemed to have its own analgesic properties and to dull the pain of the process.

As I melted into my wolf form another time after countless others, I knew it wouldn't be this easy for them the first time, and there was no way to prepare them. I remembered the screams and cries of pain when the people we'd changed had first taken on their animal form.

I padded in slowly, the clicking of my claws against the floors more pronounced in the silence. Ethan and Sebastian stood next to Dr. Jeremy in the far corner. I could see them out of my peripheral vision as I advanced to David and Trent. Changing someone, despite were-animals' denials, was similar to how a vampire sired. The only exception was that the saliva had a serum and we had to actively trigger it. Just chomping on a person wasn't going to do it. As it pooled in my mouth, tasting like an unholy mixture or rancid chicken, cayenne pepper, and mustard, I couldn't imagine someone wanting to do this often.

David walked gingerly toward me, and I looked for signs of fear, hesitation, or apprehension. Sensing my reluctance, he lowered himself to the floor and moved his arm to my face. I bit down; he howled out in pain. There wasn't any way to prepare himself for the bite or the serum that would course through his body, damaging it, changing it, and finally reforming it. Then I moved to Trent. He suppressed any display of pain from the bite. It wasn't until the serum invaded his body that he yelled out, collapsing to the ground from his crouched position.

I quickly went to the recovery room to change back and into my clothes. That was an excuse. I needed to be away from the initial process. Did it say something about their change that it happened so quickly? Now in human form, I felt queasy from hearing them cry out in pain. Again my face was in the commode, chucking up everything I'd eaten that day. After I'd used one of the spare toothbrushes, with my back pressed against the door of the recovery room, I slid to the floor.

How much longer was I going to deny it? This wasn't just about David and Trent.

"I'm pregnant," I said aloud. It seemed impossible. I couldn't be pregnant. There wasn't a way to find the joy in it, because my thoughts stayed on Maya. What would she do to our baby?

An hour had passed before I could return to the room and my gaze moved over Ethan and Sebastian, who was trying to ease David and Trent into their full form. They writhed and twisted in midform, and I cringed when I heard the bone crunching, breaking, and reassembling in order to accommodate their new bodies. As they wailed out in pain I wondered if they regretted their decision. I knelt down next to them in an attempt to ease their pain, comforting them, and I stroked the upper halves of their bodies, the part that had already gone through the change. They howled, a distorted, painful sound mingled with their human voices, before slowly transitioning into deep growls.

"Sky, step back," Ethan instructed. I took several steps back. The violent twisting and turning continued as David and Trent attempted to achieve full form. Howling continued but wasn't as torturous as before. My heart pounded and I worked to keep the bile down, watching my friends go through the transition. It seemed like I had been standing just inches from the entrance for nearly five hours, but when I looked at the clock it had only been an hour. Finally they had achieved their wolf form. Agitated, they bounced about, claws skittering along the floor, howling erratically. They kept bouncing between me and Ethan, moving around in deranged circles.

"Trent and David, calm down," Sebastian ordered. They were struggling with the ability to do so. They backed up next to me, howling as their heads rubbed against my thighs.

"What's wrong with them?" I asked, concerned. No other transformation had been like this.

Ethan and Sebastian looked at each other and then at me. "It's you," Ethan said softly.

"They don't know how to discern your emotion. It's your unease. It's humming so much they can't relax. They're distressed because you are."

I knelt down and stroked their fur, massaging them through it. "I'm okay. Shhh. I'm okay. You're okay. We're okay."

But obviously I wasn't, because they wouldn't calm down. I took a seat on the floor and they curled around me, crowding me, whining as they nuzzled into me.

Ethan finally spoke. His powerful command held hints of sympathy and concern. He spoke slowly, so they could under-stand him in their new form. "David. Trent. I need to talk to my wife." They whimpered in response and stayed put. "Now."

Heads down, they backed away a few steps but continued to hesitate, giving me furtive glances.

"I'm okay," I said, but their sullen eyes showed that they didn't believe me.

"Trent, David," Ethan commanded again. The steely power behind his words had them easing away until they were in the corner.

Ethan cleared the space between us, concern in his eyes. To him, it was just the two of us in the room. I was aware of Sebastian's and Dr. Jeremy's attention.

"Tell me," Ethan said softly. I responded with a blank look.

He tilted his head and studied me. "You didn't have a period last month."

"I did."

"No, you had one for one day. That's not normal for you. And you missed your period this month. You've been nauseous in the morning for the past six days and it only got worse with the situation with David and Trent. Sky?"

My voice quivered as I spoke the words. Not because I didn't want to have a child with Ethan but because I knew it wasn't just us having a child. Then there was Maya and everyone else who had reacted negatively to Ethan and me being together. Something as simplistic as mating—done by were-animals for years—and our union caused an uproar. It wasn't going to be easy—or normal. I'd never get my normal, even in pregnancy.

"I think I'm pregnant." Thinking it and saying it out loud were so different. It had meaning. A real thing. No longer a speculation. Something I was telling people.

Concern fell heavily over Ethan's features as he watched me carefully. "You're afraid."

"Not of having a child." Tears fell and I didn't bother wiping them away because I knew there would be more.

Ethan's fingers swiped over my face, wiping away the fallen tears. "You don't have to worry, you are going to be a great mother."

I shook my head. "I struggle daily to keep Maya in check.

She forced me to place a curse on you." My eyes drifted to Sebastian and back to Ethan. "What will she do with a baby who isn't able to protect itself? We don't know the extent of her magic. Can she perform magic through our baby?" I turned my face into Ethan's hand, appreciating the small comfort it offered.

"You need a spirit shade to survive; I have one. She will not hurt our baby."

"I'll talk to Ariel; the witches suppressed her magic before, they can do it again," Sebastian offered.

I relaxed, and so did Trent and David, who had been making low whimpers in the corner. They went quiet, curled up in the corner lying next to each other. Their eyes fluttered as they fought to keep them open, a fight they were clearly about to lose.

"That's great preparation and an excellent idea," Dr. Jeremy said. He shrugged nonchalantly. "Should we determine definitively whether or not she's pregnant?"

Ethan and I pulled away from each other.

"Yes, we should find that out as well," Ethan said, slightly embarrassed.

CHAPTER 35

eetings between the Creed and the weres always held a level of reluctant acceptance and uneasy alliance forged out of mutual need. This meeting was hostile, and even Sebastian and Ariel's personal relationship seemed to have been left at the door the moment we walked into their office. The Creed sat at their table, ready to carry out the meeting with a formality that we weren't used to. When Ethan had asked for the conference, Ariel had only agreed for it to be at their headquarters, the deceptively innocuous store with a meeting room in the back.

"How many months are you?" Ariel asked coolly.

"About twelve weeks," I said. Dr. Jeremy had deduced that after he'd examined me following my announcement two weeks ago.

She sucked in a harsh breath and closed her eyes. "Do you think it's a good idea for you and Ethan to have children?"

"Well, it's a little too late now, isn't it?" I informed her, irritated by her condescending tone. As if she was speaking with a child.

Nia interjected, "It's not too late for you to—"

"You don't want to finish that sentence," I warned, feeling my wolf come to the defense of my child. She straightened carefully, watching me as if she was with an unpredictable, dangerous animal. And she was. I imagined my eyes looked as murderous as I felt. I'd had my fill of people insulting us and assuming the worst of anything Ethan and I would create. Doomed before being given a chance to make an impression, I had started to feel helpless. I didn't want to feel that way.

Ariel touched Nia's hand to calm her as she tensed, preparing to defend herself.

Focused on a piece of metal on her desk, Ariel eventually gazed from Josh, to me, Ethan, and Sebastian, who looked confused by her newly ardent unwillingness to help. It was more than what we were used to, negotiating to put the witches in a better position or at the very least ensure they weren't being taken advantage of.

"With everything that is going on, it would have been a better idea to be more cautious. You two are under a microscope; the world is watching, apprehensive and afraid." Then she directed her attention to Sebastian. "You are all being watched."

"That's not new information, Ariel," Sebastian said, tone disarmingly warm and coaxing. "What's really going on?"

Again her eyes went to the metal, then she looked at Josh with notable indecision. Ariel wasn't being cruel; she was afraid. Inundating the air were the smells of many ingredients used in spells—amber, tannin, salt, hazelnut, and blood—but they weren't masking the smell of fear that was becoming pungent.

"You got one, too, didn't you?" Josh asked, sinking his hand in his pocket and pulling out a piece of metal with a red mark in the middle.

She nodded. "We all did. Every one of us in the Creed. It's the sign of betrayal of our kind. Denouncing us. Rayna said our alliance with you is sedition and paramount to betrayal, and we need to be held accountable. Now she has more followers, enough that she feels confident doing this. There's about to be a war, something I wanted to avoid. No one ever comes out a true victor in one. Too many casualties, and the winner is always left compromised." She shook her head, distraught over the situation.

"Why didn't you tell me about that?" Ethan asked his brother, frustrated.

Josh shrugged, dismissing the threat of the symbol. "It's nothing new. I've always been considered an enemy of some sort to Marcia's Creed witches. My loyalties have been divided since birth. I won't choose anyone over you. It's a nonissue," he admitted softly. "I'm your brother first, a witch second. If I'm their enemy, so what. They can bring whatever they have."

"We got you into this; we will get you out," Sebastian assured the witches.

Ariel gave him a weak smile. "It's not that simple. We've lost witches who once supported us; they see Rayna as a stronger leader who will uphold our rules and their perceived 'purity' of magic. You two possessing magic is one of the 'impure' things they are concerned about. Those who were on the fence have now sided with her. She has the Aufero, and like Marcia, she's made no secret of her willingness to use it. I'm sure I will be on that list eventually and so will the rest of the Creed. So, even if we do decide to restrict the magic—she'll use it to hurt you. If she removes any of our magic, the mark won't work."

"Alliances works both ways, Ariel. We've had this discussion more than once, and you've even reminded me of my own advice. Don't be afraid to ask for help. The Aufero doesn't work on us. We can find a place for you until we fix it."

"We're running and hiding?" Nia asked, mortified by the idea.

"You can devalue and reduce self-preservation to 'running and hiding' if you like. I see it as a strategic move to keep your powers until a threat is removed by people willing and capable of doing it," Sebastian offered.

Ariel smiled at Sebastian redefining what they perceived as a cowardly act to be smart, strategic planning. It was a reminder that he was more than just brute force and, in the end, he would choose survival and whatever tactic was necessary for it to be achieved. The outcome was all that mattered to him.

She looked at the others, trying to read their faces, but they remained blank, indecipherable, except for Nia's, who'd assigned us blame for it all.

"Please give us a minute?" Ariel requested of us.

We stood just outside the door, but we could follow the discussion, which quickly became a heated debate. Ariel was accused of allowing her relationship with Sebastian to influence her decision.

"They are offering to help us. The Aufero can't be used against them. Why do you have a problem with it?" Ariel asked. Although her tone was terse, her curiosity was apparent.

"Because it's them we are handing our safety to. They are the very reason we are in this position. Distancing ourselves from them might be the best option," Nia said, incensed.

"You don't see this as a power move on Rayna's part to claim the Creed for herself?" Ariel asked.

"If it is, she has every right to want to see the Creed elevated to more than just the were-animals' lackey. And that's what we've been reduced to. They call, we come, and what have we gotten from this alliance? Our names tarnished, our fealty challenged, and our morals compromised, and believe me, I see it getting worse." I could hear the rigid frown in Nia's voice.

There was a long silence and another witch spoke. "I know you wanted to be different, to have a better relationship with them, but have we considered that after all we've seen, maybe there was a reason the others would distance themselves from them? Not just that Rayna considers them a blight on the otherworld? It's not as if she is truly an acolyte of Marcia's. She left them and chose to be alone, to separate herself from Marcia and the others. She's resurfaced for a reason."

"You two seem like you are ready to do that as well, maybe even join Rayna," Ariel speculated, with a knife-sharp edge to her voice.

"We are with you. When you decided to take over, I didn't follow blindly. When I said I was with you, I meant it. To the bitter end. But I don't want this to be our end. Not disgraced and stripped of our magic because we allied ourselves with them." Nia's voice softened. "When we decided to do this, you chose people who would challenge you, be the voice of dissent when necessary. You didn't want sycophants; you wanted challengers. You may not like what I'm saying, but I'm doing the very thing you said you needed. What's changed?"

"'I won't be one of the many who falls for his allure' was the first thing you said when you were warned about Sebastian. You assured us that you wouldn't" said the other dissenting witch. "But you have. You're besotted and you don't see it, but we do."

A small smirk coursed over Sebastian's lips.

Don't smile at that. Your reputation isn't helping us, Mr. Charming. And you're not that damn alluring!

"And don't forget the child," Nia added.

Silence fell hard, as if we'd been placed in a soundproof room. The air thickened with strong magic.

Josh made a face, aware that an auditory cloaking spell had been done. I leaned toward the door and heard only the same silence.

"Can you break it?" Sebastian asked.

He nodded. "But are you sure you want me to? It can't be done without them knowing. Will that help or hurt our case? If it were me, I'd consider it an insult to have it broken by someone I was supposed to trust."

Sebastian's lips tightened and he shook his head.

Being engulfed in a strange, magical silence made the time drag, and the conversation between us seemed mundane because no one addressed the elephant in the room. People were severing ties with us, and I couldn't help but wonder if the small group of Faeries were the puppeteers making the marionettes dance—to perform in the show "Destruction of the Were-animals." Was I being paranoid?

The door of the shop blasted open, and we stiffened, waiting for someone to come through. For several tense seconds—nothing. Windows around the building received similar treatment, and broken glass covered the ground. Sebastian shifted, eyeing the openings. Nothing. Was it just a threat? A rock through the window for attention, to give notice? It wasn't. A massive hybrid creature entered with force. Winged, it had a face like a harpy eagle, and its aggressiveness reminded me of its mythical ancestor. Its hooked beak had a dagger-sharp horn emerging from it. It swooped in, talons sharpened, weapons on the attack. Sebastian shifted before the eagle hybrid could target him and bit into the descending creature's leg. Using his grip, he slung the animal to the other side of the room.

Unimpeded by the door, another travesty of nature trampled through, a cross between a rhino and a Komodo dragon. Or crocodile. I wasn't sure what creatures had been mixed into it. Samuel was pressed close to it, a hazy film of protective field covering both of them, blocking them from our magic. It was strong, and Josh, Ethan, and I surged magic against it to no avail in an attempt to break it. It was a shock-and-awe tactic, but we weren't about to move. If we did, it would leave the witches vulnerable. I could feel Rayna near and the pull of the Aufero.

Concentrating, I attempted to call it. *Mine.* It had an affinity for me. "Josh, do you have this? I need to try to get the Aufero. It's near. Rayna's near."

"Sky, don't you dare!" Ethan yelled. The deep rumble of the Alpha command made me pause, an alarming, disarming bellow. It was instinctual to pause and acknowledge it. Even Sebastian's head jerked a little at the commanding sound. Sebastian had disabled one flying hybrid, but there were two more. The door to the witches' meeting room jerked open; London's vibrantly colored hair rippled like a war flag as waves of magic flared off her. The force of the eagle's winnowing wings overpowered her. Magic was consuming her, her eyes the color of coal and virulent anger. Josh's eyes widened as he stepped back. Behind were the others. Fiery anger entwined their magic. Destructive and vengeful. Magic flowed from them in a destructive wave, destroying the protective field that Samuel had around him and the animal. I was surprised the building was still standing.

Magic bulleted through the room, slamming us all against the ground. I rolled to stand, whipping around the fighting wolf and elven atrocity at the door. Before Samuel could react, I plowed into him. He hit the ground with a thud. Hands fixed around his throat, my hold was harder than anticipated. Weak magic drifted off of him as he exerted most of his energy trying to breathe. There was a brief, lackluster pulse of magic. My grip tightened and he garbled out a sound.

Magic in me roiled, unhinged and deadly. I did nothing to rein it in. It was the same magic that I pulled from the darkest depths of my being. Without remorse or restraint, I placed it over his heart. Eyes narrowed on him, I watched the struggle. The slowing thump of his heart was euphonious. His struggle was a wonderous theatrical performance, and his fear was ambrosia. I was in that place—in the sewer, in the pits of all the darkness, without a desire to crawl out.

I leaned in closer, my eyes locked on him. "You behave as if this is a fight you are ready to die for. Is it?" I whispered.

Pallid, he could barely catch a breath, let alone speak. He had to work to preserve his life.

He shook his head.

"You're going to leave and be done with this fight. You don't want to be on this side of the war you've chosen," I urged him. "This world you want without us in it isn't going to happen, Samuel." No matter how much I wanted to abandon my humanity and snuff out the idealistic nuisance, I couldn't. His actions weren't born from cruelty but a poor tenet. He didn't want anyone to have magic. "Samuel," I started slowly. "This will be your last warning and the final time I ever grant you clemency." His eyes widened. He nodded. Desperate shallow breaths came from him as soon as I released him.

I didn't bother staying around to check on his recovery or to see if he attempted to retaliate. Perhaps there was a part of me that wanted him to. Feeling the pull of the Aufero, I kept running toward it as the aggressive sounds of fighting continued in the background. I stopped abruptly, Rayna several feet away. Beating spastically, the Aufero lurched in her hand, strong magic restraining it where Rayna was physically unable to. The muscles of her forearm strained as she held it close to her body.

"This won't end well for the weres," she said. Honesty rang in her voice. To my surprise there were whispers of supplication in her admission. "Do the spell. You have the power to end this. The Clostra was left for you." Her eyes moved to my stomach. I used that moment of distraction to magically yank at the Aufero. Colors sparked in it, like it was an excited puppy ready to return to its owner. Brutal magic punched into my chest and I hit the ground. Rolling to all fours, I was about to shift when Rayna said, "I guess you've made your decision." She disappeared.

I returned to the witches' destroyed store. Blood permeated the air. Nausea settled in as I looked at the results of the fight. The elven creatures hadn't survived it.

"Liam has chosen a side," Sebastian said.

"Are we sure he has, or is he just indifferent? I think Mason and Abigail are the ones to watch. She would have access to the Dark Forest," Ethan pointed out.

With a sigh, Sebastian turned toward the witches, who were coming down from the use of strong magic and the turbulent emotions that fueled it. Instead of addressing just Ariel, he spoke to the group. "Are you willing to accept our help?"

His offer wasn't without benefit to us as well; we needed them at full strength. But he seemed genuine in his offer and invested in their safety.

Tension strained the silence as Ariel remained mute.

"How the hell did we get here?" Nia whispered, and I knew that feeling of defeat and sorrow. The feeling of looking at devastation, mournful about the tragedies of the past, weary for those still to come, and needing some reconciliation. Wanting to pinpoint the moment when a different action could have changed the course of events. Her cautious gaze and reluctant trust of us spoke volumes. In her mind, we were that action that could have changed things. We saw it, and so did Ariel, who gave her a regretful smile of apology.

Sebastian drew in a slow, deep breath, held it, and then blew it out slowly, taking a moment before he spoke. "What you see as acquiescing and a sullied compromise of who you are as witches, isn't. Marcia's flaw was that she held to old ways, faulty ways that led to her destruction. Your strength is in the fact that you haven't. You won't be bullied into siding with someone who doesn't share your beliefs. That is a strength, not a flaw, and it will serve you well to remember that. We have resources that you don't. I have had years to build them." He turned his attention to Nia, the most vocal dissenter. "You weren't wrong—this alliance has benefited us disproportionately, but if you never give us a chance to help in an area that we excel in, then it will remain that way, unequal. I question whether your biases and fixation on our past and our flaws have narrowed your vision. If that is the case, perhaps you're not really what Ariel or the

Creed needs. If you care about the strength of the Creed, then you'd care about its survival."

Nia's deep, pensive eyes appraised him as she tried to make a decision. A decision about Sebastian. About us. Along with the others, she took several moments to deliberate, but she was the first to acknowledge Sebastian's offer. Hand raised slightly, she said, "I vote that we go with Sebastian."

CHAPTER 36

*I*t had been three and a half weeks since the witches had agreed to allow us to put them in safer housing. Rayna had been quiet, which wasn't a good thing, and Ethan was exercising a great deal of restraint in not storming Elysian, where he was convinced she was. Liam was maintaining his neutrality, which in my opinion implied he'd chosen a side— and it wasn't ours.

I didn't know where Ariel and the other witches were, and I figured Sebastian was keeping it that way. Ethan had the biggest issue with not having that information. They were in Illinois— that's all the information we had. Available to perform *interdico* when necessary.

Ethan and I were on the way home from our second visit with Dr. Jeremy since I'd formally announced my pregnancy. I was hugged out. At fifteen weeks, I still wasn't showing. Kelly's emphatic touches to my stomach cued me to look down at the still flat belly, which she assured me wouldn't be that way for long. *Yay.*

My flat stomach, or the impending stretching of it, was the last thing I needed to worry about. There were so many other things more pressing: Trent and David's upcoming full moon change, and my change now that I was pregnant. Dr. Jeremy assured me that I could do it without hurting the baby and shouldn't be concerned about that. My body would accommodate it, which was really comforting, because I couldn't imagine how painful it would be to try to hold off change until I gave birth.

The heaviness that surrounded Ethan concerned me. It could be a number of things: the possibility of becoming a father, the situation with Maya, the Aufero being in Rayna's possession, the shadow alliances forming against us.

His hand clasped mine on the drive home, his thumb rubbing rhythmically along the side of it gently. He'd never voiced concern over Maya and the baby, remaining ever-confident that it wasn't a problem. There were too many things that could go wrong, and no matter how we prepared for them nothing was certain. It wasn't just our lives involved but our child's as well.

Ethan pulled into the garage, driving past a tan Suburban parked in the driveway. We got out of the car, fingers intertwined, to meet an eclectically dressed woman with one pair of glasses on top of her head and another dangling from a chain around her neck. Because of her disheveled topknot, I assumed she had forgotten about the pair on top of her head. Her hunter-green shift dress and flats were accented by large, clunky jewelry, large earrings, and a large-faced gold watch. Her face brightened and she smiled when she saw me.

"Hi, you must be Ethan's wife." She extended her hand to shake mine. I could tell she was one of those people who hugged a lot and could make a handshake feel as warm and comforting as a hug. I had no idea how she knew Ethan and how they would get along.

When she shook Ethan's hand, it was different. A firm, quick shake. *That's how.* I probably didn't look like a rabid dog ready to take her hand off if she got too close. Ethan might not have looked like one, but most people would think *stay away*.

She focused her attention solely on me. "I'm sure we can have all the changes made in two months. Don't you worry about a thing."

It was then that a man dressed casually in jeans and a button-down and carrying a measuring tape, toolbelt, and notepad got out of the car. Ethan waved them to follow him and escorted them into the house.

"It still looks great. You're sure you don't want to consider getting a new house?" she asked, flipping open a notebook.

"No," we said at the same time, my voice more forceful and certain. She gave me a knowing smile, as if she knew I was the reason we weren't considering it.

"Changes?" I asked in a strained voice, turning to look at him.

"I'm getting an estimate on moving the bedrooms down-stairs, ours and another for the baby, and the offices upstairs so you won't have to go up and down the stairs while you're pregnant."

It took several moments before I spoke, feeling my irritation rise. I didn't want to be upset with him, he was being him. He was going to go full-on Ethan.

"I also have a list of cribs—one for the baby's room and one for travel—strollers, and car seats. You should look over them so we can have a decision by next week. Tracy will sit down with us to go over some colors for the rooms."

"Ethan." My voice was sharp enough to pull him out of the automatic state he'd been in, just making a succession of plans. "I'm three months. We have time …"

"You're almost four. We don't have lots of time, it's better to be prepared than rush to do everything at the last minute."

I sighed. "I'm pregnant, I'm not going to be an invalid. I will be able to walk up stairs and I'm sure I can carry a baby that only weighs a few pounds. Stop Tracy—" I stopped to get confirmation that the woman who would be helping me pick out colors was the same one walking around the house taking pictures, talking to the contractor, and making dramatic movements with her hands. I had a feeling she had extravagant plans for the remodel.

"Okay, but we'll look at the list later?"

It wasn't a list, it was a thesis. Each product listed had reviews from various companies and a list of pros and cons. We had five months.

"We need to get prepared." He looked around like a dispassionate overlord, ready to take down any walls, destroy part of the house, and do whatever was necessary to prepare for the baby. This was going to be a very long five and a half months.

"Ethan," I cajoled in a low, controlled voice, with a level of certainty that would ease his frustrations and bring him down a notch so that he could enjoy things instead of worrying. But the problem was, he was responding to my anxiety and I knew it. I was trying to squelch it—not think about what Maya might do, any complications, the fact that there were people unhappy about us becoming mates and that my pregnancy was going to be a huge problem. I slipped my hand over his and gave it a reassuring squeeze. "Everything will be fine."

Impressed with how steady and convincing I sounded, I continued, "We'll go through your list and pick out a stroller, crib, brand of diapers, baby mobile, diaper bag, or whatever else you have there." It had been part of the discussion on the way home. I should have known something was up, given how uninvolved he'd been in the conversation. He was expecting a remodel, and whatever "we" decided would be moot.

"I'll sit down with Tracy to pick a color for the baby's room —spoiler alert, I want yellow."

"It's a good color," he said.

"See. We have it covered. Everything's going to be fine." For a few fleeting moments, I started to believe it, too. I'd allowed my imagination to get the best of me. It could be okay ... it would be okay.

Ethan turned to face me, his fingers languidly moving over my shoulder. His touch was featherlight until it reached the pulse of my neck. "You don't believe that," he whispered.

"No," I confessed.

I wanted it to be fine and hoped it would be.

"Once I'm marked, I should be fine. It will be fine. The pregnancy will go on without any problems."

He frowned at my false optimism. "Your ordinary respiration rate is seventeen. It used to be fifteen, but since the pregnancy it's been consistently seventeen. When you weren't giving the full truth, it decreased to thirteen, now it's fifteen. Six times you've blinked; it's usually eight times. Your heart rate is a little higher since the pregnancy—it's sixty-nine, instead of sixty-four —it's now seventy-six and has been since you started claiming everything is going to be fine." He leaned forward until his forehead pressed against mine. "If you're concerned, don't pretend not to be, okay?"

I nodded, and with that I spilled it all. Everything about the pregnancy, the things Rayna had said, and how I felt the other denizens were going to respond. It was cleansing to voice every concern, even the ones that were minor. "Finally, I'm afraid I'm going to start hating red velvet cake. I've read and heard the stories about women despising the foods they once loved. What if our baby hates red velvet cake!"

He snorted a laugh, and his tone was heavy with sarcasm when he spoke. "Making sure you can eat red velvet for the rest of the pregnancy is at the top of my list, and the whole keeping Maya in check, handling Rayna and the others thing will be a strong second."

"That sounds about right."

Ethan was still smiling when he walked toward Tracy, something that shocked her for a moment. Her head tilted with surprise as if she'd seen a mythical creature and was still trying to determine if her eyes had played tricks on her. Ethan warmly smiling at her was equivalent to her seeing a unicorn.

While he spoke with Tracy, I headed for the cabinet, pulled out a bag of pretzels and a can of frosting, and started eating the disgusting combination while heading upstairs and out of sight. I attacked food like a rabid animal; Tracy didn't need to see that.

Twenty minutes later, Ethan found me on the bed, still nursing my feast. His face was impassive as he watched me, different from the look of disgust he'd given me the day before. Now I knew how Steven must have felt when I'd responded with similar looks of revulsion to the concoctions he ate.

"Frosting and pretzels, the meal of champions," he intoned in an even voice.

"I've seen you eat a deer," I pointed out between bites.

"In wolf form," he countered, the smile deepening.

Still shoving food in my face, I took a seat next to him. "This has to stop. It's too soon. I should be getting cravings at five and six months. Not three. What am I going to be like at five months?" I sighed.

"I've read the cravings start early, then they get better in the late second or third trimester," he offered as comfort.

He pressed his lips to my forehead, where they remained for a few minutes. "Better?" he asked soothingly.

No, it's not better. You're not a touch wizard. How is kissing me on the forehead supposed to make things better? I want you pregnant, too. I want you shoving weird things in your piehole. I'm pretty sure this baby is going to be a were-goat, based on the garbage I'm eating.

CHAPTER 37

I awoke to an empty bed, and I knew exactly where I would find Ethan. After brushing my teeth and showering I conceded to the new reality—I had to wear maternity clothes. It seemed like ten weeks of a barely discernible bump were gone. At close to five months, my jeans didn't fit. My yoga pants stretched, but not enough for my rapidly expanding stomach, so I wore them under it. Dr. Jeremy confirmed that I wasn't having twins, but looking at my profile made me wonder if he was wrong. Last week, Gavin had taken one look at me and suggested I have the test again. No one ever expected you to bite them. Punch, yes, but never bite them. It was barbaric, but as he'd looked at the imprint of my incisors on his skin, the amused smirk had faded quickly into shocked derision.

Memories of Gavin's wide eyes and gaping mouth brought a smile to my face as I slipped on the yoga pants and an oversized t-shirt. I followed the forbidden smell of coffee to the next room, the nursery. The room was calming. Tracy had it painted light yellow with decorative white and yellow lines. The blanket in the crib was soft yellow and mint green. I assumed it was sacrilege to have anything other than dark wood in the house, so the soft hues were complemented by the rich browns of the crib and nursery furniture. Several baby monitors were placed around the room, and a sound machine sat several feet from the baby's bed.

Just where I suspected he'd be, there was Ethan, sitting in an oversized chair in the corner, coffee in hand, with all the furniture and baby things that had come in yesterday assembled and placed. He was shirtless, and I could see the marks from me feeding from him so often. Most of my cravings had resolved, except that one. Even his enhanced healing wasn't faster than my thirst. I hoped after the pregnancy it would go back to normal. Accepting of it as part of the pregnancy and not another indictment of how abnormal our lives were, he never commented on it other than to say, "You're pregnant."

"Did Trent and David help?" I asked.

He shook his head. "They went home before I started."

Eyes narrowed on him, I asked, "Did they leave, or did you kick them out?"

Making a noncommittal sound, he gave me an indulgent smile. "They wanted to leave."

"Sure." I rolled my eyes. "We knew they were going to be around once they were turned. You can't be irritated by that now."

"It has nothing to do with that and you know it. They're handling things exceptionally well." And they were. Their enhanced senses bothered them when they were in human form. They weren't over to see me most of the time; they loved Ethan's land and being in their wolf form. It was a huge burden being responsible for their transition, but our friendship hadn't changed. That was the thing I valued the most. They were still Trent and David, just far too comfortable exposing their butt cheeks.

"Well, I could have helped you put everything together," I informed him, leaning forward to kiss him. It wasn't a peck, it was a deep kiss where I explored his mouth, enjoying his coffee-laced taste.

"I'm going to miss those peculiar morning kisses when you're able to have coffee." There wasn't a covert action of mine he wasn't willing to call me on. He uncrossed his leg, inviting me to sit.

"We should have put in a sofa instead," I admitted.

"Hmmm, like I suggested." Even with my back to him, I knew he was giving me his "I told you so" smirk. "We can change it out, but I like this. It's cozy."

It was, even ignoring the heaviness of the concerns that haunted him. He was easier to read. I wasn't sure whether it was that I was more in tune with his emotions or that he'd stopped trying so hard to hide from me.

"You did a great job picking things out."

"Yeah, I'm amazing. I just pulled out the list you gave me with the pros and cons of each product, available colors, and reviews, and enlisted the eeny-meeny-miney-moe strategy."

"Yet it took you over a month to choose," he teased.

I pressed my head against him and he pulled me closer, his hand resting over my stomach. He sighed and tightened his grip around me and the baby.

Things had been so quiet over the past few weeks that the witches were debating whether to return home, and I was hopeful that Rayna had given up. I was being naïve and exceedingly optimistic.

"I wonder why Rayna's silent."

"Perhaps her recruiting efforts are diminishing. Now that she has the Aufero, people seem content." Ethan shook his head. "I'm not sure why people are so comfortable with that zealot having it and not us. And Liam adhering to his belief that her having it constitutes ownership is concerning. He believes it shouldn't have been in your possession in the first place. The righting of a wrong." He said the last part with a reluctant concession; it was something he and Sebastian were overlooking to prevent a war at an inopportune time. A political placation.

Sebastian had questioned whether Liam had chosen a side, but the answer couldn't be any more blatant—it was with Rayna's witches. That was confirmed when we discovered that Elysian was where she was staying.

The situation was complicated. We couldn't just storm Elysian and get her without it looking like an unprovoked attack, because she hadn't attacked me—just the Creed. The Creed witches could plan a justifiable attack as retaliation, but how would they fare against Rayna and the creatures in the dark forest?

It was funny how the political landscape and rules of engagement hinged on such a simple platitude, that sticks and stones break bones but words don't hurt. Rayna's threats were just words.

Sebastian and Ethan were now dealing with the potential cost of entering Elysian by force and ruining any chance of mending the friendship between us and the elves. It was a risk they were still assessing.

"I hate this," I whispered under my breath, cuddling up closer to Ethan. It was the reiteration of something I'd said more times than I could count. I knew we'd never have human normal, I accepted that, but was it too much to ask for sort of normal? To be pregnant, going to work, dealing with morning sickness, cravings, and the inability to wear my old clothes—without the threat of someone wanting me dead or the political aftermath of doing anything possible to get the person who threatened me, my mate, and our child.

"Are you ready for today?" Ethan asked, changing the subject.

"We're still doing that?" I groaned.

"You said you would at least look. We are just looking and …" The last part, "possibly getting something," was exhaled with a nearly inaudible breath.

"The baby will probably be less than ten pounds and, even as a toddler, how much room will it need? My Honda is just fine. I don't need anything bigger."

"Must we debate this again? Winter." He invoked her name as if that was a power word that magically made my arguments disappear. He was pointing out that my use of her Navigator to crash into a creature that had attacked her was the only reason she was alive. It was a facile argument.

"We don't know that my Civic wouldn't have stopped it," I challenged defiantly.

"Yes, we know." He was confident and cool, like a person who had won the argument and just needed to remind his opponent of the matter.

"I guess I need a larger back seat so our child can roam free?" I offered, sarcastically. "Because if the baby's in a car seat, a lot of room isn't needed."

"We're only going to look. Besides, you need more room for the baby bag, travel bed, toys, and supplies." he said, nudging me to stand.

"You know babies are small, right? Tiny? They don't need a lot of room. Even as toddlers they require very little space," I argued, knowing I wasn't getting anywhere with it. "Fine. I added cars to the list and I want to look at those."

"I saw that you had. Of course we'll look at them." I knew that voice and that tone, which meant he'd added them and would spend most of the day trying to convince me not to go to the dealers that sold them.

Let's see how that works.

. . .

"I'd like to go to my choices first. If I find something there, then we don't need to go anywhere else. I love the Pilot—it's cute." I made a show of struggling to haul myself into the front seat of his new purchase. *For the baby*—he was going to wear that excuse out fast.

He groaned and frowned at my choice.

"Just because it cost the equivalent of a house doesn't make it better," I pointed out.

"It's not the cost, it's what I like, Sky."

"And since it's for me, we should get what *I* like. I like the Pilot."

He hopped out of the driver's side of the car. "You drive. If you like the way the Pilot drives over this, we get the Pilot," he said grudgingly, as if the idea of it left a bad taste in his mouth.

Pulling out of the driveway, I spoke in a low, grave voice, like the narrator on a nature show. Dark and ominous. "The woman pulls out of her driveway, protected only by the steel of the Range Rover. Hoping it will lead to her survival in the terror-torn streets of suburbia, aware that behind the brick walls and manicured landscapes lurk the infidels. They might look innocent, pushing their strollers, jogging through the trails of danger with lattes, but the woman knows the horrors. She's aware that little girls in brown and green garb are just beacons of mayhem and horror. The woman is protected from those cunning, cookie-toting monsters because she is in her big, powerful, four-wheel-drive vehicle. But she remains vigilant behind the wheel of her aptly horse-powered military grade transportation, ever aware of potential threats. Constantly on the lookout for those hooligans carrying their netted sticks, claiming they're for lacrosse though she knows they are weapons of pure evil and destruction. The woman remains steadfast. With her grand Range Rover, she knows she stands a chance of surviving the mean streets—of suburbia."

Ethan rolled his eyes. "Are you finished?"

"Until I can think of something else clever to say."

"Clever? I think you're using that word wrong," he said, smirking at me and relaxing into the passenger seat. Nestling into soft leather, appreciating the ease of navigation and the smooth ride.

"It's still unnecessary, and I still want to test-drive the other cars," I said firmly.

Annoyance was evident in his sigh.

We both felt the shift in the air. The cold freezing the window. The tires gripping the ground on ice that shouldn't be there; we were traveling at a speed faster than we would have if there had been snow or the potential for ice. My heart pounded as I pumped the brakes and held the steering wheel firmly. The hard impact of something slamming into us shook the car. Dark brown, shaggy hair covered the passenger side of the SUV, before climbing up and over it. The bipedal creature punched through the front window, spraying shards of glass in our direction. Clawed hands grabbed at me, cutting through my shirt and grazing my skin. Ethan hammered at the creature's offending hand and then held it steady to prevent it from touching me. My arm wiggled through the narrow space between the seats and I felt around for anything that could be of use. I pulled out a flashlight and pounded at the creature's restricted arm until the long claws broke. Its other hand slipped through the window to nick Ethan's bare arm. It pulled back and stabbed into Ethan's arm again. Blood spurted.

"Let him go. He's trying to escape," I told Ethan.

Restricting the creature for fear it would go after me again, he refused to let it go.

"Release it," I asserted louder. As soon as he let go it fell back off of the Range Rover, rolled to the ground, and recovered. Holding its injured arm, the massive beast, a horrid combination of sloth-like claws, gorilla-ish build, and the shaggy hair of an orangutan started to move away. The most peculiar part of the creature was the rough, shell-like covering on the shoulder and hips, which was probably why it was able to hit the car with such force. Ethan darted out, going after it.

Before I could open the door to follow, he turned mid-run. "Sky, no. Go to the house. No. Go to Josh." When I hesitated, he added a "please." It was a reminder that it wasn't just me anymore. I got back in the car. The cool air still lingered, but the ice was slushy and melting. Rayna's words were not just a threat, and we knew that she was being helped by the elves. I suspected Abigail and Mason more specifically, but I wasn't ready to exclude Gideon from the list. Abigail could be persuasive, and the tenuous relationship between us and the elves was weakened to the point of nonexistence. With enough support and allies, could Gideon be swayed?

Josh's door swung open before I could knock. His gaze dropped to the spatters of blood on my shirt, my exposed skin, and the drying blood on the healing wound on my stomach.

"Ethan's?" he asked, pointing to the blood on the side of my shirt.

"Yes."

He quickly grabbed a knife and cut away parts of the stained material. I tried to tell him what had happened, but he seemed distracted, gathering things into a small satchel.

When he moved to the threshold of the front door and pressed the knife to his palm, I reminded him. "I can do a blood protective field."

"But I won't know if it's compromised if you do it," he rushed out, slicing his hand. He let drops of blood fall toward the ground. A translucent, gossamer wall formed over the doorway between us.

I wished he'd at least let me tell him what had happened, but it would have taken valuable time. Looking at my reflection in the mirror there in the hall, I could see that things could be easily understood. We'd been attacked.

CHAPTER 38

*E*than paced the room, sucking in ragged, sharp breaths as his eyes remained gunmetal and predaceous. He'd been walking the same path since he and Josh had returned. I could ignore the spots of dried blood on his hands and the healing scars, but I couldn't dismiss the magic that rampaged off him. It was turbulent, bouncing through the room as if he'd expelled so much too forcefully and it was trying to settle into normalcy. To determine where it belonged.

Josh's magic wasn't any better. There weren't any hints of the calming oasis, the gentle breeze that beckoned my curiosity, easing me into practicing an art that was wondrous and beautiful. If the ominous storm that raged off Josh had been my first introduction to magic, I would never have tried it. Sparks of lingering magic wove between his fingers, haphazardly, like a live wire—and it seemed just as dangerous.

Josh rested against the wall, smoky gray eclipsing his blue eyes, and I feared they'd never turn back to their normal color. It was as if he'd sunk into the stygian magic, depleted what he had, and bartered for more, leaving parts of himself behind.

For the past fourteen minutes the question "what happened"

remained lodged in my throat, but did I really need details? The violence and destruction were apparent, and once I'd heard the details I couldn't unhear them. Just when I opened my mouth to ask, someone knocked on the door. Ethan answered it before I could. Sebastian took one look at Ethan, then his gaze moved over to Josh. The Alpha was noticeably distressed. His brow furrowed, and his lips dipped down into a rigid frown. He roughly ran his hand over the lower half of his face, as if he was trying to push away the frown. It didn't work. "Do I want to ask?"

"They attacked Sky," Ethan answered.

And you. But for some reason that seemed irrelevant. An attack on me seemed to warrant the destruction he'd inflicted.

"Liam has been calling me. I haven't spoken to him yet. What do I need to know?"

Three hard knocks at the door postponed any further conversation. Sebastian took several steps back to the door, looked out the peephole, then said to Ethan, "It's Chris."

"I called her," Ethan said.

Without asking for further information, Sebastian opened the door. Chris sauntered in, her face unreadable, but her midnight eyes were stern and irritated as they moved from Ethan to Josh. Lips twisted in a scowl, she crooked her finger to beacon the younger brother closer. There was censure in her movement, and a disapproving scowl ghosted over her features. Josh stood unmoving in defiance.

Standing in contemplation, she studied him for a while. It wasn't just insolence; Josh seemed gone. Not completely gone, but in a fugue state. Instead of insisting that Josh move, Chris approached him slowly, as one would an aggressive, unfamiliar animal.

"Josh," she said, her voice low and calming.

His eyes lifted to her, but he didn't move. A wispy cocoon of darkness seemed to be around him. She got close to him, pressed her lips to his neck, and bit. Hard. Josh grimaced but kept his hands at his side. It was obvious he didn't have a lot of control of the magic. Teeth gritted, he bore the distracting pain and eventually relaxed into it as the magic around him receded back. He inhaled deeply and held the breath for a long time, easing it out through tightly pursed lips. Chris had been feeding from him for a while, and the cloudiness of his eyes eased into a hypnotic haze. His hands started to move toward her waist and he jerked them back. Startled by the movement, Chris jerked, too, and pulled away. The puncture wounds weren't neat; there were little tears in his skin.

"Want me to close them?" she asked.

He'd taken several steps away from her. His eyes were closer to their original color but still off. Hints of darkness lingered behind them. Had Josh been forever changed by the magic he'd tapped into? How much had he perfected the use of dark magic? Drawn to the unknown and thirsty for new magic and power, it wasn't unthinkable that he would.

He nodded and awkwardly leaned over to give her access to his neck.

Chris ensured that nothing sensual could come of her laving over the wounds. She lapped at them like an overexcited puppy.

Josh frowned. "Gross."

She chuckled and backed away. Once she was back in front of Ethan and Sebastian, Ethan said, "Thank you for coming."

She shrugged her response. "I've been called upon by quite a few people in regards to you all." She inched over until she was standing directly in front of Ethan. "What. The. Hell. Did. You. Do?"

"They tried to kill Sky." That seemed to be his disclaimer for his actions, as if it absolved him from penalty.

"You have every right to be pissed, but Elysian will never be the same. Their animals are all destroyed—"

"They shouldn't have been creating them in the first place.

Us overlooking the creation of such dangerous animals was a courtesy," Sebastian declared. "What was their purpose? Fun? Most of those creatures were too dangerous to exist. If anything, Ethan provided an overdue service."

Chris harrumphed. "Let's see if you get some type of acknowledgment for your acts of altruism," she said snidely.

"And you"—she directed her consternation to Josh—"whatever magic you used to break their ward and prevent them from erecting it again needs to be reversed."

"I'm not reversing anything until they tell us how to find Abigail. She was there at the attack. It was her magic that initiated it. I want her stopped."

With an exasperated sigh, Chris started to pace. The gentle, rhythmic tapping of her heels against the floor became a soothing sound—white noise. "Ethan, I'm on your side. This coalition they've founded is unnerving. I've never been one to employ the preemptive approach. They are acting out of fear, and it's a great motivator and causes people to behave erratically. Rayna's smart and calculated and has enlisted some magical heavy hitters. Even witches that wouldn't fall in line with Marcia and left under her governing have allied with her. They probably would have eventually fallen in line with Ariel, but she's convinced them that the new Creed are ineffectual. You"—she jabbed her hand in Ethan's direction—"are what they fear and you've confirmed the need for it to be a concern by displays of powerful magic."

"They tried to kill me and Sky. What exactly should I have done? Let it go unchecked? I don't care about their fear—"

"You should care because it's not just them. If I wanted you dead, other than myself there are three people I would call. They've been hired. Ethan, this is only going to get worse. Do something about it." Then she directed her attention to Sebastian. "You all need to try to handle this diplomatically, because all hell's about to break loose and the very lives you are trying to protect will be the casualties of it."

Ethan's jaw clenched. "I did nothing wrong. I fell in love and I'm having a baby. Why should that be something I need to handle diplomatically?"

"As of four hours ago, you hadn't done anything wrong and others were hesitant to feed into Rayna's and the others' paranoia. With you putting on a full display of what you and your brother are capable of, they are concerned about your offspring. It's a valid concern, especially if your child will be able to do more as a combination of you and Sky and be impossible to constrain. Have you considered that your child might be able to perform magic in animal form? Be immune to it even in human form? Immortality? How hard was it to kill the Faeries? These are the concerns people have. Will you stop at one, or can they expect an army of your children, who could be dangerous and nearly unstoppable?"

She moved away from the irritated wolf and leaned against the wall. "I'm team dud. Because honestly, that could be an option, too: everyone on high alert for the unstoppable being of great magical aptitude, and you get an absolute dud. One that can't even shift. There have been cases where two shifters had a child that wasn't able to change, right?"

"That's only happened when one was a changed wereanimal. It's never happened with two born weres," Sebastian clarified.

Her head nudged in my direction and she made a face. "That one has a lot going on. No telling what you have baking in that oven. It might just come out a pup, for all we know. Use that obscurity to your advantage."

Rude!

She was right; the fear and preemptive strategies could be for naught. I could have a child that was totally human. Unable to do anything. Or a pup? *Nah, I'm not going to have a little wolf.*

Or could I? Before my imagination could go to fantastical places, I pushed it aside.

"Would you be able to set up a meeting? I'd like to talk to Rayna and Abigail," I asked her.

"Rayna, possibly. After what your mate did to Elysian, I'm sure Abigail knows he wants to talk to her and she's not amendable to listening. But without Rayna, she won't have support. Rayna's not foolish enough not to recognize that Abigail has an ulterior motive. This isn't about the health and security of the others in this world but the preservation of her people, and her people only. She's vying for her brother's position, and now that the rules have changed about women holding the position, he will not seek reelection so that she can have it." Her gaze moved from Ethan to Josh. "Some siblings will do anything for each other. I'll see what I can do."

"How will you be able to get to her?"

"Demetrius and I were invited to be part of the conventicle and we accepted." Chris dismissed her involvement with a wave of her hand, like she hadn't just told us that she was part of a group whose main focus was to kill me so my baby couldn't be born.

"Oh, calm down, wolfie," she said with barely suppressed annoyance, rolling her eyes as deep feral growls filled the room. It wasn't until I looked down at my hands—clenched, making deep indents in my palms—that I realized the aggressive sounds were coming from me. "I've made my position known but I'd be remiss in not hearing their side, nor would it look good if I sided with you all without hearing it. They are aware I don't agree and that I don't plan to take action. Their goal was to convert me; they were unsuccessful. I told them if something was an imminent threat to the Seethe, we would handle it. Your unborn is not a threat." The frown remained on her face as she departed without another word.

CHAPTER 39

*P*olitical meetings tend to have an air of indulgence and posturing. The host displays their importance with ostentatious tables, elaborate seating, displays of their power and security. This meeting was a noticeable exception, and it was concerning. I regretted the snarky comments I'd made about the Land Rover; it didn't seem like an excessive precaution now. This location wasn't a display of power, wealth, or security. The large, dilapidated gray farmhouse sat on brown, fallow land. Surrounding it were groves of dying and bare trees. The scent of farm animals and manure seeped through the SUV's windows. The raven flying over the barn near the house couldn't be a good sign.

Placing my hand over my stomach, I smoothed over the roundness of it. Protective urges heightened and I wondered if I was making a mistake by coming. Ethan had been adamant about me not going, and it had taken several long debates and cajoling to sway him my way. Was I as naïve as he'd accused me of being? Holding fast to the idea that despite our differences, at the core, we were humans? Instinctual and protective of children? It was natural.

Playing on their protective instincts wasn't the best strategy, but I needed to hear their argument. Looking at Sebastian's face, drawn into scrutiny, I wondered if he'd considered the possibility of the witches' wrath if things progressed with Ariel and he had children with her. Then another car pulled up and Ariel got out. Fatigue was heavy over her features, and she was dressed the most casually I'd ever seen her—a simple white shirt, fitted jeans, and flats. With everything she did, there was a message. Rayna hadn't even warranted her putting on her power suit.

Ariel didn't slow her pace as Gavin and Steven assumed their animal forms beside her as she walked toward the house. She gave the location the same look I had: disappointment and disgust.

"This is where Rayna wanted to meet?"

Sebastian nodded, taking up a position next to her. "Yes, it's not what I expected," he admitted.

Ariel considered it for a moment. "I'm not surprised. I'm more surprised that she agreed to the promise of no violence. Perhaps she's more prudent than she's demonstrated."

Our advance to the meeting place was slow and cautious, everyone checking surroundings and scrutinizing the environment. Assessing everything from the slight change in the strength of the wind to the small rodents that scurried away.

Chris opened the door, her look impassive as she moved aside to let us in. The display of force and power that was lacking in the meeting place was in full force inside the hollowed-out building, which was just drywall and unfinished flooring. To the right stood Chris and Demetrius. Behind a barrier of magic were the witches and their allies. I only recognized Rayna, Abigail, and Mason. Samuel was gone; inwardly I smiled that he'd heeded my warning but couldn't help but feel a pang of apprehension that he'd done so. A zealot wouldn't so easily abandon his cause when he saw the potential for success.

As I looked at Rayna's dark eyes and those of the ten witches behind her, I knew this wasn't what he'd bargained for. He wanted to get rid of magic; they wanted to control who had access to it.

The thick, gossamer wall between us pulsed and the smell of blood—their blood—coursed through the room. A blood barrier was hard to break; one created by ten powerful witches was probably impossible to destroy. Abigail was smug as she took in my appraisal of the magical wall, the one she stood securely behind, either as the instigator of this mess or the architect.

Rayna cleared her throat to get our attention, then rolled her eyes at the pack of weres in animal form behind us. "Always a display of power with you all," she spat out.

"Like your wall," Ethan retorted coolly.

"It is for our protection. I know we agreed upon a truce but, knowing your history, I considered it prudent to protect ourselves for the moment when you all have exhausted your restraint—something you seem to do regularly," she summarized breezily.

Then she turned her fiery judgment from us to Ariel. After a long, appraising look, the lines around her mouth deepened in disapproval. "Ariel. I'm sure you know as much of my history as I know of yours."

Rayna crossed her arms over her chest and looked like a displeased mentor or teacher forced to reprimand a student. "When I heard you and yours were going to make the long-needed power grab of the Creed, I was elated. Even considered returning to the witches, to be one with you all, with the confidence it would be led by one who believed in the purity of magic, the rules, and the importance of not abusing magic." She wore a disenchanted smirk of contempt. "Top of your class in magic school, gifted beyond what had been seen in years"—her gaze jumped to Josh—"gifted for someone who would use their magic for more than being the pack's magic-wielding lackey. So much promise. How long did it take before you were allied with the pack and *allied* with Sebastian?"

Ariel seemed nonplussed by most of Rayna's diatribe, but she was clearly a person who cared about her reputation, and being known as a person who'd fallen for Sebastian's infamous charming ways bothered her. Just for a moment her embarrassment showed and gave Rayna what she needed.

"Her personal life has nothing to do with her ability to lead," Sebastian interjected.

"Of course you'd say that; it benefits your pack. Not only do you have Josh but a group of powerful witches at your beck and call. And"—she waved at my stomach—"whatever that will be."

"Do you really think she's going to weaponize their child?" Ariel snapped back, incredulous. "I don't agree with a lot of things they do, and they don't have the same reverence and respect for magic as we do, but they aren't as careless or callous with it as you want people to believe. They make a mess, they clean it up."

"Not out of virtue or acceptance of responsibility," Rayna countered. "It's to save their asses. If we all came together to punish them for the carelessness and crimes, they wouldn't win."

"Who cares about the reason they do it, as long as it is handled? That's the difference between us. Why we have control of the Creed—"

"For now," Rayna interrupted.

This was just going to be hours of bickering and posturing, and my control was already pulled taut. "I'll agree to be marked," I said. "That will restrict my magic. You win, I won't have access to magic. I will be as you wish, a wolf without magic." It was a huge compromise, one that had dual benefits. I was willing to do it anyway to keep Maya away from our baby, and it would appease Rayna and stop the attacks.

"You know that's not all I want."

431

"That's why it's called a compromise. I'm not making a decision for my pack or any of the weres who enjoy what they are and are content to live in both worlds. You don't get to make the decision of whether or not they get to live that life. That's not how things work. Just like I wouldn't agree to Samuel's desire to wipe the world of magic." It would have made life so simple. We all would just be human—normal. Not have to live in two worlds, deal with the politics, the coups, and the constant unrest. I pressed my hand to my stomach; it might have been a safer place for our baby. Would the spell affect the baby as well, if the child was a were-animal? For several thoughtful moments, I considered it. I drew in a shaky breath, and when I exhaled, I blew out the thought of it. I couldn't play god with others' lives, making a decision they otherwise wouldn't have.

I held Rayna's uncompromising eyes and took in her stern, rigid appearance and defiant posturing. Overshadowing that was her hate for me.

She wasn't going to negotiate, so I tried to appeal to Abigail, who was just as much the creator of this mess as Rayna. "Do you really want this?"

Abigail scoffed, "More than she does. I've watched you all for years, knowing the menace that followed in your wake. But the return of the Faeries was the last straw. You all need to be put down, like the animals you are."

My patience was just a fragile thread weakening with each moment. I pressed my hand against the barrier, testing the strength of it. A barrier made of witches' blood, and magic was the very life of it. Life I had the ability to destroy with my magic. I could tear it down as I had Samuel's. I was positive of it. Hand pressed against it, I reached to that well of darkness and death. And stopped. I looked at Josh, his denim-blue eyes a reminder that he'd gone to that well, bargained and indulged too much, and left a piece of himself there. I'd dipped my toe in there often, too. How many times could I test that source without just leaving a piece and allowing it to engulf me? I wouldn't today just for a display of power.

"Ethan and I will get the mark, our child will wear an iridium brace once of age, and you will surrender the Aufero to someone who can't benefit from its use. Maybe the vampires. They can't use it."

"You speak on behalf of the witches now," Rayna said in an amused tone. "You do have your nose in everything, don't you?"

"I won't allow you to terrorize the Creed for no other reason than they've helped us when we needed them."

Her dark, mocking chuckle resounded in the filthy little building. "You won't 'allow' it. How presumptuous of you."

"Yes, you heard me correctly. Nothing's wrong with your ears, it's your heart and values that have the dysfunction." I stepped even closer to the barrier, pressing into it, stretching it until we were almost nose to nose. "That's the offer. You are going to want to take it."

"And if I refuse?" she challenged.

Incensed, I wondered if she could feel the heat of my rage. It felt too virulent to contain. Again, I assessed the people behind her, the ones who followed her out of fear; they didn't seem blindly loyal to Rayna, just her cause. The smug mien of their self-proclaimed purity caused them to look down their noses at us—at me. I glared at Mason; he wasn't a Makellos—a pure elf whose blood had never mixed with human. Abigail and Gideon were, but Gideon had rejected their separatist ways, like living in Elysian away from other elves because they decided they were better. Rayna's magic was strong; it was doubtful it had been diluted by human blood.

Forceful ripples moved over the wall. Rayna's gaze shifted from my face to my hand, which I unconsciously had moved to the protective field. Several of the witches cringed at the assault, their blood linking them physically to the barrier.

Ethan whispered my name, and I made an attempt to pull

my eyes from Rayna because her surly glower only served to irritate me more.

Closing my eyes, I made an effort to calm down—to handle this amicably—but I couldn't stop looking at this for what it was: an assault on me, my child, and my pack. Rage rampaged and the softness of Ethan's voice became just white noise.

"Take the offer," I repeated in a whisper.

"Begging is hardly going to change anything. Constant compromise has led to where we are now with you. Marcia was power-hungry and at times tyrannical, but she understood and did what was necessary."

The gust of magic that slammed into the barrier edged into her. Shocked, she took several steps back, closer to the other witches. Abigail and Mason moved closer to the witches as well. *Cowards.*

"What she thought was needed was cruel and unnecessary. Fine, offer rescinded. Know this: it is over. You come after me, Ethan, or anyone I care about, you make goddamn sure you say goodbye to everyone you care about, because you won't be seeing them again!" I wasn't able to gain enough control to go to the darkest recesses of my magic to find what I needed to tear down the barrier. My rage reduced me to slamming against it with my fist. Ethan's arms circled around me as he attempted to pull me back.

Chris moved into the small space Ethan had created between me and Rayna, her tone level and professional: "You should reconsider; it's a good offer. Is the *possibility* of a magical abnormality worth a war that may come of this? You made an attempt on Sky and Ethan." Her eyes moved to Mason and Abigail, to add them to the accusations. "What will be your punishment if their child is just a simple were-animal, undeserving of whatever you have in store?"

"How can you be so optimistic?" Rayna retorted. She snorted in derision. "Oh, because you all likely won't be affected. Pardon me for not taking your feedback into consideration. This"—she waved her hand dismissively—"was a courtesy in hopes I could get you to understand the importance of our stance. Obviously, your vampire conversion has changed you from the type of person I would want on my team."

"Then obviously, the rumors you heard were false. I never supported measures like this, nor will I ever. I didn't condone it when the witches did it, nor when the elves did it." Chris lobbed a sharp look in Abigail and Mason's direction.

Ethan's chest was still pressed against my back, his hands splayed across my stomach. His breathing was slow and measured and obviously something he was working hard to control, but I could feel the vibrations of his chest. The deep growl settling in it and the tension in his touch. "Let's break the field," he said.

I moved quickly, and he was seconds behind. Rayna moved her focus from Chris and watched with renewed interest as I placed my hands on the field. No more showy displays of aggression allowing my magic to rampage against it. But I didn't have the control of the magic that I wished I had. It felt different, borrowed—no, stolen. A different type of darkness kindled the magic I was using and mingled with the erected field. It wanted to destroy. Restrictions I held on Maya's magic lifted. I not only lifted the restraints, I gave her permission to rage, unconstrained by anything. It felt different—not like an explosion of unfiltered magic. It moved in my mind like a gentle rain, droplets of magic testing the boundaries, assessing the existing magic bound to the field and the life force keeping it up. A sharp breath escaped me as it seized that force and the witches gasped for air. Their eyes widened as they reached for their throats. I'd thought I just wanted to break the field and stop them—but apparently my true desires were more vicious. *They want to kill my child.* That thought wouldn't leave my mind.

The foreboding magic didn't break the field to get to them. It circumvented it. The very blood magic they'd used to secure themselves was now used against them. Broken blood vessels reddened their eyes. They choked on the little air that remained in their bubble. Warmth eased over me and I knew it was a fraction of the fire that blazed in them. Sweat pooled on their skin.

Abigail and Mason, unaffected by the magic, rushed to the witches.

"Let the protective field drop," Abigail urged. Rayna's bloodshot eyes fixed on me. Consumed by shock and hate, her protective responses were delayed. Abigail's fingers flicked with electricity and she stunned Rayna into action; so did the others, once Mason and Abigail intervened. The field fell and they all disappeared.

Chris frowned and remained silent for just a few minutes, but I could tell she was replaying in her mind what had just happened.

"Did that go the way you wanted?" she asked, hints of irritation in her voice.

"What were we supposed to do?" I snapped.

"I'm on your side on this," she reminded me, but her sharp words were a contrast to her declaration.

"I'm sure that stunt didn't help to change her mind," Ariel said, rubbing her hands over her face. Abruptly, she turned. "We are returning home; when you are ready to have the *interdico* placed, just let me know," she said, backing out of the door.

Sebastian was close behind her. "What do you mean, you're going home?"

"I'm removing my witches from the pack's protection. The price is too high. We will protect ourselves." Ariel started toward the car, where Gavin was standing, prepared to return her to the safe house where they were staying. She said something to him and his eyes immediately went to Sebastian, seeking confirmation.

Sebastian shook his head, and Gavin nodded to him and

immediately told Ariel no. Furious, she turned and walked toward Sebastian with determination. "You don't get to make decisions for us. Do you understand? I am declining your offer of assistance."

"Once again you are putting your pride before your safety. It's a foolish way to lead."

"We are not in the same situation. You've had years to establish yourself, to earn the respect that you enjoy and often exploit. I don't have that, and with Rayna commanding so much loyalty from others, I am now the cause of the very civil war I was trying to prevent."

"You let her get to you—"

"Damn right she got to me! Did you see the witches she has with her? Older, more experienced witches who had distanced themselves from Marcia and the former Creed's ways and aligned with her. I'm not enough—*we* aren't enough. They don't trust me." Her shoulders sagged.

"We trust you to do the *interdico* and we will need you all at full strength for the safety of Ethan and Sky's child. If Rayna gets to you all, she will take your magic. How is that better?" Sebastian asked.

"We'll protect ourselves." Ariel started for the car again. "Sebastian, I'm going home. Don't instruct Gavin to do anything other than that."

She hadn't heard Sebastian's approach and looked shocked when he was just a few feet from her.

His voice was mild and sympathetic, as if he understood her dilemma of being a new leader: "What are your plans?"

"That's between me and the other Creed," she rebutted fiercely, her lips pulled so taut it intensified her winged cheeks.

Sebastian blinked once, flicking away any residual anger from his dealings with Rayna. He shortened the small distance between them. His tone was somnolent, coaxing, as he spoke to her again. "It's just us," he asserted, as if that had special meaning.

Ariel chewed on her bottom lip, considering his words. The confidence that she'd displayed when we'd first met her seemed so distant. She openly struggled with what she was going to do. Now she was dealing with a compromised reputation because of her relationship with the pack and Sebastian and dwindling trust from other witches. Witches who were once neutral were now taking sides against her.

She looked in the direction of Ethan and me, and I pretended I wasn't listening. Ethan seemed to be doing a more believable job, because her scrutinizing gaze remained on me.

Come on, you know I'm going to listen.

"Things between us have to be strictly professional," she asserted, and then she clenched her lips between her teeth as she looked past Sebastian. He seemed even more relaxed, I assumed as an effort to calm her. She was showing the difficulty she was having with navigating the delicate boundaries and paths of her position. A place Sebastian had undoubtedly been many times since he had become the Alpha.

"How do you want to handle the arrangement with the witches?" Him relinquishing his control of the situation and handing it to her seemed to ease her tension.

"We stay together—but not at one of your homes. At mine."

"Okay," he conceded.

Ariel blew out a breath, and her confidence reasserted itself. Her eyes grew brighter and bolder, along with her demands. "I would like to ask the help of Gavin, Steven, and maybe a few other were-animals to track the Aufero. Rayna's witches are more experienced but not stronger—I'd feel better with that threat out of the way."

Sebastian nodded. "Will you be warding your home?"

"Of course."

"Can Josh do a second one?" he requested.

Ariel considered it and nodded.

"It sounds like a solid plan. Gavin and Steven will be with you the entire time you look for it—their ability to track is better than yours."

"I agree."

The conversation ended with a simple nod of Sebastian's head in Gavin's direction. Sebastian's face didn't show any signs that Ariel had essentially agreed to the exact same thing that was happening before. Instead of being in the pack's home, she was at hers. Making finding the Aufero a priority would ensure that the pack was with the witches at all times. If by chance something were to happen and the ward was broken, Josh would know and thus Ethan and Sebastian.

I didn't miss the reassuring way Sebastian touched Ariel's hand and she remained still, allowing it.

Sure, you're done with him. We all believe it. When you're finished peddling that tale, why don't you tell us about your Bigfoot sighting?

"Fine." Ariel finally said in response to Sebastian's touch.

CHAPTER 40

*B*efore I could knock, Sebastian invited me in. Leaning back in his chair, his fingers across his stomach, he looked expectant.

"Sorry I'm late, Ethan had to make sure I had a motorcade." I was unable to keep the irritation out of my voice. This change in my life just compounded the many reasons I hated Rayna, Abigail, Mason, and Liam. I had a detail everywhere I went, and it was excessive. Annoyingly excessive.

"He's being cautious, and rightfully so," Sebastian said, earning him a derisive snort. I blamed my bad mood on my hormones, which were all over the place. It had only been seven days since our meeting with Rayna, but my stomach was a little larger, my hips a little wider, and my personality a little bitchier. When I wasn't irritable I was more sensitive than I'd ever been. And the news Ethan had given me last night had me spiraling and was the reason I had to see Sebastian. He was considering dividing the packs and Ethan had hinted that Steven probably would be interested in a Beta position, perhaps even Alpha. Fixated on the possibility that Steven might leave to head his own pack, I'd zoned out for the rest of the conversation.

"Well, I hope you all remember to feed the snipers," I snarked. It was a joke. I hoped it was a joke, but after having two cars—one in the front of mine, another in the rear—escort me on my ride to the pack's home, nothing seemed excessive.

Sebastian's roar of laughter shocked me. I frowned; he was enjoying this too much.

"It's not funny. Seriously, who is going to make an attempt on my way to the pack's house? This is the one place I'd be safe," I rebutted.

"If it were me planning the attack, it would be on the top of my list of times to execute it for the very reason you mentioned." A dark shadow overtook his face, a glimpse of his ominous thoughts and Machiavellian ways.

Lolling in his chair, he had a half-smile on his face and a knowing gleam in his eyes. He looked around his office. "So, once again you're here in my office." The smile remained, but a hint of coolness entered his words. It was Sebastian-speak for "I have to see your face again" or "why are you bothering me," and it wasn't as if he was above bluntly saying it. I shifted as if uneasy and put my hands to my lower back, and he grudgingly waved me to a chair. I had to admit, pregnancy came with its perks. If I sighed too loudly, people assumed I was tired and scrambled to find me a place to sit. Staring at any food too long got me a larger serving. Everyone seemed wary around me, watching me with careful eyes that didn't have anything to do with Ethan's protection detail. For some reason, they felt I was just moments from breaking into a maudlin display of emotions—which wasn't a stretch, but I had them under control more than most of the pack seemed to think. I was the one pregnant, but they were the ones being freaky. "Preggos just make them weird," Winter had said after witnessing such behavior. "They're like that with everyone, too protective and jittery. Just roll with it. Once you stop being a human incubator things will go back to normal, except all the caring and attention you ever got will go to the cute package you pushed out."

Winter had a way with words.

Brows arched, Sebastian waited for me to speak, his patience becoming increasingly thin, which he let me know by exhaling a rough breath.

"Why are you sending Steven away?" My voice broke and I snapped my mouth closed. I thought he'd missed it, but of course he didn't. Tensing, his eyes widened, and he reared back in his chair, his hand clutching the side as if he was waiting for me to break down in tears or something. I was considered weird, and not their overt aversion to most distressed emotions. Display anger, rage, predatory responses—they were fine. Cry, and they were like robots with defective circuits.

"I'm not sending Steven or anyone away," he responded, his voice tepid. He leaned in, assessing me for a moment. After several moments of silent deliberation he continued, "I'm considering dividing each pack into two packs for each area. The situation with Cole exposed the vulnerabilities that can exist. More packs will ensure there isn't too much concentrated power in one area. Besides, there are too many strong members who should be Alphas of their own pack, including Steven. I'd never force him to leave. I want him to stay." He stood, slowly exhaling. He did want him to stay but he wouldn't be the one to stop him. I frowned at my selfishness.

Sebastian rested against the wall, his lips pursed into a tight moue. "It won't be for a while. Maybe a year or two to divide the territories and consolidate the extension packs and the liaisons. Of course, members vying for the positions of Alpha will be another issue. It will be a lot of work, but in the end, it will make us stronger—better." He made an attempt at a smile, but it was weak and quickly fizzled. It wasn't just the work; there would be changes in dynamics, losses of members over challenges for positions, and him having to deal with the politics in the beginning. It would be difficult but he was willing to do that hard thing, because it was the best thing for the pack. Once again, I found myself feeling sympathy for what he had to deal with in his position and bewilderment over him wanting the position.

"I hope Steven takes one of the positions—he'll be a good Alpha," I asserted, my voice stronger than I felt. If he took the position, he'd move away. I needed years to deal with that.

Sebastian's cell phone rang just as my hand touched the doorknob to leave. "Hello, Ariel." The inflection in his voice changed. It was so light and airy with tones of something that I thought I'd perhaps mistaken: eagerness. He was eager to speak with her. I stopped in my tracks and turned to face him. He'd retreated to the other side of the office, his back to me, as he spoke to her. She didn't have preternatural hearing, so he was forced to speak at a regular volume.

I was sure it was about Rayna. "She's been quiet," Ariel said. It was odd that there hadn't been a retaliation or at the very least more threats.

"I thought she'd resurface once you all got your hands on the Fatifer and the Vitae. For no other reason other than to take them from you."

"Me, too." She sounded concerned, and rightfully so. It was never a good sign when your enemies weren't active; it meant they were planning.

"Do you still feel safe at your home? You can stay—"

"No, we will stay here. We have wards up, and if she does attack we can handle it."

"I'll be there later to relieve Gavin; we can discuss things then."

I rolled my eyes. They were exhausting. How hard was it to admit they liked each other? When Sebastian turned around, it was to see me, arms crossed and eyes narrowed, scrutinizing him.

"You're really taking a hands-on approach to this, aren't you? You have a lot of members who can take Gavin's place. You don't have to inconvenience yourself."

He shrugged. "It's fine. I don't mind."

Are we really going to play this game?

His gaze shifted from me to the door.

You can look at the door all you want, Mr. Alpha, I'm not leaving.

"You and Ariel are good for each other, but it'll never work."

He blinked once but his face remained stoic. Again, he looked at the door. I made my way back to the chair, arching my back a little and making my stomach poke out more. My waddle was exaggerated and my descent into sitting labored. I used my pregnancy superpower, endearing myself to him. He wasn't going to ask the poor pregnant woman to leave.

Lips pressed into a thin line, he was apparently unimpressed by the performance. "Hmm, poor Sky, in a matter of minutes all the energy has been zapped from your body and even sitting is a struggle," he mocked.

Yeah, we both know I'm faking it. Let's get on with it.

"It's not that it can't work—it won't because of Joan. Ariel thinks there is something between you two, and it will be a source of contention. Let her know something. ... Sebastian, she needs to know that every time Joan is around, it won't be an issue. She needs to feel secure. It's not fair to her nor to you, because you'll never have a good relationship until Ariel knows Joan isn't a threat to it."

"Joan is an exceptional woman," Sebastian admitted. He turned his back to me, perusing the books on the shelf of his library, his long fingers lingering over some of the bindings. His deep baritone voice was difficult to hear at such a low volume but I stayed statue-still, afraid that any move would send him back into his cocoon of secrecy. "She found a child, when she was so young herself, and nurtured him like her own." It was her sense of responsibility that he admired, because he was the man who'd flown across the country, fought his way through a pack, to save Winter.

My lips pressed together, making sure I didn't utter a word, because I knew the wrong sound, question, or even look would have him scurrying back into his emotional safe house. "She took Steven in, raised him, and made him into what he is. He's an amazing kid."

It *was* hard to remember he wasn't a kid. Even when I watched him toss back shots of tequila like they were water. Or control a room of rowdy club patrons with a sharp look. He was just Steven. My Steven, and I guessed in a way, he was Sebastian's Steven.

"She's a good Alpha—one that the South needs. For years, she put off her challenge ..." his voice faded. We both knew why. Most Alpha challenges were to death; if she'd lost—it would have devastated Steven. "I'm fond of her," he finally admitted.

I've seen you with her. Fondness is a light touch and a "way to go, buddy." That's not what you display. There's something different. Remaining silent, I waited for him to continue. He was drawn back into his thoughts, still looking over his collection of books as a distraction.

"There won't be a relationship between Joan and me because the South is where she belongs and I belong here. We both know that."

It was another sacrifice he'd made, and I felt it was unfair. "If there were a way, would you want to?"

He turned. "No," he answered too quickly, without a thought and without the truth, either. I sensed it, but for whatever reason, he'd never pursue it. "I agree, Ariel should know that there isn't anything between me and Joan and never has been, except a kiss."

I sucked in a breath and froze. Something so small shouldn't be impactful. "What are the chances of me getting more details?" I asked, grinning.

He chuckled. I took his hand when he extended it to help me out of the chair, and he guided me to the door. He waved his goodbye and made a show of closing the door loudly and locking it.

CHAPTER 41

The silence was deafening. Chilling. We were all in a holding pattern, waiting for Rayna to strike. I had a feeling she wouldn't do anything during business hours, which is why I believed Claudia had invited me to her gallery during that time.

My hand stayed wrapped around my cup as I inhaled the scent of peppermint.

Claudia slipped a plate of cookies in front of me. That's another thing that seemed consolatory: give preggo something sweet, that'll soothe her. It was becoming increasingly annoying.

"Pregnancy can be hard for a lot of women. I can imagine it's more so for you. It's taken away some of your independence."

"And Ethan being overprotective and bat"—*shit crazy* —"overly enthusiastic about my safety is overwhelming, too."

A faint, genial smile bowed her thin lips. "I know, but you know your circumstances are quite different."

They were more than different, they were catastrophic, or that seemed to be what everyone believed. I pressed my hand to my stomach, and the baby kicked. Not hard; it was as if my baby sensed it and was giving me a nudge of "you've got this." And I did, but I didn't want to have to. The thought that my union with Ethan would've turned the other denizens against us had never crossed my mind. Theirs was an anticipatory reaction, but it was violent and unjust.

Leaning forward, Claudia covered my hand with hers. "They are overreacting to the unknown. You had no way of knowing this would be the result." Her lips pressed into a tight thin line. "Although I believe that Abigail and Mason are using this false flag and your pregnancy as some harbinger of doom to position her better among the others. I respect that she is ambitious, but her deception to achieve it is concerning. Her adoption of the witch's nefarious ways will be her undoing. There have to be boundaries, principles, and rules. When some form of those things doesn't exist, there is chaos." She shrugged, her eyes showing the depth of her experience and knowledge. "Perhaps she plans to succeed through that chaos and fear. That isn't the sign of a leader but of a tyrant. I hope her fall won't be as cruel as her ascension."

An odd flicker of delight pulsed in her eyes. Carefully, I watched her and the smile that fought to put an odd curve in her lips. Reverting to her genial, placid mood, she smiled again, but it was a Claudia smile—reserved, kind, and maternal. Not the dark grin of delight that had threatened to emerge. I needed to know what thought had brought such a look to her face, but then again, did I? She was godmother to my mate, but that didn't blind me to what she was: a bringer of death. A Faerie. Ancient strong magic.

We'd settled into a comfortable, polite exchange as we discussed Ethan, decorating for our baby, and my plans after the baby. Ethan had a plan for everything, even a contingency plan of what to do during delivery. I left that part out of it, because I didn't want to think about wearing the *interdico*.

There was one sharp knock at her door before her assistant

poked his head in. "She's not taking no for an answer and—" He was shoved out of the way by Abigail and Mason. Abigail's fair skin was flushed with anger, her eyes razor-sharp, and her lips twisted into a grimace that looked painful. She radiated anger, but not magic. Not a hint of it drifted from her. But she was so incensed it fueled its own energy.

"There is no way I'm going to believe you don't know how to fix this," Abigail barked. Extending her arm, she revealed a thumb-sized hexagram with symbols inside each point. Eyes ablaze, Mason showed his as well.

"This is neither fae, witch, nor elf magic. It can't be removed. Ten days I've been at this. Ten days I've been without magic. The spell that put this on me isn't typical magic—when it was cast, it felt dark, powerful, and old. You can't tell me that you aren't aware of it!"

Claudia was cool and indifferent as she turned in her seat to face them. Behind their overwrought emotions were under-tones of fear.

"As I told you before, I am aware of the magic that marked you, but I can't remove it. Nor can anyone else other than the *Roho*. That's their mark. If you want to find them, ask the one who sent them."

"We don't know who sent them!" Abigail shouted back. "I was awake with bodies over me, paralyzed while these ... women placed this goddamn mark on me! They got through my wards, past security, and I can't even remember what they look like to find them." Tears of frustration brimmed along the edges of her eyes. "Who would do this to me?"

"Oh darling," Claudia said, her voice sweet but lacking sympathy. "It's not a matter of who would do it, but who would be willing to go to great lengths to call on their service."

"Tell me how to find them, and I'll figure the rest out," Abigail demanded.

Claudia made a soft snort of incredulity. "I gave you their

name before. Did you bother to research them? The three sisters are gifted with magic that compares to no other. So ancient that it predates your wards and our magic. You don't 'figure the rest out,' you pass their trials and if you don't, the penalty for it is death. I think you've lived far too long in a place of privilege to endure them." She shrugged.

"They didn't touch my brother."

"Oh, how interesting," Claudia said, though her voice didn't share that same curiosity. "Rayna and Liam are marked as well, correct?"

"I've given you that information already. Yes, them as well."

Claudia rose from her chair like a perilous wave. She moved around the room, fingers gliding over statues and books. "What a peculiar group of victims."

It wasn't peculiar at all. They were all linked, and we knew how.

"Would you like the information I have on finding them? You will need a plane willing to take you into particular mountains in Tanzania. I can recommend a pilot, but he won't stay. If you survive the test, I'm sure the *Roho* will ensure you return safely. They have their flaws, but dishonor isn't one of them. You live through the trials, you are guaranteed safe return."

Claudia was at her desk, going through papers. It seemed like a contradiction for her to be behind her elegant desk, the face of refinement and grace, scribbling away on her expensive-looking vellum, writing down instructions to send Abigail and whoever was foolish enough to follow to what was possibly her death.

Claudia was steady, her eyes blank, as she extended the paper to Abigail. It was unnerving, even more so to Abigail, who was reticent as she took the paper.

"I wish you safe travels, Abigail." Claudia should have said what she wanted to, because it was painted in her words, screamed in the gentle cadence of her tone, and screeched in the stilted delivery. *It's been real.* Claudia wouldn't have said that, but it would have been the Claudia version of it. Florid and kind. A sweet, ominous farewell.

After the elves' exit, Claudia directed her attention to me. Warm eyes lingered over me. Her head tilted as she continued to study me. "You have really made your place in this world." She sucked in a breath and forced her pinched brows to release. "And your alliances are strong. How did you do it?" she whispered.

"Do what?"

"Nothing, dear." After a long assessing look, her lips curved into a mild smile. "There are people who are willing to do more than I'd imagined to make sure your baby is safe. You impress me, Skylar." The reverence with which she said my name shocked me. I had alliances that the pack didn't have? Guardians? People who could successfully pass a test where most wouldn't? Things had been so divided, I wasn't so sure of it. I would have thought it was Ethan or Sebastian, if it weren't for seeing Ethan daily and Sebastian a few days ago.

With that in mind, I found myself at Demetrius's home. Chris answered the door and immediately opened it wider to allow me entrance. Her fluidity of movement was lost, slowed to the point she was like an injured human. She tugged at her long, oversized hooded sweatshirt. She'd abandoned her heels and had on a pair of flats and comfortable-looking leggings. She stepped back when I leaned in to inspect the thick coating of makeup that poorly concealed the scars on her face.

My gaze went from her to the figure behind her. Demetrius quickly moved back into the shadows. His movement wasn't as graceful as usual, and if I wasn't mistaken it looked like he had a limp. Before he could return to the darkness of the hallway, I got a glimpse of marks and scars running along the right side of his face.

"Been on any trips lately?" I asked, taking hold of Chris's arm. When she winced, I loosened my grip and handled it more gently. Slowly and with care, I pulled back the sleeve to reveal skin that had been badly seared. So badly that even with advanced vampire healing, the burns hadn't faded.

She didn't answer the question about the trip, nor had I expected her to.

"You should have Dr. Jeremy look at these," I suggested.

"They'll heal," she said, pulling her arm away and quickly rolling her sleeve down to keep it hidden. Her eyes moved past me as if it was difficult to look at me, and perhaps it was as the tears welling in my eyes spilled. Unable to contain them no matter how I tried, I began to sob uncontrollably.

"Stop that," she hissed through clenched teeth. It was then that I noticed her lipstick was covering a split lip.

The tears came harder. I tried to control them, but it was a lost cause. It wasn't just hormones—or maybe it was. Emotions swelled and I couldn't control them. I pressed the palm of my hand to my stomach. There wasn't any movement. The baby had been active but now had found peace. The more I tried to stop, the harder the tears came.

"You are going to have to stop that." Chris led me into the living room and directed me to sit.

My hands weren't enough to wipe away the stream that kept sliding down my face. She left and returned with a box of tissues and started roughly dabbing at my face.

"Stop." I nudged her away. "I'm not a rug you're trying to get a stain out of."

"Well, stop leaking," she retorted with a snap, still dabbing at my face, but now gently.

After a few minutes the river of tears slowed to a trickle and

I wiped them away faster, hoping it would relax the scowl on Chris's face.

"I really appreciate—"

"Let's not talk about it, okay?" she whispered.

Reluctantly I complied, but I wanted to talk about it. It didn't seem like something that should go ignored. They'd risked their life to help me—and my child. How did I not talk about it?

For several minutes I sat in the room with her in an uncomfortable silence as she shifted nervously under the weight of my stare. The elephant in the room ran rampant and I had to ignore it. Chris clearly was better at doing such things. With a sigh I stood and watched her face wrinkle into a scowl.

Inch by inch, I approached her like she was a timid animal I knew would scurry away from sudden moves. I reached out to embrace her.

"If you touch me, I will bite you," she asserted.

I shrugged. "Ordinarily, that would discourage me, but I bit Gavin a couple of days ago. It was weird at first and now it's just a funny story. 'Hey, remember when I bit Gavin?'" I shrugged. "It's not a biggie."

She snorted a laugh. "You bit Gavin. That has to be an interesting story."

I told her and she laughed. It seemed like she was doing more than finding my story entertaining and was unburdening herself.

She stiffened at my touch, which wasn't unexpected. Being part of the pack, I'd gotten used to bodies stiffening at the mere thought of being touched in any way other than sparring or sex. *Yeah, and I'm the weird one.*

It was going to be quick, because I had a feeling that biting me wasn't totally off the table. Before I could pull away, she whispered, "You are doing everything you can to take care of your child. It shouldn't be this hard. I don't want it to be."

Squeezing my eyes tighter, I was finally successful at keeping the tears at bay. The hug didn't end, and Chris tensed more when I rested my head on her shoulders.

"This is getting weird," she announced. Her palm was cool as it pressed against my back. It was the closest thing I was going to get to her returning my embrace. I sighed and we stayed there for several moments.

"Yeah, it got weird two minutes ago," I admitted into her clothes, feeling the damp stains that the tears I couldn't blink away had left. "Now, it's just disturbing."

After several more moments, I took a step back and she opened the distance between us even farther.

She nodded a farewell.

CHAPTER 42

The threat of the loss of magic without any clear way of reversing it was quite the deterrent. The monitoring stopped, the tails and watchful eyes waiting for vulnerabilities halted. Ethan periodically looked out the window with the same strained look of confusion on his face. It had been there since I told him what Demetrius and Chris had done to get the others to back off. When he didn't have that on his face, he wore a look of admiration that was directed at me.

When Rayna showed up at our door, Aufero in hand, her appearance was as withdrawn and haggard as Ariel's had been weeks before. She looked oddly pale under the golden light of the sun, and her hands were marked with worn symbols used for invocations and scars where blood had been drawn for spells. That light hum of energy that surrounded most witches was gone, smothering a peculiar light from her. It was like magic was a part of them, so intertwined and essential that when it was taken, it was like part of their existence was as well.

This woman tried to kill our baby. I couldn't feel sorry for her. I wouldn't feel sorry for her. I hoped that Samuel was one of the witches assisting her with reclaiming her magic. Seeing her would encourage him to fully abandon his dream of a world without magic. This seemed to be more than just sadness over losing her magic—she seemed off.

She extended the Aufero to me, and it pulsed with bright hues of orange, maroon, silver, and blue. Returning home. I hesitated before taking ownership of it again—reluctant to reclaim such nebulous power. It seemed to function with an obscure value system, as if it had a mind of its own.

"You should have it. I want Ariel and hers to know there isn't a threat of me taking their magic."

Should I point out that she can't? Nah, she's posturing, and that's all she has. "Thank you." I took the Aufero but held it away from my body with the gentleness and caution one would handle a bomb. In silence, Rayna scrutinized Ethan and me, I assumed trying to figure out which one of us was responsible for her predicament.

"When will my magic be returned to me?" she finally asked.

"I don't know if it will. I had nothing to do with it, and I'm not sure how to have it returned."

Doubt and disbelief sharpened her gaze, which was now firmly placed on me. Pungent desperation wafted off her. Then her eyes dropped to my distended stomach, which kept prompting questions about whether I was having twins. "Your baby is safe, I've given you the Aufero, and I've made it known that you are not to be touched—I think I've more than earned it back."

Kicking a person when they were down was rude and I would never do it, but her creative spin, making her the heroine and warrior for justice, was irritating. The Aufero was returned to me for no other reason than to get her magic back. Our child was safe because she was no longer in a position to harm.

Ethan wasn't about to allow her to get away with her revisionist version of the truth. "We aren't able to return your magic, and I think it's a good thing. Your change of heart is a result of your change in circumstances. Is there anything else you want?"

Her mouth was puckered tightly, probably holding back a scathing retort. It wasn't enough. "Just because I don't have access to magic, doesn't mean I can't be a thorn in your side. In the pack's side."

So much for not kicking someone when they're down. "You're right. But you are a cautionary tale for those who might try to follow in your footsteps. It's quite a deterrent to getting the backing you need. Abigail, Mason, and you are what happens when you screw with us. Leave us alone and we'll leave you alone. You came for us; it wasn't the other way around. Contrary to how you depict us and our history, we've done more good than bad. Goodbye, Rayna." It was rude to nudge her away from the door enough to close it, but I didn't care. I wasn't feeling very hospitable.

Chris had ended this with far less bloodshed than anyone could have anticipated. I wanted to thank her again. I also needed to thank Claudia, because I had more than a suspicion that she had her hand in this as well. The rest of my pregnancy could be somewhat normal, or as normal as it could be for a were-animal who was hosting a Faerie spirit shade and occasionally had a terait as a result of being killed by a vampire at birth. Couldn't get any more normal than that.

CHAPTER 43

But of course, I wouldn't have normal, especially with my pregnancy. My wrist was on fire from the mark from the *interdico* done the day before. It had been the third one done that week. Each one performed exhausted the witches while Maya fought not to be caged by a spell. Each night, lying next to Ethan, I spoke in words that weren't my own as she removed them, leaving me feeling weary each morning.

I clenched my teeth together trying to bite back another scream from the pain of the contractions and the hellfire on my arm. My throat was sore and dry from doing it for hours.

Sweat-drenched hair matted to my forehead and I kept waiting for the crack of Ethan's hand breaking under my hold.

A delivery room should be filled with nurses, doctors, and assistants; for me it was filled with witches, protective objects, spell ingredients, and the foul odors of defeat and apprehension.

"Why are we here? The *interdico* didn't work and apparently she's no longer immune to iridium, so what are we expected to do?" Nia asked, her pragmatism and pessimism more annoying than ever before.

"Just in case, but it will be fine." Ethan's confidence should have been inspiring and emboldening, but this time it seemed like pride that would lead to our fall. I knew what we had ultimately decided to do, and playing musical chairs with shades while giving birth wasn't going to be simple. I couldn't live without a spirit shade and I had to be alive to give birth. In the back of my mind I knew I didn't have to be alive for the baby to live, and that scared me.

Sensing my concern, Ethan whispered against my ear, "Everyone's coming out of this, I promise."

His intentions were good, but he couldn't make promises like that. I closed my eyes, tears brimming and threatening to release, replaying the sincerity in his voice. Would Ethan make it out, if I didn't? He had to, but the thought of him dealing with things if everything we'd planned didn't align made my heart ache. My eyes snapped open, searching for Josh. Josh wore the burden of his own concerns and those of his brother who refused to show them.

"Ethan," Ariel said tentatively. "Do you have a worst-case scenario? Even with a C-section, Maya is still active. If at any time she can get the baby to accept her, she can be hosted. If Sky is de—"

"We know that," he interrupted, refusing to let the word *death* be said. Filler words were always used: *worst case, downward turn, a situation,* but never *death.* Winter kept looking at the clock obsessively, the way I used to right before a change, always noting that I could live only six minutes without breath. Early on when I changed, it had felt like I couldn't breathe and for minutes I was oxygen-deprived. But this was different. If Maya left my body and wasn't replaced by another shade, I wasn't without breath, I was without a life. A person couldn't be revived from that or given supplemental breaths until they could breathe on their own.

I wasn't going to be put under anesthesia, just given an epidural, a strong one, which Dr. Jeremy had warned would wear off rather quickly.

His low, paternal voice was soothing as he prepared for an incision. "I'm going to cut you, you might feel it a little—but you've had worse, haven't you? You are going to do just fine."

I nodded and couldn't squeeze Ethan's hand any harder.

Since his visit to Elysian, his eyes hadn't been the same. Steel blue was gone, replaced by a deep smoky hue. His magic was different, and there wasn't anything pure about it. I didn't know how to describe it. Was it natural magic, laced with dark, or dark imbued with drams of natural? Whatever it was, it was strong.

"Ready?" Dr. Jeremy asked. After we had nodded, Kelly moved a portable curtain over me, blocking me from seeing him make the incision. I allowed Josh's soft invocation over me, and when Ethan joined in, it became white noise, hushing me into a calm. It was more than just a soothing ease. I felt secure. Comforted with an optimism that I had forbidden myself to feel. I had Josh, eight powerful witches, a very gifted doctor, and Ethan. This had to work.

I relaxed and felt the changes in me. Maya had been part of me for so long, a vague heaviness that with each year became stronger, a noticeable part of me that had intertwined with my existence. Unlike my wolf, she wasn't a symbiotic presence; we were at odds, fighting for dominance. I remembered Ethan's words: she fights the human but can't fight the wolf. I tapped into that part of me where Maya had no reign, no control, because it couldn't be hurt by magic.

Ethan's voice was louder, more urgent; then came Josh's, just as fervent and strong. The heaviness of Maya was gone, but she wasn't leaving without a fight. I gasped at the pain. It felt like she was clawing at me for purchase. It didn't feel like the pull of an animal—it was an enchanted touch, but that didn't make it any less painful. The emptiness of departing was filled with the joy of hearing my baby cry for the first time.

"It's a girl," Dr. Jeremy announced, and it was the last thing I heard.

CHAPTER 44

$\mathcal{J}$ could no longer stand outside the door as the machines buzzed and Ethan's voice became increasingly heightened with fear and anxiety. The false bravado was misplaced—they didn't have this. It involved magic and it was never easy, consistent, or the answer. I wished it wasn't the answer for Sky.

Ethan's emotions were thick and suffocating. It had been ten minutes since I'd been standing near the door and Sky hadn't moved. It hadn't gone unnoticed by Ethan.

Kelly was in the corner with the baby, who cried longer than I thought she should. Did she know that her mother was lying in a hospital bed unconscious after performing a complicated spell? The baby wailed; I blinked back tears—feeling her sorrow. Kelly soothed her, using low, hushed tones as she cleaned her off.

She wasn't dead. Sky couldn't be dead.

"Winter, step back," Dr. Jeremy ordered, snapping me back into the moment. I'd moved too close to get a look at the monitors and watch for some discernible sign that she was there.

What the hell were they thinking?

"Why isn't she moving?" Ethan demanded. His voice quivered and his fear reeked. "Why isn't she moving?" He looked to Josh.

"Give her a minute," Josh advised.

"It's been minutes. Nine to be exact," Ethan snapped, his voice rough and panicked.

"Ethan, move," Dr. Jeremy ordered when the machines started to beep. I hated the beep. Nothing good came from the machines beeping, notifying him that her vitals were dropping too low.

"It had to have worked, because she wouldn't be breathing at all, right?" I asked. The gravelly edge to my voice seemed cold—I was okay with sounding sterile. At least it didn't break. I didn't choke on a sob.

Ethan looked as though he'd battled an army, wounded beyond repair and subsisting on will alone. He swallowed. I stared. If anything ever happened to Sebastian, Ethan would be our Alpha, and he'd always seemed prepared for it. It was hard seeing him so vulnerable and knowing that it wasn't just a threat to Josh's life that could bring him to his knees.

My attention swung to the gentle whimpering of their daughter. I could only see Kelly's profile and the slow, rhythmic elevation and depression of her shoulders. She was crying.

Stop it! I would have demanded it, but I didn't feel like having to deal with Gavin. But it wasn't just the tears—it was the awareness of death, because whether Kelly realized it or not, she seemed to be better at sensing death. It was a scary thing about her. Four out of seven times, she'd been right. The odds weren't great. It seemed like I was the only one who'd noticed it—or perhaps they all had, but no one wanted to admit her tears were the banshee's wail.

"Josh," Ethan whispered. "What do we do now?"

Josh trembled as he shook his head, his fingers aggressively clawing through his hair. "It should have worked."

I wasn't sure why they were shocked each time magic didn't respond the way they expected it to. Magic was erratic, they'd said enough times. Expect the unexpected.

We used magic too much. Once, it was our backup plan and used as a last resort. Now it seemed like it was our first choice, and it had bitten us so many times we should have learned. There was a pang in my chest over all the warnings that had gone ignored. It was a moot point. Despite what Ethan and Sky wanted to believe, they were more magic than anything; it couldn't have worked any other way.

Sky's lips were starting to lose color. Although her breathing came at a ragged clip, she had a heartbeat, and the machines weren't beeping any longer. She was clearly dying.

Kelly turned to face her, and there wasn't any denying or pretending when I saw more tears welling in her eyes.

"Stop with the damn crying or leave!" I snapped.

It was still hard to see the soft chestnut eyes turn lethal when her animal peeked through. If she didn't have the baby in her arms, I'd be preparing to protect myself. Her gaze moved from mine to behind me, where I knew Gavin was.

"She's upset, Gavin," she explained in a low, soothing voice, one that always worked on him as effectively as a command from Sebastian. Kelly turned around, her voice lowering to a caressing lilt as she continued to soothe the baby, who hadn't had a chance to be held by her own mother.

"Josh." Ethan's voice was sharp and commanding.

Josh's eyeballs were moving erratically behind his closed lids as he thought. Hand still clasped around Sky's, Ethan watched him, wearily hopeful. With each moment, my hope withered, but I knew Ethan would remain somewhat optimistic. He had to.

Josh's eyes slowly opened. "We'll do a spell reversal. That's the only thing that can work." It wasn't. There was more that could be done, but he wouldn't dare mention the *rever tempore*; reverence and apprehension always accompanied those words.

Dr. Jeremy stood over Sky, lips pressed into a cold, hard line. I knew we were sharing the same aversion to the use of magic. It was too unpredictable—nothing like science—there was always that level of uncertainty.

"It's like her body is rejecting the shade," Dr. Jeremy speculated.

Something sparked in Josh's face. "It is. Logan. When she shifted the shade from her to him, it changed dynamics." Josh paced quickly, trying to work out whatever was going through his head. He kept his eyes focused straight ahead, avoiding the image of Ethan, distraught, waiting for him to do something.

For a person ridiculed constantly for discontinuing his magic education and not "taking magic seriously," he had an impressive knowledge of it. What he lacked in formal education he seemed to make up for with creativity. Sky hated when he mixed spells—"bootlegged" magic was what she called it. There was that pang again.

It wasn't just a sharp pain, it was hurt. Sorrow. I didn't want her to die.

Josh stopped pacing. "We can't do the same spell because, unconscious, she's not able to accept the shade. So we'll have to do a spell reversal."

Ariel was cautious with her words and approach. "I want Sky to live, but—"

"Not the *rever tempore*," Josh interjected, and then continued to explain his plan. "When we did the first spell, we technically had three witches, me, you, and Sky. Dormant dark elf magic and witch from you, and Faerie from you and Sky. That's a hell of a lot of magic. To do a reversal, the magic used has to be equal or greater than what was used to perform the spell. We have enough witches to help, but we're missing Faerie magic."

"What about Claudia?" Ethan asked. "She can help."

Josh made a face. "I'm concerned that Claudia's vampirism will interfere with the magic."

"Sky is part vampire, so it's a better match, right?" I offered.

Josh scratched at the short hairs of his beard. "Maybe. That would be easier than trying to learn to mimic magic the way Sky does." He still seemed apprehensive.

"I'll call her."

Claudia's face screwed tight, causing small crinkles to form around her eyes and mouth. She wore the weary look of a mother who was listening to her children's idealistic plans and was unable to insert any practicality. I hoped she'd exert some of that maternal influence later and ban them from using magic for a while. We all could use a reprieve from it.

"Ethan, you know I don't perform magic."

"I know." He looked at Sky, who appeared even worse than she had twenty minutes ago.

"I think she's going to die if you don't," he admitted softly.

"She might die if I do," she whispered, despondent.

Ethan blanched at the idea of losing Sky. There weren't a lot of options. There was Senna, Sky's cousin, who we'd recently discovered was a Faerie, but did we have time for her to get here?

"Claudia, please try. For me."

Moving closer, she slipped the gloves from her hand. Tensing, her movements were gentle but tentative as she looked at him with maternal sorrow. His eyes glistened with the tears that had gathered in his eyes. Her hand pressed against his cheek, her thumb brushing away the ones that had streamed down his face. We all could see that she'd try to do anything to repair his shattered world.

Her alabaster skin flushed as she reviewed the spell Josh had written for her, seemingly embarrassed by her rudimentary skills with Latin. Only she would be embarrassed by that. Even flustered, she still managed to look refined. After twenty minutes of going over the spell, she let them know she was ready.

"You can do this," Josh urged in a way that would make anyone feel invincible and empowered to do anything.

His confidence in Claudia's ability, whether genuine or not, seemed to spark something in her. But I could still sense her fear and apprehension, and so could Sebastian. Intently he watched her, his face blank, something I wished I could do. I felt embarrassed that I wasn't able to hide my feelings better. I'd been hanging around David, Trent, and Sky too much. Shooting an unwarranted baleful eye at Kelly, I added her to the list. The pack was changing—and for some reason Sebastian thought it was a good thing. I had a feeling it had something to do with the long game, the threat of us being forced out, and our full integration into the real world. It was coming and Sebastian was aware of it.

The invocation had a sweet, euphonic sound. We weren't supposed to be able to detect magic, but I wasn't so sure of that. It shifted the air, increasing the pressure in my ears, as if I was on an airplane. Claudia's face strained, and Ethan's eyes moved to Sky, whose breathing was becoming sparser, and the vitals monitor, beeping a loud, alarming noise. Panic. Vitals dropping. Death impending.

"Claudia." Sebastian's voice remained low and soothing; but his wide intense gaze was a direct contrast to it. Eyes firmly placed on her, his position changed, ready to intervene if necessary. She was killing Sky. Drawing life from the living, the very thing Cole couldn't stop fixating over after seeing her do it firsthand with a plant.

She continued with the spell, aware that if she stopped, they'd have to start it over again. She raised her hand to him, indicating she was getting control. And she was: the beeping stopped. Ethan's body grew rigid as Sky's relaxed.

Sky's groan was like music. It was the sound of life—her life. I unballed my hands, something I hadn't realized I was doing. She winced when she sat up, and Dr. Jeremy had to remind her that she had just had surgery, but she didn't care. "Where's our baby?" she asked, shifting to sitting.

Ethan was by her side, pushing back her sweat-dampened hair.

"Ethan." She studied him, taking note of the glistening of his eyes.

"I'm okay, Ethan. I promise," she whispered, comforting him. He remained there, eyes closed, relaxing only after Sky pressed her hand against his cheek. "I'm okay," she whispered over and over to him in that voice that always seemed to calm him.

"I know."

They were cavity-inducing sweet and annoying. My eye roll made my head hurt.

"Here she is," Kelly said, squeezing in between them and handing Sky their baby, clearly in distress. Small face scrunched and red, she wailed. She continued until she heard Sky: "Hello, Sage."

Sage? Why the hell did they name her after a spice? I realized they needed something short. "Sage, don't play with vampires," "Sage, don't summon Faeries," "Sage, don't perform forbidden magic," "Sage, run away from danger, not toward it."

I leaned forward to get a better look; she *was* cute. Adorable, in fact. And she'd probably be the most stubborn, precocious troublemaker I'd ever encounter.

CHAPTER 45

*E*than sat on the new sofa that had replaced the chair that we'd initially put in the baby's room. Large enough for us to both curl up, and if that wasn't efficient enough, it converted to a sofa bed. Baby Sage, cradled in his arms, made soft cooing noises as she slept.

"It's her first night in her room. I don't think she likes it," he whispered.

No, you don't like it.

Her first night in her room should have been two months ago, but Ethan hadn't been able to do it. The slightest movement or perceived sound of distress had him quickly moving to her room to check on her. If he was going to get any sleep, she had to be in our room. Even with her just a foot away, his sleep was restless, and he got up throughout the night to check on her.

He was the most relaxed I'd ever seen him. A quiescent state, watching our daughter in awe, viewing the new life as if it were a foreign concept to him. Even in sleep, her hand curled around his finger in a peaceful state that relaxed him even more.

His acceptance of the harmony removed the heaviness that had weighted me down for weeks after bringing Sage home.

Our baby was in our care, needed our protection, and I hadn't been confident we could do it. I watched each day as Ethan's protective state slowly eased, coaxing him into a calm and comfortable state that was refreshing.

He pulled his gaze from her to look at me and smile. He leaned down to kiss Sage gently on the forehead. "Thank you," he whispered, and I knew it was directed at me. It was the second time he'd said it. Simple words of gratitude that meant so much. This was a life that Ethan had never expected and was appreciative of. It wasn't the life I'd expected, either. Then his gentle smile kinked into a smirk, and I knew what he was thinking; he'd made no secret of it. Me "Skying" the situation was the reason Sage was safe. I still didn't like being a verb, especially since it was a term that the pack had wholeheartedly adopted.

As I sat down next to him, Sage's eyes opened and she looked over at me. She made a little sighing sound and went back to sleep.

"She looks like you," Ethan acknowledged.

I didn't see it. She looked like a two-month-old baby: big cheeks, pinched fluffy lips, a round face, large doe eyes. Maybe she did look like me.

Sighing, I rested my head on Ethan's shoulder. "Are you sure you're okay with Chris seeing Sage?"

He tensed, but not as much as he used to at the mention of his ex's name from me. "I will have to be. You know your friendship with her is wrong on so many levels." As if to second it, Sage shifted and made a little sound that Ethan would say was assent.

"The levels of wrongness and weirdness are insurmountable, but …" *She's the reason no one will come near us, near Sage. The peace that we have on some level is because of her and Demetrius. I don't hate her.* I didn't say any of the things I thought. "She keeps calling Sage 'the offspring'—'How's the offspring?' 'Is the offspring a little Bambi?' Maybe if she sees her, she'll refer to her as Sage. It's so weird."

"I'm not going to be friends with Demetrius," Ethan asserted firmly. He seemed petulant, like he'd expected me to set them up on a playdate or something.

"I don't expect you to. He didn't stop being an ass. In fact, it's a badge that he wears with steadfast honor. He's appreciative of me saving his life, despite him being one." Arrogance, self-indulgence, and entitlement were qualities so entwined in his existence, he'd cease to be without them. "Chris and I aren't friends," I corrected. But I wished I knew what to call what we had. Assigning a distinction to what we were was hard. We weren't enemies—that seemed simple enough.

When I grew quiet, Ethan slipped his finger out of Sage's hand and rested his hand on my leg. His thumb stroked soothingly against my thigh. "There's still time with Steven," he soothed. "Even if he is Alpha of his own pack, you won't lose touch with him."

"No, I won't. I'll make sure of that. I want whatever makes him happy," I admitted. Acceptance of the inevitable was getting easier. I wasn't the same person Steven had met, the one who'd denied her wolf, hadn't been able to control her magic, and hadn't been part of a pack. The strength of the pack was necessary, and instead of liaisons they would have smaller packs. No longer the East, West, South, and Midwest. Sebastian would divide them into eight to twelve packs, and the new suggestion of it had piqued Steven's interest.

"He's a future Alpha. You knew that, Sky."

"It's just the changes. They're still hard."

Ethan looked down at Sage and pressed his lips to her chubby cheeks and then to my temple. "I like the changes," he admitted.

If I were to be honest, I did, too. It wasn't what I had expected, but it was what I wanted.

CHAPTER 46

"*L*ook who's up," Ethan said, carrying Sage, who was leaning into him, her fingers curled into his shirt.

He tried to put her down, but she wasn't having it and clung even tighter to his shirt, an indication that she was still sleepy but refused to stay asleep. Too afraid the world would pass her by.

"Hey, sweetheart." I pushed back the thicket of unruly curls that had pulled from her ponytail holder. She moved her head when I smoothed them, afraid I was going to try to braid her hair again. Her pert nose turned up and deep steely grays eyed me suspiciously. "Do you want a snack?"

She pushed from her daddy and climbed down. She took my hand and started for the kitchen with me. In her short forty-five-minute nap we'd been able to clear away her toys and any evidence that Mini T—the name Winter had given her, short for tornado—had landed. At two years, I had thought she'd consolidate all the short naps she'd taken as a baby into one long one. Obviously, Sage had missed the memo. A few feet from the kitchen she started bouncing with overzealous excitement and began to open and close her hands. Her "give me" hands, I called them. She did that when she saw me unbox her favorite snack or ... the knock came right after. Uncle Josh.

Snacks forgotten, Sage squealed when I opened the door, her legs moving double-time to get to "Uncle Dosh." She was still having difficulty with her Js. He swooped her into his arms and planted a kiss on her cheek. I gave Ethan the same inquiring look I did each time she did it. Over the past year, she seemed to know Josh was near, and I couldn't determine if she could hear him or smell him.

Josh sat next to her, legs crossed, while she had her snack. I knew that after an hour playing with him, she'd complete her nap.

"Did you get it?" Ethan asked him. He nodded, fished in the pocket of his jacket, and tossed Ethan a black jewelry box. Ethan snapped it open, revealing an engagement ring. A simple, pear-shaped stone with a white gold band. It was beautiful and very fitting for London's petite hand.

"Nice. Claudia has the best taste," Ethan acknowledged. I was appreciative of the ring she'd helped Ethan pick out for me.

"How do you know she picked it out?" Josh challenged, defiant, giving Ethan a petulant sneer.

Ignoring his brother's insolence, Ethan asked, "When do you plan to give it to her?"

A nonchalant shrug. "We're going out tonight. I guess I'll give it to her then."

"What's wrong with you two? Were you in fact raised by natural wolves? You don't just 'give it to her then.' You make it special. And it doesn't have to be anything big. You've been with London for close to three years. You don't just toss her a ring and say, 'You wanna?'" I was flabbergasted.

"I wasn't going to say 'You wanna?' I'd ask if she wanted to do this."

"Because that's infinitely better," I said sarcastically.

Josh leaned into Sage. "Is Mommy always this demanding?" he asked with a smirk.

"I'm not being demanding—I'm helping you not to repeat your brother's first proposal." I playfully glared at Ethan, reminding him of just placing a ring on the bed without any explanation. "Just do something nice, okay?"

Josh nodded, standing, after Sage did her "ready for Josh time" dance. She released his hand to go for the one thing that took precedence over their fun time—her purple bear. Given to her by Kelly, the music-playing, story-telling bear was her favorite. Hugging it to her chest, she reached for Josh's hand, but I stopped them from going off.

Eyeing Josh suspiciously, I started to pat him down.

"I'm flattered, but your husband's right there and I really love London—so, I'm going to pass," he teased, stepping out of my reach.

"You know what I'm looking for. The last time you were here, Sage smelled like Twizzlers. No candy."

His lips beveled into a miscreant grin. "She took it from me. I had no recourse. Mini T is assertive. She's like a mob boss. She asks and you have to give it to her. No questions asked."

"Nope. I haven't sanctioned that name. It's Sage. Not Mini Tornado. You and Winter are going to give her a complex," I huffed out. Now I was behaving like a petulant child.

"Okay, come on, Sage, let's go to your room and play." He mumbled under his breath, "It seems like Ethan's the nice one now."

"I heard that," I snapped.

He laughed. "You were supposed to."

As soon as Josh disappeared upstairs, Ethan and I finished cleaning. She *was* a little tornado. I wondered how one child could make such a mess; Josh wasn't wrong—Sage was obstinate and strong-willed. I assumed all toddlers wanted what they wanted, but she seemed more tenacious than most children I'd seen. "She's just an Alpha in the making," Kelly had assured me when I'd expressed my concern. Perhaps she was. It was a sight to see one toddler be so demanding of the pack: Taking Sebastian's hand, leading him to her toy box, and demanding he hold one of her bears. Tugging on Winter's shirt during nap time, urging Winter to curl up next to her and take a nap herself. And making Trent and David her partners in crime, allowing her to get away with far too much. When it came to her, *no* wasn't in their vocabulary. It was well intended but one of the reasons they weren't on the short list of babysitters.

Everyone tried to pretend that Sage was just a normal child, but I saw the way they seemed to assess her, more than interact with her. Kelly's constant visits with her weren't fooling anyone. They'd decreased significantly over the past two months, as she was now carrying twins. She didn't have the energy, and Gavin teased that she was hiding from the world because everyone kept inquiring whether she was having triplets. I'd hated it when people asked me, and I didn't think I looked like it—Kelly definitely did. I was surprised Dr. Jeremy said it was just twins.

"Ethan, Sky," Josh's strained voice came from upstairs. "I need you both to come up here. I need to show you something."

At the sound of his muted urgency, we rushed upstairs to find a small ball of gray fur, a wolf pup, fast asleep, with a purple bear under her head.

"She changed earlier than expected," Ethan surmised, unbothered by it. He'd expected it would happen earlier than it had for us, with both of her parents being wolves.

"Yeah, but *that's* not the headline of this event," Josh said, his voice continuing to have a concerned edge. He walked to Sage, knelt down, pulled the bear from her paws, and returned to his position standing next to us, more than five feet away. The pup's head popped up; she made a whimpering noise, waved her little paw, and the bear was pulled from Josh's grasp. It floated through the air in a slow and steady glide and dropped in front of the pup. She gave Josh a warning look—*don't you dare take my bear again*—before she plopped back down, placed her head on the bear, and returned to her nap.

"Hmm," I breathed out.

"Yeah, hmmm," Josh replied.

"A were-animal who can perform magic in wolf form," Ethan said softly. I was sure he was wondering the same thing I was: would she be immune to magic in human form? It was the very thing that everyone was worried about.

Ethan, impassioned and cool, went to Sage's dresser and rummaged around in it, pulled out an iridium link bracelet, and eyed it. "I think we are going to need a couple links removed."

"And a meeting with Sebastian, too."

We looked at one another and knew it was going to be a secret that stayed between us. We'd share it only with Sebastian, who we knew would protect the knowledge the way he had Ethan's secrets.

Because that was what the pack did—we protected our own.

MESSAGE TO THE READER

∼

Thank you for choosing *Midnight Sky* from the many titles available to you. My goal is to create an engaging world, compelling characters, and an interesting experience for you. I hope I've accomplished that. Reviews are very important to authors and help other readers discover our books. Please take a moment to leave a review. I'd love to know your thoughts about the book.

For notifications about new releases, *exclusive* contests and giveaways, and cover reveals, please sign up for my mailing list at McKenzieHunter.com.

Made in the USA
Las Vegas, NV
15 April 2022